Best Horror Short Stories 1850-1899
A 6a66le™ Horror Anthology

ANDREWBARGER.COM

The Best Horror Short Stories
1850-1899
A 6a66le™ Horror Anthology

First Edition
ISBN: 978-1-933747-57-6

Bottletree Books LLC
United States of America

BottletreeBooks.com

Fonts: Bookman Old Style, Chiller

"But it now struck me for the first time that there must be one great and ruling embodiment of fear, a King of Terrors to which all others must succumb."

1859 "What Was It?"
FITZ JAMES O'BRIEN

CONTENTS

A Terror Tour Guide

Good anthologists are like tour guides who take you to literary places where you want to spend time and send back postcards to your friends. They eat at the bad restaurants and sleep in bug infested hotels so you don't have to. They know from what hills you can view the best sunsets and where the secluded beaches lie. They steer you clear of the bad parts of town.

A good horror anthologist, on the other hand, steers the reader right into these bad parts of town where nightmares live. In this collection there is no shortage of them. You are about to visit places of unabashed nightmares where black cats skitter like the one in Bram Stoker's "The Squaw" and an invisible monster ruffles the muslin sheets in a charnel house that is Fitz James O'Brien's "What Was It?" Bloodstains mar the walls or, in the case of Charlotte Perkins Gilman's "The Yellow Wallpaper," body parts mar the walls and in W. C. Morrow's "His Unconquerable Enemy" *missing* body parts add to the horror.

The fifty year period from 1850-1899 is a very important time for horror stories and because of it your terror tour guide is traveling back with you on a maniacal journey into the macabre past. He places a warning hand on your shoulder when pointing out a cave like one where the giant insect of "The Spider of Guyana" lives, or perhaps houses the crypt of the creature in Sir Arthur Conan Doyle's "Lot No. 249."

Your terror tour guide pulls you away into an overgrown jungle where a goat-hooved god of nature, W. C. Morrow called "The Great God Pan," is bending next to a stream. You see other creatures in the jungle like those with piercing eyes from Joseph Le Fanu's "Green Tea." So you dash further into the jungle as palm fronds lash your face only to come upon the witchdoctor of "Pollock and the Porroh Man" by H. G. Wells. At that moment you reach a clearing that leads to the arthropod-infested mountains of Basil Tozer's "The Pioneers of Pike's Peak."

Your anthologist directs you away from the nightmares and you awake to discover that you are still alive and have made it through the tour—but just barely—and you beg to go home.

In choosing the best horror stories for this fifty year period I used the same criteria as in *Best Horror Short Stories 1800-1849: A 6a66le Horror Anthology*. Fear is first, the oldest and most dramatic of human emotions. It is intertwined in all horror stories. H. P. Lovecraft said "The oldest and strongest emotion of mankind is fear, and the oldest and strongest kind of fear is fear of the unknown."[1] And one has to agree unless the fear of *knowing* is even greater than the unknown.

A grand horror story must evoke a sense of fear at some point in the story, which is often in a shocking ending or a pervasive sense of fear or dread throughout. And there can be no fear unless feelings are garnered for the characters of the story. The deeper connection the reader has to the protagonist, the greater the ability of the writer to invoke fear in the reader. The writing of the story must further be at a high level. All of the stories picked for this anthology meet these criteria.

Since I have chosen the ten best stories in a time period, no deference is granted to older stories in the time period versus newer stories. In addition, Big Name authors pull no more weight here than unknowns, although you will find the likes of H. G. Wells and Sir Arthur Conan Doyle and Bram Stoker inside. Their horror short stories appear in these pages because they penned the best stories. Period. They stand on equal ground next to the lesser-known author Basil Tozer.

Last, the highest premium is placed on originality, which boils down to subject matter and chronological analysis. The closest example outside of the fictional realm is technical literature. Patent offices assume that every inventor submitting a new patent application for review has read *every* other patent in the technical area that came before it. Rarely is that true apart from highly specialized areas of technology, yet it has to be the standard or how else could the novelty of an invention be evaluated? Untenable is a technical world where inventors could assert that their invention was novel simply because they claimed to have not read an earlier patent. Fiction, from a novelty standpoint, must be viewed the same.

Every author must be viewed under the microscope of history as having read *every* book and *every* short story that came before theirs. Compare "What was it?" (1859) by Fitz James O'Brien, which rises to the demanding level of this collection, and Guy de Maupassant's "*Le Horla*" (1886) that falls miserably short. Both stories deal with an unseen horror. "What was it?" preceded "*Le Horla*" by twenty-seven years and is cherished for its originality of concept. If he was allowed, O'Brien should have slapped a "patent pending" on the story.

Henry James, who knew a little something about stories that build suspense in the unseen, thought "*Le Horla*" was "not a specimen of the author's best vein – the only occasion on which he has the weakness of imitation is when he strikes us as emulating Edgar Allan Poe."[2] Guy de Maupassant presumably had the advantage of having read "What was it?" as well as many other stories that followed it.

---

[1] *Supernatural Horror in Literature*, H. P. Lovecraft, 1927, 1933-1935, Introduction, pg. 1
[2] *Partial Portraits*, Henry James,1899, pg. 267

The invisibility stories continued during this import period. In 1893, some 34 years after O'Brien's tale, Algernon Blackwood published "The Damned Thing," which is another excellent story of an invisible monster, yet, for the most part, lacking in originality. Then in 1897, H. G. Wells's novel *The Invisible Man* was published and seemed to get all the attention.

True innovation in the literature has always been held at a premium. And the list of the ten best horror stories was not easily settled upon. I struggled over it over the last part of 2015 and the first months of 2016. When cutting the turkey and trimming the tree I mulled it over. On long runs I culled stories from the list and miles later would add them back in a sweaty mass of frustration. Thinking I had the final list set in stone, I would give a hard tweak to my water bottle and trudge on only to change it once more by dinner and twice before bed. The compelling horror stories tugged and pulled at my brain. Like I said, the list was not easy.

The original contained "The Fiend of the Cooperage" by Sir Arthur Conan Doyle. It found the cutting room floor when nudged out by Doyle's "Lot No. 249" that is the first evil reanimated mummy short story. Originality! I had my heart set on "The Dualists" by Bram Stoker for its sheer brutality, yet it was replaced by Arthur Machen's "The Great God Pan." It takes a more subtle approach to unrevealed horrors, with better character development and writing. Last was "A Game of Chess" by Robert Barr. I decided that the story was lacking terror throughout. Ultimately it gave way to "The Spider of Guyana" by the French duo of Émile Erckmann and Alexandre Chatrian, the oldest story in the collection and the first spider horror story I have been able to find. Did someone say "originality?"

Your terror tour guide sometimes starts down one literary path only to double back and take you on another. Ideally your guide has written their own stories in the genre and read a large selection from the time period in question. Story backgrounds and author photos are always welcome in the tour guide's publications. A list of places visited, *ala* stories read, are most helpful and so are annotations of noteworthy points along the journey.

And unlike *Best Horror Short Stories 1800-1849: A 6a66le Horror Anthology* where my research led me to read over 300 horror short stories published in the first half of the nineteenth century to find the very best, here I have read the most widely anthologized horror stories for the period in question. My strategy in doing this is that each anthologist before me has, presumably, chosen their favorite tales. It is an all-star of all-stars horror collection.

There's a lot to be said for lining up these stories up, back to back, and seeing who stands tallest. Which is the best? Everyone is my favorite in a certain way and I will leave it up to you to be the judge. So dust off your horror passports. Pack your luggage. Grab hat, sunglasses, tanning butter and mosquito repellant—and spider repellant if you have it—because a macabre journey is about to begin and it starts with the chilling air of "The Pioneers of Pike's Peak."

Andrew Barger
February 26, 2016

Basil Tozer
(1872-1949)

Englishman Basil J. Tozer was an avid sportsman who turned writer. There are very few pictures of Tozer and the one above, which is less than hi-res, was taken from an old magazine.

In 1887 he wrote an article titled "Practical Hints on Shooting. Being a Treatise on the Shot Gun and Its Management." on guns under his pseudonym "20-Bore." Ten years later he penned "Duck Shooting in Utah." He reached the height of his writing fame by publishing the non-fiction work *The Horse in History* in 1908. Given his love of sport, he was pretty adept with a gun. These loves enabled him to pen a fantastic horror story, "The Pioneers of Pike's Peak" in 1897.

This same year turned out to be an exemplary one for horror short stories because it gave the world Sir Arthur Conan Doyle's "The Fiend of the Cooperage," H.G. Wells's "Pollock and the Porroh Man," and "The Pioneers of Pike's Peak."

The later was such a popular story, it may have been plagiarized in 1934. Fellow Englishman P. E. Cleator published "Martian Madness" in the science fiction magazine *Wonder Stories* that contained many similarities to Tozer's tale, only it was set on Mars instead of Pike's Peak. A letter to the editor of the magazine called out Cleator. The editors dismissed it by claiming they were unable to get a copy of "The Pioneers of Pike's Peak" to compare.[1]

"The Pioneers of Pike's Peak" appears to be the first horror short story where there is an attack by multiple spiders whereas the earlier story by Émile Erckmann and Alexandre Chatrian titled

---

[1] *The Gernsback Days, A Study of the Evolution of Modern Science Fiction from 1911 to 1936*, Mike Ashley and Robert A. Lowndes, 2004, pg. 361

"The Spider of Guyana" (1857) addresses a human-sized spider and its horrible deeds. It is included later in this collection.

The Pioneers of Pike's Peak
1897

"IT WAS A perfect night about the end of June, the sort of night common enough in Colorado at that time of the year. I remember it, for at the end of the game I rose from the cardtable and strolled out into the cool, refreshing air.

Overhead the stars were shining with extraordinary brilliancy in a sky so clear that one seemed almost to hear them winking. The moon had not yet risen above the range of mighty peaks which tower into the heavens until their crests gradually vanish into great belts of clouds, and at night seem to touch the lowermost of the celestial bodies; but a sort of halo, gradually broadening, served to show that presently the moon herself would shed a flood of light from the very summit of the highest peaks down into the little village nestling at the feet of the mighty range, and now practically wrapt in slumber. No sound broke the perfect stillness without. The very houses seemed to sleep.

It was only when I reentered the heated atmosphere of the smoky "bar room" where my companions, grown tired of card-playing, were now quietly conversing, that I noticed an odd-looking and apparently elderly stranger seated alone beside a little window at the further end of the room. The window was open, and he was staring through it vacantly, only interrupting his reverie now and again in order to blow a long cloud of smoke into the air. As I seated myself among my companions I cast a glance of inquiry in his direction.

"He came in five minutes ago," one of them answered.

"Who is he?"

"Some crank, I suppose. He has hardly stirred since he sat down there."

Though the room was a public one, only ourselves and the stranger now occupied it.

"What is he staring at?" someone asked, presently.

"Pike's Peak, apparently," replied Watson, who had called the stranger "some crank."

Though the words were spoken in an undertone, the "crank" evidently overheard them, for he turned his head and frowned. Then he resumed his former position—his vigil. Watson tapped his forehead significantly, and presently conversation drifted. It drifted from one topic to another, until the subject of American ways and customs, of America in general, of American scenery and landscapes, came uppermost.

"And who really was the first to reach the top of Pike's Peak?" Watson asked, looking round at us.

"Not Pike himself," somebody answered, somebody who had been reading up the subject—it was Norton, I think. "They say that a man—look out, you fellows!"

For the stranger had left his seat and was approaching us with a slow, stealthy tread, his eyes oddly dilated. As he advanced we instinctively turned to face him. A man of immense proportions, and well over six feet in height, he could not have been over fifty years of age, though he looked quite sixty.

His hair was white and rather long. He had evidently been handsome in his day, but now the face, neck, and hands were disfigured with numberless little sunken blotches in some ways resembling, though in reality quite unlike, the pits left by smallpox. He wore an old drab suit, a coon cap, thick boots, and leather leggings.

"Who did you say first saw Pike's Peak?" he asked, in a threatening, hollow voice. He had dropped into a chair upon the opposite side of the table beside me. As he spoke he looked me full in the eyes, and, placing both elbows upon the table very deliberately, rested his chin upon his fists. Norton, whom he had interrupted, came to the rescue.

"I believe that------"

"*I* first saw it! But do you know the story of our ascent?"

"I know only what I have read and told," Norton said.

"You yourself have ascended Pike's Peak?"

"I have."

"You have seen the summit, then."

"Yes."

"And what did you notice there that struck you most—there, fifteen thousand feet above the sea's level?"

"Why, scenery that was perfectly grand."

"Yes, yes, I know—grand, magnificent, marvelous scenery. I know all that. But what else did you see?"

He paused. "Surely it is there," he muttered, "surely it is still there—it *must* be there—it must be there. Who could have removed it, eh?" he continued, aloud; "who *could* have taken it away? Tell me *that.*"

Norton had an inspiration. What train of thought led up to that inspiration he says that to this day he cannot guess.

"Do you mean the stone?"

Instantly the stranger's expression changed. He looked round at us all quite intelligently.

"It *is* there, then?" he inquired, eagerly, bending forward across the table.

"Of course it is there," Norton and Watson replied in one breath. "Who could have taken it away?" Watson added, glancing towards us significantly, and suppressing a smile.

We were growing interested in this poor, demented creature.

"I can give you the inscription word for word," Norton said, wishing to propitiate him.

"Do! What is it? Tell me, what is it?"

"The inscription says: 'This stone is erected in memory of William Dawkins, James Weston, and Walter Hillier, Pioneers of Pike's Peak, who were devoured by mountain rats while endeavoring to reach this summit.'"

"Ah!" he ejaculated, greatly relieved. "I am glad it is there—I am glad it is still there. Do you know the story of my friends, the story of those pioneers?"

He had grown suddenly calm. He seemed suddenly to have regained his reason.

"No; tell it to us," said Watson, carelessly blowing a cloud of smoke across the table. " But first, what will you take, sir? And won't you try a cigar?"

"Brandy," he exclaimed. "Then I will tell you all—all!"

Our interest and curiosity were now thoroughly aroused. We could see that the stranger was not a common brawler. He was quite sober, too, and though his mind was evidently unhinged, it was equally evident to us that he had intervals of lucidness. This seemed to be one of them. With provoking deliberation he reloaded his pipe. The glasses were refilled. We noticed that he poured brandy into his tumbler until it was three-parts full. Just then the moon shone over the summit of the famous Peak, and from where we sat the outline of the glorious mountain could be clearly discerned. Watson drew the stranger's attention to it. An odd, bitter smile flitted across his face. It was the first time that we had seen him smile. He sighed once, but did not utter a word. Again his gaze became riveted upon the gigantic Peak.

"Pike never would—never could have reached it. He tried to several times. Finally he stood upon a hill near the stalactite caves at the base of my mountain, and, pointing with his finger at the summit, said: 'No mortal man will ever tread that Peak!'"

Again he paused.

"But we—*we* were determined to. Our friends shook us by the hands and bade us farewell.

"'But you are fools,' they said. 'You will never come back. You don't know what you may meet in those mountains. You know what Pike said when he came back. You know the tales he told. And some things he would not tell.'

"'Don't go, oh! Don't go,' my wife cried, in agony.

"I loved her, yet I forced her from me. She was but a unit. In the success of our enterprise lay the welfare of thousands. I told her that to comfort her. It was the last time I saw her alive. My comrades—may God help them— had no wives. 'You are married,' they had said all along; 'you should not come.' But I was determined to go. Early in the morning we started. We took with us arms, food and drink for many days, and the bare necessaries of life. We carried everything ourselves. We knew where and how Pike had failed. We should succeed.

"A week later we were fairly launched, also we were fairly in the midst of difficulties. The work was terribly severe, but we had determination, strength, and courage. We had expected to find obstacles, and in this we certainly were not disappointed. Here, enormous boulders which had to be circumvented; there, unlooked-for waterfalls and ravines that delayed us, besides vegetation so thick that in places we had literally to back our way through it. All this impeded our progress enormously. And then the unknown dangers that Pike had hinted at. There might be snakes and reptiles, of sorts hitherto never heard of, concealed among those immense boulders; there might be death-dealing plants all around us—such plants flourish in South America; there might be—indeed, we did not know what there might not be. But of course we did not pause to consider these things."

He paused, however, in order to take another great gulp of brandy. It seemed to stimulate him. His eyes glistened.

"Over a fortnight went by. We were growing more and more accustomed to meeting difficulties and to overcoming them, for many obstacles at first sight insurmountable proved in the end to be less formidable than we had anticipated. And as we gradually mounted higher and higher, our spirits steadily rose as if in sympathy. Far down in the valley we had once or twice during our progress caught glimpses of this very townlet, now called Colorado Springs, also of the village of Manitou. Tiny villages, indeed, they were in those days, and as we saw them from those great heights they looked like chessboards stretched out upon the vast expanse of prairie. And still we fought our way upward, upward, always upward.

"How long our expedition had been started I cannot quite remember, when the nature of the surroundings gradually changed greatly. In place of rock and black soil we now found vast tracts of a sandy formation. The undergrowth was still dense, however, though here and there thousands upon thousands of slim fir trees lay rotting upon the ground, evidently swept down by some terrific storm—for storms in these mountains sweep down trees as a reaping machine sweeps down standing corn. Sometimes we came upon broad, open spaces—spaces swept clear apparently in early days by giant waterfalls long since dried up. Then, as we penetrated still higher, the temperature of course became colder and colder, the atmosphere more and more rarefied—the vegetation at the same time naturally decreasing in density and the trees in size. Even the boulders grew smaller. Indeed, they now looked as though in prehistoric times they had all been flung together by a tremendous seismic disturbance, many of them being crushed to pieces in the process.

"'Have you noticed,' one of my comrades remarked one day, as we prepared to rest and refresh ourselves, 'what a quantity of insects there are up here? And the rats, too, are getting more plentiful. We seldom see any of those grey squirrels now.'

"As he spoke he stamped his foot upon an immense brown spider that was running away. Its body burst with a crack, and glutinous liquid spurted out all round his boot. Almost instantly several more spiders ran out from beneath a large stone as though to ascertain what had happened. They stopped. For a moment they seemed for all the world as if they looked at us—looked at us with a malignant, vindictive expression. Then they scuttled away.

"'I believe I felt several of those spiders scampering over my face last night,' he continued. 'You fellows had better be careful; I am told they bite like the mischief. These mountains are famous for them, and—just look at that!'

"A couple of large rats were chasing an enormous spider across a long flat boulder. A moment later, spider and rats disappeared over the edge.

"'They say that mountain rats will devour any living thing,' Weston said, presently. 'They will eat us if we don't watch them,' he ended in jest.

"During the earlier part of the afternoon we had made good progress, when suddenly, to our surprise, we came upon a large sloping tract of bare white sand. The sun, still high in the heavens, shed its rays slantingly across it, and at first sight the sand seemed to be alive with small, moving bodies.

"'Talk of spiders!' Dawkins said, laughing. 'Did you ever see anything like that?'

"We had long ago, in previous expeditions, grown accustomed to surprises. Few things astonished us now. Never in our lives, however, had we seen such an assemblage of 'lucky insects,' as some senseless folk call them. There must have been thousands upon thousands of them running about in every direction, colliding with one another and tumbling over one another apparently for no particular reason. The sight made me think of a gigantic ant's nest overrun with mammoth ants, and an odd sort of smell that for several days had pervaded the air, and caused us to wonder more than once whence it came, here stuck our nostrils with renewed strength. The smell was the smell of spiders.

"Now, as we stepped forward into this open tract, a strange thing happened, for the entire space which a moment before had been alive became in an instant motionless. The spiders were all there, right before us, but of one accord they had stopped running. Oddly enough, too, every spider was now facing us. Instinctively we felt that we had become objects of intense curiosity. And as we stood there, interested and amused, we could distinctly see the spiders' great eyes sticking out and evidently watching us. The sight would have given women, and many a man for that matter, 'the creeps,' as I believe a certain sort of nervous affection is called. We rather enjoyed it.

"'Pish! you hideous things,' Dawkins said, pitching a pebble into their midst. In less than a minute hardly a spider was to be seen.

"'If we describe that sight when we get back we shall be called liars, to say the least,' Weston said, glancing at his watch. 'I've seen insects in my time, but never anything like that. Why, it's past three o'clock.'

"The offensive smell was still strong in the air, and as we progressed it increased. Once or twice it became almost unbearable. We had now a long stretch of clear going before us, so we hastened to avail ourselves of it by advancing briskly. And still we saw spiders at every turn, spiders running in under every stone, spiders by, the hundred sunning themselves on every rock and boulder—great brown spiders, with fat, oval bodies, and with thick, hairy legs bent in grotesque curves. I kicked over a stunted little tree that lay rotting—ugh! quite two or three hundred spiders must have scuttled away from under it.

"'This is getting beyond a joke,' Hillier, who seldom spoke and was generally considered surly, suddenly said. 'I tell you what it is: these spiders will go for us.'

"'Like Weston's rats!' Dawkins said, laughing at him; and we were still chaffing Hillier and Weston when Dawkins happened to look round.

"'Why, Harry!' he exclaimed.

"There was anxiety in his tone, and I felt his hand grip my shoulder. And no wonder. Though anything but a coward, Dawkins could not help at once realizing what we all realized a moment later, namely, that Hillier's evil omen was more than likely to come true, and, realizing at the same instant our utter helplessness should such a thing occur, a sickening sense of fear had come over him.

"For there, barely fifty yards away, a reddish-brown mass gradually assuming the form of a crescent was steadily, swiftly gliding over the sand, steadily and swiftly overtaking us. And as it approached we could see thousands upon thousands of spiders hastening towards it from every side and quickly increasing its size. The swarm when first we saw it must have covered between twelve and fifteen square feet. Before it had glided over another twenty yards of sand the entire mass was nearly one-third as large again. Yet a sort of horrible fascination kept us rooted to the spot where we now stood watching the swarm approach. In order to brace up our courage we told one another that the spiders could not be pursuing us at all; that if we moved aside they would pass us by. But in our hearts we knew that we tried to think a lie. And when we moved aside in order to convince ourselves, the creeping crescent immediately swayed round towards us and seemed if anything to advance more quickly."

The stranger poured out another tumblerful of brandy, swallowed about a third of it, and, growing more and more excited, continued:—"Suddenly the intense horror of the situation flashed across my mind and struck terror into our hearts. For what could we do to avert the terrible fate that threatened us? Savage animals we might have coped with; treacherous human beings, even, we might have bested; but now we were face to face ,with a peril totally unexpected, utterly loathsome and unassailable.

"'Our only chance lies in flight,' Hillier said, bitterly.

"'Flight! and where shall we fly to? The top of the mountain, I suppose! Look there, Hillier.'

"It was Dawkins who spoke, and he spoke in tones of scorn. Looking round us, we now saw what we had not noticed before. We were surrounded. Everywhere we saw spiders—spiders approaching in brown, gliding crescents of varying sizes. And over a hundred yards away the largest and darkest mass of all could clearly be distinguished, also winding its way along the sand, also approaching, also inclosing us. Arid as this great crescent surged undulatingly, unswervingly across hillocks and irregularities in the surface of the sandy soil, it resembled the great waves of a sluggish, turbid stream leaving a factory sluice.

"'Fire into them!' I exclaimed, slipping a couple of shot cartridges into my gun. The two charges cut a lane into the approaching ware, but almost instantly the lane closed up, and the undulating mass advanced as if nothing had happened. Together Dawkins and Weston fired four barrels. Rather a broader lane this time; but again it closed up. I had reloaded.

"'Give them a volley,' Weston called out; 'that may turn them.'

"We did so; but by the time the smoke had cleared away the swarm had well-nigh resumed its normal size and shape. Could we sweep a lane with our eight barrels and then rush through it? No, that was obviously impossible: the width of the waves was too great. And still recruits were pouring in upon every side, and as we fired volley after volley into the quickly approaching swarms, in the vain hope of turning them, the distant ravines rang again and again with echoes.

"'My God! we are done for,' came despairingly from Hillier, as for the twentieth time he closed his gun with a snap.

"Our barrels had now become almost too hot to hold, and still the hideous, crawling waves, which must have contained trillions of spiders, were fast approaching with a strange, swaying motion, and rapidly narrowing our little circle. In a few minutes they would be upon us, overrunning us, dragging us down. Already many straggler were running up our legs and over our bodies. Now, the first swarm was so near that we could distinctly hear it rushing upon us, and—ah! the smell, how it still hangs in my nostrils . . . ."

For a moment the stranger stopped. His pupils were widely distended. His limbs trembled. He clutched the table frantically in order to support himself.

"Suddenly I saw several spiders run up Weston's face and fix upon his eyes. With a scream he dashed them away, but as he did so his eye began to swell, for the brutes had bitten him badly."

He stopped again. He was quivering all over with the excitement. The brandy was taking effect. Suddenly he dashed from his seat to the furthermost corner of the room.

"Keep them from me! Keep them off!" he cried, glaring wildly all round the floor. "Look at them now—look at them—ah! God help me!—help me!—*help me!*"

He sprang to right and left, then towards the door. Perspiration was pouring down his face. Then suddenly he snatched blindly at imaginary spiders running up his sleeves and legs, running up his body, running over his head, over his face, over his eyes, into his mouth. It was a dreadful sight.

"Stop him!" Watson cried, jumping from his seat and rushing towards him, but as he approached the maniac a blindly directed blow from the latter's fist nearly stunned him, and the innkeeper and two rough—looking men entered the room.

"Hold him, boys," the innkeeper said, calmly, and as the two men pounced upon the stranger the innkeeper sauntered towards us.

"Poor fellow," he said, "I always have to be ready for him—look at him now, yet the doctors pronounce him sane. He often is sane, of course, but when I heard him starting on the spiders, and on brandy as well, I knew what to expect."

"Is there any truth in his spider story?"

"Any truth? It's all truth; at least, that's my belief. Though I was quite a lad at the time the expedition started, I can remember it well. Four of them there were, all strong and hearty when they set out. Two months later *he* came back."

"Did he alone escape?"

"He alone came back—came back quite done for and disfigured all over with red blotches. Afterwards they turned into pits. Look at them now on his face and neck, but they are all over his body, too—all over every inch of him. Some years later another expedition went up and reached the summit, but they always maintained that rats, not spiders, devoured those poor fellows, so they set a stone with an inscription upon it at the top of the mountain—you have seen it, no doubt?"

"What do you, yourself, think they were killed by?"

"Think? I don't think anything. As sure as you are standing there they were eaten up by swarms of great spiders, as Mad Harry has told you. I have heard him tell the story often enough, and he always tells the same story; but when he drinks brandy while he's telling it he nearly always gets into that state sooner or later, and I get these men to hold him until he recovers. Besides, those marks are not rats' bites. They are not a bit like rats' bites. No, I believe that what he says about the rats is true: that is, that a perfect army of them suddenly came down upon the spiders and routed the lot, but not before the other three men had succumbed, or had been so sucked out of blood that they soon died of exhaustion. Ah! it's a horrible place, that mountain," he said, looking at its rugged peak so clearly outlined in the moonlight. "Though you can go up one side of it now by the track, easily enough, you don't know what horrors may exist in other parts of it. Many a man has gone into those mountains, but very few have ever returned."

Sir Arthur Conan Doyle
(1859-1930)

The inventor of the ever popular Sherlock Holmes character penned a number of excellent horror stories. "The Fiend of the Cooperage" and "The Brazilian Cat" rank high on the list. As editor Richard Burton said, "If you read these of an evening, as I did, the creeps are guaranteed. Whatever may be the wholesomeness of such attacks upon the nerves, a reviewer would not be just if he overlooked the cleverness with which a strange complication is managed and a quite unlooked for denouement sprung upon the expectant reader."[1]

But perhaps Doyle's greatest horror story that he wrote in the nineteenth century belongs to "Lot No. 249." It was originally published in *Harper's Monthly Magazine* in the fall of 1892 and is the first reanimated mummy story where the mummy strikes terror. That's why it belongs squarely in this collection. To understand this significant leap in the literature, consider the evolution of the mummy story through the nineteenth century.

The first novel about a mummy was Jane Webb's 1827 novel *The Mummy! A Tale of the Twenty-Second Century*. It is interesting to note that the author was a woman who presumably was inspired by Mary Shelley's *Frankenstein* (1818) and the reanimated corpse of the novel. The little-known short story "The Leyden Professor and the Living Mummy," published in the *Englishman's Magazine* during 1837 tells of a professor who tries to embalm a living human. Next, in September of 1840, was Théophile Gautier's much

---

[1] *The Bellman's Bookshelf*, Richard Burton, Vol. 5, November 14, 1908, pg. 1279

anthologized "The Foot of the Mummy." There, a mummy's foot bought in a curiosity shop causes the spirit of an Egyptian princess to claim it from the past.

The first reanimated mummy short story is Edgar Allan Poe's 1845 tale "Some Words with a Mummy," in which a mummy comes to life and remarks on the innovations of that age. Then in 1869 Louisa May Alcott penned "Lost in a Pyramid, or the Mummy's Curse" where a character burns an instate mummy only to suffer its terrible curse. In 1890 Doyle published his first mummy short story called "The Ring of Thoth." It is a middling effort compared to his other horror.

And that brings us to "Lot No. 249" of 1892 and the first horror story where a mummy has malevolent intent. H. P. Lovecraft wasted no time in stating that in it "the reanimated mummy theme is used with more than ordinary skill."[2]

Not only does this excellent mummy story need more visibility, this Doyle spinetingler is one of the best horror short stories for the last half of the nineteenth century.

----

[2] *Supernatural Horror in Literature*, H. P. Lovecraft, 1927, 1933-1935, Introduction, pg. 5

Lot No. 249
1892

OF THE DEALINGS of Edward Bellingham with William Monkhouse Lee, and of the cause of the great terror of Abercrombie Smith, it may be that no absolute and final judgment will ever be delivered. It is true that we have the full and clear narrative of Smith himself, and such corroboration as he could look for from Thomas Styles, the servant, from the Reverend Plumptree Peterson, Fellow of Old's, and from such other people as chanced to gain some passing glance at this or that incident in a singular chain of events.

Yet, in the main, the story must rest upon Smith alone, and the most will think that it is more likely that one brain, however outwardly sane, has some subtle warp in its texture, some strange flaw in its workings, than that the path of nature has been overstepped in open day in so famed a center of learning and light as the University of Oxford. Yet when we think how narrow and how devious this path of nature is, how dimly we can trace it, for all our lamps of science, and how from the darkness which girds it round great and terrible possibilities loom ever shadowly upwards, it is a bold and confident man who will put a limit to the strange by-paths into which the human spirit may wander.

In a certain wing of what we will call Old College in Oxford there is a corner turret of an exceeding great age. The heavy arch which spans the open door has bent downwards in the center under the weight of its years, and the gray lichen-blotched blocks of stone are bound and knitted together with withes and strands of ivy, as though the old mother had set herself to brace them up against wind and weather. From the door a stone stair curves upward spirally, passing two landings, and terminating in a third one, its steps all shapeless and hallowed by the tread of so many generations of the seekers after knowledge. Life has flowed like water down this winding stair, and, waterlike, has left these smooth-worn grooves behind it. From the long-gowned pedantic scholars of Plantagenet days down to the young bloods of a later age, how full and strong has been the tide of young English life! And what was left now of all those hopes, those strivings, those fiery energies, save here and there in some old-world churchyard a few scratches upon a stone, and perchance a handful of dust in a moldering coffin? Yet here were the silent stair and the gray old wall, with bend and saltire and many another heraldic device still to be read upon its surface, like grotesque shadows thrown back from the days that had passed.

In the month of May, in the year 1884, three young men occupied the sets of rooms which opened on to the separate landings of the old stair. Each set consisted simply of a sitting room and of a bedroom, while the two corresponding rooms upon the ground-floor were used, the one as a coal-cellar, and the other as the living-room of the servant, or gyp, Thomas Styles, whose duty it was to wait upon the three men above him. To right and to left was a line of lecture-rooms and of offices, so that the dwellers in the old turret enjoyed a certain seclusion, which made the chambers popular among the more studious undergraduates. Such were the three who occupied them now—Abercrombie Smith above, Edward Bellingham beneath him, and William Monkhouse Lee upon the lowest story.

It was ten o'clock on a bright spring night, and Abercrombie Smith lay back in his arm-chair, his feet upon the fender, and his brier-root pipe between his lips. In a similar chair, and equally at his ease, there lounged on the other side of the fireplace his old school friend Jephro Hastie. Both men were in flannels, for they had spent their evening upon the river, but apart from their dress no one could look at their hard-cut alert faces without seeing that they were open-air men—men whose minds and tastes turned naturally to all that was manly and robust. Hastie, indeed, was stroke of his college boat, and Smith was an even better oar, but a coming examination had already cast its shadow over him and held him to his work, save for the few hours a week which health demanded. A litter of medical books upon the table, with scattered bones, models, and anatomical plates, pointed to the extent as well as the nature of his studies, while a couple of single-sticks and a set of boxing-glove above the mantle-piece hinted at the means by which, with Hastie's help, he might take his exercise in its most compressed and least distant form. They knew each other very well—so well that they could sit now in that soothing silence which is the very highest development of company.

"Have some whiskey," said Abercrombie Smith at last, between two cloud-bursts. "Scotch in the jug and Irish in the bottle."

"No, thanks. I'm in for the sculls.[1] I don't liquor when I'm training. How about you?"

"I'm reading hard. I think it best to leave it alone."

Hastie nodded, and they relapsed into a contented silence.

"By-the-way, Smith," asked Hastie, presently, "have you made the acquaintance of either of the fellows on your stair yet?"

"Just a nod when we pass. Nothing more."

"Hum! I should be more inclined to let it stand at that. I know something of them both. Not much, but as much as I want. I don't

---

[1] Sculling, a type of rowing popular at Oxford University

think I should take them to my bosom if I were you. Not that there's much amiss with Monkhouse Lee."

"Meaning the thin one?"

"Precisely. He is a gentlemanly little fellow. I don't think there is any vice in him. But then you can't know him without knowing Bellingham."

"Meaning the fat one?"

"Yes, the fat one. And he's a man whom I for one would rather not know."

Abercrombie Smith raised his eyebrows and glanced across at his companion. "What's up, then?" he asked. "Drink? Cards? Cad? You used not to be censorious."

"Ah! you evidently don't know the man, or you wouldn't ask. There's something damnable about him, something reptilian. My gorge always rises at him. I should put him down as a man with secret vices—an evil liver. He's no fool, though. They say that he is one of the best men in his line that they have ever had in the college."

"Medicine or classics?"

"Eastern languages. He's a demon at them. Chillingworth met him somewhere above the second cataract last long, and he told me that he just prattled to the Arabs as if he had been born and nursed and weaned among them. He talked Coptic to the Copts, and Hebrew to the Jews, and Arabic to the Bedouins, and they were all ready to kiss the hem of his frock-coat. There are some old hermit Johnnies up in those parts who sit on rocks and scowl and spit at the casual stranger. Well, when they saw this chap Bellingham, before he had said five words they just lay down on their bellies and wriggled. Chillingsworth said that he never saw anything like it. Bellingham seemed to take it as his right too, and strutted about among them and talked down to them like a Dutch uncle. Pretty good for an undergrad of Old's, wasn't it?"

"That sort of thing doesn't mean much in the East, though. It was just their way of saying that they were surprised and pleased to find a foreigner who knew something of their history and language. But how do you come to know this fellow?"

"Well, I come from Applesford, you know, and so does young Monkhouse Lee. His father is vicar there, and he has a sister, Eveline Lee, who is as nice a little girl as you could wish to see. When Lee began to be chummy with Bellingham, he asked him down to stay in the vicarage, and I saw something of him. The mischief of it is that he's managed in some way to get the better of little Eveline, and she is engaged to him. What she can see in the fellow! But it's my belief that there are many women, and Eveline Lee is among them, who are so unselfish, and so gentle, and so frightened of giving pain, that if their fathers' gardeners were to propose to them, they would accept them for fear of hurting their feelings if they refused. Well, I suppose they know their own business best, but it makes a man grind his teeth. A dove and a toad—that's what I always think of."

Abercrombie Smith grinned and knocked his ashes out against the side of the grate. "You show every card in your hand, old chap," said he. "What a prejudiced, green-eyed, evil-thinking old man it is! You have really nothing against the fellow except that."

"Well, I've known her ever since she was as long as that cherry-wood pipe, and I don't like to see her taking risks. And it is a risk. He looks beastly. And he has a beastly temper, a venomous temper. You remember his row with Long Norton?"

"No; you always forget that I am a freshman."

"Ah, it was last winter. Of course. Well, you know the towpath along by the river. There were several fellows going along it, Bellingham in front, when they came on an old market-woman coming the other way. It had been raining—you know what those fields are like when it has rained—and the path ran between the river and a great puddle that was nearly as broad. Well, what does this swine do but keep the path, and push the old girl into the mud, where she and her marketings came to terrible grief. It was a blackguard thing to do, and Long Norton, who is as gentle a fellow as ever stepped, told him what he thought of it. One word led to another, and it ended in Norton laying his stick across the fellow's shoulders. There was the deuce of a fuss about it, and it's a treat to see the way in which Bellingham looks at Norton when they meet now. By Jove, Smith, it's nearly eleven o'clock!"

"No hurry. Light up your pipe again."

"Not I. I'm supposed to be in training. Here I've been sitting gossiping like a ——— old woman when I ought to have been safely tucked up. I'll borrow your skull, if you can spare it. Williams has had mine for a month. I'll take the little bones of your ear too, if you are sure you won't need them. Thanks very much. Never mind a bag, I can carry them very well under my arm. Good-night, my son, and take my tip as to your neighbor."

When Hastie, bearing his anatomical plunder, had clattered off down the winding stair, Abercrombie Smith hurled his pipe into the waste-paper basket, and drawing his chair nearer to the lamp, plunged into a formidable green-covered volume, adorned with great colored maps of that strange internal kingdom of which we are the hapless and helpless monarchs. Though a freshman at Oxford, the student was not so in medicine, for he had worked for four years at Glasgow and at Berlin, and this coming examination would place him finally as a member of his profession. With his firm mouth, broad forehead, and clear-cut, somewhat hard-featured face, he was a man who, if he had no brilliant talent, was yet so dogged, so patient, and so strong that he might in the end overtop a more showy genius. A man who can hold his own among Scotchmen and North Germans is not a man to be easily set back. Smith had left a name at Glasgow and at Berlin, and he was bent now upon doing as much at Oxford, if hard work and devotion could accomplish it.

He had sat reading for about an hour, and the hands of the noisy carriage clock upon the side table were rapidly closing together upon the twelve, when a sudden sound fell upon the student's ear, a sharp, rather shrill sound, like the hissing intake of a man's breath who gasps under some strong emotion. Smith laid down his book and slanted his ear to listen. There was no one on either side or above him, so that the interruption came certainly from the neighbor beneath him—the same neighbor of whom Hastie had given so unsavory an account.

Smith knew him only as a flabby pale-faced man of silent and studious habits, a man, whose lamp threw a golden bar from the old turret even after he had extinguished his own. This community in lateness had formed a silent bond between them. It was soothing to Smith when the hours stole on towards dawning to feel that there was another so close who set as small a value upon his sleep as he did. He could even see him at times, for when the moon lay behind the turret, and cast its black length across the green quadrangle lawn, each window stood out upon the shadow as a yellow glimmering square, and there, in the center of this golden frame, Smith could sometimes see the blurred outline of the sunken head and rounded shoulders of the worker beneath him.

Even now, as his thoughts turned towards him, Smith's feelings were kindly. Hastie was a good fellow, but he was rough, strong-fibred, with no imagination or sympathy. He could not tolerate departures from what he looked upon as the model type of manliness. If a man could not be measured by a public-school standard, then he was beyond the pale with Hastie. Like so many who are themselves robust, he was apt to confuse constitution with character, to ascribe to want of principle what was really a want of circulation. Smith, with his stronger mind, knew his friend's habit, and made allowance for it now as his thoughts turned towards the man beneath him.

There was no return of the singular sound, and Smith was about to turn to his work once more, when suddenly there broke out in the silence of the night a hoarse cry, a positive scream, the call of a man who is moved and shaken beyond all control. Smith sprang out of his chair and dropped his book. He was a man of fairly firm fiber, but there was something in this sudden uncontrollable shriek of horror which chilled his blood and pringled in his skin. Coming in such a place and at such an hour, it brought a thousand fantastic possibilities into his head. Should he rush down, or was it better to wait? He had all the national hatred of making a scene, and he knew so little of his neighbor that he would not lightly intrude upon his affairs. For a moment he stood in doubt, and even as he balanced the matter there was a quick rattle of footsteps upon the stairs, and young Monkhouse Lee, half dressed and as white as ashes, burst into his room.

"Come down!" he gasped. "Bellingham's ill."

Abercrombie Smith followed him closely down stairs into the sitting-room which was beneath his own, and intent as he was upon the matter at hand, he could not but take an amazed glance around him as he crossed the threshold. It was such a chamber as he had never seen before—a museum rather than a study. Walls and ceiling were thickly covered with a thousand strange relics from Egypt and the East. Tall angular figures bearing burdens or weapons stalked in an uncouth frieze round the apartments. Above were bull-headed, stork-headed, cat-crowned, almond-eyed monarchs, and strange beetlelike deities cut out of the blue Egyptian lapis lazuli. Horus and Isis and Osiris peeped down from every niche and shelf, while across the ceiling a true son of Old Nile, a great hanging-jawed crocodile, was hung in a double noose.

In the center of this singular chamber was a large square table, littered with papers, bottles, and the dried leaves of some graceful palm-like plant. These varied objects had all been heaped together in order to make room for a mummy case, which had been conveyed from the wall, as was evident from the gap there, and laid across the front of the table.

The mummy itself, a horrid, black, withered thing, like a charred head on a gnarled bush, was lying half out of the case, with its clawlike hand and bony forearm resting upon the table. Propped up against the sarcophagus was an old yellow scroll of papyrus, and in front of it, in a wooded armchair, sat the owner of the room, his head thrown back, his widely opened eyes directed in a horrified stare to the crocodile above him, and his blue thick lips puffing loudly with every expiration.

"My God! He's dying!" cried Monkhouse Lee, distractedly. He was a slim, handsome young fellow, olive-skinned and dark-eyed, of a Spanish rather than of an English type, with a Celtic intensity of manner which contrasted with the Saxon phlegm of Abercrombie Smith.

"Only a faint, I think," said the medical student. "Just give me a hand with him. You take his feet. Now on to the sofa. Can you kick all those little wooden devils off? What a litter it is! Now he will be all right if we undo his collar and give him some water. What has he been up to at all?"

"I don't know. I heard him cry out as I ran up. I know him pretty well, you know. It is good of you to come down."

"His heart is going like a pair of castanets," said Smith, laying his hand on the breast of the unconscious man. "He seems to me to be frightened all to pieces. Chuck the water on him! What a face he has got on him!"

It was indeed a strange and most repellent face, for color and outline were equally unnatural. It was white, not with the ordinary pallor of fear, but with an absolutely bloodless white, like the underside of a sole. He was very fat, but gave the impression of having at some time been considerably fatter, for his skin hung loosely in creases and folds, and was shot with a mesh-work of wrinkles. Short stubbly brown hair bristled up from his scalp, with a pair of thick wrinkled ears protruding on either side. His light gray eyes were still open, the pupils dilated, and the balls projecting in a fixed and horrid stare. It seemed to Smith as he looked down upon him that he had never seen nature's danger signals flying so plainly upon a man's countenance, and his thoughts turned more seriously to the warning which Hastie had given him an hour before.

"What the deuce can have frightened him so?" he asked.

"It's the mummy."

"The mummy? How, then?"

"I don't know. It's beastly and morbid. I wish he would drop it. It's the second fright he has given me. It was the same last winter. I found him just like this, with that horrid thing in front of him."

"What does he want with the mummy, then?"

"Oh, he's a crank, you know. It's his hobby. He knows more about these things than any man in England. But I wish he wouldn't! Ah, he's beginning to come to."

A faint tinge of color had begun to steal back into Bellingham's ghastly cheeks, and his eyelids shivered like a sail after a calm. He clasped and unclasped his hands, drew a long thin breath between his teeth, and suddenly jerking up his head, threw a glance of recognition around him. As his eyes fell upon the mummy, he sprang off the sofa, seized a roll of papyrus, thrust it into a drawer, locked the drawer, and then staggered back on to the sofa.

"What's up?" he asked. "What do you chaps want?"

"You've been shrieking out and making no end of a fuss," said Monkhouse Lee. "If our neighbor here from above hadn't come down, I'm sure I don't know what I should have done with you."

"Ah, it's Mr. Abercrombie Smith," said Bellingham, glancing up at him. "How very good of you to come in! What a fool I am! Oh, my God, what a fool I am!" He sunk his head on to his hands, and burst into peal after peal of hysterical laughter.

"Look here! Drop it!" cried Smith, shaking him roughly by the shoulder. "Your nerves are all in a jangle. You must drop these little midnight games with mummies, or you'll be going off your chump. You're all on wires now."

"I wonder," said Bellingham, "whether you would be as cool as I am if you had seen—"

"What, then?"

"Oh, nothing. I meant that I wonder if you could sit up at night with a mummy without trying your nerves. I have no doubt that you are quite right. I dare say that I have been taking it out of myself too much lately. But I am all right now. Please don't go, though. Just wait for a few minutes until I am quite myself."

"The room is very close," remarked Lee, throwing open the window and letting in the cool night air.

"It's balsamic resin," said Bellingham. He lifted up one of the dried palmate leaves from the table and frizzled it up over the chimney of the lamp. It broke away into heavy smoke wreaths, and a pungent biting odor filled the chamber. "It's the sacred plant—the plant of the priests," he remarked. "Do you know anything of Eastern languages, Mr. Smith?"

"Nothing at all. Not a word."

The answer seemed to lift a weight from the Egyptologist's mind. "By-the-way," he continued, "how long was it from the time that you came down until I came to my senses?"

"Not long. Some four or five minutes."

"I thought it could not be very long," said he, drawing a long breath. "But what a strange thing unconsciousness is! There is no measurement to it. I could not tell from my own sensations if it were seconds or weeks. Now that gentleman on the table was packed up in the days of the eleventh dynasty, some forty centuries ago, and yet if he could find his tongue, he would tell us that this lapse of time has been but a closing of the eyes and a reopening of them. He is a singularly fine mummy, Mr. Smith."

Smith stepped over to the table and looked down with a professional eye at the black and twisted form in front of him. The features, though horribly discolored, were perfect, and two little nut-like eyes still lurked in the depths of the black hollow sockets. The blotched skin was drawn tightly from bone to bone, and a tangled wrap of black coarse hair fell over the ears. Two thin teeth, like those of a rat, overlay the shriveled lower lip. In its crouching position, with bent joints and craned head, there was a suggestion of energy about the horrid thing which made Smith's gorge rise. The gaunt ribs, with their parchmentlike covering, were exposed, and the sunken, leaden-hued abdomen, with the long slit where the embalmer had left his mark; but the lower limbs were wrapt round with coarse yellow bandages. A number of little clovelike pieces of myrrh and of cassia were sprinkled over the body, and lay scattered on the inside of the case.

"I don't know his name," said Bellingham, passing his hand over the shriveled head. "You see the outer sarcophagus with the inscriptions is missing. Lot 249 is all the title he has now. You see it printed on his case. That was his number in the auction at which I picked him up."

"He has been a pretty sort of fellow in his day," remarked Abercrombie Smith.

"He has been a giant. His mummy is six feet seven in length, and that would be a giant over there, for they were never a very robust race. Feel these great knotted bones too. He would be a nasty fellow to tackle."

"Perhaps these very hands helped to build the stones into the pyramids," suggested Monkhouse Lee, looking down with disgust in his eyes at the crooked, unclean talons.

"No fear. This fellow has been pickled in natron,[2] and looked after in the most approved style. They did not serve hodsmen[3] in that fashion. Salt or bitumen[4] was enough for them. It has been calculated that this sort of thing cost about seven hundred and

---

[2] Mineral salt used to preserving and made of hydrated sodium carbonate
[3] Blue collar worker
[4] A kind of dark, viscous tar

thirty pounds in our money. Our friend was a noble at the least. What do you make of that small inscription at his feet, Mr. Smith?"

"I told you that I know no Eastern tongue."

"Ah, so you did! It is the name of the embalmer, I take it. A very conscientious worker he must have been. I wonder how many modern works will survive four thousand years?"

He kept on speaking lightly and rapidly, but it was evident to Abercrombie Smith that he was still palpitating with fear. His hands shook, his lower lip trembled, and look where he would, his eye always came sliding round to his gruesome companion. Through all his fear, however, there was a suspicion of triumph in his tone and manner. His eye shone, and his footstep, as he paced the room, was brisk and jaunty. He gave the impression of a man who has gone through an ordeal the marks of which he still bears upon him, but which has helped him to his end.

"You're not going yet?" he cried, as Smith rose from the sofa. At the prospect of solitude, his fears seemed to crowd back upon him, and he stretched out a hand to detain him.

"Yes, I must go. I have my work to do. You are all right now. I think that with your nervous system you should take up some less morbid study."

"Oh, I am not nervous as a rule; and I have unwrapped mummies before."

"You fainted last time," observed Monkhouse Lee.

"Ah, yes, so I did. Well, I must have a nerve tonic or a course of electricity. You are not going, Lee?"

"I'll do whatever you wish, Ned."

"Then I'll come down with you and have a shake-down on your sofa. Good-night, Mr. Smith. I am so sorry to have disturbed you with my foolishness."

They shook hands, and as the medical student stumbled up the spiral and irregular stair he heard a key turn in a door and the steps of his two acquaintances as they descended to the lower floor.

In this strange way began the acquaintance between Edward Bellingham and Abercrombie Smith, an acquaintance which the latter, at least, had no desire to push further. Bellingham, however, appeared to have taken a fancy to his rough-spoken neighbor, and made his advances in such a way that he could hardly be repulsed without absolute brutality. Twice he called to thank Smith for his assistance, and many times afterwards he looked in with books, papers, and such other civilities as two bachelor neighbors can offer each other. He was, as Smith soon found, a man of wide reading, with catholic tastes and an extraordinary memory.

His manner, too, was so pleasing and suave that one came, after a time, to overlook his repellent appearance. For a jaded and wearied man he was no unpleasant companion, and Smith found himself, after a time, looking forward to his visits, and even returning them.

Clever as he undoubtedly was, however, the medical student seemed to detect a dash of insanity in the man. He broke out at times into a high inflated style of talk which was in contrast with the simplicity of his life.

"It is a wonderful thing," he cried, "to feel that one can command powers of good and evil—a ministering angel or a demon of vengeance." And again, of Monkhouse Lee he said: "Lee is a good fellow, an honest fellow, but he is without strength or ambition. He would not make a fit partner for a man with a great enterprise. He would not make a fit partner for me."

At such hints and innuendoes stolid Smith, puffing solemnly at his pipe, would simply raise his eyebrows and shake his head, with little interjections of medical wisdom as to earlier hours and fresher air.

One habit Bellingham had developed of late which Smith knew to be a frequent herald of a weakening mind. He appeared to be forever talking to himself. At late hours of the night, when there could be no visitor with him, Smith could still hear his voice beneath him in a low muffled monologue, sunk almost to a whisper, and yet very audible in the silence. This solitary babbling annoyed and distracted the student, so that he spoke more than once to his neighbor about it. Bellingham, however, flushed up at the charge, and denied curtly that he had uttered a sound; indeed, he showed more annoyance over the matter than the occasion seemed to demand.

Had Abercrombie Smith had any doubt as to his own ears he had not go far to find corroboration. Tom Styles, the little wrinkled manservant who had attended to the wants of the lodgers in the turret for a longer time than any man's memory could carry him, was sorely put to it over the same matter.

"If you please, sir," said he, as he tidied down the top chamber one morning, "do you think Mr. Bellingham is all right, sir?"

"All right, Styles?"

"Yes, sir. Right in the head, sir."

"Why should he not be, then?"

"Well, I don't know, sir. His habits has changed of late. He's not the same man he used to be, though I make free to say that he was never quite one of my gentlemen, like Mr. Hastie or yourself, sir. He's took to talkin' to himself something awful. I wonder it don't disturb you. And for days sometimes he'll keep his door locked, so as I can't even make the bed; and then again he'll have it open the same as ever—wide open so as all who pass can see his mummies and things. I don't know what to make of him, sir."

"I don't know what business it is of yours, Styles."

"Well, I takes an interest, Mr. Smith. It may be forward of me, but I can't help it. I feel sometimes as if I was mother and father to my young gentlemen. It all falls on me when things go wrong and the relations come. There was poor Mr. Williams, who went mad in '47. And Mr. McAlister in '62. Brain softening from overwork, they said. He lived in this very room. I don't speak of the *dliriumtremenses*[5] which I've had, three on each floor, and four on the lowest. But Mr. Bellingham, sir. I want to know what it is that walks about his room sometimes when he's out and when the door's locked on the outside."

"Eh? You're talking nonsense, Styles."

"Maybe so, sir; but I heard it more'n once with my own ears."

"Rubbish, Styles."

"Very good, sir. You'll ring the bell if you want me."

Abercrombie Smith gave little heed to the gossip of the old manservant, but a small incident occurred a few days later which left an unpleasant effect upon his mind, and brought the words of Styles forcibly to his memory.

Bellingham had come up to see him late one night, and was entertaining him with an interesting account of the rock tombs of Beni Hassan in Upper Egypt, when Smith, whose hearing was remarkably acute, distinctly heard the sound of a door opening on the landing below.

"There's some fellow gone in or out of your room," he remarked.

Bellingham sprang up and stood helpless for a moment, with the expression of a man who is half incredulous and half afraid.

"I surely locked it. I am almost positive that I locked it," he stammered. "No one could have opened it."

"Why, I hear someone coming up the steps now," said Smith.

Bellingham rushed out through the door, slammed it loudly behind him, and hurried down the stairs. About halfway down Smith heard him stop, and thought he caught the sounds of whispering. A moment later the door beneath him shut, a key creaked in a lock, and Bellingham, with beads of moisture upon his pale face, ascended the stairs once more, and re-entered the room.

"It's all right," he said, throwing himself down in a chair. "it was that fool of a dog. He had pushed the door open. I don't know how I can to forget to lock it."

"I didn't know you kept a dog," said Smith, looking very thoughtfully at the disturbed face of his companion.

"Yes. I haven't had him long. I must get rid of him. He's a great nuisance."

"He must be, if you find it so hard to shut him up. I should have thought that shutting the door would have been enough without locking it."

"I want to prevent old Styles from letting him out. He's of some value, you know, and it would be awkward to lose him."

"I am a bit of a dog-fancier myself," said Smith, still gazing hard at his companion from the corner of his eyes. "Perhaps you'll let me have a look at it."

"Certainly. But I am afraid it cannot be tonight; I have an appointment. Is that clock right? Then I am a quarter of an hour late already. You'll excuse me, I am sure." He picked up his cap

---

[5] Delirium Tremens, a nervous condition sometimes brought on by excessive drinking, which results in hallucinations and dizziness

and hurried from the room. In spite of his appointment, Smith heard him re-enter his own chamber and lock his door upon the inside.

This interview left a disagreeable impression upon the medical student's mind. Bellingham had lied to him, and lied so clumsily that it looked as if he had desperate reasons for concealing the truth. Smith knew that his neighbor had no dog. He knew, also, that the step which he had heard upon the stairs was not the step of an animal. But if it were not, then what could it be? There was old Styles's statement about the room at times when the owner was absent.

Could it be a woman?

Smith rather inclined to the view. If so, it would mean disgrace and expulsion to Bellingham if it were discovered by the authorities, so that his anxiety and falsehoods might be accounted for. And yet it was inconceivable that an undergraduate could keep a woman in his rooms without being instantly detected. Be the explanation what it might, there was something ugly about it, and Smith determined, as he turned to his books, to discourage all further attempts at intimacy on the part of his soft-spoken and ill-favored neighbor.

But his work was destined to interruption that night. He had hardly caught up the broken threads when a firm heavy footfall came three steps at a time from below, and Hastie, in blazer and flannels, burst into the room.

"Still at it!" said he, plumping down into his wonted armchair. "What a chap you are to stew! I believe an earthquake might come and knock Oxford into a cocked hat, and you would sit perfectly placid with your books among the ruins. However, I won't bore you long. Three whiffs of baccy,[6] and I am off."

"What's the news, then?" asked Smith, cramming a plug of bird's-eye[7] into his brier[8] with his forefinger.

"Nothing very much. Wilson made 70 for the freshman against the eleven. They say that they will play him instead of Buddicomb, for Buddicomb is clean off color. He used to be able to bowl a little, but it's nothing but half-vollies and long hops now."

"Medium right," suggested Smith, with the intense gravity which comes upon a 'varsity man when he speaks of athletics.

"Inclining to fast with a work from leg. Comes with the arm about three inches or so. He used to be nasty on a wet wicket. Oh, by-the-way, have you heard about Long Norton?"

"What's that?"

"He's been attacked."

"Attacked?"

"Yes; just as he was turning out of the High Street, and within a hundred yards of the gate of Old's."

---

6 Slang term for tobacco
7 Shredded tobacco
8 Smoking pipe

"But who—"

"Ah, that's the rub! If you said 'what,' you would be more grammatical. Norton swears that it was not human, and, indeed, from the scratches on his throat, I should be inclined to agree with him."

"What, then? Have we come down with the spooks?" Abercrombie Smith puffed his scientific contempt.

"Well, no; I don't think that is quite the idea, either. I am inclined to think that if any showman has lost a great ape lately, and the brute is in these parts, a jury would find a true bill against it. Norton passes that way every night, you know, about the same hour. There's a tree that hangs low over the path—the big elm from Rainy's garden. Norton thinks the thing dropped on him out of the tree. Anyhow, he was nearly strangled by two arms, which, he says, were as strong and as thin as steel bands. He saw nothing; only these beastly arms that tightened and tightened on him. He yelled his head nearly off, and a couple of chaps came running, and the thing went over the wall like a cat. He never got a fair sight of it the whole time. It gave Norton a shake up, I can tell you. I tell him it has been as good as a change at the seaside for him."

"A garrotter,[9] most likely," said Smith.

"Very possibly. Norton says not; but we don't mind what he says. The garrotter had long nails, and was pretty smart at swinging himself over walls. By-the-way, your beautiful neighbor would be pleased if he heard about it. He had a grudge against Norton, and he's not a man, from what I know about him, to forget his little debts. But hollo, old chap, what have you got in your noddle?"

"Nothing," Smith answered curtly. He had started in his chair, and the look had flashed over his face which comes upon a man who is struck suddenly by some unpleasant idea.

"You looked as if something I had said had taken you in the raw. By-the-way, you have made the acquaintance of Master B. since I looked in last, have you not? Young Monkhouse Lee told me something to that effect."

"Yes; I know him slightly. He has been up here once or twice."

"Well, you're big enough and ugly enough to take care of yourself. He's not what I should call exactly a healthy sort of Johnny, though, no doubt, he's very clever, and all that. But you'll soon find out for yourself. Lee is all right; he's a very decent little fellow. Well, so long, old chap! I row Mullins for the Vice-Chancellor's pot[10] on Wednesday week, so mind you come down, in case I don't see you before."

He clattered off, with a trail of smoke behind him like a steamer, while bovine Smith laid down his pipe and turned stolidly to his books once more. But with all the will in the world, he found it very hard to keep his mind upon his work. It would slip away to

---

9 Strangler
10 Trophy

brood upon the man beneath him, and upon the little mystery which seemed to hang round his chambers. Then his thoughts turned to this singular attack of which Hastie had spoken, and to the grudge which Bellingham was said to owe the object of it. The two ideas would persist in rising together in his mind, as though there were some close and intimate connection between them. And yet the suspicion was so dim and vague that it could not be put down in words.

"Confound the chap!" cried Smith, as he shied his book on pathology across the room. "He has spoiled my night's reading, and that's reason enough, if there were no other, why I should steer clear of him in the future."

For ten days the medical student confined himself so closely to his studies that he neither saw nor heard anything of either of the men beneath him. At the hours when Bellingham had been accustomed to visit him, he took care to sport his oak, and though he more than once heard a knocking at his outer door, he resolutely refused to answer it. One afternoon, however, he was descending the stairs when, just as he was passing it, Bellingham's door flew open, and young Monkhouse Lee came out with his eyes sparkling and a dark flush of anger upon his olive cheeks. Close at his heels followed Bellingham, his fat, unhealthy face all quivering with malignant passion.

"You fool!" he hissed. "You'll be sorry."

"Very likely," cried the other. "Mind what I say. It's off! I won't hear of it!"

"You've promised, anyhow."

"Oh, I'll keep that! I won't speak. But I'd rather little Eva was in her grave. Once for all, it's off. She'll do what I say. We don't want to see you again."

So much Smith could not avoid hearing, but he hurried on, for he had no wish to be involved in their dispute. There had been a serious breach between them, that was clear enough, and Lee was going to cause the engagement with his sister to be broken off. Smith thought of Hastie's comparison of the toad and the dove, and was glad to think that the matter was at an end. Bellingham's face when he was in a passion was not pleasant to look upon. He was not a man to whom an innocent girl could be trusted for life. As he walked, Smith wondered languidly what could have caused the quarrel, and what the promise might be which Bellingham had been so anxious that Monkhouse Lee should keep.

It was the day of the sculling match between Hastie and Mullins, and a stream of men were making their way down to the banks of the Isis. A May sun was shining brightly, and the yellow path was barred with the black shadows of the tall elm-trees. On either side of the gray colleges lay back from the road, the hoary old mothers of minds looking out from their high mullioned windows at the tide of young life which swept so merrily past them. Black-clad tutors, prim officials, pale reading men, brown-faced, straw-hatted young athletes in white sweaters or many-colored blazers, all were hurrying towards the blue winding river which curves through the Oxford meadows.

Abercrombie Smith, with the intuition of an old oarsman, chose his position at the point where he knew that the struggle, if there were a struggle, would come. Far off he heard the hum which announced the start, the gathering roar of the approach, the thunder of running feet, and the shouts of the men in the boats beneath him. A spray of half-clad, deep-breathing runners shot past him, and craning over their shoulders, he saw Hastie pulling a steady thirty-six, while his opponent, with a jerky forty, was a good boat's length behind him. Smith gave a bellow of approval, and pulling out his watch, was starting off again for his chambers, when he felt a touch upon his shoulder, and found that young Monkhouse Lee was beside him.

"I saw you there," he said, in a timid, deprecating way. "I wanted to speak to you, if you could spare me a half-hour. This cottage is mine. I share it with Harrington of King's. Come in and have a cup of tea."

"I must be back presently," said Smith. "I am hard on the grind at present. But I'll come in for a few minutes with pleasure. I wouldn't have come out only Hastie is a friend of mine."

"So he is of mine. Hasn't he a beautiful style? Mullins wasn't in it. But come into the cottage. It's a little den of a place, but it is pleasant to work in during the summer months."

It was a little square white building with green doors and shutters, and a rustic trellis-work porch, with a drapery of creepers over it, standing back some fifty yards from the river's bank. Inside, the main room was roughly fitted up as a study—deal table, unpainted shelves with books, and a few cheap oleographs upon the wall. A kettle sang upon a spirit-stove, and there were tea things upon a tray on the table.

"Try hat chair and have a cigarette," said Lee. "Let me pour you a cup of tea. It's so good of you to come in, for I know that your time is a good deal taken up. I wanted to say to you that if I were you I would change my rooms at once."

"Eh?" Smith sat staring with a lighted match in one hand and his unlit cigarette in the other.

"Yes; it must seem very extraordinary, and the worst of it is that I cannot give my reasons, for I am under a solemn promise—a very solemn promise. But I may go so far as to say that I don't think Bellingham is a very safe man to live near. I intend to camp out here as much as I can for a time."

"Not safe?" What do you mean?"

"Ah, that's what I mustn't say. But do take my advice, and move your rooms. We had a grand row today. You must have heard us, for you came down the stairs."

"I saw that you had fallen out."

"He's a horrible chap, Mr. Smith. That is the only word for him. I have had doubts about him ever since that night when he fainted—you remember, when you came down. I taxed him today, and he told me things that made my hair rise, and wanted me to stand in with him. I'm not so straight-laced, but I am a clergyman's son, you know, and I think there are some things which are quite beyond the pale. I only thank God that I found him out before it was too late, for he was to have married into my family."

"This is all very fine, Lee," said Abercrombie Smith, curtly. "But either you are saying a great deal too much or a great deal too little."

"I give you a warning."

"If there is a real reason for warning, no promise can bind you. If I see a rascal about to blow a place up with dynamite, no pledge will stand in my way of preventing him."

"Ah, but I cannot prevent him, and I can do nothing but warn you."

"Without saying what you warn me against."

"Against Bellingham."

"But that is childish. Why should I fear him, or any man?"

"I can't tell you. I can only entreat you to change your rooms. You are in danger where you are. I don't even say that Bellingham would wish to injure you. But it might happen, for he is a dangerous neighbor just now."

"Perhaps I know more than you think," said Smith, looking keenly at the young man's boyish, earnest face. "Suppose I tell you that someone else shares Bellingham's rooms."

Monkhouse Lee sprung from his chair in uncontrollable excitement. "You know, then?" he gasped.

"A woman."

Lee dropped back again with a groan. "My lips are sealed," he said. "I must not speak."

"Well, anyhow," said Smith, rising, "it is not likely that I would allow myself to be frightened out of rooms which suit me very nicely. It would be a little too feeble for me to move out all my goods and chattels because you say that Bellingham might in some unexplained way do me an injury. I think that I'll just take my chance, and stay where I am, and as I see that it's nearly five o'clock, I must ask you to excuse me." He bade the young student adieu in a few curt words, and made his way homeward through the sweet spring evening, feeling half ruffled, half amused, as any other strong, unimaginative man might who has been menaced by a vague and shadowy danger.

There was only one little indulgence which Abercrombie Smith always allowed himself, however closely his work might press upon him. Twice a week, on the Tuesday and the Friday, it was his invariable custom to walk over to Farlingford, the residence of the Reverend Plumptree Peterson, situated about a mile and a half out of Oxford. Peterson had been a close friend of Smith's elder brother Francis, and as he was a bachelor, fairly well-to-do, with a good cellar and a better library, his house was a pleasant goal for a man who was in need of a brisk walk.

Twice a week, then, the medical student would swing out there along the dark country roads, and spend a pleasant hour discussing, over a glass of old port, the gossip of the 'varsity or the latest black-letter which the book dealers had sent to his host.

On the day which followed his interview with Monkhouse Lee, Smith shut up his books at a quarter past eight, the hour when he usually started for his friend's house. As he was leaving his room, however, his eyes happened to fall upon one of the books which Bellingham had lent him, and his conscience pricked him for not having returned it. However repellent the man might be, he should not be treated with discourtesy. Taking the book, he walked down stairs and knocked at his neighbor's door. There was no answer; but on turning the handle he found that it was unlocked. Pleased at the thought of avoiding an interview, he stepped inside, and placed the book with his card upon the table.

The lamp was turned half down, but Smith could see the details of the room plainly enough. It was all much as he had seen it before—the frieze, the animal-headed gods, the hanging crocodile, and the table littered over with papers and dried leaves. The mummy case stood upright against the wall, but the mummy itself was missing. There was no sign of any second occupant of the room, and he felt as he withdrew that he had probably done Bellingham an injustice. Had he a guilty secret to preserve, he would hardly leave his door open so that all the world might enter.

The spiral stair was as black as pitch, and Smith was slowly making his way down its irregular steps, when he was suddenly conscious that something had passed him in the darkness. There was a faint sound, a whiff of air, a light brushing past his elbow, but so slight that he could scarcely be certain of it. He stopped and listened, but the wind was rustling among the ivy outside, and he could hear nothing else.

"Is that you, Styles?" he shouted.

There was no answer, and all was still behind him. It must have been a sudden gust of air, for there were crannies and cracks in the old turret. And yet he could almost have sworn that he heard a footfall by his very side. He had emerged into the quadrangle, still turning the matter over in his head, when a man came running swiftly cross the smooth-cropped lawn.

"Is that you, Smith?"

"Hullo, Hastie!"

"For God's sake come at once! Young Lee is drowned! Here's Harrington of King's with the news. The doctor is out. You'll do, but come along at once. There may be life in him."

"Have you brandy?"

"No."

"I'll bring some. There's a flask on my table."

Smith bounded up the stairs, taking three at a time, seized he flask, and was rushing down with it, when, as he passed Bellingham's room, his eyes fell upon something which left him gasping and staring upon the landing.

The door, which he had closed behind him, was now open, and right in front of him, with the lamplight shining upon it, was the mummy case. Three minutes ago it had been empty. He could swear to that. Now it framed the lank body of its horrible occupant, who stood, grim and stark, with his black shriveled face towards the door. The form was lifeless and inert, but it seemed to Smith as he gazed that there still lingered a lurid spark of vitality, some faint sign of consciousness in the little eyes which lurked in the depths of the hollow sockets. So astounded and shaken was he that he had forgotten his errand, and still stood staring at the lean sunken figure when the voice of his friend below recalled him to himself.

"Come on, Smith!" he shouted. "It's life and death, you know. Hurry up! Now, then," he added, as the medical student reappeared, "let us do a sprint. It is well under a mile, and we should do it in five minutes. A human life is better worth running for than a pot."

Away they dashed, neck and neck, through the darkness, and did not pull up until, panting and spent, they had reached the little cottage by the river. Young Lee, limp and dripping like a broken water-plant, was stretched upon the sofa, the green scum of the river upon his black hair, and a fringe of white foam upon his leaden-hued lips. Beside him knelt his fellow-student Harrington and their old housekeeper, endeavoring to chafe some warmth back into his rigid limbs.

"I think there's life in him," said Smith, with his hand to his side. "Put your watch glass to his lips. Yes, there's dimming on it. You take one arm, Hastie. Now work it as I do, and we'll soon pull him round."

For ten minutes they worked in silence, inflating and depressing the chest of the unconscious man. At the end of that time a shiver ran through his body, his lips trembled, and he opened his eyes. The three students burst out into an irrepressible cheer.

"Wake up, old chap. You've frightened us quite enough."

"Have some brandy. Take a sip from the flask."

"He's all right now," said his companion Harrington. "Heavens, what a fright I got! I was reading here, and he went out for a stroll as far as the river, when I heard a scream and a splash. Out I ran, and by the time I could find him and fish him out, all life seemed to have gone out of him. Then Mrs. Simpson couldn't get a doctor, for she has a game-leg, and I had to run, and I don't know what I'd have done without you fellows. That's right, old chap. Sit up."

Monkhouse Lee had raised himself on his hands, and looked wildly about him. "What's up?" he asked. "I've been in the water. Ah, yes; I remember." A look of fear came into his eyes, and he sank his face into his hands.

"How did you fall in?"

"I didn't fall in."

"How, then?"

"I was thrown in. I was standing by the bank, and something from behind picked me up like a feather and hurled me in. I heard nothing, and I saw nothing. But I know what it was for all that."

"And so do I," whispered Smith.

Lee looked up with a quick glance of surprise. "You've learned, then?" he said. "You remember the advice I gave you?"

"Yes, and I begin to think that I shall take it."

"I don't know what the deuce you fellows are talking about," said Hastie, "but I think if I were you, Harrington, I would get Lee to bed at once. It will be time enough to discuss the why and the wherefore when he is a little stronger. I think, Smith, you and I can leave him alone now. I am walking back to the college; if you are coming in that direction, we can have a chat."

But it was little chat that they had upon their homeward path. Smith's mind was too full of the incidents of the evening, the absence of the mummy from his neighbor's rooms, the step that passed him on the stair, the reappearance—the extraordinary, inexplicable reappearance of the grisly thing—and then this attack upon Lee, corresponding so closely to the previous outrage upon another man against whom Bellingham bore a grudge.

All this settled in his thoughts, together with the many little incidents which had previously turned him against his neighbor, and the singular circumstances under which he was first called in to him. What had been a dim suspicion, a vague fantastic conjecture, had suddenly taken form, and stood out in his mind as a grim fact, a thing not to be denied. And yet how monstrous it was! how unheard of! how entirely beyond all bounds of human experience.

An impartial judge, or even the friend who walked by his side, would simply tell him that his eyes had deceived him, that the mummy had been there all the time, that young Lee had tumbled into the river as any other man tumbles into a river, and that a blue-pill was the best thing for a disordered liver. He felt that he would have said as much if the positions had been reversed. And yet he could swear that Bellingham was a murderer at heart, and that he wielded a weapon such as no man had ever used in all the grim history of crime.

Hastie had branched off to his rooms with a few crisp and emphatic comments upon his friend's unsociability, and Abercrombie Smith crossed the quadrangle to his corner turret with a strong feeling of repulsion for his chambers and their associations. He would take Lee's advice, and move his quarters as soon as possible, for how could a man study when his ear was ever straining for every murmur or footstep in the room below? He observed, as he crossed over the lawn, that the light was still shining in Bellingham's window, and as he passed up the staircase the door opened, and the man himself looked out at him. With his fat evil face he was like some bloated spider fresh from the weaving of his poisonous web.

"Good-evening," said he. "Won't you come in?"

"No," cried Smith, fiercely.

"No?" You are busy as ever? I wanted to ask you about Lee. I was sorry to hear that there was a rumor that something was amiss with him." His features were grave, but there was the gleam of a hidden laugh in his eyes as he spoke. Smith saw it, and he could have knocked him down for it.

"You'll be sorrier still to hear that Mr. Monkhouse Lee is doing very well, and is out of all danger," he answered. "Your hellish tricks have not come off, this time. Oh, you needn't try to brazen it out. I know all about it."

Bellingham took a step back from the angry student, and half closed the door as if to protect himself. "You are mad," he said. "What do you mean? Do you assert that I had anything to do with Lee's accident?"

"Yes," thundered Smith. "You and that bag of bones behind you; you worked it between you. I tell you what it is, Master B., they have given up burning folk like you, but we still keep a hangman, and, by George! if any man in this college meets his death while you are here, I'll have you up, and if you don't swing for it, it won't be my fault. You'll find that your filthy Egyptian tricks won't answer in England."

"You're a raving lunatic," said Bellingham.

"All right. You just remember what I say, for you'll find that I'll be better than my word."

The door slammed, and Smith went fuming up to his chamber, where he spent half the night smoking his old brier and brooding over the strange events of the evening.

On the next day Abercrombie Smith heard nothing of his neighbor, but Harrington called upon him in the afternoon to say that Lee was almost himself again. All day Smith stuck fast to his work, but in the evening he determined to pay the visit to his friend Peterson which he had started upon the night before. It was he first time that he had failed to put in an appearance, and he knew that Peterson would be expecting an explanation for his absence the previous evening. A good walk and a friendly chat would be welcome to his jangled nerves after all that had occurred.

Bellingham's door was shut as he passed, but glancing back when he was some distance from the turret, he saw his neighbor's head at the window outlined against the lamplight, his face pressed apparently against the glass as he gazed out into the darkness. It was a blessing to be away from all contact with him, if but for a few hours, and Smith stepped out briskly, and breathed the soft spring air into his lungs. The half-moon lay in the west between two Gothic pinnacles, and threw upon the silvered street a dark tracery from the stone-work above. There was a brisk breeze, and light fleecy clouds drifted swiftly across the sky. Old's was on the very border of the town, and in five minutes Smith found himself beyond the houses and between the hedges of a May-scented Oxfordshire lane.

It was a lonely and little-frequented road which led to his friend's house. Early as it was, Smith did not meet a single soul upon his way. He walked briskly along until he came to the avenue gate, which opened into the long gravel drive leading up to Farlingford. In front of him he could see the cozy red light of the windows glimmering through the foliage. He stood with his hand upon the iron latch of the swinging gate, and he glanced back at the road along which he had come. Something was coming swiftly down it.

It moved in the shadow of the hedge, silently and furtively, a dark crouching figure, dimly visible against the black background. Even as he gazed back at it it had lessened its distance by twenty paces, and was fast closing upon him. Out of the darkness he had a glimpse of a scraggy neck, and of two eyes that will ever haunt him in his dreams. He turned, and with a cry of terror he ran for his life up the avenue. There were the red lights, the signals of safety, almost within a stone's-throw of him. He was a famous runner, but never had he run as he ran that night.

The heavy gate had swung into place behind him, but he heard it dash open again before his pursuer. As he rushed madly and wildly through the night he could hear a swift dry patter behind him, and could see, as he threw back a glance, that this horror was bounding like a tiger at his heels, with blazing eyes and stringy arms out-thrown. Thank God, the door was ajar.

He could see the thin bar of light which shot from the lamp in the hall. Nearer yet sounded the clatter from behind. He heard a hoarse gurgling at his very shoulder. With a shriek he flung himself against the door, slammed and bolted it behind him, and sank half-fainting on to the hall chair.

"My goodness, Smith, what's the matter?" asked Peterson, appearing at the door of his study.

"Give me some brandy!"

Peterson disappeared, and came rushing out again with a glass and a decanter.

"You need it," he said, as his visitor drank off what he poured out for him. "Why, man, you are as white as a cheese."

Smith laid down his glass, rose up, and took a deep breath. "I am my own man again now," said he. "I was never so unmanned before. But, with your leave, Peterson, I will sleep here tonight, for I don't think I could face that road again except by daylight. It's weak, I know, but I can't help it."

Peterson looked at his visitor with a very questioning eye. "Of course you shall sleep here if you wish. I'll tell Mrs. Burney to make up the spare bed. Where are you off to now?"

"Come with me to the window that overlooks the door. I want you to see what I have seen."

They went up to the window of the upper hall, whence they could overlook the whole front of the house. The drive and the fields on either side lay quiet and still, bathed in the peaceful moonlight.

"Well, really, Smith," remarked Peterson, "it is well that I know you to be an abstemious man. What in the world can have frightened you?"

"I'll tell you presently. But where can it have gone? Ah, now look, look! See the curve of the road just beyond your gate."

"Yes, I see: you needn't pinch my arm off. I saw some one pass. I should say a man, rather thin apparently, and tall, very tall. But what of him? And what of yourself? You are still shaking like an aspen leaf."

"I have been within the hand-grip of the devil, that's all. But come down to your study, and I shall tell you the whole story."

He did so. Under the cheery lamplight, with a glass of wine on the table beside him, and the portly form and florid face of his friend in front, he narrated, in their order, all the events, great and small, which had formed so singular a chain, from the night on which he had found Bellingham fainting in front of the mummy case until his horrid experience of an hour ago.

"There, now," he said, as he concluded, "that's the whole black business. It is monstrous and incredible, but it is true."

The Reverend Plumptree Peterson sat for some time in silence with a very puzzled expression upon his face.

"I never heard of such a thing in my life, never!" he said at last. "You have told me the facts. Now tell me your inferences."

"You can draw your own."

"But I should like to hear yours. You have thought over the matter, and I have not."

"Well, it must be a little vague in detail, but the main points seem to me to be clear enough. This fellow Bellingham in his Eastern studies has got hold of some infernal secret by which a mummy—or possibly only this particular mummy—can be temporarily bought to life. He was trying this disgusting business on the night he fainted. No doubt the sight of the creature moving had shaken his nerve, even though he had expected it.

"You remember that almost the first words he said was to call out upon himself as a fool. Well, he got more hardened afterwards, and carried the matter through without fainting. The vitality which he could put into it was evidently only a passing thing, for I have seen it continually in its case as dead as this table. He has some elaborate process, I fancy, by which he brings the thing to pass. Having done it, he naturally bethought him that he might use the creature as an agent. It has intelligence and it has strength.

"For some purpose he took Lee into his confidence; but Lee, like a decent Christian, would have nothing to do with such a business. Then they had a row, and Lee vowed that he would tell his sister of Bellingham's true character. Bellingham's game was to prevent him, and he nearly managed it, by setting this creature of his on his track. He had already tried its powers upon another man—Norton—towards whom he had a grudge. It is the merest chance that he has not two murders upon his soul.

"Then, when I taxed him with the matter, he had the strongest reasons for wishing to get me out of the way before I could convey my knowledge to anyone else. He got his chance when I went out, for he knew my habits, and where I was bound for. I have had a narrow shave, Peterson, and it is mere luck you didn't find me on your doorstep this morning. I'm not a nervous man as a rule, and I never thought to have the fear of death put upon me as it was tonight."

"My dear boy, you take the matter too seriously," said his companion. "Your nerves are out of order with your work, and you make too much of it. How could such a thing as this stride about the streets of Oxford, even at night, without being seen?"

"It has been seen. There is quite a scare in the town about an escaped ape, as they imagine the creature to be. It is the talk of the place."

"Well, it's a striking chain of events. And yet, my dear fellow, you must allow that each incident in itself is capable of a more natural explanation."

"What! even my adventure of tonight?"

"Certainly. You come out with your nerves all unstrung, and your head full of this theory of yours. Some gaunt, half-famished tramp steals after you, and seeing you run is emboldened to pursue you. Your fears and imagination do the rest."

"It won't do, Peterson; it won't do."

"And again in the instance of your finding the mummy case empty, and then a few moments later an occupant, you know that it was lamplight, that the lamp was half turned down, and that you had no special reason to look hard at the case. It is quite possible that you may have overlooked the creature in the first instance."

"No, no; it is out of the question."

"And then Lee may have fallen into the river, and Norton been garroted. It is certainly a formidable indictment that you have made against Bellingham; but if you were to place it before a police magistrate, he could simply laugh in your face."

"I know he would. That is why I mean to take the matter into my own hands."

"Eh?"

"Yes; I feel that a public duty rests upon me. And besides, I must do it for my own safety, unless I choose to allow myself to be hunted by this beast out of the college, and that would be a little too feeble. I have quite made up my mind what I shall do. And first of all, may I use your paper and pens for an hour?"

"Most certainly. You will find all that you want upon that side table."

Abercrombie Smith sat down before a sheet of fool's-cap, and for an hour, and then for a second hour, his pen traveled swiftly over it. Page after page was finished and tossed aside, while his friend leaned back in his arm-chair, looking across at him with patient curiosity. At last, with an exclamation of satisfaction, Smith sprang to his feet, gathered his papers up into order, and laid the last one upon Peterson's desk.

"Kindly sign this as witness," he said.

"A witness? Of what?"

"Of my signature, and of the date. The date is the most important. Why, Peterson, my life might hang upon it."

"My dear Smith, you are talking wildly. Let me beg you to go to bed."

"On the contrary, I never spoke so deliberately in my life. And I will promise to go to bed the moment you have signed it."

"But what is it?"

"It is a statement of all that I have been telling you tonight. I wish you to witness it."

"Certainly," said Peterson, signing his name under that of his companion. "There you are! But what is the idea?"

"You will kindly retain it, and produce it in case I am arrested."

"Arrested? For what?"

"For murder. It is quite on the cards. I wish to be ready for every event. There is only one course open to me, and I am determined to take it."

"For Heaven's sake, don't do anything rash!"

"Believe me, it would be far more rash to adopt any other course. I hope that we won't need to bother you, but it will ease my mind to know that you have this statement of my motives. And now I am ready to take your advice and to go to roost, for I want to be at my best in the morning."

Abercrombie Smith was not an entirely pleasant man to have as an enemy. Slow and easy-tempered, he was formidable when driven to action. He brought to every purpose in life the same deliberate resoluteness which had distinguished him as a scientific student. He had laid his studies aside for a day, but he intended that the day should not be wasted. Not a word did he say to his host as to his plans, but by nine o'clock he was well on his way to Oxford.

In the High Street he stopped at Clifford's, the gun-maker's, and bought a heavy revolver, with a box of central-fire cartridges. Six of them he slipped into the chambers, and half-cocking the weapon, placed it in the pocket of his coat. He then made his way to Hastie's rooms, where the big oarsman was lounging over his breakfast, with the *Sporting Times*[11] propped up against the coffeepot.

"Hullo! What's up?" he asked. "Have some coffee?"

"No, thank you. I want you to come with me, Hastie, and do what I ask you."

"Certainly, my boy."

"And bring a heavy stick with you."

---

[11] Weekly British publication founded in 1865 with focused articles on sports

"Hullo!" Hastie stared. "Here's a hunting-crop that would fell an ox."

"One other thing. You have a box of amputating-knives. Give me the longest of them."

"There you are. You seem to be fairly on the war trail. Anything else?"

"No; that will do." Smith placed the knife inside his coat, and led the way to the quadrangle. "We are neither of us chickens, Hastie," said he. "I think I can do this job alone, but I take you as a precaution. I am going to have a little talk with Bellingham. If I have only him to deal with, I won't, of course, need you. If I shout, however, up you come, and lam out with your whip as hard as you can lick. Do you understand?"

"All right. I'll come if I hear you bellow."

"Stay here, then. I may be a little time, but don't budge until I come down."

"I'm a fixture."

Smith ascended the stairs, opened Bellingham's door, and stepped in. Bellingham was seated behind his table, writing. Beside him, among his litter of strange possessions, towered the mummy case, with its sale number 249 still stuck upon its front, and its hideous occupant stiff and stark within it. Smith looked very deliberately round him, closed the door, locked it, and took the key from the inside, and then stepping across to the fireplace, struck a match and set the fire alight. Bellingham sat staring, with amazement and rage upon his bloated face.

"Well, really now. You make yourself at home," he gasped.

Smith sat himself deliberately down, placed his watch upon the table, drew out his pistol, cocked it, and laid it in his lap. Then he took the long amputating-knife from his bosom, and threw it down in front of Bellingham. "Now, then," said he. "Just get to work and cut up that mummy."

"Oh, is that it?" said Bellingham, with a sneer.

"Yes, that is it. They tell me that the law can't touch you. But I have a law that will set matters straight. If in five minutes you have not set to work, I swear by the God who made me that I will put a bullet through your brain!"

"You would murder me?" Bellingham had half risen, and his face was the color of clay.

"Yes."

"And for what?"

"To stop your mischief. One minute has gone."

"But what have I done?"

"I know and you know."

"This is mere bullying."

"Two minutes are gone."

"But you must give reasons. You are a madman—a dangerous madman. Why should I destroy my own property? It is a valuable mummy."

"You must cut it up, and you must burn it."

"I will do no such thing."

"Four minutes are gone. Smith took up the pistol, and he looked towards Bellingham with an inexorable face. As the second-hand stole round, he raised his hand, and the finger twitched upon he trigger.

"There! there! I'll do it!" screamed Bellingham. In frantic haste he caught up the knife and hacked at the figure of the mummy, ever glancing round to see the eye and the weapon of his terrible visitor bent upon him. The creature crackled and snapped under every stab of the keen blade. A thick yellow dust rose up from it. Spices and dried essences rained down upon he floor. Suddenly, with a rending crack, its backbone snapped asunder, and it fell, a brown heap of sprawling limbs, upon the floor.

"Now into the fire!" said Smith.

The flames leaped and roared as the dried and tinderlike *débris* was piled upon it. The little room was like the stokehole of a steamer,[12] and the sweat ran down the faces of the two men; but still the one stooped and worked, while the other sat watching him with a set face. A thick fat smoke oozed out from the fire, and a heavy smell of burned rosin and singed hair filled the air. In a quarter of an hour a few charred and brittle sticks were all that was left of Lot No. 249.

"Perhaps that will satisfy you," snarled Bellingham, with hate and fear in his little gray eyes as he glanced back at his tormentor.

"No; I must make a clean sweep of all your materials. We must have no more devil's tricks. In with all these leaves! They may have something to do with it."

"And what now?" asked Bellingham, when the leaves also had been added to the blaze.

"Now the roll of papyrus which you had on the table that night. It is in that drawer I think.

"No, no," shouted Bellingham. "Don't burn that! Why, man, you don't know what you do! It is unique; it contains wisdom which is nowhere else to be found."

"Out with it!"

"But look here, Smith, you can't really mean it. I'll share the knowledge with you. I'll teach you all that is in it. Or, stay, let me only copy it before you burn it!"

Smith stepped forward and turned the key in the drawer. Taking out the yellow curled roll of paper, he threw it into the fire, and pressed it down with his heel. Bellingham screamed, and grabbed at it; but Smith pushed him back, and stood over it until it was reduced to a formless gray ash.

"Now, Master B.," said he, "I think I have pretty well drawn your teeth. You'll hear from me again, if you go back to your old tricks. And now, good-morning, for I must go back to my studies."

---

12 Coal-fired steamship

And such is the narrative of Abercrombie Smith as to the singular events which occurred in Old College, Oxford, in the spring of '84. As Bellingham left the university immediately afterwards, and was last heard of in the Soudan, there is no one who can contradict his statement. But the wisdom of men is small, and the ways of nature are strange, and who shall put a bound to the dark things which may be found by those who seek for them?

Charlotte Perkins Gilman
(1860-1935)

In the horror story buffet laid out during the latter half of the nineteenth century, women started taking their rightful place at table. These were fantastic authors like Amelia B. Edwards, Elizabeth Gaskell, Louisa May Alcott, Lady Emilia Frances Dilke, Edith Nesbit, and Ellen Wood. For the first time Victorian reserve and sensibilities began to be slowly pushed aside to clear the way for women who penned stories in the horror and ghost story genres. Many of them started using their real names instead of writing under pseudonyms or using just letters before their surnames so the sex of the author was unclear.

Charlotte Perkins Gilman was neither afraid of using her real name nor publishing in the supernatural genre that had primarily been the haunt of men. Gilman was one of the best in crafting storylines and getting inside the heads of fictional characters. Despite her overwhelming talents as a fiction author and the increasing number of women authors entering the supernatural scene, Gilman was acutely aware she was an outsider in the Victorian Age.

She was an early American feminist who wrote excellent poems and short stories, including "The Rocking Chair" (1893) and "The Unwatched Door" (1894). Her ghost story "The Giant Wistaria," one of three she penned, was published in 1890 in the *New England Magazine*. That same magazine would publish her most famous story, "The Yellow Wallpaper," two years later.

"The Yellow Wallpaper" draws from a dark time in her life when she suffered postpartum depression and became bedridden. It was published three years after she divorced her husband and nearly eight years after she gave birth to her daughter Katharine. The horror thriller draws certain parallels to Anton Chekov's tightly-wound tale "Sleepyhead"(1888). Yet "Sleepyhead," though more sinister, fails in both character generation and writing style.

The nervous protagonist of "The Yellow Wallpaper" further draws parallels to Edgar Allan Poe's "The Tell-Tale Heart" (1843), published some 50 years earlier. The nervousness, however, builds more slowly in Gilman's story, and to great effect. The first line in Poe's story reads:

True!—nervous—very, very dreadfully nervous I had been and am; but why will you say that I am mad?

Unlike "The Tell-Tale Heart," the first line of "The Yellow Wallpaper" foretells nothing of what is to come in the story. This provides ample space for Gilman to build her story into one of the creepiest endings in horror literature.

The Yellow Wallpaper
1892

IT IS VERY seldom that mere ordinary people like John and myself secure ancestral halls for the summer.

A colonial mansion, a hereditary estate, I would say a haunted house, and reach the height of romantic felicity,—but that would be asking too much of fate!

Still I will proudly declare that there is something queer about it. Else, why should it be let so cheaply? And why have stood so long untenanted?

John laughs at me, of course, but one expects that in marriage. John is practical in the extreme. He has no patience with faith, an intense horror of superstition, and he scoffs openly at any talk of things not to be felt and seen and put down in figures.

John is a physician, and *perhaps*—(I would not say it to a living soul, of course, but this is dead paper and a great relief to my mind)—*perhaps* that is one reason I do not get well faster.

You see, he does not believe I am sick! And what can one do?

If a physician of high standing, and one's own husband, assures friends and relatives that there is really nothing the matter with one but temporary nervous depression,—a slight hysterical tendency,—what is one to do?

My brother is also a physician, and also of high standing, and he says the same thing. So I take phosphates or phosphites,[1]—whichever it is,—and tonics, and journeys, and air, and exercise, and am absolutely forbidden to "work" until I am well again.

Personally I disagree with their ideas.

Personally I believe that congenial work, with excitement and change, would do me good.

But what is one to do?

I did write for a while in spite of them; but it *does* exhaust me a good deal—having to be so sly about it, or else meet with heavy opposition.

I sometimes fancy that in my condition if I had less opposition and more society and stimulus—but John says the very worst thing I can do is to think about my condition, and I confess it always makes me feel bad.

So I will let it alone and talk about the house.

---

[1] Salt having minerals and used as an oral tonic to rejuvenate health

The most beautiful place! It is quite alone, standing well back from the road, quite three miles from the village. It makes me think of English places that you read about, for there are hedges and walls and gates that lock, and lots of separate little houses for the gardeners and people.

There is a *delicious* garden! I never saw such a garden—large and shady, full of box-bordered paths, and lined with long grape-covered arbors with seats under them. There were greenhouses, too, but they are all broken now. There was some legal trouble, I believe, something about the heirs and co-heirs; anyhow, the place has been empty for years.

That spoils my ghostliness, I am afraid; but I don't care—there is something strange about the house—I can feel it.

I even said so to John one moonlight evening, but he said what I felt was a *draught,* and shut the window.

I get unreasonably angry with John sometimes. I'm sure I never used to be so sensitive. I think it is due to this nervous condition. But John says if I feel so I shall neglect proper self-control; so I take pains to control myself,—before him, at least,—and that makes me very tired.

I don't like our room a bit. I wanted one downstairs that opened on the piazza and had roses all over the window, and such pretty, old-fashioned chintz hangings! but John would not hear of it.

He said there was only one window and not room for two beds, and no near room for him if he took another. He is very careful and loving, and hardly lets me stir without special direction.

I have a schedule prescription for each hour in the day; he takes all care from me, and so I feel basely ungrateful not to value it more.

He said we came here solely on my account, that I was to have perfect rest and all the air I could get. "Your exercise depends on your strength, my dear," said he, "and your food somewhat on your appetite; but air you can absorb all the time." So we took the nursery, at the top of the house.

It is a big, airy room, the whole floor nearly, with windows that look all ways, and air and sunshine galore. It was nursery first and then playground and gymnasium, I should judge; for the windows are barred for little children, and there are rings and things in the walls.

The paint and paper look as if a boys' school had used it. It is stripped off—the paper—in great patches all around the head of my bed, about as far as I can reach, and in a great place on the other side of the room low down. I never saw a worse paper in my life.

One of those sprawling flamboyant patterns committing every artistic sin.

It is dull enough to confuse the eye in following, pronounced enough to constantly irritate, and provoke study, and when you follow the lame, uncertain curves for a little distance they suddenly commit suicide—plunge off at outrageous angles, destroy themselves in unheard-of contradictions.

The color is repellant, almost revolting; a smoldering, unclean yellow, strangely faded by the slow-turning sunlight. It is a dull yet lurid orange in some places, a sickly sulphur tint in others.

No wonder the children hated it! I should hate it myself if I had to live in this room long.

There comes John, and I must put this away,—he hates to have me write a word.

***

WE HAVE BEEN here two weeks, and I haven't felt like writing before, since that first day.

I am sitting by the window now, up in this atrocious nursery, and there is nothing to hinder my writing as much as I please, save lack of strength.

John is away all day, and even some nights when his cases are serious.

I am glad my case is not serious!

But these nervous troubles are dreadfully depressing.

John does not know how much I really suffer. He knows there is no *reason* to suffer, and that satisfies him.

Of course it is only nervousness. It does weigh on me so not to do my duty in any way!

I meant to be such a help to John, such a real rest and comfort, and here I am a comparative burden already! Nobody would believe what an effort it is to do what little I am able—to dress and entertain, and order things.

It is fortunate Mary is so good with the baby. Such a dear baby!

And yet I *cannot* be with him, it makes me so nervous.

I suppose John never was nervous in his life. He laughs at me so about this wallpaper!

At first he meant to repaper the room, but afterwards he said that I was letting it get the better of me, and that nothing was worse for a nervous patient than to give way to such fancies.

IIc said that after the wallpaper was changed it would be the heavy bedstead, and then the barred windows, and then that gate at the head of the stairs, and so on.

"You know the place is doing you good," he said, "and really, dear, I don't care to renovate the house just for a three months' rental."

"Then do let us go downstairs," I said, "there are such pretty rooms there."

Then he took me in his arms and called me a blessed little goose, and said he would go down cellar if I wished, and have it whitewashed into the bargain.

But he is right enough about the beds and windows and things. It is as airy and comfortable a room as any one need wish, and, of course, I would not be so silly as to make him uncomfortable just for a whim.

I'm really getting quite fond of the big room, all but that horrid paper.

Out of one window I can see the garden, those mysterious deep-shaded arbors, the riotous old-fashioned flowers, and bushes and gnarly trees.

Out of another I get a lovely view of the bay and a little private wharf belonging to the estate. There is a beautiful shaded lane that runs down there from the house. I always fancy I see people walking in these numerous paths and arbors, but John has cautioned me not to give way to fancy in the least. He says that with my imaginative power and habit of storymaking a nervous weakness like mine is sure to lead to all manner of excited fancies, and that I ought to use my will and good sense to check the tendency. So I try.

I think sometimes that if I were only well enough to write a little it would relieve the press of ideas and rest me.

But I find I get pretty tired when I try.

It is so discouraging not to have any advice and companionship about my work. When I get really well John says we will ask Cousin Henry and Julia down for a long visit; but he says he would as soon put fireworks in my pillowcase as to let me have those stimulating people about now.

I wish I could get well faster.

But I must not think about that. This paper looks to me as if it *knew* what a vicious influence it had!

There is a recurrent spot where the pattern lolls like a broken neck and two bulbous eyes stare at you upside down.

I got positively angry with the impertinence of it and the everlastingness. Up and down and sideways they crawl, and those absurd, unblinking eyes are everywhere. There is one place where two breadths didn't match, and the eyes go all up and down the line, one a little higher than the other.

I never saw so much expression in an inanimate thing before, and we all know how much expression they have! I used to lie awake as a child and get more entertainment and terror out of blank walls and plain furniture than most children could find in a toy store.

I remember what a kindly wink the knobs of our big old bureau used to have, and there was one chair that always seemed like a strong friend. I used to feel that if any of the other things looked too fierce I could always hop into that chair and be safe.

The furniture in this room is no worse than inharmonious, however, for we had to bring it all from downstairs. I suppose when this was used as a playroom they had to take the nursery things out, and no wonder! I never saw such ravages as the children have made here.

The wallpaper, as I said before, is torn off in spots, and it sticketh closer than a brother—they must have had perseverance as well as hatred.

Then the floor is scratched and gouged and splintered, the plaster itself is dug out here and there, and this great heavy bed, which is all we found in the room, looks as if it had been through the wars.

But I don't mind it a bit—only the paper.

There comes John's sister. Such a dear girl as she is, and so careful of me! I must not let her find me writing.

She is a perfect, an enthusiastic housekeeper, and hopes for no better profession. I verily believe she thinks it is the writing which made me sick!

But I can write when she is out, and see her a long way off from these windows.

There is one that commands the road, a lovely, shaded, winding road, and one that just looks off over the country. A lovely country, too, full of great elms and velvet meadows.

This wallpaper has a kind of subpattern in a different shade, a particularly irritating one, for you can only see it in certain lights, and not clearly then.

But in the places where it isn't faded, and where the sun is just so, I can see a strange, provoking, formless sort of figure, that seems to sulk about behind that silly and conspicuous front design.

There's sister on the stairs!

***

WELL, THE FOURTH of July is over! The people are all gone and I am tired out. John thought it might do me good to see a little company, so we just had mother and Nellie and the children down for a week.

Of course I didn't do a thing. Jennie sees to everything now.

But it tired me all the same.

John says if I don't pick up faster he shall send me to Weir Mitchell in the fall. But I don't want to go there at all. I had a friend who was in his hands once, and she says he is just like John and my brother, only more so!

Besides, it is such an undertaking to go so far.

I don't feel as if it was worthwhile to turn my hand over for anything, and I'm getting dreadfully fretful and querulous.

I cry at nothing, and cry most of the time.

Of course I don't when John is here, or anybody else, but when I am alone.

And I am alone a good deal just now. John is kept in town very often by serious cases, and Jennie is good and lets me alone when I want her to.

So I walk a little in the garden or down that lovely lane, sit on the porch under the roses, and lie down up here a good deal.

I'm getting really fond of the room in spite of the wallpaper. Perhaps *because* of the wallpaper.

It dwells in my mind so!

I lie here on this great immovable bed—it is nailed down, I believe—and follow that pattern about by the hour. It is as good as gymnastics, I assure you. I start, we'll say, at the bottom, down in the corner over there where it has not been touched, and I determine for the thousandth time that I *will* follow that pointless pattern to some sort of a conclusion.

I know a little of the principles of design, and I know this thing was not arranged on any laws of radiation, or alternation, or repetition, or symmetry, or anything else that I ever heard of.

It is repeated, of course, by the breadths, but not otherwise.

Looked at in one way, each breadth stands alone, the bloated curves and flourishes—a kind of "debased Romanesque"[2] with *delirium tremens*[3]—go waddling up and down in isolated columns of fatuity.

But, on the other hand, they connect diagonally, and the sprawling outlines run off in great slanting waves of optic horror, like a lot of wallowing seaweeds in full chase.

The whole thing goes horizontally, too, at least it seems so, and I exhaust myself in trying to distinguish the order of its going in that direction. They have used a horizontal breadth for a frieze,[4] and that adds wonderfully to the confusion.

There is one end of the room where it is almost intact, and there, when the cross-lights fade and the low sun shines directly upon it, I can almost fancy radiation, after all,—the interminable grotesques seem to form around a common center and rush off in headlong plunges of equal distraction.

It makes me tired to follow it. I will take a nap, I guess.

I don't know why I should write this.

I don't want to.

I don't feel able.

And I know John would think it absurd. But I *must* say what I feel and think in some way—it is such a relief!

But the effort is getting to be greater than the relief.

Half the time now I am awfully lazy, and lie down ever so much.

John says I mustn't lose my strength, and has me take cod-liver oil and lots of tonics and things, to say nothing of ale and wine and rare meat.

Dear John! He loves me very dearly, and hates to have me sick. I tried to have a real earnest reasonable talk with him the other day, and tell him how I wished he would let me go and make a visit to Cousin Henry and Julia.

---

[2] Type of architectural punctuated by semi-circular arches
[3] Quick onset of frustration or confusion, usually caused by alcohol or stimulant withdrawal
[4] Artsy horizontal paper strip

But he said I wasn't able to go, nor able to stand it after I got there; and I did not make out a very good case for myself, for I was crying before I had finished.

It is getting to be a great effort for me to think straight. Just this nervous weakness, I suppose.

And dear John gathered me up in his arms, and just carried me upstairs and laid me on the bed, and sat by me and read to me till he tired my head.

He said I was his darling and his comfort and all he had, and that I must take care of myself for his sake, and keep well. He says no one but myself can help me out of it, that I must use my will and self-control and not let my silly fancies run away with me.

There's one comfort, the baby is well and happy, and does not have to occupy this nursery with the horrid wallpaper.

If we had not used it that blessed child would have! What a fortunate escape! Why, I wouldn't have a child of mine, an impressionable little thing, live in such a room for worlds.

I never thought of it before, but it is lucky that John kept me here, after all. I can stand it so much easier than a baby, you see. Of course I never mention it to them anymore,—I am too wise,—but I keep watch of it all the same.

There are things in that paper that nobody knows but me, or ever will.

Behind that outside pattern the dim shapes get clearer every day.

It is always the same shape, only very numerous.

And it is like a woman stooping down and creeping about behind that pattern. I don't like it a bit. I wonder—I begin to think—I wish John would take me away from here!

It is so hard to talk with John about my case, because he is so wise, and because he loves me so.

But I tried it last night.

It was moonlight. The moon shines in all around, just as the sun does.

I hate to see it sometimes, it creeps so slowly, and always comes in by one window or another.

John was asleep and I hated to waken him, so I kept still and watched the moonlight on that undulating wallpaper till I felt creepy.

The faint figure behind seemed to shake the pattern, just as if she wanted to get out.

I got up softly and went to feel and see if the paper *did* move, and when I came back John was awake.

"What is it, little girl?" he said. "Don't go walking about like that—you'll get cold."

I thought it was a good time to talk, so I told him that I really was not gaining here, and that I wished he would take me away.

"Why, darling!" said he, "our lease will be up in three weeks, and I can't see how to leave before.

"The repairs are not done at home, and I cannot possibly leave town just now. Of course if you were in any danger I could and would, but you really are better, dear, whether you can see it or not. I am a doctor, dear, and I know. You are gaining flesh and color, your appetite is better. I feel really much easier about you."

"I don't weigh a bit more," said I, "nor as much; and my appetite may be better in the evening, when you are here, but it is worse in the morning, when you are away."

"Bless her little heart!" said he with a big hug; "she shall be as sick as she pleases. But now let's improve the shining hours by going to sleep, and talk about it in the morning."

"And you won't go away?" I asked gloomily.

"Why, how can I, dear? It is only three weeks more and then we will take a nice little trip of a few days while Jennie is getting the house ready. Really, dear, you are better!"

"Better in body, perhaps"—I began, and stopped short, for he sat up straight and looked at me with such a stern, reproachful look that I could not say another word.

"My darling," said he, "I beg of you, for my sake and for our child's sake, as well as for your own, that you will never for one instant let that idea enter your mind! There is nothing so dangerous, so fascinating, to a temperament like yours. It is a false and foolish fancy. Can you not trust me as a physician when I tell you so?"

So of course I said no more on that score, and we went to sleep before long. He thought I was asleep first, but I wasn't,—I lay there for hours trying to decide whether that front pattern and the back pattern really did move together or separately.

On a pattern like this, by daylight, there is a lack of sequence, a defiance of law, that is a constant irritant to a normal mind.

The color is hideous enough, and unreliable enough, and infuriating enough, but the pattern is torturing.

You think you have mastered it, but just as you get well under way in following, it turns a back somersault, and there you are. It slaps you in the face, knocks you down, and tramples upon you. It is like a bad dream.

The outside pattern is a florid arabesque,[5] reminding one of a fungus. If you can imagine a toadstool in joints, an interminable string of toadstools, budding and sprouting in endless convolutions,—why, that is something like it.

That is, sometimes!

There is one marked peculiarity about this paper, a thing nobody seems to notice but myself, and that is that it changes as the light changes.

When the sun shoots in through the east window—I always watch for that first long, straight ray—it changes so quickly that I never can quite believe it.

That is why I watch it always.

---

[5] Floral surface decoration set in linear patterns

By moonlight—the moon shines in all night when there is a moon—I wouldn't know it was the same paper. At night in any kind of light, in twilight, candlelight, lamplight, and worst of all by moonlight, it becomes bars! The outside pattern, I mean, and the woman behind it is as plain as can be.

I didn't realize for a long time what the thing was that showed behind,—that dim sub-pattern,—but now I am quite sure it is a woman.

By daylight she is subdued, quiet. I fancy it is the pattern that keeps her so still. It is so puzzling. It keeps me quiet by the hour.

I lie down ever so much now. John says it is good for me, and to sleep all I can. Indeed, he started the habit by making me lie down for an hour after each meal.

It is a very bad habit, I am convinced, for, you see, I don't sleep.

And that cultivates deceit, for I don't tell them I'm awake,— oh, no!

The fact is, I am getting a little afraid of John.

He seems very queer sometimes, and even Jennie has an inexplicable look. It strikes me occasionally, just as a scientific hypothesis, that perhaps it is the paper!

I have watched John when he did not know I was looking, and come into the room suddenly on the most innocent excuses, and I've caught him several times *looking at the paper* and Jennie too. I caught Jennie with her hand on it once.

She didn't know I was in the room, and when I asked her in a quiet, a very quiet voice, with the most restrained manner possible, what she was doing with the paper she turned around as if she had been caught stealing, and looked quite angry—asked me why I should frighten her so!

Then she said that the paper stained everything it touched, that she had found yellow smooches on all my clothes and John's, and she wished we would be more careful!

Did not that sound innocent? But I know she was studying that pattern, and I am determined that nobody shall find it out but myself!

Life is very much more exciting now than it used to be. You see I have something more to expect, to look forward to, to watch. I really do eat better, and am more quiet than I was.

John is so pleased to see me improve! He laughed a little the other day, and said I seemed to be flourishing in spite of my wallpaper.

I turned it off with a laugh. I had no intention of telling him it was *because* of the wallpaper—he would make fun of me. He might even want to take me away.

I don't want to leave now until I have found it out. There is a week more, and I think that will be enough.

I'm feeling ever so much better! I don't sleep much at night, for it is so interesting to watch developments; but I sleep a good deal in the daytime.

In the daytime it is tiresome and perplexing. There are always new shoots on the fungus, and new shades of yellow all over it. I cannot keep count of them, though I have tried conscientiously.

It is the strangest yellow, that wallpaper! It makes me think of all the yellow things I ever saw—not beautiful ones like buttercups, but old foul, bad yellow things.

But there is something else about that paper—the smell! I noticed it the moment we came into the room, but with so much air and sun it was not bad. Now we have had a week of fog and rain, and whether the windows are open or not the smell is here.

It creeps all over the house.

I find it hovering in the dining-room, skulking in the parlor, hiding in the hall, lying in wait for me on the stairs.

It gets into my hair.

Even when I go to ride, if I turn my head suddenly and surprise it—there is that smell! Such a peculiar odor, too! I have spent hours in trying to analyze it, to find what it smelled like.

It is not bad—at first, and very gentle, but quite the subtlest, most enduring odor I ever met. In this damp weather it is awful. I wake up in the night and find it hanging over me. It used to disturb me at first. I thought seriously of burning the house—to reach the smell.

But now I am used to it. The only thing I can think of that it is like is the *color* of the paper—a yellow smell!

There is a very funny mark on this wall, low down, near the mopboard. A streak that runs around the room. It goes behind every piece of furniture, except the bed, a long, straight, even *smooch,* as if it had been rubbed over and over.

I wonder how it was done and who did it, and what they did it for. Round and round and round—round and round and round—it makes me dizzy!

I really have discovered something at last.

Through watching so much at night, when it changes so, I have finally found out.

The front pattern *does* move—and no wonder! The woman behind shakes it!

Sometimes I think there are a great many women behind, and sometimes only one, and she crawls around fast, and her crawling shakes it all over.

Then in the very bright spots she keeps still, and in the very shady spots she just takes hold of the bars and shakes them hard.

And she is all the time trying to climb through. But nobody could climb through that pattern—it strangles so; I think that is why it has so many heads.

They get through, and then the pattern strangles them off and turns them upside-down, and makes their eyes white!

If those heads were covered or taken off it would not be half so bad.

I think that woman gets out in the daytime!

And I'll tell you why—privately—I've seen her!

I can see her out of every one of my windows! It is the same woman, I know, for she is always creeping, and most women do not creep by daylight.

I see her in that long shaded lane, creeping up and down. I see her in those dark grape arbors, creeping all around the garden. I see her on that long road under the trees, creeping along, and when a carriage comes she hides under the blackberry vines. I don't blame her a bit. It must be very humiliating to be caught creeping by daylight! I always lock the door when I creep by daylight. I can't do it at night, for I know John would suspect something at once.

And John is so queer, now, that I don't want to irritate him. I wish he would take another room! Besides, I don't want anybody to get that woman out at night but myself.

I often wonder if I could see her out of all the windows at once. But, turn as fast as I can, I can only see out of one at one time. And though I always see her she *may* be able to creep faster than I can turn!

I have watched her sometimes away off in the open country, creeping as fast as a cloud shadow in a high wind.

If only that top pattern could be gotten off from the under one! I mean to try it, little by little.

I have found out another funny thing, but I shan't tell it this time! It does not do to trust people too much.

There are only two more days to get this paper off, and I believe John is beginning to notice. I don't like the look in his eyes.

And I heard him ask Jennie a lot of professional questions about me. She had a very good report to give.

She said I slept a good deal in the daytime.

John knows I don't sleep very well

at night, for all I'm so quiet!

He asked me all sorts of questions, too, and pretended to be very loving and kind.

As if I couldn't see through him!

Still, I don't wonder he acts so, sleeping under this paper for three months.

It only interests me, but I feel sure John and Jennie are secretly affected by it.

***

HURRAH! THIS IS the last day, but it is enough. John is to stay in town overnight, and won't be out until this evening.

Jennie wanted to sleep with me—the sly thing! but I told her I should undoubtedly rest better for a night all alone. That was clever, for really I wasn't alone a bit! As soon as it was moonlight, and that poor thing began to crawl and shake the pattern, I got up and ran to help her.

I pulled and she shook, I shook and she pulled, and before morning we had peeled off yards of that paper.

A strip about as high as my head and half around the room.

And then when the sun came and that awful pattern began to laugh at me I declared I would finish it today!

We go away tomorrow, and they are moving all my furniture down again to leave things as they were before.

Jennie looked at the wall in amazement, but I told her merrily that I did it out of pure spite at the vicious thing. She laughed and said she wouldn't mind doing it herself, but I must not get tired.

How she betrayed herself that time!

But I am here, and no person touches this paper but me— not *alive!*

She tried to get me out of the room—it was too patent! But I said it was so quiet and empty and clean now that I believed I would lie down again and sleep all I could; and not to wake me even for dinner—I would call when I woke.

So now she is gone, and the servants are gone, and the things are gone, and there is nothing left but that great bedstead nailed down, with the canvas mattress we found on it.

We shall sleep downstairs tonight, and take the boat home tomorrow.

I quite enjoy the room, now it is bare again.

How those children did tear about here!

This bedstead is fairly gnawed! But I must get to work. I have locked the door and thrown the key down into the front path.

I don't want to go out, and I don't want to have anybody come in, till John comes.

I want to astonish him.

I've got a rope up here that even Jennie did not find. If that woman does get out, and tries to get away, I can tie her! But I forgot I could not reach far without anything to stand on!

This bed will *not* move!

I tried to lift and push it until I was lame, and then I got so angry I bit off a little piece at one corner—but it hurt my teeth.

Then I peeled off all the paper I could reach standing on the floor. It sticks horribly and the pattern just enjoys it! All those strangled heads and bulbous eyes and waddling fungus growths just shriek with derision!

I am getting angry enough to do something desperate. To jump out of the window would be admirable exercise, but the bars are too strong even to try.

Besides, I wouldn't do it. Of course not. I know well enough that a step like that is improper and might be misconstrued.

I don't like to *look* out of the windows even—there are so many of those creeping women, and they creep so fast.

I wonder if they all come out of that wallpaper, as I did?

But I am securely fastened now by my well-hidden rope—you don't get *me* out in the road there!

I suppose I shall have to get back behind the pattern when it comes night, and that is hard!

It is so pleasant to be out in this great room and creep around as I please!

I don't want to go outside. I won't, even if Jennie asks me to.

For outside you have to creep on the ground, and everything is green instead of yellow.

But here I can creep smoothly on the floor, and my shoulder just fits in that long smooch around the wall, so I cannot lose my way.

Why, there's John at the door!

It is no use, young man, you can't open it!

How he does call and pound!

Now he's crying for an axe.

It would be a shame to break down that beautiful door!

"John, dear!" said I in the gentlest voice, "the key is down by the front steps, under a plantain leaf!"

That silenced him for a few moments.

Then he said—very quietly indeed, "Open the door, my darling!"

"I can't," said I. "The key is down by the front door, under a plantain leaf!"

And then I said it again, several times, very gently and slowly, and said it so often that he had to go and see, and he got it, of course, and came in. He stopped short by the door.

"What is the matter?" he cried. "For God's sake, what are you doing!"

I kept on creeping just the same, but I looked at him over my shoulder.

"I've got out at last," said I, "in spite of you and Jane. And I've pulled off most of the paper, so you can't put me back!"

Now why should that man have fainted? But he did, and right across my path by the wall, so that I had to creep over him every time!

Joseph Le Fanu
(1814-1873)

No author had a bigger impact during the middle part of the nineteenth century on supernatural fiction than Irishman Joseph Thomas Sheridan Le Fanu. His female vampire story "Carmilla" (1872) influenced Bram Stoker when chiseling the foundations of *Dracula* and it is still a literary force to be reckoned with today.

Fanu's ghost stories influenced the likes of M. R. James, the leading ghost short story writer of the last half of the nineteenth century. James unabashedly placed Fanu "in the first rank as a writer of ghost stories. That is my deliberate verdict, after reading all the supernatural tales I have been able to get hold of."[1] A "Strange Event in the Life of Schalken the Painter" (1839) was included in *BlooDeath: Best Vampire Short Stories 1800-1849* with James saying "'Schalken' conforms more strictly to my own ideals. It is indeed one of the best of Le Fanu's good things."[2] The paintings of Schalken are even mentioned in "Green Tea."

A story about the hallucinatory effects of green tea seems odd in our present day mindset that green tea is very healthy and should be drunk often. Everyday a new article appears on its health benefits, including recommendations on drinking the strong, ground up, tea leaves of Matcha green tea.

Green tea had a much different reputation in the Victorian age, which many deemed worse than cocaine. In the story Fanu artfully

---

[1] Prologue to *Madame Crowl's Ghost and Other Tales of Mystery*, 1923
[2] Introduction to *Ghosts and Marvels: A Selection of Uncanny Tales from Daniel Defoe to Algernon Blackwood*, M. R. James, 1924, pg. 2

plays off Victorian fears of green tea that started with a mistrust of the Chinese suppliers, some of which mixed Prussian blue—a poison—in with the green tea to give it a vibrant color. "They mix Prussian blue with what is sold to foreigners, which gives it the greenish blue color it so often has, and something of its astringent qualities."[3] In recommending black tea from China, the author went on to state, "It is very much better, and has not the same stimulating effect on the nerves that many people suffer from, when they drink the green. If you were here you might drink as much green tea as you like, for the Chinese are too wise to put drugs into their own tea."[4]

Charlotte Bronte who appears to have borrowed liberally from Fanu's "A Chapter in the History of a Tyrone Family" (1839)[5] when fashioning the attic inhabitant of *Jane Eyre*, refused to drink tea having "the least particle of green leaf"[6] because of its strength. This didn't stop Elizabeth Gaskell, her literary friend, from serving it to her when that was all she had left and Bronte, who drank it without knowing, showed no ill effects.[7]

Charles Dickens liked "Green Tea" so much that he originally printed the rather long story in his weekly magazine *All the Year Round* in serial fashion (Oct. 23-Nov. 13, 1869). The Fanu horror story was so well-received, Dickens went on to publish five other supernatural Fanu tales the very next year, including "The Child that Went with the Fairies," "The White Cat of Drumgunniol," "Stories of Lough Guir," "The Vision of Tom Chuff," and "Madame Crowl's Ghost."

But it was M. R. James who designated "Green Tea" to be "of paramount excellence."[8]

---

[3] "Green Tea and Black Tea", *Semi-Monthly Courant*, reprinted in The *New England Botanic, Medical and Surgical Journal*, Calvin Newton, M.D., Vol. 2, Dec 16, 1848, pg. 381

[4] Ibid. at 382

[5] See Afterword to "A Chapter in the History of a Tyrone Family," *Phantasmal: The Best Ghost Short Stories 1800-1849*, Andrew Barger, 2011, pgs. 171-172

[6] *Mrs. Gaskell: Haunts, Homes, and Stories*, Mrs. Ellis H. Chadwick, 1910 pg. 260

[7] Ibid

[8] "Some Remarks on Ghost Stories," M. R. James, *The Bookman*, 1929, pg. 171

Green Tea
1869

**Prologue
Martin Hesselius
The German Physician**

THOUGH CAREFULLY EDUCATED in medicine and surgery, I have never practiced either. The study of each continues, nevertheless, to interest me profoundly. Neither idleness nor caprice caused my secession from the honorable calling which I had just entered. The cause was a very trifling scratch inflicted by a dissecting knife. This trifle cost me the loss of two fingers, amputated promptly, and the more painful loss of my health, for I have never been quite well since, and have seldom been twelve months together in the same place.

In my wanderings I became acquainted with Dr. Martin Hesselius, a wanderer like myself, like me a physician, and like me an enthusiast in his profession. Unlike me in this, that his wanderings were voluntary, and he a man, if not of fortune, as we estimate fortune in England, at least in what our forefathers used to term "easy circumstances."

He was an old man when I first saw him; nearly five-and-thirty years my senior. In Dr. Martin Hesselius, I found my master. His knowledge was immense, his grasp of a case was an intuition. He was the very man to inspire a young enthusiast, like me, with awe and delight. My admiration has stood the test of time and survived the separation of death. I am sure For nearly twenty years I acted as his medical secretary. His immense collection of papers he has left in my care, to be arranged, indexed and bound.

His treatment of some of these cases is curious. He writes in two distinct characters. He describes what he saw and heard as an intelligent layman might, and when in this style of narrative he had seen the patient either through his own hall-door, to the light of day, or through the gates of darkness to the caverns of the dead, he returns upon the narrative, and in the terms of his art, and with all the force and originality of genius, proceeds to the work of analysis, diagnosis and illustration.

Here and there a case strikes me as of a kind to amuse or horrify a lay reader with an interest quite different from the peculiar one which it may possess for an expert. With slight modifications, chiefly of language, and of course a change of names, I copy the following.

The narrator is Dr. Martin Hesselius. I find it among the voluminous notes of cases which he made during a tour in England about sixty-four years ago. It is related in a series of letters to his friend Professor Van Loo of Leyden. The professor was not a physician, but a chemist, and a man who read history and metaphysics and medicine, and had, in his day, written a play. The narrative is therefore, if somewhat less valuable as a medical record, necessarily written in a manner more likely to interest an unlearned reader. These letters, from a memorandum attached, appear to have been returned on the death of the professor, in 1819, to Dr. Hesselius. They are written, some in English, some in French, but the greater part in German. I am a faithful, though I am conscious, by no means a graceful translator, and although here and there, I omit some passages, and shorten others and disguise names, I have interpolated nothing.

Chapter I.
Dr. Hesselius Relates How
He Met the Rev. Mr. Jennings

THE REV. MR. Jennings is tall and thin. He is middle-aged, and dresses with a natty, old-fashioned, high-church precision. He is naturally a little stately, but not at all stiff. His features, without being handsome, are well formed, and their expression extremely kind, but also shy. I met him one evening at Lady Mary Heyduke's. The modesty and benevolence of his countenance are extremely prepossessing.

We were but a small party, and he joined agreeably enough in the conversation. He seems to enjoy listening very much more than contributing to the talk; but what he says is always to the purpose and well said. He is a great favorite of Lady Mary's, who it seems, consults him upon many things, and thinks him the most happy and blessed person on earth. Little knows she about him.

The Rev. Mr. Jennings is a bachelor, and has, they say, sixty thousand pounds in the funds. He is a charitable man. He is most anxious to be actively employed in his sacred profession, and yet though always tolerably well elsewhere, when he goes down to his vicarage[1] in Warwickshire, to engage in the actual duties of his sacred calling his health soon fails him, and in a very strange way. So says Lady Mary.

There is no doubt that Mr. Jennings's health does break down in, generally a sudden and mysterious way, sometimes in the very act of officiating in his old and pretty church at Kenlis. It may be his heart, it may be his brain. But so it has happened three or four times, or oftener, that after proceeding a certain way in the service,

---

[1] Home of a clergy member

he has on a sudden stopped short, and after a silence, apparently quite unable to resume, he has fallen into solitary, inaudible prayer, his hands and eyes uplifted, and then pale as: death, and in the agitation of a strange shame and horror, descended trembling, and got into the vestry-room, leaving his congregation, without explanation, to themselves. This occurred when his curate was absent. When he goes down to Kenlis, now, he always takes care to provide a clergyman to share his duty, and to supply his place on the instant should he become thus suddenly incapacitated.

When Mr. Jennings breaks down quite, and beats a retreat from the vicarage, and returns to London, where, in a dark street off Piccadilly, he inhabits a very narrow house. Lady Mary says that he is always perfectly well. I have my own opinion about that. There are degrees of course. We shall see.

Mr. Jennings is a perfectly gentlemanlike man. People, however, remark something odd. There is an impression a little ambiguous. One thing which certainly contributes to it, people I think don't remember; or, perhaps, distinctly remark. But I did, almost immediately. Mr. Jennings has a way of looking sidelong upon the carpet, as if his eye followed the movements of something there. This, of course, is not always. It occurs only now and then.

But often enough to give a certain oddity, as I have said to his manner, and in this glance travelling along the floor there is something both shy and anxious. A medical philosopher, as you are good enough to call me, elaborating theories by the aid of cases sought out by himself, and by him watched and scrutinized with more time at command, and consequently infinitely more minuteness than the ordinary practitioner can afford, falls insensibly into habits of observation, which accompany him everywhere, and are exercised, as some people would say, impertinently, upon every subject that presents itself with the least likelihood of rewarding inquiry. There was a promise of this kind in the slight, timid, kindly, but reserved gentleman, whom I met for the first time at this agreeable little evening gathering. I observed, of course, more than I here set down; but I reserve all that borders on the technical for a strictly scientific paper.

I may remark, that when I hear speak of medical science, I do so, as I hope someday to see it more generally understood, in a much more comprehensive sense than its generally material treatment would warrant. I believe the entire natural world is but the ultimate expression of that spiritual world from which, and in which alone, it has its life. I believe that the essential man is a spirit, that the spirit is an organized substance, but as different in point of material from what we ordinarily understand by matter, as light or electricity is; that the material body is, in the most literal sense, a vesture, and death consequently no interruption of the living man's existence, but simply his extrication from the natural body—a process which commences at the moment of what we term death, and the completion of which, at furthest a few days later, is the resurrection "in power."

The person who weighs the consequences of these positions will probably see their practical bearing upon medical science. This is, however, by no means the proper place for displaying the proofs and discussing the consequences of this too generally unrecognized state of facts.

In pursuance of my habit, I was covertly observing Mr. Jennings, with all my caution—I think he perceived it—and I saw plainly that he was as cautiously observing me. Lady Mary happening to address me by my name, as Dr. Hesselius, I saw that he glanced at me more sharply, and then became thoughtful for a few minutes.

After this, as I conversed with a gentleman at the other end of the room, I saw him look at me more steadily, and with an interest which I thought I understood. I then saw him take an opportunity of chat ting with Lady Mary, and was, as one always is, perfectly aware of being the subject of a distant inquiry and answer. This tall clergyman approached me by-and-by, and in a little time we had got into conversation. When two people, who like reading, and know books and places, having travelled, wish to converse, it is very strange if they can't find topics. It was not accident that brought him near me, and led him into conversation.

He knew German, and had read my *Essays on Metaphysical Medicine* which suggest more than they actually say. This courteous man, gentle, shy, plainly a man of thought and reading, who moving and talking among us, was not altogether of us, and whom I already suspected of leading a life whose transactions and alarms were carefully concealed, with an impenetrable reserve from, not only the world, but his best beloved friends—was cautiously weighing in his own mind the idea of taking a certain step with regard to me.

I penetrated his thoughts without his being aware of it, and was careful to say nothing which could betray to his sensitive vigilance my suspicions respecting his position, or my surmises about his plans respecting myself. We chatted upon indifferent subjects for a time; but at last he said: "I was very much interested by some papers of yours, Dr. Hesselius, upon what you term Metaphysical Medicine—I read them in German, ten or twelve years ago—have they been translated?"

"No, I'm sure they have not—I should have heard. They would have asked my leave, I think."

"I asked the publishers here, a few months ago, to get the book for me in the original German; but they tell me it is out of print."

"So it is, and has been for some years; but it flatters me as an author to find that you have not forgotten my little book, although," I added, laughing, "ten or twelve years is a considerable time to have managed without it; but I suppose you have been turning the subject over again in your mind, or something has happened lately to revive your interest in it."

At this remark, accompanied by a glance of inquiry, a sudden embarrassment disturbed Mr. Jennings, analogous to that which makes a young lady blush and look foolish. He dropped his eyes, and folded his hands together uneasily, and looked oddly, and you would have said, guiltily for a moment.

I helped him out of his awkwardness in the best way, by appearing not to observe it, and going straight on, I said: "Those revivals of interest in a subject happen to me often; one book suggests another, and often sends me back a wild-goose chase over an interval of twenty years. But if you still care to possess a copy, I shall be only too happy to provide you; I have still got two or three by me—and if you allow me to present one I shall be very much honored."

"You are very good indeed," he said, quite at his ease again, in a moment: "I almost despaired—I don't know how to thank you."

"Pray don't say a word; the thing is really so little worth that I am only ashamed of having offered it, and if you thank me any more I shall throw it into the fire in a fit of modesty."

Mr. Jennings laughed. He inquired where I was staying in London, and after a little more conversation on a variety of subjects, he took his departure.

Chapter II
The Doctor Questions Lady Mary and She Answers

"LIKE YOUR VICAR so much, Lady Mary," said I, so soon as he was gone. "He has read, travelled, and thought, and having also suffered, he ought to be an accomplished companion."

"So he is, and, better still, he is a really good man," said she. "His advice is invaluable about my schools, and all my little undertakings at Dawlbridge, and he's so painstaking, he takes so much trouble—you have no idea—wherever he thinks he can be of use: he's so good-natured and so sensible."

"It is pleasant to hear so good an account of his neighborly virtues. I can only testify to his being an agreeable and gentle companion, and in addition to what you have told me, I think I can tell you two or three things about him," said I.

"Really!"

"Yes, to begin with, he's unmarried."

"Yes, that's right,—go on."

"He has been writing, that is he *was,* but for two or three years perhaps, he has not gone on with his work, and the book was upon some rather abstract subject—perhaps theology."

"Well, he was writing a book, as you say; I'm not quite sure what it was about, but only that it was nothing that I cared for, very likely you are right, and he certainly did stop—yes."

"And although he only drank a little coffee here tonight, he likes tea, at least, did like it, extravagantly."

"Yes, that's *quite* true."

"He drank green tea, a good deal, didn't he?" I pursued.

"Well, that's very odd! Green tea was a subject on which we used almost to quarrel."

"But he has quite given that up," said I.

"So he has."

"And, now, one more fact. His mother or his father, did you know them?"

"Yes, both; his father is only ten years dead, and their place is near Dawlbridge. We knew them very well," she answered.

"Well, either his mother or his father—I should rather think his father, saw a ghost," said I.

"Well, you really are a conjurer, Dr. Hesselius."

"Conjurer or no, haven't I said right?"

I answered merrily. "You certainly have, and it *was* his father: he was a silent, whimsical man, and he used to bore my father about his dreams, and at last he told him a story about a ghost he had seen and talked with, and a very odd story it was. I remember it particularly, because I was so afraid of him. This story was long before he died—when I was quite a child—and his ways were so silent and moping, and he used to drop in, sometimes, in the dusk, when I was alone in the drawing-room, and I used to fancy there were ghosts about him." I smiled and nodded. "And now having established my character as a conjurer I think I must say goodnight," said I.

"But how *did* you find it out?"

"By the planets of course, as the gypsies do," I answered, and so, gaily, we said goodnight. Next morning I sent the little book he had been inquiring after, and a note to Mr. Jennings, and on returning late that evening, I found that he had called, at my lodgings, and left his card.

He asked whether I was at home, and asked at what hour he would be most likley to find me. Does he intend opening his case, and consulting me "professionally," as they say? I hope so. I have already conceived a theory about him. It is supported by Lady Mary's answers to my parting questions. I should like much to ascertain from his own lips. But what can I do consistently with good breeding to invite, a confession? Nothing. I rather think he meditates one. At all events, my dear Van L., I shan't make myself difficult of access; I mean to return his visit tomorrow. It will be only civil in return for his politeness, to ask to see him. Perhaps something may come of it. Whether much, little, or nothing, my dear Van L., you shall hear.

CHAPTER III.
Dr. Hesselius Picks Up Something in Latin Books.

WELL, I HAVE called at Blank Street.

On inquiring at the door, the servant told me that Mr. Jennings was engaged very particularly with a gentleman, a clergyman from

Kenlis, his parish in the country. Intending to reserve my privilege and to call again, I merely intimated that I should try another time, and had turned to go, when the servant begged my pardon, and asked me, looking at me a little more attentively than well-bred persons of his order usually do, whether I was Dr. Hesselius; and, on learning that I was, he said, "Perhaps then, sir, you would allow me to mention it to Mr. Jennings, for I am sure he wishes to see you."

The servant returned in a moment, with a message from Mr. Jennings, asking me to go into his study, which was in effect his back drawing-room, promising to be with me in a very few minutes. This was really a study—almost a library. The room was lofty, with two tall slender windows, and rich dark curtains. It was much larger than I had expected, and stored with books on every side, from the floor to the ceiling. The upper carpet—for to my tread it felt that there were two or three—was a Turkey carpet. My steps fell noiselessly. The bookcases standing out, placed the windows, particularly narrow ones, in deep recesses.

The effect of the room was, although extremely comfortable, and even luxurious, decidedly gloomy, and aided by the silence, almost oppressive. Perhaps, however, I ought to have allowed something for association. My mind had connected peculiar ideas with Mr. Jennings. I stepped into this perfectly silent room, of a very silent house, with a peculiar foreboding; and its darkness, and solemn clothing of books, for except where two narrow looking-glasses were set in the wall, they were everywhere, helped this somber feeling.

While awaiting Mr. Jennings arrival, I amused myself by looking into some of the books with which his shelves were laden. Not among these, but immediately under them, with their backs upward, on the floor, I lighted upon a complete set of Swedenborg's *Arcana Caelestia*,[2] in the original Latin, a very fine folio set, bound in the natty livery[3] which theology affects, pure vellum,[4] namely, gold letters, and carmine edges.[5] There were paper markers in several of these volumes, I raised and placed them, one after the other, upon the table, and opening where these papers were placed, I read in the solemn Latin phraseology, a series of sentences indicated by a penciled line at the margin. Of these I copy here a few, translating them into English.

"When man's interior sight is opened, which is that of his spirit, then there appear the things of another life, which cannot possibly be made visible to the bodily sight." . . .

---

[2] Emanuel Swedenborg's (1688-1772) theological book *Arcana Caelestia, quae in Scriptura Sacra seu Verbo Domini sunt, detecta* (*Arcana Caelestia,* Heavenly Mysteries or Secrets of Heaven), 1749-1756 describes spiritual growth or mysticism for the stories contained in the first two books of the Bible: *Genesis* and *Exodus*

[3] Uniform

[4] Fine parchment

[5] Crimson color

"By the internal sight it has been granted me to see the things that are in the other life, more clearly than I see those that are in the world. From these considerations, it is evident that external vision exists from interior vision, and this from a vision still more interior, and so on." . . . .

"There are with every man at least two evil spirits." . . . .

"With wicked genii there is also a fluent speech, but harsh and grating. There is also among them a speech which is not fluent, wherein the dissent of the thoughts is perceived as something secretly creeping along within it." . . . .

"The evil spirits associated with man are, indeed, from the hells, but when with man they are not then in hell, but are taken out thence. The place where they then are is in the midst between heaven and hell, and is called the world of spirits—when the evil spirits who are with man, are in that world, they are not in any infernal torment, but in every thought and affection of the man, and so, in all that the man himself enjoys. But when they are remitted into their hell, they return to their former state." . . . .

"If evil spirits could perceive that they were associated with man, and yet that they were spirits separate from him, and if they could flow in into the things of his body, they would attempt by a thousand means to destroy him; for they hate man with a deadly hatred." . . . .

"Knowing, therefore, that I was a man in the body, they were continually striving to destroy me, not as to the body only, but especially as to the soul; for to destroy any man or spirit is the very delight of the life of all who are in hell; but I have been continually protected by the Lord. Hence it appears how dangerous it is for man to be in a living consort with spirits, unless he be in the good of faith." . . . .

"Nothing is more carefully guarded from the knowledge of associate spirits than their being thus conjoint with a man, for if they knew it they would speak to him, with the intention to destroy him." . . . .

"The delight of hell is to do evil to man, and to hasten his eternal ruin."

A long note, written with a very sharp and fine pencil, in Mr. Jennings's neat hand, at the foot of the page, caught my eye. Expecting his criticism upon the text, I read a word or two, and stopped, for it was something quite different, and began with these words, *Deus misereatur mei*—"May God compassionate me."

Thus warned of its private nature, I averted my eyes, and shut the book, replacing all the volumes as I had found them, except one which interested me, and in which, as men studious and solitary in their habits will do, I grew so absorbed as to take no cognizance of the outer world, nor to remember where I was.

I was reading some pages which refer to "representatives" and "correspondents," in the technical language of Swedenborg, and had arrived at a passage, the substance of which is, that evil spirits, when seen by other eyes than those of their infernal associates, present themselves, by "correspondence," in the shape of the beast *(fera)* which represents their particular lust and life, in aspect direful and atrocious. This is a long passage, and particularizes a number of those bestial forms.

CHAPTER IV.
Four Eyes Were Reading the Passage.

I WAS RUNNING the head of my pencil case along the line as I read it, and something caused me to raise my eyes. Directly before me was one of the mirrors I have mentioned, in which I saw reflected the tall shape of my friend Mr. Jennings leaning over my shoulder, and reading the page at which I was busy, and with a face so dark and wild that I should hardly have known him. I turned and rose. He stood erect also, and with an effort laughed a little, saying:

"I came in and asked you how you did, but without succeeding in awaking you from your book; so I could not restrain my curiosity, and very impertinently, I'm afraid, peeped over your shoulder. This is not your first time of looking into those pages. You have looked into Swedenborg, no doubt, long ago?"

"Oh dear, yes! I owe Swedenborg a great deal; you will discover traces of him in the little book on *Metaphysical Medicine*, which you were so good as to remember."

Although my friend affected a gaiety of manner, there was a slight flush in his face, and I could perceive that he was inwardly much perturbed. "I'm scarcely yet qualified, I know so little of Swedenborg. I've only had them a fortnight," he answered, "and I think they are rather likely to make a solitary man nervous—that is, judging from the very little I have read—I don't say that they have made me so," he laughed; "and I'm so very much obliged for the book. I hope you got my note."

I made all proper acknowledgments and modest disclaimers.

"I never read a book that I go with, so entirely, as that of yours," he continued. "I saw at once there is more in it than is quite unfolded. Do you know Dr. Harley?" he asked, rather abruptly.

In passing, the editor remarks that the physician here named was one of the most eminent who had ever practiced in England. I did, having had letters to him, and had experienced from him great courtesy and considerable assistance during my visit to England.

"I think that man one of the very greatest fools I ever met in my life," said Mr. Jennings.

This was the first time I had ever heard him say a sharp thing of anybody, and such a term applied to so high a name a little startled me. "Really and in what way?" I asked.

"In his profession," he answered. I smiled. "I mean this," he said: "he seems to me, one half, blind—I mean one half of all he looks at is dark—preternaturally bright and vivid all the rest; and the worst of it is, it seems *willful*. I can't get him—I mean he won't—

I've had some experience of him as a physician, but I look on him as, in that sense, no better than a paralytic mind, an intellect half dead, I'll tell you—I know I shall some time—all about it," he said, with a little agitation. "You stay some months longer in England. If I should be out of town during your stay for a little time, would you allow me to trouble you with a letter?"

"I should be only too happy," I assured him.

"Very good of you. I am so utterly dissatisfied with Harley."

"A little leaning to the materialistic school," I said.

"A *mere* materialist," he corrected me; "you can't think how that sort of thing worries one who knows better. You won't tell anyone— any of my friends you know—that I am hippish; now, for instance, no one knows—not even Lady Mary—that I have seen Dr. Harley, or any other doctor. So pray don't mention it; and, if I should have any threatening of an attack, you'll kindly let me write, or, should I be in town, have a little talk with you."

I was full of conjecture, and unconsciously I found I had fixed my eyes gravely on him, for he lowered his for a moment, and he said: "I see you think I might as well tell you now, or else you are forming a conjecture; but you may as well give it up. If you were guessing all the rest of your life, you will never hit on it." He shook his head smiling, and over that wintry sunshine a black cloud suddenly came down, and he drew his breath in, through his teeth as men do in pain. "Sorry, of course, to learn that you apprehend occasion to consult any of us; but, command me when and how you like, and I need not assure you that your confidence is sacred."

He then talked of quite other things, and in a comparatively cheerful way and after a little time, I took my leave.

CHAPTER V.
Doctor Hesselius is Summoned to Richmond.

HE PARTED CHEERFULLY, but he was not cheerful, nor was I. There are certain expressions of that powerful organ of spirit—the human face—which, although I have seen them often, and possess a doctor's nerve, yet disturb me profoundly. One look of Mr. Jennings haunted me. It had seized my imagination with so dismal a power that I changed my plans for the evening, and went to the opera, feeling that I wanted a change of ideas.

I heard nothing of or from him for two or three days, when a note in his hand reached me. It was cheerful, and full of hope. He said that he had been for some little time so much better—quite well, in fact—that he was going to make a little experiment, and run down for a month or so to his parish, to try whether a little work might not quite set him up. There was in it a fervent religious expression of gratitude for his restoration, as he now almost hoped he might call it.

A day or two later I saw Lady Mary, who repeated what his note had announced, and told me that he was actually in Warwickshire, having resumed his clerical duties at Kenlis; and she added, "I begin to think that he is really perfectly well, and that there never was anything the matter, more than nerves and fancy; we are all nervous, but I fancy there is nothing like a little hard work for that kind of weakness, and he has made up his mind to try it. I should not be surprised if he did not come back for a year."

Notwithstanding all this confidence, only two days later I had this note, dated from his house off Piccadilly:[6] "Dear Sir.—I have returned disappointed. If I should feel at all able to see you, I shall write to ask you kindly to call. At present I am too low, and, in fact, simply unable to say all I wish to say. Pray don't mention my name to my friends. I can see no one. By-and-by, please God, you shall hear from me. I mean to take a run into Shropshire, where some of my people are. God bless you! May we, on my return, meet more happily than I can now write."

About a week after this I saw Lady Mary at her own house, the last person, she said, left in town, and just on the wing for Brighton, for the London season was quite over. She told me that she had heard from Mr. Jennings's niece, Martha, in Shropshire. There was nothing to be gathered from her letter, more than that he was low and nervous. In those words, of which healthy people think so lightly, what a world of suffering is sometimes hidden.

Nearly five weeks passed without any further news of Mr. Jennings. At the end of that time I received a note from him. He wrote: "I have been in the country, and have had change of air, change of scene, change of faces, change of everything and in everything—but *myself.* I have made up my mind, so far as the most irresolute creature on earth can do it, to tell my case fully to you. If your engagements will permit, pray come to me today, tomorrow, or the next day; but, pray defer as little as possible. You know not how much I need help. I have a quiet house at Richmond, where I now am. Perhaps you can manage to come to dinner, or to luncheon, or even to tea. You shall have no trouble in finding me out. The servant at Blank Street, who takes this note, will have a carriage at your door at any hour you please; and I am always to be found. You will say that I ought not to be alone. I have tried everything. Come and see."

I called up the servant, and decided on going out the same evening, which accordingly I did. He would have been much better in a lodging-house, or hotel, I thought, as I drove up through a short double row of somber elms to a very old-fashioned brick house, darkened by the foliage of these trees, which over-topped, and nearly surrounded it. It was a perverse choice, for nothing could be imagined more triste and silent. The house, I found, belonged to him. He had stayed for a day or two in town, and, finding it for some cause insupportable, had come out here,

---

[6] Piccadilly was a wealthy part of London in the last half of the nineteenth century

probably because being furnished and his own, he was relieved of the thought and delay of selection, by coming here.

The sun had already set, and the red reflected light of the western sky illuminated the scene with the peculiar effect with which we are all familiar. The hall seemed very dark, but, getting to the back drawing-room, whose windows command the west, I was again in the same dusky light. I sat down, looking out upon the richly wooded landscape that glowed in the grand and melancholy light which was every moment fading. The corners of the room were already dark; all was growing dim, and the gloom was insensibly toning my mind, already prepared for what was sinister. I was waiting alone for his arrival, which soon took place. The door communicating with the front room opened, and the tall figure of Mr. Jennings, faintly seen in the ruddy twilight, came, with quiet stealthy steps, into the room. We shook hands, and, taking a chair to the window, where there was still light enough to enable us to see each other's faces, he sat down beside me, and, placing his hand upon my arm, with scarcely a word of preface began his narrative.

CHAPTER VI.
How Mr. Jennings Met His Companion.

THE FAINT GLOW of the west, the pomp of the then lonely woods of Richmond, were before us, behind and about us the darkening room, and on the stony face of the sufferer—for the character of his face, though still gentle and sweet, was changed—rested that dim, odd glow which seems to descend and produce, where it touches, lights, sudden though faint, which are lost, almost without gradation, in darkness.

The silence, too, was utter; not a distant wheel, or bark, or whistle from without; and within the depressing stillness of an invalid bachelor's house. I guessed well the nature, though not even vaguely the particulars of the revelations I was about to receive, from that fixed face of suffering that so oddly flushed stood out, like a portrait of Schalken's,[7] before its background of darkness.

"It began," he said, "on the 15th of October, three years and eleven weeks ago, and two days—I keep very accurate count, for every day is torment. If I leave anywhere a chasm in my narrative tell me. "About four years ago I began a work, which had cost me very much thought and reading. It was upon the religious metaphysics of the ancients."

---

[7] Godfried Schalcken (1643-1706) was a Dutch painter whose Gothic style was to have his subjects bathed in darkness with only a light illuminating their face; Fanu drew upon this effect in his 1839 vampire story "Strange Event in the Life of Schalken the Painter" found annotated in *BlooDeath: Best Vampire Short Stories 1800-1849*

"I know," said I; "the actual religion of educated and thinking paganism, quite apart from symbolic worship? A wide and very interesting field."

"Yes; but not good for the mind—the Christian mind, I mean. Paganism is all bound together in essential unity, and, with evil sympathy, their religion involves their art, and both their manners, and the subject is a degrading fascination and the nemesis sure. God forgive me!

"I wrote a great deal; I wrote late at night. I was always thinking on the subject, walking about, wherever I was, everywhere. It thoroughly infected me. You are to remember that all the material ideas connected with it were more or less of the beautiful, the subject itself delightfully interesting, and I, then, without a care." He sighed heavily. "I believe that everyone who sets about writing in earnest does his work, as a friend of mine phrased it, *on* something—tea, or coffee, or tobacco. I suppose there is a material waste that must be hourly supplied in such occupations, or that we should grow too abstracted, and the mind, as it were, pass out of the body, unless it were reminded often of the connection by actual sensation.

"At all events, I felt the want, and I supplied it. Tea was my companion—at first the ordinary black tea, made in the usual way, not too strong: but I drank a good deal, and increased its strength as I went on. I never experienced an uncomfortable symptom from it. I began to take a little green tea. I found the effect pleasanter, it cleared and intensified the power of thought so. I had come to take it frequently, but not stronger than one might take it for pleasure. I wrote a great deal out here, it was so quiet, and in this room. I used to sit up very late, and it became a habit with me to sip my tea—green tea—every now and then as my work proceeded. I had a little kettle on my table, that swung over a lamp, and made tea two or three times between eleven o'clock and two or three in the morning, my hours of going to bed. I used to go into town every day. I was not a monk, and, although I spent an hour or two in a library, hunting up authorities and looking out lights upon my theme, I was in no morbid state as far as I can judge. I met my friends pretty much as usual, and enjoyed their society, and, on the whole, existence had never been, I think, so pleasant before.

"I had met with a man who had some odd old books, German editions in mediaeval Latin, and I was only too happy to be permitted access to them. This obliging person's books were in the City, a very out-of-the way part of it. I had rather out-stayed my intended hour, and, on coming out, seeing no cab near, I was tempted to get into the omnibus which used to drive past this house. It was darker than this by the time the bus had reached an old house, you may have remarked, with four poplars at each side of the door, and there the last passenger but myself got out. We drove along rather faster. It was twilight now. I leaned back in my corner next the door ruminating pleasantly.

"The interior of the omnibus was nearly dark. I had observed in the corner opposite to me at the other side, and at the end next the horses, two small circular reflections, as it seemed to me of a reddish light. They were about two inches apart, and about the size of those small brass buttons that yachting men used to put upon their jackets. I began to speculate, as listless men will, upon this trifle, as it seemed. From what center did that faint but deep red light come, and from what—glass beads, buttons, toy decorations—was it reflected? We were lumbering along gently, having nearly a mile still to go. I had not solved the puzzle, and it became in another minute more odd, for these two luminous points, with a sudden jerk, descended nearer the floor, keeping still their relative distance and horizontal position, and then, as suddenly, they rose to the level of the seat on which I was sitting, and I saw them no more.

"My curiosity was now really excited, and, before I had time to think, I saw again these two dull lamps, again together near the floor; again they disappeared, and again in their old corner I saw them.

"So, keeping my eyes upon them, I edged quietly up my own side, towards the end at which I still saw these tiny discs of red.

"There was very little light in the bus. It was nearly dark. I leaned forward to aid my endeavor to discover what these little circles really were. They shifted their position a little as I did so. I began now to perceive an outline of something black, and I soon saw with tolerable distinctness the outline of a small black monkey, pushing its face forward in mimicry to meet mine; those were its eyes, and I now dimly saw its teeth grinning at me.

"I drew back, not knowing whether it might not meditate a spring. I fancied that one of the passengers had forgot this ugly pet, and wishing to ascertain something of its temper, though not caring to trust my fingers to it, I poked my umbrella softly towards it. It remained immovable—up to *it*—*through* it! For through it, and back and forward, it passed, without the slightest resistance.

"I can't, in the least, convey to you the kind of horror that I felt. When I had ascertained that the thing was an illusion, as I then supposed, there came a misgiving about myself and a terror that fascinated me in impotence to remove my gaze from the eyes of the brute for some moments. As I looked, it made a little skip back, quite into the corner, and I, in a panic, found myself at the door, having put my head out, drawing deep breaths of the outer air, and staring at the lights and trees we were passing, too glad to reassure myself of reality.

"I stopped the bus and got out. I perceived the man look oddly at me as I paid him. I daresay there was something unusual in my looks and manner, for I had never felt so strangely before."

CHAPTER VII.
The Journey: First Stage.

"THEN THE OMNIBUS drove on, and I was alone upon the road, I looked carefully round to ascertain whether the monkey had followed me. To my indescribable relief I saw it nowhere. I can't describe easily what a shock I had received, and my sense of genuine gratitude on finding myself, as I supposed, quite rid of it.

"I had got out a little before we reached this house, two or three hundred steps. A brick wall runs along the footpath, and inside the wall is a hedge of yew or some dark evergreen of that kind, and within that again the row of fine trees which you may have remarked as you came.

"This brick wall is about as high as my shoulder, and happening to raise my eyes I saw the monkey, with that stooping gait, on all fours, walking or creeping, close beside me on top of the wall. I stopped looking at it with a feeling of loathing and horror. As I stopped so did it. It sat up on the wall with its long hands on its knees looking at me. There was not light enough to see it much more than in outline, nor was it dark enough to bring the peculiar light of its eyes into strong relief. I still saw, however, that red foggy light plainly enough. It did not show its teeth, nor exhibit any sign of irritation, but seemed jaded and sulky, and was observing me steadily.

"I drew back into the middle of the road. It was an unconscious recoil, and there I stood, still looking at it, it did not move.

"With an instinctive determination to try something—anything, I turned about and walked briskly towards town with a skance look, all the time, watching the movements of the beast. It crept swiftly along the wall, at exactly my pace.

"Where the wall ends, near the turn of the road, it came down and with a wiry spring or two brought itself close to my feet, and continued to keep up with me, as I quickened my pace. It was at my left side, so close to my leg that I felt every moment as if I should tread upon it.

"The road was quite deserted and silent, and it was darker every moment. I stopped dismayed and bewildered, turning as I did so, the other way—I mean, towards this house, away from which I had been walking. When I stood still, the monkey drew back to a distance of, I suppose, about five or six yards, and remained stationary, watching me.

"I had been more agitated than I have said. I had read, of course, as everyone has, something about 'spectral illusions,' as you physicians term the phenomena of such cases. I considered my situation, and looked my misfortune in the face.

"These affections, I had read, are sometimes transitory and sometimes obstinate. I had read of cases in which the appearance, at first harmless, had, step by step, degenerated into something direful and insupportable, and ended by wearing its victim out. Still as I stood there, but for my bestial companion, quite alone, I tried to comfort myself by repeating again and again the assurance, 'the thing is purely disease, a well-known physical affection, as distinctly as small-pox or neuralgia. Doctors are all agreed on that, philosophy demonstrates it. I must not be a fool. I've been sitting up too late, and I daresay my digestion is quite wrong, and with God's help, I shall be all right, and this is but a symptom of nervous dyspepsia. Did I believe all this? Not one word of it, no more than any other miserable being ever did who is once seized and riveted in this satanic captivity. Against my convictions, I might say my knowledge, I was simply bullying myself into a false courage.

"I now walked homeward. I had only a few hundred yards to go. I had forced myself into a sort of resignation, but I had not got over the sickening shock and the flurry of the first certainty of my misfortune.

"I made up my mind to pass the night at home. The brute moved close beside me, and I fancied there was the sort of anxious drawing toward the house, which one sees in tired horses or dogs, sometimes as they come toward home.

"I was afraid to go into town, I was afraid of any one's seeing and recognizing me. I was conscious of an irrepressible agitation in my manner. Also, I was afraid of any violent change in my habits, such as going to a place of amusement, or walking from home in order to fatigue myself. At the hall door it waited till I mounted the steps, and when the door was opened entered with me.

"I drank no tea that night. I got cigars and some brandy-and-water. My idea was that I should act upon my material system, and by living for a while in sensation apart from thought, send myself forcibly, as it were, into a new groove. I came up here to this drawing-room. I sat just here. The monkey then got upon a small table that then stood *there.* It looked dazed and languid. An irrepressible uneasiness as to its movements kept my eyes always upon it.

"Its eyes were half closed, but I could see them glow. It was looking steadily at me. In all situations, at all hours, it is awake and looking at me. That never changes.

"I shall not continue in detail my narrative of this particular night. I shall describe, rather, the phenomena of the first year, which never varied, essentially. I shall describe the monkey as it appeared in daylight. In the dark, as you shall presently hear, there are peculiarities. It is a small monkey, perfectly black. It had only one peculiarity—a character of malignity—unfathomable malignity. During the first year it looked sullen and sick. But this character of intense malice and vigilance was always underlying that surly languor. During all that time it acted as if on a plan of giving me as little trouble as was consistent with watching me. Its eyes were never off me, I have never lost sight of it, except in my sleep, light or dark, day or night, since it came here, excepting when it withdraws for some weeks at a time, unaccountably.

"In total dark it is visible as in daylight. I do not mean merely its eyes. It is *all* visible distinctly in a halo that resembles a glow of red embers, and which accompanies it in all its movements.

"When it leaves me for a time, it is always at night, in the dark, and in the same way. It grows at first uneasy, and then furious, and then advances towards me, grinning and shaking its paws clenched, and, at the same time, there comes the appearance of fire in the grate. I never have any fire. I can't sleep in the room where there is any, and it draws nearer and nearer to the chimney, quivering, it seems, with rage, and when its fury rises to the highest pitch, it springs into the grate, and up the chimney, and I see it no more.

"When first this happened I thought I was released. I was a new man. A day passed—a night—and no return, and a blessed week— a week—another week. I was always on my knees, Dr. Hesselius, always, thanking God and praying. A whole month passed of liberty, but on a sudden, it was with me again."

CHAPTER VIII.
The Second Stage.

"IT WAS WITH me, and the malice which before was torpid under a sullen exterior, was now active. It was perfectly unchanged in every other respect. This new energy was apparent in its activity and its looks, and soon in other ways.

"For a time, you will understand, the change was shown only in an increased vivacity, and an air of menace, as if it was always brooding over some atrocious plan. Its eyes, as before, were never off me."

"Is it here now?" I asked.

"No," he replied, "it has been absent exactly a fortnight and a day-fifteen days. It has sometimes been away so long as nearly two months, once for three. Its absence always exceeds a fortnight, although it may be but by a single day. Fifteen days having passed since I saw it last, it may return now at any moment."

"Is its return," I asked, "accompanied by any peculiar manifestation?"

"Nothing—no," he said. "It is simply with me again. On lifting my eyes from a book, or turning my head, I see it, as usual, looking at me, and then it remains, as before, for its appointed time. I have never told so much and so minutely before to anyone."

I perceived that he was agitated, and looking like death, and he repeatedly applied his handkerchief to his forehead; I suggested that he might be tired, and told him that I would call, with pleasure, in the morning, but he said: "No, if you don't mind hearing it all now. I have got so far, and I should prefer making one effort of it. When I spoke to Dr. Harley, I had nothing like so much to tell. You are a philosophic physician. You give spirit its proper rank. If this thing is real—" he paused, looking at me with agitated inquiry.

"We can discuss it by-and-by, and very fully. I will give you all I think," I answered, after an interval.

"Well—very well. If it is anything real, I say, it is prevailing, little by little, and drawing me more interiorly into hell. Optic nerves, he talked of. Ah! well—there are other nerves of communication. May God Almighty help me! You shall hear.

"Its power of action, I tell you, had increased. It's malice became, in a way aggressive. About two years ago, some questions that were pending between me and the bishop having been settled, I went down to my parish in Warwickshire, anxious to find occupation in my profession. I was not prepared for what happened, although I have since thought I might have apprehended something like it. The reason of my saying so, is this——"

He was beginning to speak with a great deal more effort and reluctance, and sighed often, and seemed at times nearly overcome. But at this time his manner was not agitated. It was more like that of a sinking patient, who has given himself up.

"Yes, but I will first tell you about Kenlis, my parish.

"It was with me when I left this place for Dawlbridge. It was my silent travelling companion, and it remained with me at the vicarage. When I entered on the discharge of my duties, another change took place. The thing exhibited an atrocious determination to thwart me. It was with me in the church—in the reading-desk— in the pulpit— within the communion rails. At last, it reached this extremity, that while I was reading to the congregation, it would spring upon the open book and squat there, so that I was unable to see the page. This happened more than once.

"I left Dawlbridge for a time. I placed myself in Dr. Harley's hands. I did everything he told me. He gave my case a great deal of thought. It interested him, I think. He seemed successful. For nearly three months I was perfectly free from a return. I began to think I was safe. With his full assent I returned to Dawlbridge.

"I travelled in a chaise.[8] I was in good spirits. I was more—I was happy and grateful. I was returning, as I thought delivered from a dreadful hallucination, to the scene of duties which I longed to enter upon. It was a beautiful sunny evening, everything looked serene and cheerful, and I was delighted. I remember looking out of the window to see the spire of my church at Kenlis among the trees, at the point where one has the earliest view of it. It is exactly where the little stream that bounds the parish passes under the road by a culvert, and where it emerges at the roadside, a stone with an old inscription is placed. As we passed this point, I drew my head in and sat down, and in the corner of the chaise was the monkey.

---

[8] Horse-drawn carriage usually having no roof

"For a moment I felt faint, and then quite wild with despair and horror. I called to the driver, and got out, and sat down at the road-side, and prayed to God silently for mercy. A despairing resignation supervened. My companion was with me as I re-entered the vicarage. The same persecution followed. After a short struggle I submitted, and soon I left the place.

"I told you," he said, "that the beast has before this become in certain ways aggressive. I will explain a little. It seemed to be actuated by intense and increasing fury, whenever I said my prayers, or even meditated prayer. It amounted at last to a dreadful interruption. You will ask, how could a silent immaterial phantom effect that? It was thus, whenever I meditated praying; it was always before me, and nearer and nearer.

"It used to spring on a table, on the back of a chair, on the chimney-piece, and slowly to swing itself from side to side, looking at me all the time. There is in its motion an indefinable power to dissipate thought, and to contract one's attention to that monotony, till the ideas shrink, as it were, to a point, and at last to nothing—and unless I had started up, and shook off the catalepsy I have felt as if my mind were on the point of losing itself. There are other ways," he sighed heavily; "thus, for instance, while I pray with my eyes closed, it comes closer and closer, and I see it. I know it is not to be accounted for physically, but I do actually see it, though my lids are closed, and so it rocks my mind, as it were, and overpowers me, and I am obliged to rise from my knees. If you had ever yourself known this, you would be acquainted with desperation."

CHAPTER IX.
The Third Stage.

"SEE, DR. HESSELIUS, that you don't lose one word of my statement. I need not ask you to listen specially to what I am now going to tell you. They talk of the optic nerves, and of spectral illusions, as if the organ of sight was the only point assailable by the influences that have fastened upon me—I know better. For two years in my direful case that limitation prevailed. But as food is taken in softly at the lips, and then brought under the teeth, as the tip of the little finger caught in a mill crank will draw in the hand, and the arm, and the whole body, so the miserable mortal who has been once caught firmly by the end of the finest fiber of his nerve, is drawn in and in, by the enormous machinery of hell, until he is as I am. Yes, Doctor, as *I* am, for while I talk to you, and implore relief, I feel that my prayer is for the impossible, and my pleading with the inexorable."

I endeavored to calm his visibly increasing agitation, and told him that he must not despair. While we talked the night had overtaken us. The filmy moonlight was wide over the scene which the window commanded, and I said: "Perhaps you would prefer having candles. This light, you know, is odd. I should wish you, as much as possible, under your usual conditions while I make my diagnosis, shall I call it—otherwise I don't care."

"All lights are the same to me," he said: "except when I read or write, I care not if night were perpetual. I am going to tell you what happened about a year ago. The thing began to speak to me."

"Speak! How do you mean—speak as a man does, do you mean?"

"Yes; speak in words and consecutive sentences, with perfect coherence and articulation; but there is a peculiarity. It is not like the tone of a human voice. It is not by my ears it reaches me—it comes like a singing through my head.

"This faculty, the power of speaking to me, will be my undoing. It won't let me pray, it interrupts me with dreadful blasphemies. I dare not go on, I could not. Oh! Doctor, can the skill, and thought, and prayers of man avail me nothing!"

"You must promise me, my dear sir, not to trouble yourself with unnecessarily exciting thoughts; confine yourself strictly to the narrative of *facts*; and recollect, above all, that even if the thing that infests you be as you seem to suppose, a reality with an actual independent life and will, yet it can have no power to hurt you, unless it be given from above: its access to your senses depends mainly upon your physical condition—this is, under God, your comfort and reliance: we are all alike environed. It is only that in your case, the *'paries,* the veil of the flesh, the screen, is a little out of repair, and sights and sounds are transmitted. We must enter on a new course, sir—be encouraged. I'll give tonight to the careful consideration of the whole case."

"You are very good, sir; you think it worth trying, you don't give me quite up; but, sir, you don't know, it is gaining such an influence over me: it orders me about, it is such a tyrant, and I'm growing so helpless. May God deliver me!"

"It orders you about—of course you mean by speech?"

"Yes, yes; it is always urging me to crimes, to injure others, or myself. You see, Doctor, the situation is urgent, it is indeed. When I was in Shropshire, a few weeks ago" (Mr. Jennings was speaking rapidly and trembling now, holding my arm with one hand, and looking in my face.)

"I went out one day with a party of friends for a walk: my persecutor, I tell you, was with me at the time. I lagged behind the rest: the country near the Dee,[9] you know, is beautiful. Our path happened to lie near a coal mine, and at the verge of the wood is a perpendicular shaft, they say, a hundred and fifty feet deep. My niece had remained behind with me—she knows, of course, nothing of the nature of my sufferings. She knew, however, that I had been ill, and was low, and she remained to prevent my being quite alone. As we loitered slowly on together the brute that accompanied me was urging me to throw myself down the shaft. I

---

[9] River Dee in Wales, England

tell you now—oh, sir, think of it!—the one consideration that saved me from that hideous death was the fear lest the shock of witnessing the occurrence should be too much for the poor girl. I asked her to go on and take her walk with her friends, saying that I could go no further. She made excuses, and the more I urged her the firmer she became. She looked doubtful and frightened. I suppose there was something in my looks or manner that alarmed her; but she would not go, and that literally saved me. You had no idea, sir, that a living man could be made so abject a slave of Satan," he said, with a ghastly groan and a shudder.

There was a pause here, and I said, "You *were* preserved nevertheless. It was the act of God. You are in his hands and in the power of no other being: be therefore confident for the future."

CHAPTER X.
Home.

I MADE HIM have candles lighted, and saw the room looking cheery and inhabited before I left him. I told him that he must regard his illness strictly as one dependent on physical, though *subtle* physical, causes. I told him that he had evidence of God's care and love in the deliverance which he had just described, and that I had perceived with pain that he seemed to regard its peculiar features as indicating that he had been delivered over to spiritual reprobation. Than such a conclusion nothing could be, I insisted, less warranted; and not only so, but more contrary to facts, as disclosed in his mysterious deliverance from that murderous influence during his Shropshire excursion.

First, his niece had been retained by his side without his intending to keep her near him; and, secondly, there had been infused into his mind an irresistible repugnance to execute the dreadful suggestion in her presence. As I reasoned this point with him, Mr. Jennings wept. He seemed comforted. One promise I exacted, which was that should the monkey at any time return, I should be sent for immediately; and, repeating my assurance that I would give neither time nor thought to any other subject until I had thoroughly investigated his case, and that tomorrow he should hear the result, I took my leave.

Before getting into the carriage I told the servant that his master was far from well, and that he should make a point of frequently looking into his room. My own arrangements I made with a view to being quite secure from interruption. I merely called at my lodgings, and with a travelling-desk and carpetbag, set off in a hackney-carriage[10] for an inn about two miles out of town, called The Horns, a very quiet and comfortable house, with good thick walls. And there I resolved, without the possibility of intrusion or

---

[10] Horse-drawn taxi

distraction, to devote some hours of the night, in my comfortable sitting-room, to Mr. Jennings's case, and so much of the morning as it might require. (There occurs here a careful note of Dr. Hesselius's opinion upon the case and of the habits, dietary, and medicines which he prescribed. It is curious—some persons would say mystical. But on the whole I doubt whether it would sufficiently interest a reader of the kind I am likely to meet with, to warrant its being here reprinted.

The whole letter was plainly written at the inn where he had hid himself for the occasion. The next letter is dated from his town lodgings. I left town for the inn where I slept last night at half-past nine, and did not arrive at my room in town until one o'clock this afternoon. I found a letter in Mr. Jennings's hand upon my table. It had not come by post, and, on inquiry, I learned that Mr. Jennings's servant had brought it, and on learning that I was not to return until today, and that no one could tell him my address, he seemed very uncomfortable, and said that his orders from his master were that he was not to return without an answer.

I opened the letter, and read:

"Dear Dr. Hesselius. It is here. You had not been an hour gone when it returned. It is speaking. It knows all that has happened. It knows everything—it knows you, and is frantic and atrocious. It reviles. I send you this. It knows every word I have written—I write. This I promised, and I therefore write, but I fear very confused, very incoherently. I am so interrupted, disturbed.

"Ever yours, sincerely yours,

"Robert Lynder Jennings."

"When did this come?" I asked.

"About eleven last night: the man was here again, and has been here three times today. The last time is about an hour. since."

Thus answered, and with the notes I had made upon his case in my pocket, I was in a few minutes driving towards Richmond, to see Mr. Jennings.

I by no means, as you perceive, despaired of Mr. Jennings case. He had himself remembered and applied, though quite in a mistaken way, the principle which I lay down in my *Metaphysical Medicine,* and which governs all such cases. I was about to apply it in earnest. I was profoundly interested, and very anxious to see and examine him while the "enemy" was actually present.

I drove up to the somber house, and ran up the steps, and knocked. The door, in a little time, was opened by a tall woman in black silk. She looked ill, and as if she had been crying. She curtseyed, and heard my question, but she did not answer. She turned her face away, extending her hand towards two men who were coming downstairs; and thus having, as it were, tacitly made me over to them, she passed through a side-door hastily and shut it.

The man who was nearest the hall, I at once accosted, but being now close to him, I was shocked to see that both his hands were covered with blood. I drew back a little, and the man passing downstairs merely said in a low tone, "Here's the servant, sir." The servant had stopped on the stairs, confounded and dumb at seeing me. He was rubbing his hands in a handkerchief, and it was steeped in blood.

"Jones, what is it, what has happened?" I asked, while a sickening suspicion overpowered me. The man asked me to come up to the lobby. I was beside him in a moment, and frowning and pallid, with contracted eyes, he told me the horror which I already half guessed. His master had made away with himself. I went upstairs with him to the room—what I saw there I won't tell you. He had cut his throat with his razor. It was a frightful gash.

The two men had laid him on the bed and composed his limbs. It had happened as the immense pool of blood on the floor declared, at some distance between the bed and the window. There was carpet round his bed, and a carpet under his dressing table, but none on the rest of the floor, for the man said he did not like a carpet on his bedroom. In this somber, and now terrible room, one of the great elms that darkened the house was slowly moving the shadow of one of its great boughs upon this dreadful floor. I beckoned to the servant and we went downstairs together. I turned off the hall into an old-fashioned paneled room, and there standing, I heard all the servant had to tell. It was not a great deal.

"I concluded, sir, from your words, and looks, sir, as you left last night, that you thought my master seriously ill. I thought it might be that you were afraid of a fit, or something. So I attended very close to your directions. He sat up late, till past three o'clock. He was not writing or reading. He was talking a great deal to himself, but that was nothing unusual. At about that hour I assisted him to undress, and left him in his slippers and dressing-gown. I went back softly in about half an hour. He was in his bed, quite undressed, and a pair of candles lighted on the table beside his bed. He was leaning on his elbow and looking out at the other side of the bed when I came in. I asked him if he wanted anything, and he said no.

"I don't know whether it was what you said to me, sir, or something a little unusual about him, but I was uneasy, uncommon uneasy about him last night.

"In another half hour, or it might be a little more, I went up again. I did not hear him talking as before. I opened the door a little. The candles were both out, which was not usual. I had a bedroom candle, and I let the light in, a little bit, looking softly round. I saw him sitting in that chair beside the dressing-table with his clothes on again. He turned round and looked at me. I thought it strange he should get up and dress, and put out the candles to sit in the dark, that way. But I only asked him again if I could do anything for him. He said, no, rather sharp, I thought. I asked if I might light the candles, and he said, 'Do as you like, Jones.' So I lighted them, and I lingered about the room, and he said, 'Tell me truth, Jones, why did you come again, you did not hear any one cursing?' 'No, sir,' I said, wondering what he could mean.

"'No,' said he, after me, of course, 'no;' and I said to him, 'Wouldn't it be well, sir, you went to bed? It's just five o'clock;' and he said nothing but, 'Very likely; goodnight, Jones.' So I went, sir, but in less than hour I came again. The door was fast, and he heard me, and called as I thought from the bed to know what I wanted, and he desired me not to disturb him again. I lay down and slept for a little. It must have been between six and seven when I went up again.

"The door was still fast, and he made no answer, so I did not like to disturb him, and thinking he was asleep, I left him till nine. It was his custom to ring when he wished me to come, and I had no particular hour for calling him. I tapped very gently, and getting no answer, I stayed away a good while, supposing he was getting some rest then. It was not till eleven o'clock I grew really uncomfortable about him—for at the latest he was never, that I could remember, later than half-past ten. I got no answer. I knocked and called, and still no answer. So not being able to force the door, I called Thomas from the stables, and together we forced it, and found him in the shocking way you saw."

Jones had no more to tell. Poor Mr. Jennings was very gentle, and very kind. All his people were fond of him. I could see that the servant was very much moved.

So, dejected and agitated, I passed from that terrible house, and its dark canopy of elms, and I hope I shall never see it more. While I write to you I feel like a man who has but half waked from a frightful and monotonous dream. My memory rejects the picture with incredulity and horror. Yet I know it is true. It is the story of the process of a poison, a poison which excites the reciprocal action of spirit and nerve, and paralyses the tissue that separates those cognate functions of the senses, the external and the interior. Thus we find strange bedfellows, and the mortal and immortal prematurely make acquaintance.

CONCLUSION.
A Word for Those Who Suffer.

MY DEAR VAN L, you have suffered from an affection similar to that which I have just described. You twice complained of a return of it. Who, under God, cured you? Your humble servant, Martin Hesselius. Let me rather adopt the more emphasized piety of a certain good old French surgeon of three hundred years ago: "I treated, and God cured you."

Come, my friend, you are not to be hippish. Let me tell you a fact. I have met with, and treated, as my book shows, fifty-seven cases of this kind of vision, which I term indifferently "sublimated," "precocious," and "interior." There is another class of affections which are truly termed—though commonly confounded with those which I describe—spectral illusions. These latter I look upon as being no less simply curable than a cold in the head or a trifling dyspepsia.[11] It is those which rank in the first category that test our promptitude of thought. Fifty seven such cases have I encountered, neither more nor less.

And in how many of these have I failed? In no one single instance. There is no one affliction of mortality more easily and certainly reducible, with a little patience, and a rational confidence in the physician. With these simple conditions, I look upon the cure as absolutely certain. You are to remember that I had not even commenced to treat Mr. Jennings's case. I have not any doubt that I should have cured him perfectly in eighteen months, or possibly it might have extended to two years. Some cases are very rapidly curable, others extremely tedious. Every intelligent physician who will give thought and diligence to the task, will effect a cure. You know my tract on *The Cardinal Functions of the Brain.* I there, by the evidence of innumerable facts, prove, as I think, the high probability of a circulation arterial and venous in its mechanism, through the nerves. Of this system, thus considered, the brain is the heart. The fluid, which is propagated hence through one class of nerves, returns in an altered state through another, and the nature of that fluid is spiritual, though not immaterial, any more than, as I before remarked, light or electricity are so.

By various abuses, among which the habitual use of such agents as green tea is one, this fluid may be affected as to its quality, but it is more frequently disturbed as to equilibrium. This fluid being that which we have in common with spirits, a congestion found upon the masses of brain or nerve, connected with the interior sense, forms a surface unduly exposed, on which disembodied spirits may operate: communication is thus more or less effectually established. Between this brain circulation and the heart circulation there is an intimate sympathy. The seat, or rather the instrument of exterior vision, is the eye. The seat of interior vision is the nervous tissue and brain, immediately about and above the eyebrow. You remember how effectually I dissipated your pictures by the simple application of iced *eau-de cologne.*[12]

Few cases, however, can be treated exactly alike with anything like rapid success. Cold acts powerfully as a repellant of the nervous fluid. Long enough continued it will even produce that permanent insensibility which we call numbness, and a little longer, muscular as well as sensational paralysis. I have not, I repeat, the slightest doubt that I should have first dimmed and ultimately sealed that inner eye which Mr. Jennings had inadvertently opened.

---

[11] Indigestion
[12] Perfume

The same senses are opened in *delirium tremens*,[13] and entirely shut up again when the over-action of the cerebral heart, and the prodigious nervous congestions that attend it, are terminated by a decided change in the state of the body. It is by acting steadily upon the body, by a simple process, that this result is produced—and inevitably produced—I have never yet failed.

Poor Mr. Jennings made away with himself. But that catastrophe was the result of totally different malady, which, as it were, projected itself upon that disease which was established. His case was in the distinctive manner a complication, and the complaint under which he really succumbed, was hereditary suicidal mania. Poor Mr. Jennings I cannot call a patient of mine, for I had not even begun to treat his case, and he had not yet given me, I am convinced, his full and unreserved confidence. If the patient do not array himself on the side of the disease, his cure is certain.

---

[13] Nervousness and perhaps visions brought on by stimulants, which are typically alcohol, but in this case green tea

Fitz James O'Brien
(1828-1862)

Yet another Irishman appears in this anthology of the best horror short story writers. Fitz James O'Brien was born in Cork, Ireland. His father was an attorney and O'Brien later attended Dublin University where Joseph Le Fanu published many of his stories in *The Dublin University Magazine*.

O'Brien subsequently moved to the United States where well-known publications like the *New York Times*, *Vanity Fair*, and *Harper's Magazine* discovered his supernatural fiction.

He was also a poet and wrote a number of poems in the horror genre including "The Gory Gnome" and "The Demon of the Gibbet." In 1853 his first short story, "The Two-Skulls," possessed elements of horror.

The years 1858 and 1859 were watershed years for O'Brien's fictional short stories in the horror and fantasy genres. His most popular was "The Diamond Lens" (1858), published in the *Atlantic Monthly*, which tells of a secret world found under a microscope. He also penned that same year "From Hand to Mouth," which is a precursor to *Alice's Adventures in Wonderland* (1865) in surrealistic fiction. In 1859 the *Atlantic Monthly* also printed O'Brien's "The Wondersmith" where dolls are brought to life in a macabre fashion.

That same year is when O'Brien published one of the best horror stories for the last half of the nineteenth century in "What Was it? A Mystery." Apart from ghost stories, "What Was It?" employs the first use of invisibility in a horror story and perhaps the first in fiction. Invisibility would be used in the stories of many great authors.

In 1881 Bram Stoker published "The Invisible Giant." "What Was it?" also influenced Guy de Maupassant's "Le Horla" (1886) and H. G. Wells's *The Invisible Man* (1897), the popular author of the next story.

"What Was It?" shows that the power of the unseen can be the most frightening of all. It is the second oldest story in this collection and plays its part in the annals of monster horror.

The story was a smashing success. As one editor put it, "Would you believe me, such an impression did this story make upon the American public, that inside of six week's (sic) time, (20,000) twenty thousand letters came to the *Harpers'* (sic) office, full of queries and requests for further news."[1] It is set in New York on Twenty-sixth Street between Seventh and Eighth Avenues.

---

[1] *The Shield: Official Publication of the Theta Delta Chi Fraternity*, Vol. XI, 1895, pg. 292

What Was It?
1859

IT IS I confess, with considerable diffidence that I approach the strange narrative which I am about to relate. The events which I purpose detailing are of so extraordinary and unheard-of a character that I am quite prepared to meet with an unusual amount of incredulity and scorn. I accept all such beforehand. I have, I trust, the literary courage to face unbelief. I have, after mature consideration, resolved to narrate, in as simple and straightforward a manner as I can compass, some facts that passed under my observation in the month of July last, and which, in the annals of the mysteries of physical science, are wholly unparalleled.

I live at No. — Twenty-sixth Street, in this city. The house is in some respects a curious one. It has enjoyed for the last two years the reputation of being haunted. It is a large and stately residence, surrounded by what was once a garden, but which is now only a green enclosure used for bleaching clothes. The dry basin of what has been a fountain, and a few fruit-trees, ragged and unpruned, indicate that this spot, in past days, was a pleasant, shady retreat, filled with fruits and flowers and the sweet murmur of waters.

The house is very spacious. A hall of noble size leads to a vast spiral staircase winding through its center, while the various apartments are of imposing dimensions. It was built some fifteen or twenty years since by Mr. A — the well-known New York merchant, who five years ago threw the commercial world into convulsions by a stupendous bank fraud. Mr. A — as everyone knows, escaped to Europe, and died not long after of a broken heart. Almost immediately after the news of his decease reached this country, and was verified, the report spread in Twenty-sixth Street that No. —— was haunted. Legal measures had dispossessed the widow of its former owner, and it was inhabited merely by a care taker and his wife, placed there by the house agent into whose hands it had passed for purposes of renting or sale. These people declared that they were troubled with unnatural noises.

Doors were opened without any visible agency. The remnants of furniture scattered through the various rooms were, during the night, piled one upon the other by unknown hands. Invisible feet passed up and down the stairs in broad daylight, accompanied by the rustle of unseen silk dresses, and the gliding of viewless hands along the massive balusters. The caretaker and his wife declared that they would live there no longer. The house agent laughed, dismissed them, and put others in their place. The noises and supernatural manifestations continued. The neighborhood caught up the story, and the house remained untenanted for three years. Several persons negotiated for it; but somehow, always before the bargain was closed, they heard the unpleasant rumors, and declined to treat any further.

It was in this state of things that my landlady—who at that time kept a boardinghouse in Bleecker Street, and who wished to move farther up town—conceived the bold idea of renting No. —— Twenty-sixth Street. Happening to have in her house rather a plucky and philosophical set of boarders, she laid down her scheme before us, stating candidly everything she had heard respecting the ghostly qualities of the establishment to which she wished to remove us. With the exception of two timid persons—a sea captain and a returned Californian, who immediately gave notice that they would leave—all of Mrs. Moffat's guests declared that they would accompany her in her chivalric incursion into the abode of spirits.

Our removal was effected in the month of May, and we were all charmed with our new residence. The portion of Twenty-sixth Street where our house is situated—between Seventh and Eighth Avenues—is one of the pleasantest localities in New York. The gardens back of the houses, running down nearly to the Hudson, form, in the summer time, a perfect avenue of verdure. The air is pure and invigorating, sweeping, as it does, straight across the river from the Weehawken heights, and even the ragged garden which surrounded the house on two sides, although displaying on washing days rather too much clothesline, still gave us a piece of greensward to look at, and a cool retreat in the summer evenings, where we smoked our cigars in the dusk, and watched the fireflies flashing their dark-lanterns in the long grass.

Of course we had no sooner established ourselves at No. —— than we began to expect the ghosts. We absolutely awaited their advent with eagerness. Our dinner conversation was supernatural. One of the boarders, who had purchased Mrs. Crowe's *Night Side of Nature*[1] for his own private delectation, was regarded as a public enemy by the entire household for not having bought twenty copies. The man led a life of supreme wretchedness while he was reading this volume. A system of espionage was established, of which he was the victim. If he incautiously laid the book down for an instant and left the room, it was immediately seized and read aloud in secret places to a select few.

I found myself a person of immense importance, it having leaked out that I was tolerably well versed in the history of supernaturalism, and had once written a story, entitled "The Pot of

---

[1] Catherine Crowe (1803-1876) who published in 1848 a book of supernatural events titled *The Night-side of Nature* and in 1854 was found wandering naked in Edinburg, Scotland, claiming spirits had made her invisible

Tulips," for *Harper's Monthly*,[2] the foundation of which was a ghost. If a table or a wainscot panel happened to warp when we were assembled in the large drawing-room, there was an instant silence, and everyone was prepared for an immediate clanking of chains and a spectral form.

After a month of psychological excitement, it was with the utmost dissatisfaction that we were forced to acknowledge that nothing in the remotest degree approaching the supernatural had manifested itself. Once the black butler asseverated that his candle had been blown out by some invisible agency while he was undressing himself for the night; but as I had more than once discovered this colored gentleman in a condition when one candle must have appeared to him like two, I thought it possible that, by going a step farther in his potations, he might have reversed his phenomenon, and seen no candle at all where he ought to have beheld one.

Things were in this state when an incident took place so awful and inexplicable in its character that my reason fairly reels at the bare memory of the occurrence. It was the tenth of July. After dinner was over I repaired with my friend, Dr. Hammond, to the garden to smoke my evening pipe. The Doctor and myself found ourselves in an unusually metaphysical mood. We lit our large meerschaums,[3] filled with fine Turkish tobacco; we paced to and fro, conversing.

A strange perversity dominated the currents of our thought. They would not flow through the sunlit channels into which we strove to divert them. For some unaccountable reason they constantly diverged into dark and lonesome beds, where a continual gloom brooded. It was in vain that, after our old fashion, we flung ourselves on the shores of the East, and talked of its gay bazaars, of the splendors of the time of Haroun,[4] of harems and golden palaces. Black afreets[5] continually arose from the depths of our talk, and expanded, like the one the fisherman released from the copper vessel,[6] until they blotted everything bright from our vision.

Insensibly, we yielded to the occult force that swayed us, and indulged in gloomy speculation. We had talked some time upon the proneness of the human mind to mysticism, and the almost universal love of the Terrible, when Hammond suddenly said to me, "What do you consider to be the greatest element of Terror?"

The question, I own, puzzled me. That many things were terrible, I knew. Stumbling over a corpse in the dark; beholding, as I once did, a woman floating down a deep and rapid river, with

---

[2] "The Pot of Tulips," *Harper's Monthly Magazine*, Fitz James O'Brien, 1855
[3] Pipe with bowl made from white claylike material
[4] Harun al-Rashid 763-809 was an Abbasid Caliph and the arts flourished under his reign from 786-809
[5] Ifrits are mythical winged creatures that live under the earth
[6] Reference to Eastern myth of an Ifrit locked in a copper vessel and thrown in the sea only to be found by a fisherman who let the creature out

wildly lifted arms, and awful, upturned face, uttering, as she sank, shrieks that rent one's heart, while we, the spectators, stood frozen at a window which overhung the river at a height of sixty feet, unable to make the slightest effort to save her, but dumbly watching her last supreme agony and her disappearance. A shattered wreck, with no life visible, encountered floating listlessly on the ocean, is a terrible object, for it suggests a huge terror, the proportions of which are veiled. But it now struck me for the first time that there must be one great and ruling embodiment of fear, a King of Terrors to which all others must succumb. What might it be? To what train of circumstances would it owe its existence?

"I confess, Hammond," I replied to my friend, "I never considered the subject before. That there must be one Something more terrible than any other thing, I feel. I cannot attempt, however, even the most vague definition."

"I am somewhat like you, Harry," he answered. "I feel my capacity to experience a terror greater than anything yet conceived by the human mind—something combining in fearful and unnatural amalgamation hitherto supposed incompatible elements. The calling of the voices in Brockden Brown's novel of *Wieland*[7] is awful; so is the picture of the Dweller of the Threshold, in Bulwer's *Zanoni*;[8] but," he added, shaking his head gloomily, "there is something more horrible still than these."

"Look here, Hammond," I rejoined, "let us drop this kind of talk, for Heaven's sake!"

"I don't know what's the matter with me tonight," he replied, "but my brain is running upon all sorts of weird and awful thoughts. I feel as if I could write a story like Hoffman[9] tonight, if I were only master of a literary style."

"Well, if we are going to be Hoffmanesque in our talk, I'm off to bed. How sultry it is! Goodnight, Hammond."

"Goodnight, Harry. Pleasant dreams to you."

"To you, gloomy wretch, afreets, ghouls, and enchanters."

We parted, and each sought his respective chamber. I undressed quickly and got into bed, taking with me, according to my usual custom, a book, over which I generally read myself to sleep. I opened the volume as soon as I had laid my head upon the pillow, and instantly flung it to the other side of the room. It was Goudon's *History of Monsters*[10]—a curious French work, which I had lately imported from Paris, but which, in the state of mind I had then reached, was anything but an agreeable companion. I resolved to go to sleep at once; so, turning down my gas until

---

[7] *Wieland, or the Transformation, an American Tale*, Charles Brockden Brown (1771-1810), 1798

[8] Zanoni, Edward Bulwer-Lytton (1803-1873), 1842

[9] E. T. A. Hoffmann (1776-1822) German forerunner of weird tales that influenced the likes of Edgar Allan Poe and many others

[10] Perhaps mistaken author attribution by O'Brien, the proper reference is to Paris Doctor Ernest Martin's book *Histoire des Monstres Depuis L'Antiquite Jusqu'a Nos Jours*, 1800

nothing but a little blue point of light glimmered on the top of the tube, I composed myself to rest.

The room was in total darkness. The atom of gas that still remained lighted did not illuminate a distance of three inches round the burner. I desperately drew my arm across my eyes, as if to shut out even the darkness, and tried to think of nothing. It was in vain. The confounded themes touched on by Hammond in the garden kept obtruding themselves on my brain. I battled against them. I erected ramparts of would-be blankness of intellect to keep them out. They still crowded upon me. While I was lying still as a corpse, hoping that by a perfect physical inaction I should hasten mental repose, an awful incident occurred. A Something dropped, as it seemed, from the ceiling, plumb upon my chest, and the next instant I felt two bony hands encircling my throat, endeavoring to choke me.

I am no coward, and am possessed of considerable physical strength. The suddenness of the attack, instead of stunning me, strung every nerve to its highest tension. My body acted from instinct, before my brain had time to realize the terrors of my position. In an instant I wound two muscular arms around the creature, and squeezed it, with all the strength of despair, against my chest. In a few seconds the bony hands that had fastened on my throat loosened their hold, and I was free to breathe once more. Then commenced a struggle of awful intensity.

Immersed in the most profound darkness, totally ignorant of the nature of the Thing by which I was so suddenly attacked, finding my grasp slipping every moment, by reason, it seemed to me, of the entire nakedness of my assailant, bitten with sharp teeth in the shoulder, neck, and chest, having every moment to protect my throat against a pair of sinewy, agile hands, which my utmost efforts could not confine—these were a combination of circumstances to combat which required all the strength and skill and courage that I possessed.

At last, after a silent, deadly, exhausting struggle, I got my assailant under by a series of incredible efforts of strength. Once pinned, with my knee on what I made out to be its chest, I knew that I was victor. I rested for a moment to breathe. I heard the creature beneath me panting in the darkness, and felt the violent throbbing of a heart. It was apparently as exhausted as I was; that was one comfort. At this moment I remembered that I usually placed under my pillow, before going to bed, a large yellow silk pocket handkerchief, for use during the night. I felt for it instantly; it was there. In a few seconds more I had, after a fashion, pinioned the creature's arms.

I now felt tolerably secure. There was nothing more to be done but to turn on the gas, and, having first seen what my midnight assailant was like, arouse the household. I will confess to being actuated by a certain pride in not giving the alarm before; I wished to make the capture alone and unaided.

Never losing my hold for an instant, I slipped from the bed to the floor, dragging my captive with me. I had but a few steps to make to reach the gas-burner; these I made with the greatest caution, holding the creature in a grip like a vice. At last I got within arm's-length of the tiny speck of blue light which told me where the gas-burner lay. Quick as lightning I released my grasp with one hand and let on the full flood of light. Then I turned to look at my captive.

I cannot even attempt to give any definition of my sensations the instant after I turned on the gas. I suppose I must have shrieked with terror, for in less than a minute afterward my room was crowded with the inmates of the house. I shudder now as I think of that awful moment. I saw nothing! Yes; I had one arm firmly clasped round a breathing, panting, corporeal shape, my other hand gripped with all its strength a throat as warm, and apparently fleshly, as my own; and yet, with this living substance in my grasp, with its body pressed against my own, and all in the bright glare of a large jet of gas, I absolutely beheld nothing! Not even an outline—a vapor!

I do not, even at this hour, realize the situation in which I found myself. I cannot recall the astounding incident thoroughly. Imagination in vain tries to compass the awful paradox.

It breathed. I felt its warm breath upon my cheek. It struggled fiercely. It had hands. They clutched me. Its skin was smooth, like my own. There it lay, pressed close up against me, solid as stone—and yet utterly invisible!

I wonder that I did not faint or go mad on the instant. Some wonderful instinct must have sustained me; for, absolutely, in place of loosening my hold on the terrible Enigma, I seemed to gain an additional strength in my moment of horror, and tightened my grasp with such wonderful force that I felt the creature shivering with agony.

Just then Hammond entered my room at the head of the household. As soon as he beheld my face—which, I suppose, must have been an awful sight to look at—he hastened forward, crying, "Great heaven, Harry! what has happened?"

"Hammond! Hammond!" I cried, "come here. Oh! this is awful! I have been attacked in bed by something or other, which I have hold of; but I can't see it—I can't see it!"

Hammond, doubtless struck by the unfeigned horror expressed in my countenance, made one or two steps forward with an anxious yet puzzled expression. A very audible titter burst from the remainder of my visitors. This suppressed laughter made me furious. To laugh at a human being in my position! It was the worst species of cruelty. Now, I can understand why the appearance of a man struggling violently, as it would seem, with an airy nothing, and calling for assistance against a vision, should have appeared ludicrous. Then, so great was my rage against the mocking crowd that had I the power I would have stricken them dead where they stood.

"Hammond! Hammond!" I cried again, despairingly, "for God's sake come to me. I can hold the—the Thing but a short while longer. It is overpowering me. Help me! Help me!"

"Harry," whispered Hammond, approaching me, "you have been smoking too much."

"I swear to you, Hammond, that this is no vision," I answered, in the same low tone. "Don't you see how it shakes my whole frame with its struggles? If you don't believe me, convince yourself. Feel it—touch it."

Hammond advanced and laid his hand on the spot I indicated. A wild cry of horror burst from him. He had felt it!

In a moment he had discovered somewhere in my room a long piece of cord, and was the next instant winding it and knotting it about the body of the unseen being that I clasped in my arms.

"Harry," he said, in a hoarse, agitated voice, for, though he preserved his presence of mind, he was deeply moved, "Harry, it's all safe now. You may let go, old fellow, if you're tired. The Thing can't move."

I was utterly exhausted, and I gladly loosed my hold.

Hammond stood holding the ends of the cord that bound the Invisible, twisted round his hand, while before him, self-supporting as it were, he beheld a rope laced and interlaced, and stretching tightly round a vacant space. I never saw a man look so thoroughly stricken with awe. Nevertheless his face expressed all the courage and determination which I knew him to possess. His lips, although white, were set firmly, and one could perceive at a glance that, although stricken with fear, he was not daunted.

The confusion that ensued among the guests of the house who were witnesses of this extraordinary scene between Hammond and myself—who beheld the pantomime of binding this struggling Something—who beheld me almost sinking from physical exhaustion when my task of jailer was over—the confusion and terror that took possession of the bystanders, when they saw all this, was beyond description. The weaker ones fled from the apartment. The few who remained clustered near the door, and could not be induced to approach Hammond and his Charge. Still incredulity broke out through their terror.

They had not the courage to satisfy themselves, and yet they doubted. It was in vain that I begged of some of the men to come near and convince themselves by touch of the existence in that room of a living being which was invisible. They were incredulous, but did not dare to undeceive themselves. How could a solid, living, breathing body be invisible, they asked. My reply was this. I gave a sign to Hammond, and both of us—conquering our fearful repugnance to touch the invisible creature—lifted it from the ground, manacled as it was, and took it to my bed. Its weight was about that of a boy of fourteen.

"Now, my friends," I said, as Hammond and myself held the creature suspended over the bed, "I can give you self-evident proof that here is a solid, ponderable body which, nevertheless, you cannot see. Be good enough to watch the surface of the bed attentively."

I was astonished at my own courage in treating this strange event so calmly; but I had recovered from my first terror, and felt a sort of scientific pride in the affair which dominated every other feeling.

The eyes of the bystanders were immediately fixed on my bed. At a given signal Hammond and I let the creature fall. There was the dull sound of a heavy body alighting on a soft mass. The timbers of the bed creaked. A deep impression marked itself distinctly on the pillow, and on the bed itself. The crowd who witnessed this gave a sort of low, universal cry, and rushed from the room. Hammond and I were left alone with our Mystery.

We remained silent for some time, listening to the low, irregular breathing of the creature on the bed, and watching the rustle of the bedclothes as it impotently struggled to free itself from confinement. Then Hammond spoke.

"Harry, this is awful."

"Aye, awful."

"But not unaccountable."

"Not unaccountable! What do you mean? Such a thing has never occurred since the birth of the world. I know not what to think, Hammond. God grant that I am not mad, and that this is not an insane fantasy!"

"Let us reason a little, Harry. Here is a solid body which we touch, but which we cannot see. The fact is so unusual that it strikes us with terror. Is there no parallel, though, for such a phenomenon? Take a piece of pure glass. It is tangible and transparent. A certain chemical coarseness is all that prevents its being so entirely transparent as to be totally invisible. It is not theoretically impossible, mind you, to make a glass which shall not reflect a single ray of light—a glass so pure and homogeneous in its atoms that the rays from the sun shall pass through it as they do through the air, refracted but not reflected. We do not see the air, and yet we feel it."

"That's all very well, Hammond, but these are inanimate substances. Glass does not breathe, air does not breathe. This thing has a heart that palpitates—a will that moves it—lungs that play, and inspire and respire."

"You forget the strange phenomena of which we have so often heard of late," answered the Doctor, gravely. "At the meetings called 'spirit circles,' invisible hands have been thrust into the hands of those persons round the table—warm, fleshly hands that seemed to pulsate with mortal life."

"What? Do you think, then, that this thing is—"

"I don't know what it is," was the solemn reply; "but please the gods I will, with your assistance, thoroughly investigate it."

We watched together, smoking many pipes, all night long, by the bedside of the unearthly being that tossed and panted until it was apparently wearied out. Then we learned by the low, regular breathing that it slept.

The next morning the house was all astir. The boarders congregated on the landing outside my room, and Hammond and myself were lions. We had to answer a thousand questions as to the state of our extraordinary prisoner, for as yet not one person in the house except ourselves could be induced to set foot in the apartment.

The creature was awake. This was evidenced by the convulsive manner in which the bedclothes were moved in its efforts to escape. There was something truly terrible in beholding, as it were, those secondhand indications of the terrible writhings and agonized struggles for liberty which themselves were invisible.

Hammond and myself had racked our brains during the long night to discover some means by which we might realize the shape and general appearance of the Enigma. As well as we could make out by passing our hands over the creature's form, its outlines and lineaments were human. There was a mouth; a round, smooth head without hair; a nose, which, however, was little elevated above the cheeks; and its hands and feet felt like those of a boy. At first we thought of placing the being on a smooth surface and tracing its outline with chalk, as shoemakers trace the outline of the foot. This plan was given up as being of no value. Such an outline would give not the slightest idea of its conformation.

A happy thought struck me. We would take a cast of it in plaster of Paris. This would give us the solid figure, and satisfy all our wishes. But how to do it? The movements of the creature would disturb the setting of the plastic covering, and distort the mold. Another thought. Why not give it chloroform?[11] It had respiratory organs—that was evident by its breathing. Once reduced to a state of insensibility, we could do with it what we would. Doctor X—— was sent for; and after the worthy physician had recovered from the first shock of amazement, he proceeded to administer the chloroform.

In three minutes afterward we were enabled to remove the fetters from the creature's body, and a well-known modeler of this city was busily engaged in covering the invisible form with the moist clay. In five minutes more we had a mold, and before evening a rough facsimile of the mystery. It was shaped like a man— distorted, uncouth, and horrible, but still a man. It was small, not over four feet and some inches in height, and its limbs revealed a muscular development that was unparalleled. Its face surpassed in hideousness anything I had ever seen.

Gustave Doré,[12] or Callot,[13] or Tony Johannot,[14] never conceived anything so horrible. There is a face in one of the latter's

---

[11] Anesthetic administered in gas form that places the patient in a sleeplike state

[12] Paul Gustave Doré (1832-1883) was a French artist and illustrator who etched Gothic scenes into wood such as those by Edgar Allan Poe and Dante Alighieri

illustrations to *"Un Voyage où il vous plaira,"*[15] which somewhat approaches the countenance of this creature, but does not equal it. It was the physiognomy of what I should have fancied a ghoul to be. It looked as if it was capable of feeding on human flesh.

Having satisfied our curiosity, and bound everyone in the house to secrecy, it became a question what was to be done with our Enigma. It was impossible that we should keep such a horror in our house; it was equally impossible that such an awful being should be let loose upon the world. I confess that I would have gladly voted for the creature's destruction. But who would shoulder the responsibility? Who would undertake the execution of this horrible semblance of a human being? Day after day this question was deliberated gravely. The boarders all left the house. Mrs. Moffat was in despair, and threatened Hammond and myself with all sorts of legal penalties if we did not remove the Horror. Our answer was, "We will go if you like, but we decline taking this creature with us. Remove it yourself if you please. It appeared in your house. On you the responsibility rests."

To this there was, of course, no answer. Mrs. Moffat could not obtain for love or money a person who would even approach the Mystery.

The most singular part of the transaction was that we were entirely ignorant of what the creature habitually fed on. Everything in the way of nutriment that we could think of was placed before it, but was never touched. It was awful to stand by, day after day, and see the clothes toss, and hear the hard breathing, and know that it was starving.

Ten, twelve days, a fortnight passed, and it still lived. The pulsations of the heart, however, were daily growing fainter, and had now nearly ceased altogether. It was evident that the creature was dying for want of sustenance. While this terrible life struggle was going on, I felt miserable. I could not sleep of nights. Horrible as the creature was, it was pitiful to think of the pangs it was suffering.

At last it died. Hammond and I found it cold and stiff one morning in the bed. The heart had ceased to beat, the lungs to inspire. We hastened to bury it in the garden. It was a strange funeral, the dropping of that viewless corpse into the damp hole. The cast of its form I gave to Dr. X — who keeps it in his museum in Tenth Street.

As I am on the eve of a long journey from which I may not return, I have drawn up this narrative of an event the most singular that has ever come to my knowledge.

---

[13] Jacques Callot (1592-1635) was a Flemish illustrator

[14] Tony Johannot (1803-1852) was a French engraver who crafted Gothic images of famous stories including Lord Byron's works, Honoré de Balzac and *Faust* by Johann Wolfgang von Goethe

[15] Translated "Travel Where you Want to Go" is an illustration of work by Alfred de Musset and P.-J. Stahl of 1843

NOTE. —It was rumored that the proprietors of a well-known museum in this city had made arrangements with Dr. X—— to exhibit to the public the singular cast which Mr. Escott deposited with him. So extraordinary a history cannot fail to attract universal attention.

H. G. Wells
(1866-1946)

Herbert George Wells was part of the intelligencia of science fiction writing. He was educated at the Royal College of Science in England. He wrote under a high voice that was not always well-received by the masses. He published his most popular works between 1895 and 1898 though he continued to write for many years thereafter. They included *The Time Machine* (1895), *The Island of Doctor Moreau* (1896), *The Invisible Man* (1897) and *The War of the Worlds* (1898).

As a result, he is often called one of the fathers of science fiction along with Jules Verne who wrote during the same period, but this is going a step too far. Both those authors are known for their science fiction *novels*. Edgar Allan Poe, with his many short stories in the science fiction genre, is more properly deemed the father of the science fiction *short story*—or perhaps the grandfather.

Wells penned a number of other fine horror stories including "The Country of the Blind" (1904), which is a precursor to Shirley Jackson's "The Lottery" (1948). In 1896 he published "The Sea Raiders" (1896) and "The Red Room," which is his most chilling ghost story.

The year Wells penned *The Invisible Man* he wrote one of the most shocking horror stories in "Pollock and the Porroh Man" for the last half of the nineteenth century. Note that if the P in Porroh was changed to an R, it would spell horror backwards. The descriptions of the jungle draw from *The Island of Doctor Moreau* that Wells published the year prior. Who knows from where the visions of the inverted severed head came?

The story was originally published in the British magazine *New Budget* on May 23, 1895. Early in the twentieth century it had a strong showing in a number of anthologies.

Pollock and the Porroh Man
1897

IT WAS IN a swampy village on the lagoon river behind the Turner Peninsula that Pollock's first encounter with the Porroh man[1] occurred.

The women of that country are famous for their good looks— they are Gallinas with a dash of European blood that dates from the days of Vasco da Gama[2] and the English slave-traders, and the Porroh man too, was possibly inspired by a faint Caucasian taint in his composition. (It's a curious thing to think that some of us may have distant cousins eating men on Sherboro Island or raiding with the Sofas.) At any rate, the Porroh man stabbed the woman to the heart as though he had been a mere low-class Italian, and very narrowly missed Pollock. But Pollock, using his revolver to parry the lightning stab which was aimed at his deltoid muscle, sent the iron dagger flying, and firing, hit the man in the hand.

He fired again and missed, knocking a sudden window out of the wall of the hut. The Porroh man stooped in the doorway, glancing under his arm at Pollock. Pollock caught a glimpse of his inverted face in the sunlight, and then the Englishman was alone, sick and trembling with the excitement of the affair, in the twilight of the place. It had all happened in less time than it takes to read about it.

The woman was quite dead, and having ascertained this, Pollock went to the entrance of the hut and looked out. Things outside were dazzling bright. Half a dozen of the porters of the expedition were standing up in a group near the green huts they occupied, and staring towards him, wondering what the shots might signify. Behind the little group of men was the broad stretch of black fetid mud by the river, a green carpet of rafts of papyrus and water-grass, and then the leaden water. The mangroves beyond the stream loomed indistinctly through the blue haze. There were no signs of excitement in the squat village, whose fence was just visible above the cane-grass.

Pollock came out of the hut cautiously and walked towards the river, looking over his shoulder at intervals. But the Porroh man had vanished. Pollock clutched his revolver nervously in his hand.

---

[1] Witchdoctor of a tribal pagan religion based on voodoo and superstition
[2] Vasco da Gama (1469-1524) was a great Portuguese explorer that visited India and Africa

One of his men came to meet him, and as he came, pointed to the bushes behind the hut in which the Porroh man had disappeared. Pollock had an irritating persuasion of having made an absolute fool of himself; he felt bitter, savage, at the turn things had taken. At the same time, he would have to tell Waterhouse—the moral, exemplary, cautious Waterhouse—who would inevitably take the matter seriously. Pollock cursed bitterly at his luck, at Waterhouse, and especially at the West Coast of Africa. He felt consummately sick of the expedition. And in the back of his mind all the time was a speculative doubt where precisely within the visible horizon the Porroh man might be.

It is perhaps rather shocking, but he was not at all upset by the murder that had just happened. He had seen so much brutality during the last three months, so many dead women, burnt huts, drying skeletons, up the Kittam River in the wake of the Sofa cavalry, that his senses were blunted. What disturbed him was the persuasion that this business was only beginning.

He swore savagely at the black, who ventured to ask a question, and went on into the tent under the orange-trees where Waterhouse was lying, feeling exasperatingly like a boy going into the headmaster's study.

Waterhouse was still sleeping off the effects of his last dose of chlorodyne, and Pollock sat down on a packing-case beside him, and lighting his pipe, waited for him to awake. About him were scattered the pots and weapons Waterhouse had collected from the Mendi people, and which he had been repacking for the canoe voyage to Sulyma.

Presently Waterhouse woke up, and after judicial stretching, decided he was all right again. Pollock got him some tea. Over the tea, the incidents of the afternoon were described by Pollock, after some preliminary beating about the bush. Waterhouse took the matter even more seriously than Pollock had anticipated. He did not simply disapprove, he scolded, he insulted.

"You're one of those infernal fools who think a black man isn't a human being," he said. "I can't be ill a day without you must get into some dirty scrape or other. This is the third time in a month that you have come crossways-on with a native, and this time you're in for it with a vengeance. Porroh, too! They're down upon you enough as it is, about that idol you wrote your silly name on. And they're the most vindictive devils on earth! You make a man ashamed of civilization. To think you come of a decent family! If ever I cumber myself up with a vicious, stupid young lout like you again—"

"Steady on, now," snarled Pollock, in the tone that always exasperated Waterhouse; "steady on."

At that Waterhouse became speechless. He jumped to his feet.

"Look here, Pollock," he said, after a struggle to control his breath. "You must go home. I won't have you any longer. I'm ill enough as it is, through you—"

"Keep your hair on," said Pollock, staring in front of him. "I'm ready enough to go."

Waterhouse became calmer again. He sat down on the campstool. "Very well," he said. "I don't want a row, Pollock you know, but it's confoundedly annoying to have one's plans put out by this kind of thing. I'll come to Sulyma with you, and see you safe aboard—"

"You needn't," said Pollock. "I can go alone. From here."

"Not far," said Waterhouse. "You don't understand this Porroh business."

"How should I know she belonged to a Porroh man?" said Pollock bitterly.

"Well, she did," said Waterhouse; "and you can't undo the thing. Go alone, indeed! I wonder what they'd do to you. You don't seem to understand that this Porroh hokey-pokey rules this country, is its law, religion, constitution, medicine, magic . . . They appoint the chiefs. The Inquisition,[3] at its best, couldn't hold a candle to these chaps. He will probably set Awajale, the chief here, on to us. It's lucky our porters are Mendis.[4] We shall have to shift this little settlement of ours . . . Confound you, Pollock! And, of course, you must go and miss him."

He thought, and his thoughts seemed disagreeable. Presently he stood up and took his rifle. "I'd keep close for a bit, if I were you," he said, over his shoulder, as he went out. "I'm going out to see what I can find out about it."

Pollock remained sitting in the tent, meditating. "I was meant for a civilized life," he said to himself, regretfully, as he filled his pipe. "The sooner I get back to London or Paris the better for me."

His eye fell on the sealed case in which Waterhouse had put the featherless poisoned arrows they had bought in the Mendi country. "I wish I had hit the beggar somewhere vital," said Pollock viciously.

Waterhouse came back after a long interval. He was not communicative, though Pollock asked him questions enough. The Porroh man, it seems was a prominent member of that mystical society. The village was interested, but not threatening. No doubt the witchdoctor had gone into the bush. He was a great witchdoctor. "Of course, he's up to something," said Waterhouse, and became silent.

"But what can he do?" asked Pollock, unheeded.

"I must get you out of this. There's something brewing, or things would not be so quiet," said Waterhouse, after a gap of silence. Pollock wanted to know what the brew might be. "Dancing in a circle of skulls," said Waterhouse; "brewing a stink in a copper pot." Pollock wanted particulars. Waterhouse was vague, Pollock

---

[3] Spanish Inquisition that consisted of a Grand Inquisitor, junior members and tribunals for judging whether a person was guilty of a crime without a jury of their peers, and disbanded in 1834

[4] Egyptian who worshipped Egyptian gods from the ancient city of the same name

pressing. At last Waterhouse lost his temper. "How the devil should I know?" he said to Pollock's twentieth inquiry what the Porroh man would do. "He tried to kill you off-hand in the hut. Now, I fancy he will try something more elaborate. But you'll see fast enough. I don't want to help unnerve you. It's probably all nonsense."

That night, as they were sitting at their fire, Pollock again tried to draw Waterhouse out on the subject of Porroh methods. "Better get to sleep," said Waterhouse, when Pollock's bent became apparent; "we start early tomorrow. You may want all your nerve about you."

"But what line will he take?"

"Can't say. They're versatile people. They know a lot of rum dodges. You'd better get that copper-devil, Shakespeare, to talk."

There was a flash and a heavy bang, out of the darkness behind the huts, and a clay bullet came whistling close to Pollock's head. This, at least, was crude enough. The blacks and half-breeds sitting and yarning round their own fire jumped up, and someone fired into the dark.

"Better go into one of the huts," said Waterhouse quietly, still sitting unmoved.

Pollock stood up by the fire and drew his revolver. Fighting, at least, he was not afraid of. But a man in the dark is in the best of armor. Realizing the wisdom of Waterhouse's advice, Pollock went into the tent and lay down there.

What little sleep he had was disturbed by dreams, variegated dreams, but chiefly of the Porroh man's face, upside down, as he went out of the hut, and looked up under his arm. It was odd that this transitory impression should have stuck so firmly in Pollock's memory. Moreover, he was troubled by queer pains in his limbs.

In the white haze of the early morning, as they were loading the canoes, a barbed arrow suddenly appeared quivering in the ground close to Pollock's foot. The boys made a perfunctory effort to clear out the thicket, but it led to no capture.

After these two occurrences, there was a disposition on the part of the expedition to leave Pollock to himself, and Pollock became, for the first time in his life, anxious to mingle with blacks. Waterhouse took one canoe, and Pollock, in spite of a friendly desire to chat with Waterhouse, had to take the other. He was left all alone in the front part of the canoe, and he had the greatest trouble to make the men—who did not love him—keep to the middle of the river, a clear hundred yards or more from either shore. However, he made Shakespeare, the Freetown half-breed, come up to his own end of the canoe and tell him about Porroh, which Shakespeare, failing in his attempts to leave Pollock alone, presently did with considerable freedom and gusto.

The day passed. The canoe glided swiftly along the ribbon of lagoon water, between the drift of water-figs, fallen trees, papyrus, and palm-wine palms, and with the dark mangrove swamp to the left, through which one could hear now and then the roar of the

Atlantic surf. Shakespeare told in his soft, blurred English of how the Porroh could cast spells; how men withered up under their malice; how they could send dreams and devils; how they tormented and killed the sons of Ijibu; how they kidnapped a white trader from Sulyma who had maltreated one of the sect, and how his body looked when it was found. And Pollock after each narrative cursed under his breath at the want of missionary enterprise that allowed such things to be, and at the inert British Government that ruled over this dark heathendom of Sierra Leone.

In the evening they came to the Kasi Lake, and sent a score of crocodiles lumbering off the island on which the expedition camped for the night.

The next day they reached Sulyma, and smelt the sea breeze, but Pollock had to put up there for five days before he could get on to Freetown. Waterhouse, considering him to be comparatively safe here, and within the pale of Freetown influence, left him and went back with the expedition to Gbemma, and Pollock became very friendly with Perera, the only resident white trader at Sulyma—so friendly, indeed, that he went about with him everywhere. Perera was a little Portuguese Jew, who had lived in England, and he appreciated the Englishman's friendliness as a great compliment.

For two days nothing happened out of the ordinary; for the most part Pollock and Perera played Nap[5]—the only game they had in common—and Pollock got into debt. Then, on the second evening, Pollock had a disagreeable intimation of the arrival of the Porroh man in Sulyma by getting a flesh-wound in the shoulder from a lump of filed iron. It was a long shot, and the missile had nearly spent its force when it hit him. Still it conveyed its message plainly enough. Pollock sat up in his hammock, revolver in hand, all that night, and next morning confided, to some extent, in the Anglo–Portuguese.

Perera took the matter seriously. He knew the local customs pretty thoroughly. "It is a personal question, you must know. It is revenge. And of course he is hurried by your leaving de country. None of de natives or half-breeds will interfere wid him very much— unless you make it wort deir while. If you come upon him suddenly, you might shoot him. But den he might shoot you. Den dere's dis-infernal magic," said Perera. "Of course, I don't believe in it—superstition—but still it's not nice to tink dat wherever you are, dere is a black man, who spends a moonlight night now and den a-dancing about a fire to send you bad dreams . . . Had any bad dreams?"

"Rather," said Pollock. "I keep on seeing the beggar's head upside down grinning at me and showing all his teeth as he did in the hut, and coming close up to me, and then going ever so far off, and coming back. It's nothing to be afraid of, but somehow it simply paralyses me with terror in my sleep. Queer things—

---

[5] A British card game also called Napoleon

dreams. I know it's a dream all the time, and I can't wake up from it."

"It's probably only fancy," said Perera. "Den my niggers say Porroh men can send snakes. Seen any snakes lately?"

"Only one. I killed him this morning, on the floor near my hammock. Almost trod on him as I got up."

"Ah!" said Perera, and then, reassuringly, "Of course it is a—coincidence. Still I would keep my eyes open. Den dere's pains in de bones."

"I thought they were due to miasma,"[6] said Pollock.

"Probably dey are. When did dey begin?"

Then Pollock remembered that he first noticed them the night after the fight in the hut. "It's my opinion he don't want to kill you," said Perera—"at least not yet. I've heard deir idea is to scare and worry a man wid deir spells, and narrow misses, and rheumatic pains, and bad dreams, and all dat, until he's sick of life. Of course, it's all talk, you know. You mustn't worry about it . . . But I wonder what he'll be up to next."

"I shall have to be up to something first," said Pollock, staring gloomily at the greasy cards that Perera was putting on the table. "It don't suit my dignity to be followed about, and shot at, and blighted in this way. I wonder if Porroh hokey-pokey upsets your luck at cards."

He looked at Perera suspiciously.

"Very likely it does," said Perera warmly, shuffling. "Dey are wonderful people."

That afternoon Pollock killed two snakes in his hammock, and there was also an extraordinary increase in the number of red ants that swarmed over the place; and these annoyances put him in a fit temper to talk over business with a certain Mendi rough he had interviewed before. The Mendi rough showed Pollock a little iron dagger, and demonstrated where one struck in the neck, in a way that made Pollock shiver, and in return for certain considerations Pollock promised him a double-barreled gun with an ornamental lock.

In the evening, as Pollock and Perera were playing cards, the Mendi rough came in through the doorway, carrying something in a blood-soaked piece of native cloth.

"Not here!" said Pollock very hurriedly. "Not here!"

But he was not quick enough to prevent the man, who was anxious to get to Pollock's side of the bargain, from opening the cloth and throwing the head of the Porroh man upon the table. It bounded from there on to the floor, leaving a red trail on the cards, and rolled into the corner, where it came to rest upside down, but glaring hard at Pollock.

Perera jumped up as the thing fell among the cards, and began in his excitement to gabble in Portuguese. The Mendi was bowing, with the red cloth in his hand. "De gun!" he cried. Pollock stared

---

[6] Humid jungle atmosphere

back at the head in the corner. It bore exactly the expression it had in his dreams. Something seemed to snap in his own brain as he looked at it.

Then Perera found his English again.

"You got him killed?" he said. "You did not kill him yourself?"

"Why should I?" said Pollock.

"But he will not be able to take it off now!"

"Take what off?" said Pollock.

"And all dese cards are spoiled!"

"What do you mean by taking off?" said Pollock.

"You must send me a new pack from Freetown. You can buy dem dere.

"But—'take it off'?"

"It is only superstition. I forgot. De niggers say dat if de witches—he was a witch—But it is rubbish . . . You must make de Porroh man take it off, or kill him yourself . . . It is very silly."

Pollock swore under his breath, still staring hard at the head in the corner.

"I can't stand that glare," he said. Then suddenly he rushed at the thing and kicked it. It rolled some yards or so, and came to rest in the same position as before, upside down, and looking at him.

"He is ugly," said the Anglo–Portuguese. "Very ugly. Dey do it on deir faces with little knives."

Pollock would have kicked the head again, but the Mendi man touched him on the arm. "De gun?" he said, looking nervously at the head.

"Two—if you will take that beastly thing away," said Pollock.

The Mendi shook his head, and intimated that he only wanted one gun now due to him, and for which he would be obliged. Pollock found neither cajolery nor bullying any good with him. Perera had a gun to sell (at a profit of three hundred per cent), and with that the man presently departed. Then Pollock's eyes, against his will, were recalled to the thing on the floor.

"It is funny dat his head keeps upside down," said Perera, with an uneasy laugh. "His brains must be heavy, like de weight in de little images one sees dat keep always upright wid lead in dem. You will take him wiv you when you go presently. You might take him now. De cards are all spoilt. Dere is a man sell dem in Freetown. De room is in a filthy mess as it is. You should have killed him yourself."

Pollock pulled himself together, and went and picked up the head. He would hang it up by the lamp-hook in the middle of the ceiling of his room, and dig a grave for it at once. He was under the impression that he hung it up by the hair, but that must have been wrong, for when he returned for it, it was hanging by the neck upside down.

He buried it before sunset on the north side of the shed he occupied, so that he should not have to pass the grave after dark when he was returning from Perera's. He killed two snakes before he went to sleep. In the darkest part of the night he awoke with a start, and heard a pattering sound and something scraping on the floor. He sat up noiselessly, and felt under his pillow for his revolver. A mumbling growl followed, and Pollock fired at the sound. There was a yelp, and something dark passed for a moment across the hazy blue of the doorway. "A dog!" said Pollock, lying down again.

In the early dawn he awoke again with a peculiar sense of unrest. The vague pain in his bones had returned. For some time he lay watching the red ants that were swarming over the ceiling, and then, as the light grew brighter, he looked over the edge of his hammock and saw something dark on the floor. He gave such a violent start that the hammock overset and flung him out.

He found himself lying, perhaps, a yard away from the head of the Porroh man. It had been disinterred by the dog, and the nose was grievously battered. Ants and flies swarmed over it. By an odd coincidence, it was still upside down, and with the same diabolical expression in the inverted eyes.

Pollock sat paralyzed, and stared at the horror for some time. Then he got up and walked round it—giving it a wide berth—and out of the shed. The clear light of the sunrise, the living stir of vegetation before the breath of the dying land-breeze, and the empty grave with the marks of the dog's paws, lightened the weight upon his mind a little.

He told Perera of the business as though it was a jest—a jest to be told with white lips. "You should not have frighten de dog," said Perera, with poorly simulated hilarity.

The next two days, until the steamer came, were spent by Pollock in making a more effectual disposition of his possession. Overcoming his aversion to handling the thing, he went down to the river mouth and threw it into the seawater, but by some miracle it escaped the crocodiles, and was cast up by the tide on the mud a little way up the river, to be found by an intelligent Arab half-breed, and offered for sale to Pollock and Perera as a curiosity, just on the edge of night. The native hung about in the brief twilight, making lower and lower offers, and at last, getting scared in some way by the evident dread these wise white men had for the thing, went off, and passing Pollock's shed, threw his burden in there for Pollock to discover in the morning.

At this Pollock got into a kind of frenzy. He would burn the thing. He went out straightway into the dawn, and had constructed a big pyre of brushwood before the heat of the day. He was interrupted by the hooter of the little paddle steamer from Monrovia to Bathurst, which was coming through the gap in the bar.

"Thank Heaven!" said Pollock, with infinite piety, when the meaning of the sound dawned upon him. With trembling hands he lit his pile of wood hastily, threw the head upon it, and went away to pack his portmanteau[7] and make his *adieux* to Perera.

---

[7] Suitcase

That afternoon, with a sense of infinite relief, Pollock watched the flat swampy foreshore of Sulyma grow small in the distance. The gap in the long line of white surge became narrower and narrower. It seemed to be closing in and cutting him off from his trouble. The feeling of dread and worry began to slip from him bit by bit. At Sulyma belief in Porroh malignity and Porroh magic had been in the air, his sense of Porroh had been vast, pervading, threatening, dreadful. Now manifestly the domain of Porroh was only a little place, a little black band between the sea and the blue cloudy Mendi uplands.

"Goodbye, Porroh!" said Pollock. "Goodbye—certainly not *au revoir.*"

The captain of the steamer came and leant over the rail beside him, and wished him good-evening, and spat at the froth of the wake in token of friendly ease.

"I picked up a rummy curio on the beach this go," said the captain. "It's a thing I never saw done this side of Indy before."

"What might that be?" said Pollock.

"Pickled 'ed," said the captain.

"What!" said Pollock.

"'Ed—smoked. 'Ed of one of those Porroh chaps, all ornamented with knife-cuts. Why! What's up? Nothing? I shouldn't have took you for a nervous chap. Green in the face. By gosh! You're a bad sailor. All right, eh? Lord, how funny you went . . .! Well, this 'ed I was telling you of is a bit rum in a way. I've got it, along with some snakes, in a jar of spirit in my cabin what I keeps for such curios, and I'm hanged if it don't float upsy down. Hullo!"

Pollock had given an incoherent cry, and had his hands in his hair. He ran towards the paddle-boxes with a half-formed idea of jumping into the sea, and then he realized his position and turned back towards the captain.

"Here!" said the captain. "Jack Philips, just keep him off me! Stand off! No nearer, mister! What's the matter with you? Are you mad?"

Pollock put his hand to his head. It was no good explaining. "I believe I am pretty nearly mad at times," he said. "It's a pain I have here. Comes suddenly. You'll excuse me, I hope."

He was white and in a perspiration. He saw suddenly very clearly all the danger he ran of having his sanity doubted. He forced himself to restore the captain's confidence, by answering his sympathetic inquiries, noting his suggestions, even trying a spoonful of neat brandy in his cheek, and that matter settled, asking a number of questions about the captain's private trade in curiosities. The captain described the head in detail. All the while Pollock was struggling to keep under a preposterous persuasion that the ship was as transparent as glass, and that he could distinctly see the inverted face looking at him from the cabin beneath his feet.

Pollock had a worse time almost on the steamer than he had at Sulyma. All day he had to control himself in spite of his intense perception of the imminent presence of that horrible head that was overshadowing his mind. At night his old nightmare returned, until, with a violent effort, he would force himself awake, rigid with the horror of it, and with the ghost of a hoarse scream in his throat.

He left the actual head behind at Bathurst, where he changed ship for Teneriffe, but not his dreams nor the dull ache in his bones. At Teneriffe, Pollock transferred to a Cape liner, but the head followed him.

He gambled, he tried chess, he even read books, but he knew the danger of drink. Yet whenever a round black shadow, a round black object came into his range, there he looked for the head, and—saw it.

He knew clearly enough that his imagination was growing traitor to him, and yet at times it seemed the ship he sailed in, his fellow-passengers, the sailors, the wide sea, was all part of a filmy phantasmagoria that hung, scarcely veiling it, between him and a horrible real world. Then the Porroh man, thrusting his diabolical face through that curtain, was the one real and undeniable thing. At that he would get up and touch things, taste something, gnaw something, burn his hand with a match, or run a needle into himself.

So, struggling grimly and silently with his excited imagination, Pollock reached England. He landed at Southampton, and went on straight from Waterloo to his banker's in Cornhill in a cab. There he transacted some business with the manager in a private room, and all the while the head hung like an ornament under the black marble mantel and dripped upon the fender. He could hear the drops fall, and see the red on the fender.

"A pretty fern," said the manager, following his eyes. "But it makes the fender rusty."

"Very," said Pollock; "a very pretty fern. And that reminds me. Can you recommend me a physician for mind troubles? I've got a little—what is it—? Hallucination."

The head laughed savagely, wildly. Pollock was surprised the manager did not notice it. But the manager only stared at his face.

With the address of a doctor, Pollock presently emerged in Cornhill. There was no cab in sight, and so he went on down to the western end of the street, and essayed the crossing opposite the Mansion House. The crossing is hardly easy even for the expert Londoner; cabs, vans, carriages, mail-carts, omnibuses go by in one incessant stream; to anyone fresh from the malarious solitudes of Sierra Leone it is a boiling, maddening confusion.

But when an inverted head suddenly comes bouncing, like an India rubber ball, between your legs, leaving distinct smears of blood every time it touches the ground, you can scarcely hope to avoid an accident. Pollock lifted his feet convulsively to avoid it, and then kicked at the thing furiously. Then something hit him violently in the back, and a hot pain ran up his arm.

He had been hit by the pole of an omnibus, and three of the fingers of his left hand smashed by the hoof of one of the horses—the very fingers, as it happened, that he shot from the Porroh man. They pulled him out from between the horse's legs, and found the address of the physician, in his crushed hand.

For a couple of days Pollock's sensations were full of the sweet, pungent smell of chloroform,[8] of painful operations that caused him no pain, of lying still and being given food and drink. Then he had a slight fever, and was very thirsty, and his old nightmare came back. It was only when it returned that he noticed it had left him for a day.

"If my skull had been smashed instead of my fingers, it might have gone altogether," said Pollock, staring thoughtfully at the dark cushion that had taken on for the time the shape of the head.

Pollock at the first opportunity told the physician of his mind trouble. He knew clearly that he must go mad unless something should intervene to save him. He explained that he had witnessed a decapitation in Dahomey, and was haunted by one of the heads. Naturally, he did not care to state the actual facts. The physician looked grave.

Presently he spoke hesitatingly. "As a child, did you get very much religious training?"

"Very little," said Pollock.

A shade passed over the physician's face. "I don't know if you have heard of the miraculous cures—it may be, of course, they are not miraculous—at Lourdes."

"Faith-healing will hardly suit me, I am afraid," said Pollock, with his eye on the dark cushion.

The head distorted its scarred features in an abominable grimace. The physician went upon a new track. "It's all imagination," he said, speaking with sudden briskness. "A fair case for faith-healing, anyhow. Your nervous system has run down, you're in that twilight state of health when the bogles come easiest. The strong impression was too much for you. I must make you up a little mixture that will strengthen your nervous system—especially your brain. And you must take exercise."

"I'm no good for faith-healing," said Pollock.

"And therefore we must restore tone. Go in search of stimulating air—Scotland, Norway, the Alps—"

"Jericho, if you like," said Pollock—"where Naaman[9] went."

However, so soon as his fingers would let him, Pollock made a gallant attempt to follow out the doctor's suggestion. It was now November. He tried football, but to Pollock the game consisted in kicking a furious inverted head about a field. He was no good at the game. He kicked blindly, with a kind of horror, and when they put

---

[8] Anesthetic administered in gas form that places the patient in a sleeplike state

[9] Naaman the Aramean was the king of Aram-Damascus who had leprosy and was told to bathe in the River Jordan seven times to heal himself

him back into goal, and the ball came swooping down upon him, he suddenly yelled and got out of its way.

The discreditable stories that had driven him from England to wander in the tropics shut him off from any but men's society, and now his increasingly strange behavior made even his man friends avoid him. The thing was no longer a thing of the eye merely; it gibbered at him, spoke to him. A horrible fear came upon him that presently, when he took hold of the apparition, it would no longer become some mere article of furniture, but would feel like a real dissevered head. Alone, he would curse at the thing, defy it, entreat it; once or twice, in spite of his grim self-control, he addressed it in the presence of others. He felt the growing suspicion in the eyes of the people that watched him—his landlady, the servant, his man.

One day early in December his cousin Arnold—his next of kin—came to see him and draw him out, and watch his sunken yellow face with narrow eager eyes. And it seemed to Pollock that the hat his cousin carried in his hand was no hat at all, but a Gorgon head[10] that glared at him upside down, and fought with its eyes against his reason.

However, he was still resolute to see the matter out. He got a bicycle, and, riding over the frosty road from Wandsworth to Kingston, found the thing rolling along at his side, and leaving a dark trail behind it. He set his teeth and rode faster. Then suddenly, as he came down the hill towards Richmond Park, the apparition rolled in front of him and under his wheel, so quickly that he had no time for thought, and, turning quickly to avoid it, was flung violently against a heap of stones and broke his left wrist.

The end came on Christmas morning.

All night he had been in a fever, the bandages encircling his wrist like a band of fire, his dreams more vivid and terrible than ever. In the cold, colorless, uncertain light that came before the sunrise, he sat up in his bed, and saw the head upon the bracket in the place of the bronze jar that had stood there overnight.

"I know that is a bronze jar," he said, with a chill doubt at his heart. Presently the doubt was irresistible. He got out of bed slowly, shivering, and advanced to the jar with his hand raised. Surely he would see now his imagination had deceived him, recognize the distinctive sheen of bronze. At last, after an age of hesitation, his fingers came down on the patterned cheek of the head. He withdrew them spasmodically. The last stage was reached. His sense of touch had betrayed him.

Trembling, stumbling against the bed, kicking against his shoes with his bare feet, a dark confusion eddying round him, he groped his way to the dressing-table, took his razor from the drawer, and sat down on the bed with this in his hand. In the looking-glass he saw his own face, colorless, haggard, full of the ultimate bitterness of despair.

---

[10] Horrific carved head that Greek gods, primarily Athena and Zeus, wore to ward off evil

He beheld in swift succession the incidents in the brief tale of his experience. His wretched home, his still more wretched schooldays, the years of vicious life he had led since then, one act of selfish dishonor leading to another; it was all clear and pitiless now, all its squalid folly, in the cold light of the dawn. He came to the hut, to the fight with the Porroh man, to the retreat down the river to Sulyma, to the Mendi assassin and his red parcel, to his frantic endeavors to destroy the head, to the growth of his hallucination.

It was a hallucination! He knew it was. A hallucination merely. For a moment he snatched at hope. He looked away from the glass, and on the bracket, the inverted head grinned and grimaced at him . . . With the stiff fingers of his bandaged hand he felt at his neck for the throb of his arteries.

The morning was very cold, the steel blade felt like ice.

Émile Erckmann & Alexandre Chatrian
(1822-1899 & 1826-1890)

Émile Erckmann and Alexandre Chatrian were two Frenchman who met in 1847 and became close friends. Erckmann was the son of a bookseller and Chatrain's father was a glass maker.[1] They began their careers as journalists and started writing together in 1850 under the recognizable pseudonym Erckmann-Chatrian. Success was elusive and they did not start getting popular in the horror genre until 1857 when they published their first collection of supernatural short stories *Contes Fantastiques* (*Fantastic Tales*). They were praised by the likes of M. R. James and H. P. Lovecraft.

"The Spider of Guyana" is their best horror short story, followed closely by "The Invisible Eye." The former is the oldest story in this collection. The duo also published the ever-popular werewolf novella known today as "The Man-Wolf," and called it "Hugh the Wolf" (*"Hugues-le-loup"*) in the original of 1857.

In 1864, "The Spider of Guyana" was translated into English for the first time in a monthly rag called *Frank Leslie's Ten Cent Monthly*. It was printed under the title "The Crab-Spider,"[2] the name the duo chose for the original French edition in *Contes Fantastiques*. The 1864 translation was wrongly attributed to John B. Williams, M.D., who may have been the English translator, but sadly no mention was made of Émile Erckmann or Alexandre Chatrian. The next English publication appears to be in 1893 when it appeared in *Romance Magazine* and then in *The Strand* of 1899, which is the version published below.

---

[1] "Popular Writers-Past and Present: VII.-Erckmann-Chatrian," *The American Stationer*, 1879, pg. 10

[2] "The Crab-Spider," *Frank Leslie's Ten Cent Monthly*, 1864, pg. 289

In 2014 the world's largest spider was found in Guyana—the South American Goliath birdeater (*Theraphosa blondi*). It was the size of a puppy having legs up to one foot in length. The insect in "The Spider of Guyana" is much larger and certainly the huge spiders in the country influenced Erckmann and Chatrian when conceiving the story.

Despite their sporadic success in writing, the duo was still unable to live solely off their stories. Later in life Chatrian got a position at a railway company and started writing plays by himself while Erckmann suffered through mental disorders.

Their last work together was in 1885. Chatrian would die some five years later and Erckmann followed in 1899.

The Spider of Guyana
1857

THE MINERAL WATERS of Spinbronn, in Hundsruck, a few leagues from Pirmesans, formerly enjoyed an excellent reputation, for Spinbronn was the rendezvous of all the gouty and rheumatic members of the German aristocracy. The wild nature of the surrounding country did not deter the visitors, for they were lodged in charming villas at the foot of the mountain. They bathed in the cascade which fell in large sheets of foam from the summit of the rocks, and drank two or three pints of the water every day. Dr. Daniel Haselnoss, who prescribed for the sick and those who thought they were, received his patients in a large wig, brown coat, and ruffles, and was rapidly making his fortune.

Today, however, Spinbronn is no longer a favorite watering-place. The fashionable visitors have disappeared; Dr. Haselnoss has given up his practice; and the town is only inhabited by a few poor, miserable woodcutters. All this is the result of a succession of strange and unprecedented catastrophes, which Councillor Bremen, of Pirmesans, recounted to me the other evening.

"You know, Mr. Fritz," he said, "that the source of the Spinbronn flows from a sort of cavern about 5ft. high, and from 10ft. to 15ft. across; the water, which has a temperature of 67 deg. centigrade,[1] is salt. The front of the cavern is half hidden by moss, ivy, and low shrubs, and it is impossible to find out the depth of it, because of the thermal exhalations which prevent any entrance.

"In spite of that, it had been remarked for a century that the birds of the locality, hawks, thrushes, and turtledoves, were engulphed in full flight, and no one knew of what mysterious influence it was the result. During the season of 1801, for some unexplained reason, the source became more abundant, and the visitors one evening, taking their constitutional promenade on the lawns at the foot of the rocks, saw a human skeleton descend from the cascade.

"You can imagine the general alarm, Mr. Fritz. It was naturally supposed that a murder had been committed at Spinbronn some years before, and that the victim had been thrown into the source. But the skeleton, which was blanched as white as snow, only weighed twelve pounds: and Dr. Haselnoss concluded that, in all

---

[1] 152.6 Degrees Fahrenheit

probability, it had been in the sand more than three centuries to have arrived at that state of desiccation.

"Plausible as his reasoning was, it did not prevent many visitors leaving that same day, horrified to have drunk the waters. The really gouty and rheumatic ones, however, stayed on, and consoled themselves with the doctor's version. But the following days the cavern disgorged all that it contained of detritus; and a veritable ossuary descended the mountain—skeletons of animals of all sorts, quadrupeds, birds, reptiles. In fact, all the most horrible things that could be imagined.

"Then Haselnoss wrote and published a pamphlet to prove that all these bones were relics of the antediluvian world,[2] that they were fossil skeletons, accumulated there in a sort of funnel during the universal Deluge, that is to say, four thousand years before Christ; and, consequently, could only be regarded as stones, and not as anything repulsive.

"But his work had barely reassured the gouty ones, when one fine morning the corpse of a fox, and then of a hawk, with all its plumage, fell from the cascade. Impossible to maintain that these had existed before the Deluge, and the exodus became general.

"'How horrible!' cried the ladies. 'That is where the so-called virtue of mineral waters springs from. Better die of rheumatism than continue such a remedy.'

"At the end of a week the only visitor left was a stout Englishman, Commodore Sir Thomas Hawerbrook, who lived on a grand scale, as most Englishmen do. He was tall and very stout, and of a florid complexion. His hands were literally knotted with gout, and he would have drunk no matter what if he thought it would cure him. He laughed loudly at the desertion of the sufferers, installed himself in the best of the villas, and announced his intention of spending the winter at Spinbronn."

Here Councilor Bremen leisurely took a large pinch of snuff to refresh his memory, and with the tips of his fingers shook off the tiny particles which fell on his delicate lace jabot. Then he went on:—"Five or six years before the revolution of 1789,[3] a young doctor of Pirmesans, called Christian Weber, went to St. Domingo to seek his fortune. He had been very successful, and was about to retire, when the revolt of the negroes occurred. Happily he escaped the massacre, and was able to save part of his fortune. He travelled for a time in South America, and about the period of which I speak, returned to Pirmesans, and bought the house and what remained of the practice of Dr. Haselnoss.

"Dr. Christian Weber brought with him an old negress called Agatha; a very ugly old woman, with a flat nose, and enormous lips. She always enveloped her head in a sort of turban of the most startling colors; and wore rings in her ears which reached to her

---

[2] Prior to the Deluge, the Biblical flood that destroyed the earth
[3] French Revolution (1789-1799)

shoulders. Altogether she was such a singular-looking creature, that the mountaineers came from miles around just to look at her.

"The doctor himself was a tall, thin man, invariably dressed in a blue swallow-tailed coat and leather breeches. He talked very little, his laugh was dry and nervous, and his habits most eccentric. During his wanderings he had collected a number of insects of almost every species, and seemed to be much more interested in them than in his patients. In his daily rambles among the mountains he often found butterflies to add to his collection, and these he brought home pinned to the lining of his hat.

"Dr. Weber, Mr. Fritz, was my cousin and my guardian, and directly he returned to Germany he took me from school, and settled me with him at Spinbronn. Agatha was a great friend of mine, though at first she frightened me, but she was a good creature, knew how to make the most delicious sweets, and could sing the most charming songs.

"Sir Thomas and Dr. Weber were on friendly terms, and spent long hours together talking of subjects beyond my comprehension—of transmission of fluids, and mysterious things which they had observed in their travels. Another mystery to me was the singular influence which the doctor appeared to have over the negress, for though she was generally particularly lively, ready to be amused at the slightest thing, yet she trembled like a leaf if she encountered her masters eyes fixed upon her.

"I have told you that birds, and even large animals, were engulphed in the cavern. After the disappearance of the visitors, some of the old inhabitants remembered that about fifty years before a young girl, Loisa Muller, who lived with her grandmother in a cottage near the source, had suddenly disappeared. She had gone out one morning to gather herbs, and was never seen or heard of again, but her apron had been found a few days later near the mouth of the cavern. From that it was evident to all that the skeleton about which Dr. Haselnoss had written so eloquently was that of the poor girl, who had, no doubt, been drawn into the cavern by the mysterious influence which almost daily acted upon more feeble creatures. What that influence was nobody could tell. The superstitious mountaineers believed that the devil inhabited the cavern, and terror spread throughout the district.

"One afternoon, in the month of July, my cousin was occupied in classifying his insects and rearranging them in their cases. He had found some curious ones the night before, at which he was highly delighted. I was helping by making a needle red-hot in the flame of a candle.

"Sir Thomas, lying back in a chair near the window and smoking a big cigar, was regarding us with a dreamy air. The commodore was very fond of me. He often took me driving with him, and used to like to hear me chatter in English. When the doctor had labelled all his butterflies, he opened the box of larger insects.

"'I caught a magnificent horn-beetle yesterday,' he said, 'the *lucanus cervus* of the Hartz oaks. It is a rare kind.'

"As he spoke I gave him the hot needle, which he passed through the insect preparatory to fixing it on the cork. Sir

Thomas, who had taken no notice till then, rose and came to the table on which the case of specimens stood. He looked at the spider of Guyana, and an expression of horror passed over his rubicund features.

"'There,' he said, 'is the most hideous work of the Creator. I tremble only to look at it.'

"And, sure enough, a sudden pallor spread over his face.

"'Bah!' said my guardian, 'all that is childish nonsense. You heard your nurse scream at a spider, you were frightened, and the impression has remained. But if you regard the creature with a strong microscope, you would be astonished at the delicacy of its organs, at their admirable arrangement, and even at their beauty.'

"'It disgusts me,' said the commodore, brusquely. 'Pouff!'

"And he walked away.

"'I don't know why,' he continued, 'but a spider always freezes my blood.'

"Dr. Weber burst out laughing, but I felt the same as Sir Thomas, and sympathized with him.

"'Yes, cousin, take away that horrid creature,' I cried. 'It is frightful, and spoils all the others.'

"'Little stupid,' said he, while his eyes flashed, 'nobody compels you to look at them. If you are not pleased you can go.'

"Evidently he was angry, and Sir Thomas, who was standing by the window regarding the mountains, turned suddenly round, and took me by the hand.

"'Your guardian loves his spiders, Frantz,' he said, kindly. 'We prefer the trees and the grass. Come with me for a drive.'

"'Yes, go,' returned the doctor, 'and be back to dinner at six.' Then, raising his voice, 'No offence, Sir Thomas,' he said.

"Sir Thomas turned and laughed, and we went out to the carriage.

"The commodore decided to drive himself, and sent back his servant. He placed me on the seat beside him, and we started for Rothalps. While the carriage slowly mounted the sandy hill, I was quiet and sad. Sir Thomas, too, was grave, but my silence seemed to strike him.

"'You don't like the spiders, Frantz; neither do I. But, thank Heaven! there are no dangerous ones in this country. The spider which your cousin has in his box is found in the swampy forests of Guyana, which is always full of hot vapors and burning exhalations, for it needs a high temperature to support its existence. Its immense web, or rather its net, would surround an ordinary thicket, and birds are caught in it, the same as flies in our spiders' webs. But do not think any more about it; let us drink a glass of Burgundy.'

"As he spoke he lifted the cover of the seat, and, taking out a flask of wine, poured me out a full leathern goblet.

"I felt better when I had drunk it, and we continued our way. The carriage was drawn by a little Ardennes pony, which climbed the steep incline as lightly and actively as a goat. The air was full of the murmur of myriads of insects. At our right was the forest of Rothalps. At our left was the cascade of Spinbronn; and the higher we mounted, the bluer became the silver sheets of water foaming in the distance, and the more musical the sound as the water passed over the rocks.

"Both Sir Thomas and I were captivated by the spectacle, and, lost in a reverie, allowed the pony to go on as he would. Soon we were within a hundred paces of the cavern of Spinbronn. The shrubs around the entrance were remarkably green. The water, as it flowed from the cavern, passed over the top of the rock, which was slightly hollowed, and there formed a small lake, from which it again burst forth and descended into the valley below. This lake was shallow, the bottom of it composed of sand and black pebbles, and, although covered with a slight vapor, the water was clear and limpid as crystal.

"The pony stopped to breathe. Sir Thomas got out and walked about for a few seconds.

"'How calm it is,' he said.

"Then, after a minute's silence, he continued: 'Frantz, if you were not here, I should have a bathe in that lake.'

"'Well, why not?' I answered. 'I will take a walk the while. There are numbers of strawberries to be found a little way up that mountain. I can go and get some, and be back in an hour.'

"'Capital idea, Frantz. Dr. Weber pretends that I drink too much Burgundy; we must counteract that with mineral water. This little lake looks inviting.'

"Then he fastened the pony to the trunk of a tree, and waved his hand in *adieu*. Sitting down on the moss, he commenced to take off his boots, and, as I walked away, he called after me:—"'In an hour, Frantz.'

"They were his last words.

"An hour after I returned. The pony, the carriage, and Sir Thomas's clothes were all that I could see. The sun was going down and the shadows were lengthening. Not a sound of bird or of insect, and a silence as of death filled the solitude. This silence frightened me. I climbed on to the rock above the cavern, and looked right and left. There was nobody to be seen. I called; no one responded. The sound of my voice repeated by the echoes filled me with terror. Night was coming on. All of a sudden I remembered the disappearance of Loisa Muller, and I hurried down to the front of the cavern. There I stopped in affright, and glancing towards the entrance, I saw two red, motionless points.

"A second later I distinguished some dark moving object farther back in the cavern, farther perhaps than human eye had ever before penetrated; for fear had sharpened my sight, and given all my senses an acute ness of perception which I had never before experienced.

"During the next minute I distinctly heard the chirp, chirp of a grasshopper, and the bark of a dog in the distant village. Then my heart, which had been frozen with terror, commenced to beat furiously, and I heard nothing more. With a wild cry I fled, leaving pony and carriage.

"In less than twenty minutes, bounding over rocks and shrubs, I reached my cousin's door.

"'Run, run,' I cried, in a choking tone, as I burst into the room where Dr. Weber and some invited friends were waiting for us. 'Run, run; Sir Thomas is dead; Sir Thomas is in the cavern,' and I fell fainting on the floor.

"All the village turned out to search for the commodore. At ten o'clock they returned, bringing back Sir Thomas's clothes, the pony, and carriage. They had found nothing, seen nothing, and it was impossible to go ten paces into the cavern.

"During their absence Agatha and I remained in the chimney-corner, I still trembling with fear, she, with wide-open eyes, going from time to time to the window, from which we could see the torches passing to and fro on the mountain, and hear the searchers shout to one another in the still night air.

"At her master's approach Agatha began to tremble. The doctor entered brusquely, pale, with set lips. He was followed by about twenty woodcutters, shaking out the last remnants of their nearly extinguished torches.

"He had barely entered before, with flashing eyes, he glanced round the room, as if in search of something. His eyes fell on the negress, and without a word being exchanged between them the poor woman began to cry.

"'No, no, I will not,' she shrieked.

"'But I will,' returned the doctor, in a hard tone.

"The negress shook from head to foot, as though seized by some invisible power. The doctor pointed to a seat, and she sat down as rigid as a corpse.

"The woodcutters, good, simple people, full of pious sentiments, crossed themselves, and I, who had never yet heard of the hypnotic force, began to tremble, thinking Agatha was dead.

"Dr. Weber approached the negress, and passed his hands over her forehead.

"'Are you ready?' he said.

"'Yes. sir.'

"'Sir Thomas Hawerbrook.'

"At these words she shivered again.

"'Do you see him?

"'Yes, yes,' she answered, in a gasping voice, 'I see him.'

"'Where is he?'

"'Up there, in the depths of the cavern, dead!'

"'Dead!' said the doctor; 'how?'

"'The spider I oh, the spider!'

"'Calm yourself,' said the doctor, who was very pale. 'Tell us clearly.'

"'The spider holds him by the throat—in the depths of the cavern—under the rock—enveloped in its web—Ah!'

"Dr. Weber glanced round on the people, who, bending forward, with eyes starting out of their heads, listened in horror.

"Then he continued: 'You see him?'

"'I see him.'

"'And the spider. Is it a big one?'

"'O Master, never, never, have I seen such a big one. Neither on the banks of the Mocaris, nor in the swamps of Konanama. It is as large as my body.'

"There was a long silence. Everybody waited with livid face and hair on end. Only the doctor kept calm. Passing his hand two or three times over the woman's forehead, he recommenced his questions. Agatha described how Sir Thomas's death happened.

"'He was bathing in the lake of the source. The spider saw his bare back from behind. It had been fasting for a long time, and was hungry. Then it saw Sir Thomas's arm on the water. All of a sudden it rushed out, put its claws round the commodore's neck. He cried out, "*Mon Dieu, Mon Dieu*."

The spider stung him and went back, and Sir Thomas fell into the water and died. Then the spider returned, spun its web round him, and swam slowly, gently back to the extremity of the cavern; drawing Sir Thomas after it by the thread attached to its own body.'

"I was still sitting in the chimney-corner, overwhelmed with fright. The doctor turned to me.

"'Is it true, Frantz, that the commodore was going to bathe?'

"'Yes, cousin.'

"'At what time?'

"'At four o'clock.'

"'At four o'clock? It was very hot then, was it not?'

"'Yes; oh, yes.'

"'That's it. The monster was not afraid to come out then.'

"He spoke a few unintelligible words, and turned to the peasants.

"'My friends,' he cried, 'that is where the mass of *debris* and those skeletons come from. It is the spider which has frightened away your visitors, and ruined you all. It is there hidden in its web, entrapping its prey into the depths of the cavern. Who can say the number of its victims?'

"He rushed impetuously from the house, and all the woodcutters hurried after him.

"'Bring fagots, bring fagots!' he cried.

"Ten minutes later two immense carts, laden with fagots, slowly mounted the hill; a long file of woodcutters followed, with hatchets on their shoulders. My guardian and I walked in front, holding the horses by the bridle; while the moon lent a vague, melancholy light to the funeral procession.

"At the entrance of the cavern the *cortege* stopped. The torches were lighted and the crowd advanced. The limpid water flowed over the sand, reflecting the blue light of the resinous torches, the rays of which illuminated the tops of the dark, overhanging pines on the rocks above us.

"'It is here you must unload,' said the doctor. 'We must block up the entrance of the cavern.'

"It was not without a feeling of dread that they commenced to execute his order. The fagots fell from the tops of the carts, and the men piled them up before the opening, placing some stakes against them to prevent their being carried away by the water. Towards midnight the opening was literally closed by the fagots. The hissing water below them flowed right and left over the moss, but those on the top were perfectly dry.

"Then Dr. Weber took a lighted torch, and himself set fire to the pile. The flames spread from twig to twig, and rose towards the sky, preceded by dense clouds of smoke. It was a wild, strange sight, and the woods lighted by the crackling flames had a weird effect. Thick volumes of smoke proceeded from the cavern, while the men standing round, gloomy and motionless, waited with their eyes fixed on the opening. As for me, though I trembled from head to foot, I could not withdraw my gaze.

"We waited quite a quarter of an hour, and Dr. Weber began to be impatient, when a black object, with long, crooked claws, suddenly appeared in the shadow, and then threw itself forward towards the opening. One of the men, fearing that it would leap over the fire, threw his hatchet, and aimed at the creature so well that, for an instant, the blood which flowed from its wound half-quenched the fire, but soon the flame revived, and the horrible insect was consumed.

"Evidently driven by the heat, the spider had taken refuge in its den. Then, suffocated by the smoke, it had returned to the charge, and rushed into the middle of the flames. The body of the horrible creature was as large as a man's, reddish violet in color, and most repulsive in appearance.

"That, Mr. Fritz, is the strange event which destroyed the reputation of Spinbronn. I can swear to the exactitude of my story, but it would be impossible for me to give you an explanation. Nevertheless, admitting that the high temperature of certain thermal springs furnishes the same conditions of existence as the burning climate of Africa and South America, it is not unreasonable to suppose that insects, subject to its influence, can attain an enormous development.

"Whatever may have been the cause, my guardian decided that it would be useless to attempt the resuscitate the waters of Spinbronn; so he sold his house, and returned to America with his negress and his collection."

Bram Stoker
(1847-1912)

Apart from Edgar Allan Poe, there was no bigger name in horror fiction during the nineteenth century than one Bram Stoker. He was born in Dublin, Ireland and the third of seven children. He suffered from an unknown illness and spent most his days bedridden until he recovered at the age of seven. Later he attended Trinity College, Dublin where he studied mathematics. Stoker became the personal assistant to the popular stage actor Henry Irving. He is mentioned by one of the characters in "The Squaw."

Bram Stoker started his writing career by writing short stories. "The Crystal Cup" was his first. It was published in 1872 when Stoker was twenty-five. Later, rats were his animal of choice in a number of his tales, including, of course, "The Burial of the Rats" (1896) and his best ghost story, "The Judge's House" (1891).

He also used cats (black ones) to weave the most fiendish cat horror tale since Edgar Allan Poe's "The Black Cat" (1843) published 50 years earlier. "The Squaw" will never be mistaken for a warm holiday story, yet it was published in the December 2nd Christmas issue of *The Illustrated Sporting of Dramatic News* magazine, titled "Holly Leaves" on its cover.

In 1893, Stoker took a break from writing *Dracula* to publish "The Squaw." He viewed the story as being that important. It includes an American with a thick Southern accent that can be overbearing at times.

"The Squaw" was first published in book form by Stoker's wife, Florence, during 1914. This was two years after Stoker's death. The anthology titled *Dracula's Guest and Other Stories* further contained the first publication of "Dracula's Guest," a segment cut from the *Dracula* novel due to length.

Given the excellent writing, character generation and shocking ending, "The Squaw" is one of Bram Stoker's greatest horror short stories.

The Squaw
1893

NURNBERG AT THE time was not so much exploited as it has been since then. Irving had not been playing *Faust*,[1] and the very name of the old town was hardly known to the great bulk of the travelling public.

My wife and I being in the second week of our honeymoon, naturally wanted someone else to join our party, so that when the cheery stranger, Elias P. Hutcheson, hailing from Isthmian City, Bleeding Gulch, Maple Tree County, Neb.[2] turned up at the station at Frankfort, and casually remarked that he was going on to see the most all-fired old Methuselah[3] of a town in Yurrup, and that he guessed that so much travelling alone was enough to send an intelligent, active citizen into the melancholy ward of a daft house, we took the pretty broad hint and suggested that we should join forces.

We found, on comparing notes afterwards, that we had each intended to speak with some diffidence or hesitation so as not to appear too eager, such not being a good compliment to the success of our married life; but the effect was entirely marred by our both beginning to speak at the same instant—stopping simultaneously and then going on together again.

Anyhow, no matter how, it was done; and Elias P. Hutcheson became one of our party. Straightway Amelia and I found the pleasant benefit; instead of quarrelling, as we had been doing, we found that the restraining influence of a third party was such that we now took every opportunity of spooning in odd corners. Amelia declares that ever since she has, as the result of that experience, advised all her friends to take a friend on the honeymoon. Well, we "did" Nurnberg together, and much enjoyed the racy remarks of our Transatlantic friend, who, from his quaint speech and his wonderful stock of adventures, might have stepped out of a novel. We kept for the last object of interest in the city to be visited the Burg, and on the day appointed for the visit strolled round the outer wall of the city by the eastern side.

---

[1] Sir Henry Irving (1838-1905) was a British actor-manager who performed *Faust* during the 1886-87 season and it was so popular it was revived again in three later years

[2] Fictitious place in Nebraska, U.S.A.

[3] Biblical reference to Methuselah who lived to the age 969

The Burg is seated on a rock dominating the town and an immensely deep fosse guards it on the northern side. Nurnberg has been happy in that it was never sacked;[4] had it been it would certainly not be so spick and span perfect as it is at present. The ditch has not been used for centuries, and now its base is spread with teagardens and orchards, of which some of the trees are of quite respectable growth.

As we wandered round the wall, dawdling in the hot July sunshine, we often paused to admire the views spread before us, and in especial the great plain covered with towns and villages and bounded with a blue line of hills, like a landscape of Claude Lorraine.[5]

From this we always turned with new delight to the city itself, with its myriad of quaint old gables and acre-wide red roofs dotted with dormer windows, tier upon tier. A little to our right rose the towers of the Burg, and nearer still, standing grim, the Torture Tower,[6] which was, and is, perhaps, the most interesting place in the city. For centuries the tradition of the Iron Virgin of Nurnberg[7] has been handed down as an instance of the horrors of cruelty of which man is capable; we had long looked forward to seeing it; and here at last was its home.

In one of our pauses we leaned over the wall of the moat and looked down. The garden seemed quite fifty or sixty feet below us, and the sun pouring into it with an intense, moveless heat like that of an oven. Beyond rose the grey, grim wall seemingly of endless height, and losing itself right and left in the angles of bastion[8] and counterscarp.[9] Trees and bushes crowned the wall, and above again towered the lofty houses on whose massive beauty Time has only set the hand of approval. The sun was hot and we were lazy; time was our own, and we lingered, leaning on the wall. Just below us was a pretty sight—a great black cat lying stretched in the sun, whilst round her gamboled prettily a tiny black kitten. The mother would wave her tail for the kitten to play with, or would raise her feet and push away the little one as an encouragement to further play. They were just at the foot of the wall, and Elias P. Hutcheson, in order to help the play, stooped and took from the walk a moderate sized pebble.

"See!" he said, "I will drop it near the kitten, and they will both wonder where it came from."

---

[4] Never damaged in a war, but this would change 51 years later when it was bombed during World War II

[5] Claude Lorraine (1600-1682) was a French painter of cities and countryside landscapes

[6] The Nuremberg Castle, or the Imperial Castle, was first indicated on historical records in 1050 and contains a large tower with a torture room

[7] The torture room of Nuremberg Castle contained an Iron Virgin know today as an Iron Maiden torture device built in 1802, which was destroyed in 1944 during World War II

[8] Angled top of a castle wall used for defensive purposes

[9] Outer or facing wall of a castle moat

"Oh, be careful," said my wife; "you might hit the dear little thing!"

"Not me, ma'am," said Elias P. "Why, I'm as tender as a Maine cherry-tree. Lor, bless ye. I wouldn't hurt the poor pooty little critter more'n I'd scalp a baby. An' you may bet your variegated socks on that! See, I'll drop it fur away on the outside so's not to go near her!"

Thus saying, he leaned over and held his arm out at full length and dropped the stone. It may be that there is some attractive force which draws lesser matters to greater; or more probably that the wall was not plump but sloped to its base—we not noticing the inclination from above; but the stone fell with a sickening thud that came up to us through the hot air, right on the kitten's head, and shattered out its little brains then and there. The black cat cast a swift upward glance, and we saw her eyes like green fire fixed an instant on Elias P. Hutcheson; and then her attention was given to the kitten, which lay still with just a quiver of her tiny limbs, whilst a thin red stream trickled from a gaping wound.

With a muffled cry, such as a human being might give, she bent over the kitten licking its wounds and moaning. Suddenly she seemed to realize that it was dead, and again threw her eyes up at us. I shall never forget the sight, for she looked the perfect incarnation of hate. Her green eyes blazed with lurid fire, and the white, sharp teeth seemed to almost shine through the blood which dabbled her mouth and whiskers.

She gnashed her teeth, and her claws stood out stark and at full length on every paw. Then she made a wild rush up the wall as if to reach us, but when the momentum ended fell back, and further added to her horrible appearance for she fell on the kitten, and rose with her black fur smeared with its brains and blood. Amelia turned quite faint, and I had to lift her back from the wall.

There was a seat close by in shade of a spreading plane-tree, and here I placed her whilst she composed herself. Then I went back to Hutcheson, who stood without moving, looking down on the angry cat below.

As I joined him, he said:

"Wall, I guess that air the savagest beast I ever see—'cept once when an Apache squaw[10] had an edge on a half-breed what they nicknamed 'Splinters' 'cos of the way he fixed up her papoose[11] which he stole on a raid just to show that he appreciated the way they had given his mother the fire torture. She got that kinder look so set on her face that it jest seemed to grow there. She followed Splinters mor'n three year till at last the braves got him and handed him over to her. They did say that no man, white or Injun, had ever been so long a-dying under the tortures of the Apaches. The only time I ever see her smile was when I wiped her out. I kem on the camp just in time to see Splinters pass in his checks, and he

---

[10] American Indian woman of the Southwest United States
[11] Sling or bag used to carry a baby on a back

wasn't sorry to go either. He was a hard citizen, and though I never could shake with him after that papoose business—for it was bitter bad, and he should have been a white man, for he looked like one—I see he had got paid out in full. Durn me, but I took a piece of his hide from one of his skinnin' posts an' had it made into a pocketbook. It's here now!" and he slapped the breast pocket of his coat.

Whilst he was speaking the cat was continuing her frantic efforts to get up the wall. She would take a run back and then charge up, sometimes reaching an incredible height. She did not seem to mind the heavy fall which she got each time but started with renewed vigor; and at every tumble her appearance became more horrible. Hutcheson was a kind-hearted man—my wife and I had both noticed little acts of kindness to animals as well as to persons—and he seemed concerned at the state of fury to which the cat had wrought herself.

"Wall, now!" he said, "I du declare that that poor critter seems quite desperate. There! there! poor thing, it was all an accident—though that won't bring back your little one to you. Say! I wouldn't have had such a thing happen for a thousand! Just shows what a clumsy fool of a man can do when he tries to play! Seems I'm too darned slipper-handed to even play with a cat. Say Colonel!" it was a pleasant way he had to bestow titles freely—"I hope your wife don't hold no grudge against me on account of this unpleasantness? Why, I wouldn't have had it occur on no account."

He came over to Amelia and apologized profusely, and she with her usual kindness of heart hastened to assure him that she quite understood that it was an accident. Then we all went again to the wall and looked over.

The cat missing Hutcheson's face had drawn back across the moat, and was sitting on her haunches as though ready to spring. Indeed, the very instant she saw him she did spring, and with a blind unreasoning fury, which would have been grotesque, only that it was so frightfully real. She did not try to run up the wall, but simply launched herself at him as though hate and fury could lend her wings to pass straight through the great distance between them. Amelia, womanlike, got quite concerned, and said to Elias P. in a warning voice:

"Oh! you must be very careful. That animal would try to kill you if she were here; her eyes look like positive murder."

He laughed out jovially. "Excuse me, ma'am," he said, "but I can't help laughin'. Fancy a man that has fought grizzlies an' Injuns bein' careful of bein' murdered by a cat!"

When the cat heard him laugh, her whole demeanor seemed to change. She no longer tried to jump or run up the wall, but went quietly over, and sitting again beside the dead kitten began to lick and fondle it as though it were alive.

"See!" said I, "the effect of a really strong man. Even that animal in the midst of her fury recognizes the voice of a master, and bows to him!"

"Like a squaw!" was the only comment of Elias P. Hutcheson, as we moved on our way round the city fosse.

Every now and then we looked over the wall and each time saw the cat following us. At first she had kept going back to the dead kitten, and then as the distance grew greater took it in her mouth and so followed. After a while, however, she abandoned this, for we saw her following all alone; she had evidently hidden the body somewhere. Amelia's alarm grew at the cat's persistence, and more than once she repeated her warning; but the American always laughed with amusement, till finally, seeing that she was beginning to be worried, he said:

"I say, ma'am, you needn't be skeered over that cat. I go heeled, I du!" Here he slapped his pistol pocket at the back of his lumbar region. "Why sooner'n have you worried, I'll shoot the critter, right here, an' risk the police interferin' with a citizen of the United States for carryin' arms contrairy to reg'lations!" As he spoke he looked over the wall, but the cat on seeing him, retreated, with a growl, into a bed of tall flowers, and was hidden. He went on: "Blest if that ar critter ain't got more sense of what's good for her than most Christians. I guess we've seen the last of her! You bet, she'll go back now to that busted kitten and have a private funeral of it, all to herself!"

Amelia did not like to say more, lest he might, in mistaken kindness to her, fulfil his threat of shooting the cat: and so we went on and crossed the little wooden bridge leading to the gateway whence ran the steep paved roadway between the Burg and the pentagonal Torture Tower. As we crossed the bridge we saw the cat again down below us. When she saw us her fury seemed to return, and she made frantic efforts to get up the steep wall. Hutcheson laughed as he looked down at her, and said:

"Goodbye, old girl. Sorry I injured your feelin's, but you'll get over it in time! So long!" And then we passed through the long, dim archway and came to the gate of the Burg.

When we came out again after our survey of this most beautiful old place which not even the well-intentioned efforts of the Gothic restorers of forty years ago have been able to spoil—though their restoration was then glaring white—we seemed to have quite forgotten the unpleasant episode of the morning. The old lime tree with its great trunk gnarled with the passing of nearly nine centuries, the deep well cut through the heart of the rock by those captives of old, and the lovely view from the city wall whence we heard, spread over almost a full quarter of an hour, the multitudinous chimes of the city, had all helped to wipe out from our minds the incident of the slain kitten.

We were the only visitors who had entered the Torture Tower that morning—so at least said the old custodian—and as we had the place all to ourselves were able to make a minute and more satisfactory survey than would have otherwise been possible. The custodian, looking to us as the sole source of his gains for the day, was willing to meet our wishes in any way. The Torture Tower is truly a grim place, even now when many thousands of visitors have sent a stream of life, and the joy that follows life, into the place; but at the time I mention it wore its grimmest and most gruesome aspect. The dust of ages seemed to have settled on it, and the darkness and the horror of its memories seem to have become sentient in a way that would have satisfied the Pantheistic[12] souls of Philo[13] or Spinoza.[14]

The lower chamber where we entered was seemingly, in its normal state, filled with incarnate darkness; even the hot sunlight streaming in through the door seemed to be lost in the vast thickness of the walls, and only showed the masonry rough as when the builder's scaffolding had come down, but coated with dust and marked here and there with patches of dark stain which, if walls could speak, could have given their own dread memories of fear and pain. We were glad to pass up the dusty wooden staircase, the custodian leaving the outer door open to light us somewhat on our way; for to our eyes the one long-wick'd, evil-smelling candle stuck in a sconce on the wall gave an inadequate light.

When we came up through the open trap in the corner of the chamber overhead, Amelia held on to me so tightly that I could actually feel her heart beat. I must say for my own part that I was not surprised at her fear, for this room was even more gruesome than that below. Here there was certainly more light, but only just sufficient to realize the horrible surroundings of the place. The builders of the tower had evidently intended that only they who should gain the top should have any of the joys of light and prospect. There, as we had noticed from below, were ranges of windows, albeit of mediaeval smallness, but elsewhere in the tower were only a very few narrow slits such as were habitual in places of mediaeval defense.

A few of these only lit the chamber, and these so high up in the wall that from no part could the sky be seen through the thickness of the walls. In racks, and leaning in disorder against the walls, were a number of headsmen's swords, great double-handed weapons with broad blade and keen edge. Hard by were several blocks whereon the necks of the victims had lain, with here and there deep notches where the steel had bitten through the guard of flesh and shored into the wood.

Round the chamber, placed in all sorts of irregular ways, were many implements of torture which made one's heart ache to see— chairs full of spikes which gave instant and excruciating pain; chairs and couches with dull knobs whose torture was seemingly less, but which, though slower, were equally efficacious; racks, belts, boots, gloves, collars, all made for compressing at will; steel

---

[12] Pantheists believe that the universe is a group of gods and God is not an individual, but rather everything in the universe is a god
[13] Philo of Alexandria (25 B.C. – 50 A.D.) was a Jewish philosopher who sought to rationalize Greek philosophy with Jewish philosophy
[14] Baruch Spinoza (1632-1677) was a Jewish Dutch philosopher who set forth arguments against the authenticity of the Hebrew Bible

baskets in which the head could be slowly crushed into a pulp if necessary; watchmen's hooks with long handle and knife that cut at resistance—this a specialty of the old Nurnberg police system; and many, many other devices for man's injury to man.

Amelia grew quite pale with the horror of the things, but fortunately did not faint, for being a little overcome she sat down on a torture chair, but jumped up again with a shriek, all tendency to faint gone. We both pretended that it was the injury done to her dress by the dust of the chair, and the rusty spikes which had upset her, and Mr. Hutcheson acquiesced in accepting the explanation with a kind-hearted laugh.

But the central object in the whole of this chamber of horrors was the engine known as the Iron Virgin, which stood near the center of the room. It was a rudely-shaped figure of a woman, something of the bell order, or, to make a closer comparison, of the figure of Mrs. Noah in the children's Ark, but without that slimness of waist and perfect *rondeur* of hip which marks the aesthetic type of the Noah family.[15] One would hardly have recognized it as intended for a human figure at all had not the founder shaped on the forehead a rude semblance of a woman's face. This machine was coated with rust without, and covered with dust; a rope was fastened to a ring in the front of the figure, about where the waist should have been, and was drawn through a pulley, fastened on the wooden pillar which sustained the flooring above.

The custodian pulling this rope showed that a section of the front was hinged like a door at one side; we then saw that the engine was of considerable thickness, leaving just room enough inside for a man to be placed. The door was of equal thickness and of great weight, for it took the custodian all his strength, aided though he was by the contrivance of the pulley, to open it. This weight was partly due to the fact that the door was of manifest purpose hung so as to throw its weight downwards, so that it might shut of its own accord when the strain was released.

The inside was honeycombed with rust—nay more, the rust alone that comes through time would hardly have eaten so deep into the iron walls; the rust of the cruel stains was deep indeed! It was only, however, when we came to look at the inside of the door that the diabolical intention was manifest to the full. Here were several long spikes, square and massive, broad at the base and sharp at the points, placed in such a position that when the door should close the upper ones would pierce the eyes of the victim, and the lower ones his heart and vitals.

The sight was too much for poor Amelia, and this time she fainted dead off, and I had to carry her down the stairs, and place her on a bench outside till she recovered. That she felt it to the quick was afterwards shown by the fact that my eldest son bears to

---

[15] Noah's wife is classically depicted as having a pear (or bell) shape in illustrated children's books

this day a rude birthmark on his breast, which has, by family consent, been accepted as representing the Nurnberg Virgin.

When we got back to the chamber we found Hutcheson still opposite the Iron Virgin; he had been evidently philosophizing, and now gave us the benefit of his thought in the shape of a sort of exordium.

"Wall, I guess I've been learnin' somethin' here while madam has been gettin' over her faint. 'Pears to me that we're a long way behind the times on our side of the big drink.[16] We uster think out on the plains that the Injun could give us points in tryin' to make a man uncomfortable; but I guess your old mediaeval law-and-order party could raise him every time. Splinters was pretty good in his bluff on the squaw, but this here young miss held a straight flush all high on him. The points of them spikes air sharp enough still, though even the edges air eaten out by what uster be on them. It'd be a good thing for our Indian section to get some specimens of this here play-toy to send round to the Reservations[17] jest to knock the stuffin' out of the bucks, and the squaws too, by showing them as how old civilization lays over them at their best. Guess but I'll get in that box a minute jest to see how it feels!"

"Oh no! no!" said Amelia. "It is too terrible!"

"Guess, ma'am, nothin's too terrible to the explorin' mind. I've been in some queer places in my time. Spent a night inside a dead horse while a prairie fire swept over me in Montana Territory—an' another time slept inside a dead buffler when the Comanches[18] was on the war path an' I didn't keer to leave my kyard on them. I've been two days in a caved-in tunnel in the Billy Broncho gold mine in New Mexico, an' was one of the four shut up for three parts of a day in the caisson what slid over on her side when we was settin' the foundations of the Buffalo Bridge. I've not funked an odd experience yet, an' I don't propose to begin now!"

We saw that he was set on the experiment, so I said: "Well, hurry up, old man, and get through it quick!"

"All right, General," said he, "but I calculate we ain't quite ready yet. The gentlemen, my predecessors, what stood in that thar canister, didn't volunteer for the office—not much! And I guess there was some ornamental tyin' up before the big stroke was made. I want to go into this thing fair and square, so I must get fixed up proper first. I dare say this old galoot can rise some string and tie me up accordin' to sample?"

This was said interrogatively to the old custodian, but the latter, who understood the drift of his speech, though perhaps not appreciating to the full the niceties of dialect and imagery, shook his head. His protest was, however, only formal and made to be overcome.

---

[16] Atlantic Ocean

[17] Land drawn up by the United States government on which the American Indians could live to the exclusion of all others

[18] American Indian branch of the Southwest United States

The American thrust a gold piece into his hand, saying: "Take it, pard! it's your pot; and don't be skeer'd. This ain't no necktie party that you're asked to assist in!"

He produced some thin frayed rope and proceeded to bind our companion with sufficient strictness for the purpose. When the upper part of his body was bound, Hutcheson said:

"Hold on a moment, Judge. Guess I'm too heavy for you to tote into the canister. You jest let me walk in, and then you can wash up regardin' my legs!"

Whilst speaking he had backed himself into the opening which was just enough to hold him. It was a close fit and no mistake. Amelia looked on with fear in her eyes, but she evidently did not like to say anything. Then the custodian completed his task by tying the American's feet together so that he was now absolutely helpless and fixed in his voluntary prison. He seemed to really enjoy it, and the incipient smile which was habitual to his face blossomed into actuality as he said:

"Guess this here Eve[19] was made out of the rib of a dwarf! There ain't much room for a full-grown citizen of the United States to hustle. We uster make our coffins more roomier in Idaho territory. Now, Judge, you jest begin to let this door down, slow, on to me. I want to feel the same pleasure as the other jays had when those spikes began to move toward their eyes!"

"Oh no! no! no!" broke in Amelia hysterically. "It is too terrible! I can't bear to see it!—I can't! I can't!"

But the American was obdurate. "Say, Colonel," said he, "why not take Madame for a little promenade? I wouldn't hurt her feelin's for the world; but now that I am here, havin' kem eight thousand miles, wouldn't it be too hard to give up the very experience I've been pinin' an' pantin' fur? A man can't get to feel like canned goods every time! Me and the Judge here'll fix up this thing in no time, an' then you'll come back, an' we'll all laugh together!"

Once more the resolution that is born of curiosity triumphed, and Amelia stayed holding tight to my arm and shivering whilst the custodian began to slacken slowly inch by inch the rope that held back the iron door. Hutcheson's face was positively radiant as his eyes followed the first movement of the spikes.

"Wall!" he said, "I guess I've not had enjoyment like this since I left Noo York. Bar a scrap with a French sailor at Wapping—an' that warn't much of a picnic neither—I've not had a show fur real pleasure in this dod-rotted Continent, where there ain't no b'ars nor no Injuns, an' wheer nary man goes heeled. Slow there, Judge! Don't you rush this business! I want a show for my money this game—I du!"

The custodian must have had in him some of the blood of his predecessors in that ghastly tower, for he worked the engine with a deliberate and excruciating slowness which after five minutes, in

---

[19] Biblical reference to Eve who was made the rib of Adam, the first person God created on Earth

which the outer edge of the door had not moved half as many inches, began to overcome Amelia.

I saw her lips whiten, and felt her hold upon my arm relax. I looked around an instant for a place whereon to lay her, and when I looked at her again found that her eye had become fixed on the side of the Virgin. Following its direction I saw the black cat crouching out of sight. Her green eyes shone like danger lamps in the gloom of the place, and their color was heightened by the blood which still smeared her coat and reddened her mouth.

I cried out: "The cat! look out for the cat!" for even then she sprang out before the engine. At this moment she looked like a triumphant demon. Her eyes blazed with ferocity, her hair bristled out till she seemed twice her normal size, and her tail lashed about as does a tiger's when the quarry is before it.

Elias P. Hutcheson when he saw her was amused, and his eyes positively sparkled with fun as he said: "Darned if the squaw hain't got on all her war paint! Jest give her a shove off if she comes any of her tricks on me, for I'm so fixed everlastingly by the boss, that durn my skin if I can keep my eyes from her if she wants them! Easy there, Judge! don't you slack that ar rope or I'm euchered!"

At this moment Amelia completed her faint, and I had to clutch hold of her round the waist or she would have fallen to the floor. Whilst attending to her I saw the black cat crouching for a spring, and jumped up to turn the creature out.

But at that instant, with a sort of hellish scream, she hurled herself, not as we expected at Hutcheson, but straight at the face of the custodian. Her claws seemed to be tearing wildly as one sees in the Chinese drawings of the dragon rampant, and as I looked I saw one of them light on the poor man's eye, and actually tear through it and down his cheek, leaving a wide band of red where the blood seemed to spurt from every vein.

With a yell of sheer terror which came quicker than even his sense of pain, the man leaped back, dropping as he did so the rope which held back the iron door. I jumped for it, but was too late, for the cord ran like lightning through the pulley-block, and the heavy mass fell forward from its own weight.

As the door closed I caught a glimpse of our poor companion's face. He seemed frozen with terror. His eyes stared with a horrible anguish as if dazed, and no sound came from his lips.

And then the spikes did their work. Happily the end was quick, for when I wrenched open the door they had pierced so deep that they had locked in the bones of the skull through which they had crushed, and actually tore him—it—out of his iron prison till, bound as he was, he fell at full length with a sickly thud upon the floor, the face turning upward as he fell.

I rushed to my wife, lifted her up and carried her out, for I feared for her very reason if she should wake from her faint to such a scene. I laid her on the bench outside and ran back. Leaning against the wooden column was the custodian moaning in pain whilst he held his reddening handkerchief to his eyes. And sitting on the head of the poor American was the cat, purring loudly as she licked the blood which trickled through the gashed socket of his eyes.

I think no one will call me cruel because I seized one of the old executioner's swords and shore her in two as she sat.

Arthur Machen
(1863-1947)

Welsh-born Arthur Machen is one of the greatest, largely unknown, horror story writers to emerge from the Victorian gothic revival period in the last half of the nineteenth century. His given name was Arthur Llewellyn Jones and he chose Arthur Machen to write his supernatural fiction under.

He was raised in the Llanddewi Rectory, being the son of a minister, and had access to various occult books that his father used as defense against Satan. He began writing in the "weird fiction" genre and penned what would be the first chapter of his most enduring work in 1890, which he titled "The Great God Pan." This early publication of the story was printed in *The Whirlwind* weekly newspaper.[1] A few years later Machen filled out the rest of the horror story and found a publisher in December of 1893. This later version is included here. It was first sent to *Blackwood's Magazine* where its editors summarily declined to publish it after "shrinking" away "from the central idea."[2] This is odd from a magazine that had no issues with publishing horror stories about severed heads and torture.

"The Great God Pan" met with overwhelming criticism when published the second time to a wider audience. The editors of the *Westminister (Second Notice)* remarked: "It is an incoherent nightmare of sex and the supposed horrible mysteries behind it, such as might conceivably possess a man who was given to a

---

[1] "The Great God Pan," Arthur Machen, Introduction, 1916, pg. 6
[2] Ibid

morbid brooding over these matters, but which would soon lead to insanity if unrestrained . . . innocuous from its absurdity."[3]

Modern horror writers felt differently. "The Great God Pan" has been referred to as "Maybe the best in the English language."[4] H. P. Lovecraft, in his thesis *Supernatural Horror in Literature*, said this about the story, "[T]he sensitive reader reaches the end with only an appreciative shudder and a tendency to repeat the words of one of the characters: 'It is too incredible, too monstrous; such things can never be in this quiet world.'" In a 1923 letter[5] he stated "Machen is a Titan—perhaps the greatest living author—and I must read everything of his."

"The Great God Pan" deserves its place among Joseph Le Fanu's "Carmilla" (1872), Robert Louis Stevenson's *The Strange Case of Dr. Jekyll and Mr. Hyde* (1886), Oscar Wilde's *The Picture of Dorian Gray* (1890) and Bram Stoker's *Dracula* (1897).

It is that special.

---

[3] Ibid. at 8
[4] "Self-Interview," Stephen King, Sep. 4, 2008, website StephenKing.com
[5] H. P. Lovecraft to Frank Belknap Long, June 3, 1923

The Great God Pan
1894

I

THE EXPERIMENT

"I AM GLAD you came, Clarke; very glad indeed. I was not sure you could spare the time."

"I was able to make arrangements for a few days; things are not very lively just now. But have you no misgivings, Raymond? Is it absolutely safe?"

The two men were slowly pacing the terrace in front of Dr. Raymond's house. The sun still hung above the western mountain-line, but it shone with a dull red glow that cast no shadows, and all the air was quiet; a sweet breath came from the great wood on the hillside above, and with it, at intervals, the soft murmuring call of the wild doves. Below, in the long lovely valley, the river wound in and out between the lonely hills, and, as the sun hovered and vanished into the west, a faint mist, pure white, began to rise from the hills. Dr. Raymond turned sharply to his friend.

"Safe? Of course it is. In itself the operation is a perfectly simple one; any surgeon could do it."

"And there is no danger at any other stage?"

"None; absolutely no physical danger whatsoever, I give you my word. You are always timid, Clarke, always; but you know my history. I have devoted myself to transcendental medicine[1] for the last twenty years. I have heard myself called a quack and charlatan and impostor, but all the while I knew I was on the right path. Five years ago I reached the goal, and since then every day has been a preparation for what we shall do tonight."

"I should like to believe it is all true." Clarke knit his brows, and looked doubtfully at Dr. Raymond. "Are you perfectly sure, Raymond, that your theory is not a phantasmagoria—a splendid vision, certainly, but a mere vision after all?"

Dr. Raymond stopped in his walk and turned sharply. He was a middle-aged man, gaunt and thin, of a pale yellow complexion, but as he answered Clarke and faced him, there was a flush on his cheek.

---

[1] The practice of medicine where the patient is put in a state of relaxed awareness

"Look about you, Clarke. You see the mountain, and hill following after hill, as wave on wave, you see the woods and orchard, the fields of ripe corn, and the meadows reaching to the reed-beds by the river. You see me standing here beside you, and hear my voice; but I tell you that all these things—yes, from that star that has just shone out in the sky to the solid ground beneath our feet—I say that all these are but dreams and shadows; the shadows that hide the real world from our eyes. There is a real world, but it is beyond this glamour and this vision, beyond these 'chases in Arras, dreams in a career,'[2] beyond them all as beyond a veil. I do not know whether any human being has ever lifted that veil; but I do know, Clarke, that you and I shall see it lifted this very night from before another's eyes. You may think this all strange nonsense; it may be strange, but it is true, and the ancients knew what lifting the veil means. They called it seeing the god Pan."[3]

Clarke shivered; the white mist gathering over the river was chilly.

"It is wonderful indeed," he said. "We are standing on the brink of a strange world, Raymond, if what you say is true. I suppose the knife is absolutely necessary?"

"Yes; a slight lesion in the grey matter, that is all; a trifling rearrangement of certain cells, a microscopical alteration that would escape the attention of ninety-nine brain specialists out of a hundred. I don't want to bother you with 'shop,' Clarke; I might give you a mass of technical detail which would sound very imposing, and would leave you as enlightened as you are now. But I suppose you have read, casually, in out-of-the-way corners of your paper, that immense strides have been made recently in the physiology of the brain.

"I saw a paragraph the other day about Digby's theory,[4] and Browne[5] Faber's discoveries.[6] Theories and discoveries! Where they are standing now, I stood fifteen years ago, and I need not tell you

---

[2] A combined quote from the first stanza of George Herbert's "The Temple" poem of 1633, which states "Chases in Arras, guilded emptiness, Shadows well mounted, dreams in a career," referring to animal hunts in Arras, France that are in vain, yet there is surety in shadows and dreams

[3] Greek god of forests and pastures and his lower body is goatlike with hooves as feet and horns sprouting from his head

[4] Everard Digby's (1578-1606) *Theoria Analytica viam ad monarchiam scientiarum demonstrans . . .totius Philosophiae & reliquarum scientiarum* of 1579 quantifies the sciences based on active perception of matter by the mind using senses, see *Dictionary of National Biography*, edited by Leslie Stephen, Vol. XV, 1888, pg. 50

[5] Sir Thomas Browne (1605-1682) published *Religio Medici* in 1642 that purports if a person of science will follow the Christian religion on faith, he may examine the material world of nature with skepticism, see *Sir Thomas Browne*, edited by Edmund Gosse, 1905 pg. 29

[6] Johann Faber (1478-1541) who coauthored *De Anima Rationali Disputatio Philosophica* in 1588 that sets forth a system of philosophy based in rational or tangible observances apart from religion

that I have not been standing still for the last fifteen years. It will be enough if I say that five years ago I made the discovery that I alluded to when I said that ten years ago I reached the goal. After years of labor, after years of toiling and groping in the dark, after days and nights of disappointments and sometimes of despair, in which I used now and then to tremble and grow cold with the thought that perhaps there were others seeking for what I sought, at last, after so long, a pang of sudden joy thrilled my soul, and I knew the long journey was at an end.

"By what seemed then and still seems a chance, the suggestion of a moment's idle thought followed up upon familiar lines and paths that I had tracked a hundred times already, the great truth burst upon me, and I saw, mapped out in lines of sight, a whole world, a sphere unknown; continents and islands, and great oceans in which no ship has sailed (to my belief) since a Man first lifted up his eyes and beheld the sun, and the stars of heaven, and the quiet earth beneath. You will think this all high-flown language, Clarke, but it is hard to be literal. And yet; I do not know whether what I am hinting at cannot be set forth in plain and lonely terms. For instance, this world of ours is pretty well girded now with the telegraph wires and cables; thought, with something less than the speed of thought, flashes from sunrise to sunset, from north to south, across the floods and the desert places.

"Suppose that an electrician of today were suddenly to perceive that he and his friends have merely been playing with pebbles and mistaking them for the foundations of the world; suppose that such a man saw uttermost space lie open before the current, and words of men flash forth to the sun and beyond the sun into the systems beyond, and the voice of articulate-speaking men echo in the waste void that bounds our thought. As analogies go, that is a pretty good analogy of what I have done; you can understand now a little of what I felt as I stood here one evening; it was a summer evening, and the valley looked much as it does now; I stood here, and saw before me the unutterable, the unthinkable gulf that yawns profound between two worlds, the world of matter and the world of spirit; I saw the great empty deep stretch dim before me, and in that instant a bridge of light leapt from the earth to the unknown shore, and the abyss was spanned.

"You may look in Browne Faber's book, if you like, and you will find that to the present day men of science are unable to account for the presence, or to specify the functions of a certain group of nerve-cells in the brain. That group is, as it were, land to let, a mere waste place for fanciful theories. I am not in the position of Browne Faber and the specialists, I am perfectly instructed as to the possible functions of those nerve-centers in the scheme of things. With a touch I can bring them into play, with a touch, I say, I can set free the current, with a touch I can complete the communication between this world of sense and—we shall be able to finish the sentence later on. Yes, the knife is necessary; but think what that knife will effect. It will level utterly the solid wall of sense, and probably, for the first time since man was made, a spirit will gaze on a spirit-world. Clarke, Mary will see the god Pan!"

"But you remember what you wrote to me? I thought it would be requisite that she—"

He whispered the rest into the doctor's ear.

"Not at all, not at all. That is nonsense. I assure you. Indeed, it is better as it is; I am quite certain of that."

"Consider the matter well, Raymond. It's a great responsibility. Something might go wrong; you would be a miserable man for the rest of your days."

"No, I think not, even if the worst happened. As you know, I rescued Mary from the gutter, and from almost certain starvation, when she was a child; I think her life is mine, to use as I see fit. Come, it's getting late; we had better go in."

Dr. Raymond led the way into the house, through the hall, and down a long dark passage. He took a key from his pocket and opened a heavy door, and motioned Clarke into his laboratory. It had once been a billiard-room, and was lighted by a glass dome in the center of the ceiling, whence there still shone a sad grey light on the figure of the doctor as he lit a lamp with a heavy shade and placed it on a table in the middle of the room.

Clarke looked about him. Scarcely a foot of wall remained bare; there were shelves all around laden with bottles and phials of all shapes and colors, and at one end stood a little Chippendale book-case. Raymond pointed to this.

"You see that parchment by Oswald Crollius?[7] He was one of the first to show me the way, though I don't think he ever found it himself. That is a strange saying of his: 'In every grain of wheat there lies hidden the soul of a star.'"

There was not much furniture in the laboratory. The table in the center, a stone slab with a drain in one corner, the two armchairs on which Raymond and Clarke were sitting; that was all, except an odd-looking chair at the furthest end of the room. Clarke looked at it, and raised his eyebrows.

"Yes, that is the chair," said Raymond. "We may as well place it in position." He got up and wheeled the chair to the light, and began raising and lowering it, letting down the seat, setting the back at various angles, and adjusting the foot-rest. It looked comfortable enough, and Clarke passed his hand over the soft green velvet, as the doctor manipulated the levers.

"Now, Clarke, make yourself quite comfortable. I have a couple hours' work before me; I was obliged to leave certain matters to the last."

Raymond went to the stone slab, and Clarke watched him drearily as he bent over a row of phials and lit the flame under the crucible. The doctor had a small hand-lamp, shaded as the larger

---

[7] Oswald Crollius (1560-1604) was an alchemist who published in *Basilica Chymica* in 1608 that extolled the use of natural herbs and chemicals in medicine, which came from God, see *A Select Bibliography of Chemistry, 1492-1892*, Vol. 2, 1893 pg. 971

one, on a ledge above his apparatus, and Clarke, who sat in the shadows, looked down at the great shadowy room, wondering at the bizarre effects of brilliant light and undefined darkness contrasting with one another.

Soon he became conscious of an odd odor, at first the merest suggestion of odor, in the room, and as it grew more decided he felt surprised that he was not reminded of the chemist's shop or the surgery.

Clarke found himself idly endeavoring to analyze the sensation, and half conscious, he began to think of a day, fifteen years ago, that he had spent roaming through the woods and meadows near his own home. It was a burning day at the beginning of August, the heat had dimmed the outlines of all things and all distances with a faint mist, and people who observed the thermometer spoke of an abnormal register, of a temperature that was almost tropical.

Strangely that wonderful hot day of the fifties rose up again in Clarke's imagination; the sense of dazzling all-pervading sunlight seemed to blot out the shadows and the lights of the laboratory, and he felt again the heated air beating in gusts about his face, saw the shimmer rising from the turf, and heard the myriad murmur of the summer.

"I hope the smell doesn't annoy you, Clarke; there's nothing unwholesome about it. It may make you a bit sleepy, that's all."

Clarke heard the words quite distinctly, and knew that Raymond was speaking to him, but for the life of him he could not rouse himself from his lethargy. He could only think of the lonely walk he had taken fifteen years ago; it was his last look at the fields and woods he had known since he was a child, and now it all stood out in brilliant light, as a picture, before him.

Above all there came to his nostrils the scent of summer, the smell of flowers mingled, and the odor of the woods, of cool shaded places, deep in the green depths, drawn forth by the sun's heat; and the scent of the good earth, lying as it were with arms stretched forth, and smiling lips, overpowered all. His fancies made him wander, as he had wandered long ago, from the fields into the wood, tracking a little path between the shining undergrowth of beech-trees; and the trickle of water dropping from the limestone rock sounded as a clear melody in the dream.

Thoughts began to go astray and to mingle with other thoughts; the beech alley was transformed to a path between ilex-trees, and here and there a vine climbed from bough to bough, and sent up waving tendrils and drooped with purple grapes, and the sparse grey-green leaves of a wild olive-tree stood out against the dark shadows of the ilex. Clarke, in the deep folds of dream, was conscious that the path from his father's house had led him into an undiscovered country, and he was wondering at the strangeness of it all, when suddenly, in place of the hum and murmur of the summer, an infinite silence seemed to fall on all things, and the wood was hushed, and for a moment in time he stood face to face there with a presence, that was neither man nor beast, neither the living nor the dead, but all things mingled, the form of all things but devoid of all form. And in that moment, the sacrament of body and soul was dissolved, and a voice seemed to cry "Let us go hence," and then the darkness of darkness beyond the stars, the darkness of everlasting.

When Clarke woke up with a start he saw Raymond pouring a few drops of some oily fluid into a green phial, which he stoppered tightly.

"You have been dozing," he said. "The journey must have tired you out. It is done now. I am going to fetch Mary; I shall be back in ten minutes."

Clarke lay back in his chair and wondered. It seemed as if he had but passed from one dream into another. He half expected to see the walls of the laboratory melt and disappear, and to awake in London, shuddering at his own sleeping fancies. But at last the door opened, and the doctor returned, and behind him came a girl of about seventeen, dressed all in white. She was so beautiful that Clarke did not wonder at what the doctor had written to him. She was blushing now over face and neck and arms, but Raymond seemed unmoved.

"Mary," he said, "the time has come. You are quite free. Are you willing to trust yourself to me entirely?"

"Yes, dear."

"Do you hear that, Clarke? You are my witness. Here is the chair, Mary. It is quite easy. Just sit in it and lean back. Are you ready?"

"Yes, dear, quite ready. Give me a kiss before you begin."

The doctor stooped and kissed her mouth, kindly enough. "Now shut your eyes," he said. The girl closed her eyelids, as if she were tired, and longed for sleep, and Raymond placed the green phial to her nostrils. Her face grew white, whiter than her dress; she struggled faintly, and then with the feeling of submission strong within her, crossed her arms upon her breast as a little child about to say her prayers.

The bright light of the lamp fell full upon her, and Clarke watched changes fleeting over her face as the changes of the hills when the summer clouds float across the sun. And then she lay all white and still, and the doctor turned up one of her eyelids. She was quite unconscious. Raymond pressed hard on one of the levers and the chair instantly sank back. Clarke saw him cutting away a circle, like a tonsure, from her hair, and the lamp was moved nearer. Raymond took a small glittering instrument from a little case, and Clarke turned away shudderingly. When he looked again the doctor was binding up the wound he had made.

"She will awake in five minutes." Raymond was still perfectly cool. "There is nothing more to be done; we can only wait."

The minutes passed slowly; they could hear a slow, heavy, ticking. There was an old clock in the passage. Clarke felt sick and faint; his knees shook beneath him, he could hardly stand.

Suddenly, as they watched, they heard a long-drawn sigh, and suddenly did the color that had vanished return to the girl's cheeks, and suddenly her eyes opened. Clarke quailed before them. They shone with an awful light, looking far away, and a great wonder fell upon her face, and her hands stretched out as if to touch what was invisible; but in an instant the wonder faded, and gave place to the most awful terror. The muscles of her face were hideously convulsed, she shook from head to foot; the soul seemed struggling and shuddering within the house of flesh. It was a horrible sight, and Clarke rushed forward, as she fell shrieking to the floor.

Three days later Raymond took Clarke to Mary's bedside. She was lying wide-awake, rolling her head from side to side, and grinning vacantly.

"Yes," said the doctor, still quite cool, "it is a great pity; she is a hopeless idiot. However, it could not be helped; and, after all, she has seen the Great God Pan."

II
MR. CLARKE'S MEMOIRS

MR. CLARKE, THE gentleman chosen by Dr. Raymond to witness the strange experiment of the god Pan, was a person in whose character caution and curiosity were oddly mingled; in his sober moments he thought of the unusual and eccentric with undisguised aversion, and yet, deep in his heart, there was a wide-eyed inquisitiveness with respect to all the more recondite and esoteric elements in the nature of men.

The latter tendency had prevailed when he accepted Raymond's invitation, for though his considered judgment had always repudiated the doctor's theories as the wildest nonsense, yet he secretly hugged a belief in fantasy, and would have rejoiced to see that belief confirmed.

The horrors that he witnessed in the dreary laboratory were to a certain extent salutary; he was conscious of being involved in an affair not altogether reputable, and for many years afterwards he clung bravely to the commonplace, and rejected all occasions of occult investigation. Indeed, on some homeopathic principle, he for some time attended the séances of distinguished mediums, hoping that the clumsy tricks of these gentlemen would make him altogether disgusted with mysticism of every kind, but the remedy, though caustic, was not efficacious.

Clarke knew that he still pined for the unseen, and little by little, the old passion began to reassert itself, as the face of Mary, shuddering and convulsed with an unknown terror, faded slowly from his memory. Occupied all day in pursuits both serious and lucrative, the temptation to relax in the evening was too great, especially in the winter months, when the fire cast a warm glow over his snug bachelor apartment, and a bottle of some choice claret stood ready by his elbow.

His dinner digested, he would make a brief pretense of reading the evening paper, but the mere catalogue of news soon palled upon him, and Clarke would find himself casting glances of warm desire in the direction of an old Japanese bureau, which stood at a pleasant distance from the hearth. Like a boy before a jam-closet, for a few minutes he would hover indecisive, but lust always prevailed, and Clarke ended by drawing up his chair, lighting a candle, and sitting down before the bureau.

Its pigeonholes and drawers teemed with documents on the most morbid subjects, and in the well reposed a large manuscript volume, in which he had painfully entered the gems of his collection. Clarke had a fine contempt for published literature; the most ghostly story ceased to interest him if it happened to be printed; his sole pleasure was in the reading, compiling, and rearranging what he called his "Memoirs to prove the Existence of the Devil," and engaged in this pursuit the evening seemed to fly and the night appeared too short.

On one particular evening, an ugly December night, black with fog, and raw with frost, Clarke hurried over his dinner, and scarcely deigned to observe his customary ritual of taking up the paper and laying it down again. He paced two or three times up and down the room, and opened the bureau, stood still a moment, and sat down. He leant back, absorbed in one of those dreams to which he was subject, and at length drew out his book, and opened it at the last entry. There were three or four pages densely covered with Clarke's round, set penmanship, and at the beginning he had written in a somewhat larger hand:

Singular Narrative told me by my Friend, Dr. Phillips. He assures me that all the facts related therein are strictly and wholly True, but refuses to give either the Surnames of the Persons Concerned, or the Place where these Extraordinary Events occurred.

Mr. Clarke began to read over the account for the tenth time, glancing now and then at the pencil notes he had made when it was told him by his friend. It was one of his humors to pride himself on a certain literary ability; he thought well of his style, and took pains in arranging the circumstances in dramatic order. He read the following story:—

The persons concerned in this statement are Helen V., who, if she is still alive, must now be a woman of twenty-three, Rachel M., since deceased, who was a year younger than the above, and Trevor W., an imbecile, aged eighteen. These persons were at the period of the story inhabitants of a village on the borders of Wales, a place of some importance in the time of the Roman occupation, but now a scattered hamlet, of not more than five hundred souls. It is situated on rising ground, about six miles from the sea, and is sheltered by a large and picturesque forest.

Some eleven years ago, Helen V. came to the village under rather peculiar circumstances. It is understood that she, being an orphan, was adopted in her infancy by a distant relative, who brought her up in his own house until she was twelve years old. Thinking, however, that it would be better for the child to have playmates of her own age, he advertised in several local papers for a good home in a comfortable farmhouse for a girl of twelve, and this advertisement was answered by Mr. R., a well-to-do farmer in the above-mentioned village.

His references proving satisfactory, the gentleman sent his adopted daughter to Mr. R., with a letter, in which he stipulated that the girl should have a room to herself, and stated that her guardians need be at no trouble in the matter of education, as she was already sufficiently educated for the position in life which she would occupy.

In fact, Mr. R. was given to understand that the girl be allowed to find her own occupations and to spend her time almost as she liked. Mr. R. duly met her at the nearest station, a town seven miles away from his house, and seems to have remarked nothing extraordinary about the child except that she was reticent as to her former life and her adopted father. She was, however, of a very different type from the inhabitants of the village; her skin was a pale, clear olive, and her features were strongly marked, and of a somewhat foreign character.

She appears to have settled down easily enough into farmhouse life, and became a favorite with the children, who sometimes went with her on her rambles in the forest, for this was her amusement. Mr. R. states that he has known her to go out by herself directly after their early breakfast, and not return till after dusk, and that, feeling uneasy at a young girl being out alone for so many hours, he communicated with her adopted father, who replied in a brief note that Helen must do as she chose.

In the winter, when the forest paths are impassable, she spent most of her time in her bedroom, where she slept alone, according to the instructions of her relative. It was on one of these expeditions to the forest that the first of the singular incidents with which this girl is connected occurred, the date being about a year after her arrival at the village. The preceding winter had been remarkably severe, the snow drifting to a great depth, and the frost continuing for an unexampled period, and the summer following was as noteworthy for its extreme heat.

On one of the very hottest days in this summer, Helen V. left the farmhouse for one of her long rambles in the forest, taking with her, as usual, some bread and meat for lunch. She was seen by some men in the fields making for the old Roman Road, a green causeway which traverses the highest part of the wood, and they were astonished to observe that the girl had taken off her hat, though the heat of the sun was already tropical. As it happened, a laborer, Joseph W. by name, was working in the forest near the Roman Road, and at twelve o'clock his little son, Trevor, brought the man his dinner of bread and cheese.

After the meal, the boy, who was about seven years old at the time, left his father at work, and, as he said, went to look for flowers in the wood, and the man, who could hear him shouting with delight at his discoveries, felt no uneasiness. Suddenly, however, he was horrified at hearing the most dreadful screams, evidently the result of great terror, proceeding from the direction in which his son had gone, and he hastily threw down his tools and ran to see what had happened. Tracing his path by the sound, he met the little boy, who was running headlong, and was evidently terribly frightened, and on questioning him the man elicited that after picking a posy of flowers he felt tired, and lay down on the grass and fell asleep.

He was suddenly awakened, as he stated, by a peculiar noise, a sort of singing he called it, and on peeping through the branches he saw Helen V. playing on the grass with a "strange naked man," who he seemed unable to describe more fully. He said he felt dreadfully frightened and ran away crying for his father. Joseph W. proceeded in the direction indicated by his son, and found Helen V. sitting on the grass in the middle of a glade or open space left by charcoal burners.

He angrily charged her with frightening his little boy, but she entirely denied the accusation and laughed at the child's story of a "strange man," to which he himself did not attach much credence. Joseph W. came to the conclusion that the boy had woke up with a sudden fright, as children sometimes do, but Trevor persisted in his story, and continued in such evident distress that at last his father took him home, hoping that his mother would be able to soothe him.

For many weeks, however, the boy gave his parents much anxiety; he became nervous and strange in his manner, refusing to leave the cottage by himself, and constantly alarming the household by waking in the night with cries of "The man in the wood! Father! Father!"

In course of time, however, the impression seemed to have worn off, and about three months later he accompanied his father to the home of a gentleman in the neighborhood, for whom Joseph W. occasionally did work. The man was shown into the study, and the little boy was left sitting in the hall, and a few minutes later, while the gentleman was giving W. his instructions, they were both horrified by a piercing shriek and the sound of a fall, and rushing out they found the child lying senseless on the floor, his face contorted with terror. The doctor was immediately summoned, and after some examination he pronounced the child to be suffering from a kind of fit, apparently produced by a sudden shock.

The boy was taken to one of the bedrooms, and after some time recovered consciousness, but only to pass into a condition described by the medical man as one of violent hysteria. The doctor exhibited a strong sedative, and in the course of two hours pronounced him fit to walk home, but in passing through the hall the paroxysms of fright returned and with additional violence. The father perceived that the child was pointing at some object, and heard the old cry, "The man in the wood," and looking in the direction indicated saw a stone head of grotesque appearance, which had been built into the wall above one of the doors. It seems the owner of the house had recently made alterations in his premises, and on digging the foundations for some offices, the men had found a curious head, evidently of the Roman period, which had been placed in the manner described. The head is pronounced by the most experienced archaeologists of the district to be that of a faun[8] or satyr.[9] [Dr. Phillips tells me that he has seen the head in question, and assures me that he has never received such a vivid presentment of intense evil.]

From whatever cause arising, this second shock seemed too severe for the boy Trevor, and at the present date he suffers from a weakness of intellect, which gives but little promise of amending. The matter caused a good deal of sensation at the time, and the girl Helen was closely questioned by Mr. R., but to no purpose, she steadfastly denying that she had frightened or in any way molested Trevor.

The second event with which this girl's name is connected took place about six years ago, and is of a still more extraordinary character.

At the beginning of the summer of 1882, Helen contracted a friendship of a peculiarly intimate character with Rachel M., the daughter of a prosperous farmer in the neighborhood. This girl, who was a year younger than Helen, was considered by most people to be the prettier of the two, though Helen's features had to a great extent softened as she became older.

The two girls, who were together on every available opportunity, presented a singular contrast, the one with her clear, olive skin and almost Italian appearance, and the other of the proverbial red and white of our rural districts. It must be stated that the payments made to Mr. R. for the maintenance of Helen were known in the village for their excessive liberality, and the impression was general that she would one day inherit a large sum of money from her relative. The parents of Rachel were therefore not averse from their daughter's friendship with the girl, and even encouraged the intimacy, though they now bitterly regret having done so.

Helen still retained her extraordinary fondness for the forest, and on several occasions Rachel accompanied her, the two friends setting out early in the morning, and remaining in the wood until dusk. Once or twice after these excursions Mrs. M. thought her daughter's manner rather peculiar; she seemed languid and

---

[8] In Greek mythology these creatures had the lower half of a goat and upper half being human with horns of a goat that help or hurt humans at leisure
[9] In Greek mythology these human figures with the tails and ears of a horse would roam the forest

dreamy, and as it has been expressed, "different from herself," but these peculiarities seem to have been thought too trifling for remark. One evening, however, after Rachel had come home, her mother heard a noise which sounded like suppressed weeping in the girl's room, and on going in found her lying, half undressed, upon the bed, evidently in the greatest distress.

As soon as she saw her mother, she exclaimed, "Ah, mother, mother, why did you let me go to the forest with Helen?" Mrs. M. was astonished at so strange a question, and proceeded to make inquiries. Rachel told her a wild story. She said—

Clarke closed the book with a snap, and turned his chair towards the fire. When his friend sat one evening in that very chair, and told his story, Clarke had interrupted him at a point a little subsequent to this, had cut short his words in a paroxysm of horror. "My God!" he had exclaimed, "think, think what you are saying. It is too incredible, too monstrous; such things can never be in this quiet world, where men and women live and die, and struggle, and conquer, or maybe fail, and fall down under sorrow, and grieve and suffer strange fortunes for many a year; but not this, Phillips, not such things as this. There must be some explanation, some way out of the terror. Why, man, if such a case were possible, our earth would be a nightmare."

But Phillips had told his story to the end, concluding:

"Her flight remains a mystery to this day; she vanished in broad sunlight; they saw her walking in a meadow, and a few moments later she was not there."

Clarke tried to conceive the thing again, as he sat by the fire, and again his mind shuddered and shrank back, appalled before the sight of such awful, unspeakable elements enthroned as it were, and triumphant in human flesh. Before him stretched the long dim vista of the green causeway in the forest, as his friend had described it; he saw the swaying leaves and the quivering shadows on the grass, he saw the sunlight and the flowers, and far away, far in the long distance, the two figures moved toward him. One was Rachel, but the other?

Clarke had tried his best to disbelieve it all, but at the end of the account, as he had written it in his book, he had placed the inscription:

ET DIABOLUS INCARNATE EST. ET HOMO FACTUS EST.[10]

---

[10] And the devil is made flesh. And become human.

III
THE CITY OF RESURRECTIONS

"HERBERT! GOOD GOD! Is it possible?"

"Yes, my name's Herbert. I think I know your face, too, but I don't remember your name. My memory is very queer."

"Don't you recollect Villiers of Wadham?"

"So it is, so it is. I beg your pardon, Villiers, I didn't think I was begging of an old college friend. Good-night."

"My dear fellow, this haste is unnecessary. My rooms are close by, but we won't go there just yet. Suppose we walk up Shaftesbury Avenue a little way? But how in heaven's name have you come to this pass, Herbert?"

"It's a long story, Villiers, and a strange one too, but you can hear it if you like."

"Come on, then. Take my arm, you don't seem very strong."

The ill-assorted pair moved slowly up Rupert Street; the one in dirty, evil-looking rags, and the other attired in the regulation uniform of a man about town, trim, glossy, and eminently well-to-do. Villiers had emerged from his restaurant after an excellent dinner of many courses, assisted by an ingratiating little flask of Chianti, and, in that frame of mind which was with him almost chronic, had delayed a moment by the door, peering round in the dimly-lighted street in search of those mysterious incidents and persons with which the streets of London teem in every quarter and every hour.

Villiers prided himself as a practiced explorer of such obscure mazes and byways of London life, and in this unprofitable pursuit he displayed an assiduity which was worthy of more serious employment. Thus he stood by the lamppost surveying the passersby with undisguised curiosity, and with that gravity known only to the systematic diner, had just enunciated in his mind the formula: "London has been called the city of encounters; it is more than that, it is the city of Resurrections," when these reflections were suddenly interrupted by a piteous whine at his elbow, and a deplorable appeal for alms.

He looked around in some irritation, and with a sudden shock found himself confronted with the embodied proof of his somewhat stilted fancies. There, close beside him, his face altered and disfigured by poverty and disgrace, his body barely covered by greasy ill-fitting rags, stood his old friend Charles Herbert, who had matriculated on the same day as himself, with whom he had been merry and wise for twelve revolving terms. Different occupations and varying interests had interrupted the friendship, and it was six years since Villiers had seen Herbert; and now he looked upon this wreck of a man with grief and dismay, mingled with a certain inquisitiveness as to what dreary chain of circumstances had dragged him down to such a doleful pass. Villiers felt together with compassion all the relish of the amateur in mysteries, and congratulated himself on his leisurely speculations outside the restaurant.

They walked on in silence for some time, and more than one passerby stared in astonishment at the unaccustomed spectacle of a well-dressed man with an unmistakable beggar hanging on to his arm, and, observing this, Villiers led the way to an obscure street in Soho.[11] Here he repeated his question.

"How on earth has it happened, Herbert? I always understood you would succeed to an excellent position in Dorsetshire. Did your father disinherit you? Surely not?"

"No, Villiers; I came into all the property at my poor father's death; he died a year after I left Oxford. He was a very good father to me, and I mourned his death sincerely enough. But you know what young men are; a few months later I came up to town and went a good deal into society. Of course I had excellent introductions, and I managed to enjoy myself very much in a harmless sort of way. I played a little, certainly, but never for heavy stakes, and the few bets I made on races brought me in money—only a few pounds, you know, but enough to pay for cigars and such petty pleasures. It was in my second season that the tide turned. Of course you have heard of my marriage?"

"No, I never heard anything about it."

"Yes, I married, Villiers. I met a girl, a girl of the most wonderful and most strange beauty, at the house of some people whom I knew. I cannot tell you her age; I never knew it, but, so far as I can guess, I should think she must have been about nineteen when I made her acquaintance. My friends had come to know her at Florence; she told them she was an orphan, the child of an English father and an Italian mother, and she charmed them as she charmed me. The first time I saw her was at an evening party. I was standing by the door talking to a friend, when suddenly above the hum and babble of conversation I heard a voice which seemed to thrill to my heart. She was singing an Italian song. I was introduced to her that evening, and in three months I married Helen. Villiers, that woman, if I can call her woman, corrupted my soul. The night of the wedding I found myself sitting in her bedroom in the hotel, listening to her talk. She was sitting up in bed, and I listened to her as she spoke in her beautiful voice, spoke of things which even now I would not dare whisper in the blackest night, though I stood in the midst of a wilderness. You, Villiers, you may think you know life, and London, and what goes on day and night in this dreadful city; for all I can say you may have heard the talk of the vilest, but I tell you, you can have no conception of what I know, not in your most fantastic, hideous dreams can you have imaged forth the faintest shadow of what I have heard—and seen. Yes, seen. I have seen the incredible, such horrors that even I myself sometimes stop in the middle of the street and ask whether

---

[11] In the late nineteenth century Soho was considered the slums of London

it is possible for a man to behold such things and live. In a year, Villiers, I was a ruined man, in body and soul—in body and soul."

"But your property, Herbert? You had land in Dorset."

"I sold it all; the fields and woods, the dear old house—everything."

"And the money?"

"She took it all from me."

"And then left you?"

"Yes; she disappeared one night. I don't know where she went, but I am sure if I saw her again it would kill me. The rest of my story is of no interest; sordid misery, that is all. You may think, Villiers, that I have exaggerated and talked for effect; but I have not told you half. I could tell you certain things which would convince you, but you would never know a happy day again. You would pass the rest of your life, as I pass mine, a haunted man, a man who has seen hell."

Villiers took the unfortunate man to his rooms, and gave him a meal. Herbert could eat little, and scarcely touched the glass of wine set before him. He sat moody and silent by the fire, and seemed relieved when Villiers sent him away with a small present of money.

"By the way, Herbert," said Villiers, as they parted at the door, "what was your wife's name? You said Helen, I think? Helen what?"

"The name she passed under when I met her was Helen Vaughan, but what her real name was I can't say. I don't think she had a name. No, no, not in that sense. Only human beings have names, Villiers; I can't say anymore. Goodbye; yes, I will not fail to call if I see any way in which you can help me. Goodnight."

The man went out into the bitter night, and Villiers returned to his fireside. There was something about Herbert which shocked him inexpressibly; not his poor rags nor the marks which poverty had set upon his face, but rather an indefinite terror which hung about him like a mist. He had acknowledged that he himself was not devoid of blame; the woman, he had avowed, had corrupted him body and soul, and Villiers felt that this man, once his friend, had been an actor in scenes evil beyond the power of words. His story needed no confirmation: he himself was the embodied proof of it. Villiers mused curiously over the story he had heard, and wondered whether he had heard both the first and the last of it. "No," he thought, "certainly not the last, probably only the beginning. A case like this is like a nest of Chinese boxes; you open one after the other and find a quainter workmanship in every box. Most likely poor Herbert is merely one of the outside boxes; there are stranger ones to follow."

Villiers could not take his mind away from Herbert and his story, which seemed to grow wilder as the night wore on. The fire seemed to burn low, and the chilly air of the morning crept into the room; Villiers got up with a glance over his shoulder, and, shivering slightly, went to bed.

A few days later he saw at his club a gentleman of his acquaintance, named Austin, who was famous for his intimate knowledge of London life, both in its tenebrous and luminous phases. Villiers, still full of his encounter in Soho and its consequences, thought Austin might possibly be able to shed some light on Herbert's history, and so after some casual talk he suddenly put the question:

"Do you happen to know anything of a man named Herbert—Charles Herbert?"

Austin turned round sharply and stared at Villiers with some astonishment.

"Charles Herbert? Weren't you in town three years ago? No; then you have not heard of the Paul Street case? It caused a good deal of sensation at the time."

"What was the case?"

"Well, a gentleman, a man of very good position, was found dead, stark dead, in the area of a certain house in Paul Street, off Tottenham Court Road. Of course the police did not make the discovery; if you happen to be sitting up all night and have a light in your window, the constable will ring the bell, but if you happen to be lying dead in somebody's area, you will be left alone. In this instance, as in many others, the alarm was raised by some kind of vagabond; I don't mean a common tramp, or a public-house loafer, but a gentleman, whose business or pleasure, or both, made him a spectator of the London streets at five o'clock in the morning.

"This individual was, as he said, 'going home,' it did not appear whence or whither, and had occasion to pass through Paul Street between four and five a.m. Something or other caught his eye at Number 20; he said, absurdly enough, that the house had the most unpleasant physiognomy he had ever observed, but, at any rate, he glanced down the area and was a good deal astonished to see a man lying on the stones, his limbs all huddled together, and his face turned up. Our gentleman thought his face looked peculiarly ghastly, and so set off at a run in search of the nearest policeman.

"The constable was at first inclined to treat the matter lightly, suspecting common drunkenness; however, he came, and after looking at the man's face, changed his tone, quickly enough. The early bird, who had picked up this fine worm, was sent off for a doctor, and the policeman rang and knocked at the door till a slatternly servant girl came down looking more than half asleep. The constable pointed out the contents of the area to the maid, who screamed loudly enough to wake up the street, but she knew nothing of the man; had never seen him at the house, and so forth. Meanwhile, the original discoverer had come back with a medical man, and the next thing was to get into the area.

"The gate was open, so the whole quartet stumped down the steps. The doctor hardly needed a moment's examination; he said the poor fellow had been dead for several hours, and it was then the case began to get interesting. The dead man had not been robbed, and in one of his pockets were papers identifying him as—

well, as a man of good family and means, a favorite in society, and nobody's enemy, as far as could be known. I don't give his name, Villiers, because it has nothing to do with the story, and because it's no good raking up these affairs about the dead when there are no relations living. The next curious point was that the medical men couldn't agree as to how he met his death. There were some slight bruises on his shoulders, but they were so slight that it looked as if he had been pushed roughly out of the kitchen door, and not thrown over the railings from the street or even dragged down the steps.

"But there were positively no other marks of violence about him, certainly none that would account for his death; and when they came to the autopsy there wasn't a trace of poison of any kind. Of course the police wanted to know all about the people at Number 20, and here again, so I have heard from private sources, one or two other very curious points came out. It appears that the occupants of the house were a Mr. and Mrs. Charles Herbert; he was said to be a landed proprietor, though it struck most people that Paul Street was not exactly the place to look for country gentry.

"As for Mrs. Herbert, nobody seemed to know who or what she was, and, between ourselves, I fancy the divers after her history found themselves in rather strange waters. Of course they both denied knowing anything about the deceased, and in default of any evidence against them they were discharged. But some very odd things came out about them. Though it was between five and six in the morning when the dead man was removed, a large crowd had collected, and several of the neighbors ran to see what was going on. They were pretty free with their comments, by all accounts, and from these it appeared that Number 20 was in very bad odor in Paul Street. The detectives tried to trace down these rumors to some solid foundation of fact, but could not get hold of anything. People shook their heads and raised their eyebrows and thought the Herberts rather 'queer,' 'would rather not be seen going into their house,' and so on, but there was nothing tangible.

"The authorities were morally certain the man met his death in some way or another in the house and was thrown out by the kitchen door, but they couldn't prove it, and the absence of any indications of violence or poisoning left them helpless. An odd case, wasn't it? But curiously enough, there's something more that I haven't told you. I happened to know one of the doctors who was consulted as to the cause of death, and sometime after the inquest I met him, and asked him about it. 'Do you really mean to tell me,' I said, 'that you were baffled by the case, that you actually don't know what the man died of?' 'Pardon me,' he replied, 'I know perfectly well what caused death. Blank died of fright, of sheer, awful terror; I never saw features so hideously contorted in the entire course of my practice, and I have seen the faces of a whole host of dead.' The doctor was usually a cool customer enough, and a certain vehemence in his manner struck me, but I couldn't get anything more out of him. I suppose the Treasury didn't see their way to prosecuting the Herberts for frightening a man to death; at any rate, nothing was done, and the case dropped out of men's minds. Do you happen to know anything of Herbert?"

"Well," replied Villiers, "he was an old college friend of mine."

"You don't say so? Have you ever seen his wife?"

"No, I haven't. I have lost sight of Herbert for many years."

"It's queer, isn't it, parting with a man at the college gate or at Paddington, seeing nothing of him for years, and then finding him pop up his head in such an odd place. But I should like to have seen Mrs. Herbert; people said extraordinary things about her."

"What sort of things?"

"Well, I hardly know how to tell you. Everyone who saw her at the police court said she was at once the most beautiful woman and the most repulsive they had ever set eyes on. I have spoken to a man who saw her, and I assure you he positively shuddered as he tried to describe the woman, but he couldn't tell why. She seems to have been a sort of enigma; and I expect if that one dead man could have told tales, he would have told some uncommonly queer ones. And there you are again in another puzzle; what could a respectable country gentleman like Mr. Blank (we'll call him that if you don't mind) want in such a very queer house as Number 20? It's altogether a very odd case, isn't it?"

"It is indeed, Austin; an extraordinary case. I didn't think, when I asked you about my old friend, I should strike on such strange metal. Well, I must be off; good-day."

Villiers went away, thinking of his own conceit of the Chinese boxes; here was quaint workmanship indeed.

IV

THE DISCOVERY IN PAUL STREET

A FEW MONTHS after Villiers's meeting with Herbert, Mr. Clarke was sitting, as usual, by his after-dinner hearth, resolutely guarding his fancies from wandering in the direction of the bureau. For more than a week he had succeeded in keeping away from the "Memoirs," and he cherished hopes of a complete self-reformation; but, in spite of his endeavors, he could not hush the wonder and the strange curiosity that the last case he had written down had excited within him. He had put the case, or rather the outline of it, conjecturally to a scientific friend, who shook his head, and thought Clarke getting queer, and on this particular evening Clarke was making an effort to rationalize the story, when a sudden knock at the door roused him from his meditations.

"Mr. Villiers to see you sir."

"Dear me, Villiers, it is very kind of you to look me up; I have not seen you for many months; I should think nearly a year. Come in, come in. And how are you, Villiers? Want any advice about investments?"

"No, thanks, I fancy everything I have in that way is pretty safe. No, Clarke, I have really come to consult you about a rather curious matter that has been brought under my notice of late. I am afraid you will think it all rather absurd when I tell my tale. I sometimes think so myself, and that's just what I made up my mind to come to you, as I know you're a practical man."

Mr. Villiers was ignorant of the "Memoirs to prove the Existence of the Devil."

"Well, Villiers, I shall be happy to give you my advice, to the best of my ability. What is the nature of the case?"

"It's an extraordinary thing altogether. You know my ways; I always keep my eyes open in the streets, and in my time I have chanced upon some queer customers, and queer cases too, but this, I think, beats all. I was coming out of a restaurant one nasty winter night about three months ago; I had had a capital dinner and a good bottle of Chianti, and I stood for a moment on the pavement, thinking what a mystery there is about London streets and the companies that pass along them.

"A bottle of red wine encourages these fancies, Clarke, and I dare say I should have thought a page of small type, but I was cut short by a beggar who had come behind me, and was making the usual appeals. Of course I looked round, and this beggar turned out to be what was left of an old friend of mine, a man named Herbert. I asked him how he had come to such a wretched pass, and he told me. We walked up and down one of those long and dark Soho streets, and there I listened to his story.

"He said he had married a beautiful girl, some years younger than himself, and, as he put it, she had corrupted him body and soul. He wouldn't go into details; he said he dare not, that what he had seen and heard haunted him by night and day, and when I looked in his face I knew he was speaking the truth. There was something about the man that made me shiver. I don't know why, but it was there. I gave him a little money and sent him away, and I assure you that when he was gone I gasped for breath. His presence seemed to chill one's blood."

"Isn't this all just a little fanciful, Villiers? I suppose the poor fellow had made an imprudent marriage, and, in plain English, gone to the bad."

"Well, listen to this." Villiers told Clarke the story he had heard from Austin.

"You see," he concluded, "there can be but little doubt that this Mr. Blank, whoever he was, died of sheer terror; he saw something so awful, so terrible, that it cut short his life. And what he saw, he most certainly saw in that house, which, somehow or other, had got a bad name in the neighborhood. I had the curiosity to go and look at the place for myself. It's a saddening kind of street; the houses are old enough to be mean and dreary, but not old enough to be quaint. As far as I could see most of them are let in lodgings, furnished and unfurnished, and almost every door has three bells to it.

"Here and there the ground floors have been made into shops of the commonest kind; it's a dismal street in every way. I found Number 20 was to let, and I went to the agent's and got the key. Of course I should have heard nothing of the Herberts in that quarter, but I asked the man, fair and square, how long they had left the house and whether there had been other tenants in the meanwhile. He looked at me queerly for a minute, and told me the Herberts had left immediately after the unpleasantness, as he called it, and since then the house had been empty."

Mr. Villiers paused for a moment.

"I have always been rather fond of going over empty houses; there's a sort of fascination about the desolate empty rooms, with the nails sticking in the walls, and the dust thick upon the windowsills. But I didn't enjoy going over Number 20, Paul Street. I had hardly put my foot inside the passage when I noticed a queer, heavy feeling about the air of the house.

"Of course all empty houses are stuffy, and so forth, but this was something quite different; I can't describe it to you, but it seemed to stop the breath. I went into the front room and the back room, and the kitchens downstairs; they were all dirty and dusty enough, as you would expect, but there was something strange about them all. I couldn't define it to you, I only know I felt queer. It was one of the rooms on the first floor, though, that was the worst. It was a largish room, and once on a time the paper must have been cheerful enough, but when I saw it, paint, paper, and everything were most doleful.

"But the room was full of horror; I felt my teeth grinding as I put my hand on the door, and when I went in, I thought I should have fallen fainting to the floor. However, I pulled myself together, and stood against the end wall, wondering what on earth there could be about the room to make my limbs tremble, and my heart beat as if I were at the hour of death. In one corner there was a pile of newspapers littered on the floor, and I began looking at them; they were papers of three or four years ago, some of them half torn, and some crumpled as if they had been used for packing. I turned the whole pile over, and amongst them I found a curious drawing; I will show it to you presently. But I couldn't stay in the room; I felt it was overpowering me. I was thankful to come out, safe and sound, into the open air.

"People stared at me as I walked along the street, and one man said I was drunk. I was staggering about from one side of the pavement to the other, and it was as much as I could do to take the key back to the agent and get home. I was in bed for a week, suffering from what my doctor called nervous shock and exhaustion. One of those days I was reading the evening paper, and happened to notice a paragraph headed: 'Starved to Death.' It was the usual style of thing; a model lodging-house in Marylebone, a door locked for several days, and a dead man in his chair when they broke in. 'The deceased,' said the paragraph, 'was known as Charles Herbert, and is believed to have been once a prosperous country gentleman. His name was familiar to the public three years ago in connection with the mysterious death in Paul Street, Tottenham Court Road, the deceased being the tenant of the house Number 20, in the area of which a gentleman of good position was found dead under circumstances not devoid of suspicion.' A tragic ending, wasn't it? But after all, if what he told me were true, which I am sure it was, the man's life was all a tragedy, and a tragedy of a stranger sort than they put on the boards."

"And that is the story, is it?" said Clarke musingly.

"Yes, that is the story."

"Well, really, Villiers, I scarcely know what to say about it. There are, no doubt, circumstances in the case which seem peculiar, the finding of the dead man in the area of Herbert's house, for instance, and the extraordinary opinion of the physician as to the cause of death; but, after all, it is conceivable that the facts may be explained in a straightforward manner. As to your own sensations, when you went to see the house, I would suggest that they were due to a vivid imagination; you must have been brooding, in a semi-conscious way, over what you had heard. I don't exactly see what more can be said or done in the matter; you evidently think there is a mystery of some kind, but Herbert is dead; where then do you propose to look?"

"I propose to look for the woman; the woman whom he married. She is the mystery."

The two men sat silent by the fireside; Clarke secretly congratulating himself on having successfully kept up the character of advocate of the commonplace, and Villiers wrapped in his gloomy fancies.

"I think I will have a cigarette," he said at last, and put his hand in his pocket to feel for the cigarette-case.

"Ah!" he said, starting slightly, "I forgot I had something to show you. You remember my saying that I had found a rather curious sketch amongst the pile of old newspapers at the house in Paul Street? Here it is."

Villiers drew out a small thin parcel from his pocket. It was covered with brown paper, and secured with string, and the knots were troublesome. In spite of himself Clarke felt inquisitive; he bent forward on his chair as Villiers painfully undid the string, and unfolded the outer covering. Inside was a second wrapping of tissue, and Villiers took it off and handed the small piece of paper to Clarke without a word.

There was dead silence in the room for five minutes or more; the two men sat so still that they could hear the ticking of the tall old-fashioned clock that stood outside in the hall, and in the mind of one of them the slow monotony of sound woke up a far, far memory. He was looking intently at the small pen-and-ink sketch of the woman's head; it had evidently been drawn with great care, and by a true artist, for the woman's soul looked out of the eyes, and the lips were parted with a strange smile.

Clarke gazed still at the face; it brought to his memory one summer evening, long ago; he saw again the long lovely valley, the river winding between the hills, the meadows and the cornfields, the dull red sun, and the cold white mist rising from the water. He heard a voice speaking to him across the waves of many years, and saying "Clarke, Mary will see the god Pan!" and then he was standing in the grim room beside the doctor, listening to the heavy ticking of the clock, waiting and watching, watching the figure lying on the green chair beneath the lamplight. Mary rose up, and he looked into her eyes, and his heart grew cold within him.

"Who is this woman?" he said at last. His voice was dry and hoarse.

"That is the woman who Herbert married."

Clarke looked again at the sketch; it was not Mary after all. There certainly was Mary's face, but there was something else, something he had not seen on Mary's features when the white-clad girl entered the laboratory with the doctor, nor at her terrible awakening, nor when she lay grinning on the bed. Whatever it was, the glance that came from those eyes, the smile on the full lips, or the expression of the whole face, Clarke shuddered before it at his inmost soul, and thought, unconsciously, of Dr. Phillip's words, "the most vivid presentment of evil I have ever seen." He turned the paper over mechanically in his hand and glanced at the back.

"Good God! Clarke, what is the matter? You are as white as death."

Villiers had started wildly from his chair, as Clarke fell back with a groan, and let the paper drop from his hands.

"I don't feel very well, Villiers, I am subject to these attacks. Pour me out a little wine; thanks, that will do. I shall feel better in a few minutes."

Villiers picked up the fallen sketch and turned it over as Clarke had done.

"You saw that?" he said. "That's how I identified it as being a portrait of Herbert's wife, or I should say his widow. How do you feel now?"

"Better, thanks, it was only a passing faintness. I don't think I quite catch your meaning. What did you say enabled you to identify the picture?"

"This word—'Helen'—was written on the back. Didn't I tell you her name was Helen? Yes; Helen Vaughan."

Clarke groaned; there could be no shadow of doubt.

"Now, don't you agree with me," said Villiers, "that in the story I have told you tonight, and in the part this woman plays in it, there are some very strange points?"

"Yes, Villiers," Clarke muttered, "it is a strange story indeed; a strange story indeed. You must give me time to think it over; I may be able to help you or I may not. Must you be going now? Well, goodnight, Villiers, goodnight. Come and see me in the course of a week."

V
THE LETTER OF ADVICE

"DO YOU KNOW, Austin," said Villiers, as the two friends were pacing sedately along Piccadilly one pleasant morning in May, "do you know I am convinced that what you told me about Paul Street and the Herberts is a mere episode in an extraordinary history? I may as well confess to you that when I asked you about Herbert a few months ago I had just seen him."

"You had seen him? Where?"

"He begged of me in the street one night. He was in the most pitiable plight, but I recognized the man, and I got him to tell me his history, or at least the outline of it. In brief, it amounted to this—he had been ruined by his wife."

"In what manner?"

"He would not tell me; he would only say that she had destroyed him, body and soul. The man is dead now."

"And what has become of his wife?"

"Ah, that's what I should like to know, and I mean to find her sooner or later. I know a man named Clarke, a dry fellow, in fact a man of business, but shrewd enough. You understand my meaning; not shrewd in the mere business sense of the word, but a man who really knows something about men and life. Well, I laid the case before him, and he was evidently impressed. He said it needed consideration, and asked me to come again in the course of a week. A few days later I received this extraordinary letter."

Austin took the envelope, drew out the letter, and read it curiously. It ran as follows:—

"MY DEAR VILLIERS,—I have thought over the matter on which you consulted me the other night, and my advice to you is this. Throw the portrait into the fire, blot out the story from your mind. Never give it another thought, Villiers, or you will be sorry. You will think, no doubt, that I am in possession of some secret information, and to a certain extent that is the case. But I only know a little; I am like a traveler who has peered over an abyss, and has drawn back in terror. What I know is strange enough and horrible enough, but beyond my knowledge there are depths and horrors more frightful still, more incredible than any tale told of winter nights about the fire. I have resolved, and nothing shall shake that resolve, to explore no whit farther, and if you value your happiness you will make the same determination.

"Come and see me by all means; but we will talk on more cheerful topics than this."

Austin folded the letter methodically, and returned it to Villiers.

"It is certainly an extraordinary letter," he said, "what does he mean by the portrait?"

"Ah! I forgot to tell you I have been to Paul Street and have made a discovery."

Villiers told his story as he had told it to Clarke, and Austin listened in silence. He seemed puzzled.

"How very curious that you should experience such an unpleasant sensation in that room!" he said at length. "I hardly gather that it was a mere matter of the imagination; a feeling of repulsion, in short."

"No, it was more physical than mental. It was as if I were inhaling at every breath some deadly fume, which seemed to penetrate to every nerve and bone and sinew of my body. I felt racked from head to foot, my eyes began to grow dim; it was like the entrance of death."

"Yes, yes, very strange certainly. You see, your friend confesses that there is some very black story connected with this woman. Did you notice any particular emotion in him when you were telling your tale?"

"Yes, I did. He became very faint, but he assured me that it was a mere passing attack to which he was subject."

"Did you believe him?"

"I did at the time, but I don't know. He heard what I had to say with a good deal of indifference, till I showed him the portrait. It was then that he was seized with the attack of which I spoke. He looked ghastly, I assure you."

"Then he must have seen the woman before. But there might be another explanation; it might have been the name, and not the face, which was familiar to him. What do you think?"

"I couldn't say. To the best of my belief it was after turning the portrait in his hands that he nearly dropped from the chair. The name, you know, was written on the back."

"Quite so. After all, it is impossible to come to any resolution in a case like this. I hate melodrama, and nothing strikes me as more commonplace and tedious than the ordinary ghost story of commerce; but really, Villiers, it looks as if there were something very queer at the bottom of all this."

The two men had, without noticing it, turned up Ashley Street, leading northward from Piccadilly. It was a long street, and rather a gloomy one, but here and there a brighter taste had illuminated the dark houses with flowers, and gay curtains, and a cheerful paint on the doors. Villiers glanced up as Austin stopped speaking, and looked at one of these houses; geraniums, red and white, drooped from every sill, and daffodil-colored curtains were draped back from each window.

"It looks cheerful, doesn't it?" he said.

"Yes, and the inside is still more cheery. One of the pleasantest houses of the season, so I have heard. I haven't been there myself, but I've met several men who have, and they tell me it's uncommonly jovial."

"Whose house is it?"

"A Mrs. Beaumont's."

"And who is she?"

"I couldn't tell you. I have heard she comes from South America, but after all, who she is is of little consequence. She is a very wealthy woman, there's no doubt of that, and some of the best people have taken her up. I hear she has some wonderful claret, really marvelous wine, which must have cost a fabulous sum. Lord Argentine was telling me about it; he was there last Sunday evening. He assures me he has never tasted such a wine, and Argentine, as you know, is an expert. By the way, that reminds me, she must be an oddish sort of woman, this Mrs. Beaumont. Argentine asked her how old the wine was, and what do you think she said? 'About a thousand years, I believe.' Lord Argentine thought she was chaffing him, you know, but when he laughed she said she was speaking quite seriously and offered to show him the jar. Of course, he couldn't say anything more after that; but it seems rather antiquated for a beverage, doesn't it? Why, here we are at my rooms. Come in, won't you?"

"Thanks, I think I will. I haven't seen the curiosity-shop for a while."

It was a room furnished richly, yet oddly, where every jar and bookcase and table, and every rug and jar and ornament seemed to be a thing apart, preserving each its own individuality.

"Anything fresh lately?" said Villiers after a while.

"No; I think not; you saw those queer jugs, didn't you? I thought so. I don't think I have come across anything for the last few weeks."

Austin glanced around the room from cupboard to cupboard, from shelf to shelf, in search of some new oddity. His eyes fell at last on an odd chest, pleasantly and quaintly carved, which stood in a dark corner of the room.

"Ah," he said, "I was forgetting, I have got something to show you." Austin unlocked the chest, drew out a thick quarto volume, laid it on the table, and resumed the cigar he had put down.

"Did you know Arthur Meyrick the painter, Villiers?"

"A little; I met him two or three times at the house of a friend of mine. What has become of him? I haven't heard his name mentioned for some time."

"He's dead."

"You don't say so! Quite young, wasn't he?"

"Yes; only thirty when he died."

"What did he die of?"

"I don't know. He was an intimate friend of mine, and a thoroughly good fellow. He used to come here and talk to me for hours, and he was one of the best talkers I have met. He could even talk about painting, and that's more than can be said of most painters. About eighteen months ago he was feeling rather overworked, and partly at my suggestion he went off on a sort of roving expedition, with no very definite end or aim about it. I believe New York was to be his first port, but I never heard from him. Three months ago I got this book, with a very civil letter from an English doctor practicing at Buenos Ayres, stating that he had attended the late Mr. Meyrick during his illness, and that the deceased had expressed an earnest wish that the enclosed packet should be sent to me after his death. That was all."

"And haven't you written for further particulars?"

"I have been thinking of doing so. You would advise me to write to the doctor?"

"Certainly. And what about the book?"

"It was sealed up when I got it. I don't think the doctor had seen it."

"It is something very rare? Meyrick was a collector, perhaps?"

"No, I think not, hardly a collector. Now, what do you think of these Ainu jugs?"[12]

"They are peculiar, but I like them. But aren't you going to show me poor Meyrick's legacy?"

"Yes, yes, to be sure. The fact is, it's rather a peculiar sort of thing, and I haven't shown it to anyone. I wouldn't say anything about it if I were you. There it is."

Villiers took the book, and opened it at haphazard.

"It isn't a printed volume, then?" he said.

"No. It is a collection of drawings in black and white by my poor friend Meyrick."

Villiers turned to the first page, it was blank; the second bore a brief inscription, which he read:

Silet per diem universus, nec sine horrore secretus est; lucet nocturnis ignibus, chorus Aegipanum undique personatur: audiuntur et cantus tibiarum, et tinnitus cymbalorum per oram maritimam.[13]

On the third page was a design which made Villiers start and look up at Austin; he was gazing abstractedly out of the window. Villiers turned page after page, absorbed, in spite of himself, in the frightful Walpurgis Night of evil,[14] strange monstrous evil, that the dead artist had set forth in hard black and white. The figures of Fauns and Satyrs and Aegipans[15] danced before his eyes, the darkness of the thicket, the dance on the mountaintop, the scenes by lonely shores, in green vineyards, by rocks and desert places, passed before him: a world before which the human soul seemed to

---

[12] Pottery made the Ainu group of people of Northern Japan

[13] Quote from Gaius Julius Solinus's (Mid-third century) De Mirabilibus Mundi 24 as translated "The universe is silent throughout the day , and the horrible thoughts remain secret; its fire shines at night, and an Aegipan chorus rings on every side, pronounces , and songs are heard, sounds of pipes and the ringing of cymbals by the coast of the sea." The paragraph tells of a Bachian orgy at night.

[14] In the eighth century a British nun travelled to Germany and supposedly participated in a pagan ritual on the eve of May 1st and it became a pagan holiday when evil spirits were abroad

[15] Also called Pans with the legs of a goat and horns, see *Studies of the Gods in Greece at Certain Sanctuaries Recently Excavated Being Eight Lectures Given in 1890* at the Lowell Institute, Louis Dyer, 1891 pg. 98

shrink back and shudder. Villiers whirled over the remaining pages; he had seen enough, but the picture on the last leaf caught his eye, as he almost closed the book.

"Austin!"

"Well, what is it?"

"Do you know who that is?"

It was a woman's face, alone on the white page.

"Know who it is? No, of course not."

"I do."

"Who is it?"

"It is Mrs. Herbert."

"Are you sure?"

"I am perfectly sure of it. Poor Meyrick! He is one more chapter in her history."

"But what do you think of the designs?"

"They are frightful. Lock the book up again, Austin. If I were you I would burn it; it must be a terrible companion even though it be in a chest."

"Yes, they are singular drawings. But I wonder what connection there could be between Meyrick and Mrs. Herbert, or what link between her and these designs?"

"Ah, who can say? It is possible that the matter may end here, and we shall never know, but in my own opinion this Helen Vaughan, or Mrs. Herbert, is only the beginning. She will come back to London, Austin; depend on it, she will come back, and we shall hear more about her then. I doubt it will be very pleasant news."

VI
THE SUICIDES

LORD ARGENTINE WAS a great favorite in London Society. At twenty he had been a poor man, decked with the surname of an illustrious family, but forced to earn a livelihood as best he could, and the most speculative of moneylenders would not have entrusted him with fifty pounds on the chance of his ever changing his name for a title, and his poverty for a great fortune. His father had been near enough to the fountain of good things to secure one of the family livings, but the son, even if he had taken orders, would scarcely have obtained so much as this, and moreover felt no vocation for the ecclesiastical estate.

Thus he fronted the world with no better armor than the bachelor's gown and the wits of a younger son's grandson, with which equipment he contrived in some way to make a very tolerable fight of it. At twenty-five Mr. Charles Aubernon saw himself still a man of struggles and of warfare with the world, but out of the seven who stood before him and the high places of his family three only remained.

These three, however, were "good lives," but yet not proof against the Zulu assegais and typhoid fever, and so one morning Aubernon woke up and found himself Lord Argentine, a man of thirty who had faced the difficulties of existence, and had conquered. The situation amused him immensely, and he resolved that riches should be as pleasant to him as poverty had always been. Argentine, after some little consideration, came to the conclusion that dining, regarded as a fine art, was perhaps the most amusing pursuit open to fallen humanity, and thus his dinners became famous in London, and an invitation to his table a thing covetously desired.

After ten years of lordship and dinners Argentine still declined to be jaded, still persisted in enjoying life, and by a kind of infection had become recognized as the cause of joy in others, in short, as the best of company. His sudden and tragical death therefore caused a wide and deep sensation. People could scarcely believe it, even though the newspaper was before their eyes, and the cry of "Mysterious Death of a Nobleman" came ringing up from the street. But there stood the brief paragraph: "Lord Argentine was found dead this morning by his valet under distressing circumstances. It is stated that there can be no doubt that his lordship committed suicide, though no motive can be assigned for the act. The deceased nobleman was widely known in society, and much liked for his genial manner and sumptuous hospitality. He is succeeded by," etc., etc.

By slow degrees the details came to light, but the case still remained a mystery. The chief witness at the inquest was the deceased's valet, who said that the night before his death Lord Argentine had dined with a lady of good position, whose name was suppressed in the newspaper reports.

At about eleven o'clock Lord Argentine had returned, and informed his man that he should not require his services till the next morning. A little later the valet had occasion to cross the hall and was somewhat astonished to see his master quietly letting himself out at the front door. He had taken off his evening clothes, and was dressed in a Norfolk coat[16] and knickerbockers,[17] and wore a low brown hat.

The valet had no reason to suppose that Lord Argentine had seen him, and though his master rarely kept late hours, thought little of the occurrence till the next morning, when he knocked at the bedroom door at a quarter to nine as usual. He received no answer, and, after knocking two or three times, entered the room, and saw Lord Argentine's body leaning forward at an angle from the bottom of the bed. He found that his master had tied a cord securely to one of the short bedposts, and, after making a running noose and slipping it round his neck, the unfortunate man must have resolutely fallen forward, to die by slow strangulation.

---

[16] Single-breasted jacket having a belt and large front pockets
[17] Baggy pants that end at the knees

He was dressed in the light suit in which the valet had seen him go out, and the doctor who was summoned pronounced that life had been extinct for more than four hours. All papers, letters, and so forth seemed in perfect order, and nothing was discovered which pointed in the most remote way to any scandal either great or small. Here the evidence ended; nothing more could be discovered. Several persons had been present at the dinner-party at which Lord Argentine had assisted, and to all these he seemed in his usual genial spirits. The valet, indeed, said he thought his master appeared a little excited when he came home, but confessed that the alteration in his manner was very slight, hardly noticeable, indeed. It seemed hopeless to seek for any clue, and the suggestion that Lord Argentine had been suddenly attacked by acute suicidal mania was generally accepted.

It was otherwise, however, when within three weeks, three more gentlemen, one of them a nobleman, and the two others men of good position and ample means, perished miserably in the almost precisely the same manner. Lord Swanleigh was found one morning in his dressing-room, hanging from a peg affixed to the wall, and Mr. Collier-Stuart and Mr. Herries had chosen to die as Lord Argentine. There was no explanation in either case; a few bald facts; a living man in the evening, and a body with a black swollen face in the morning.

The police had been forced to confess themselves powerless to arrest or to explain the sordid murders of Whitechapel; but before the horrible suicides of Piccadilly and Mayfair they were dumbfounded, for not even the mere ferocity which did duty as an explanation of the crimes of the East End, could be of service in the West. Each of these men who had resolved to die a tortured shameful death was rich, prosperous, and to all appearances in love with the world, and not the acutest research should ferret out any shadow of a lurking motive in either case.

There was a horror in the air, and men looked at one another's faces when they met, each wondering whether the other was to be the victim of the fifth nameless tragedy. Journalists sought in vain for their scrapbooks for materials whereof to concoct reminiscent articles; and the morning paper was unfolded in many a house with a feeling of awe; no man knew when or where the next blow would light.

A short while after the last of these terrible events, Austin came to see Mr. Villiers. He was curious to know whether Villiers had succeeded in discovering any fresh traces of Mrs. Herbert, either through Clarke or by other sources, and he asked the question soon after he had sat down.

"No," said Villiers, "I wrote to Clarke, but he remains obdurate, and I have tried other channels, but without any result. I can't find out what became of Helen Vaughan after she left Paul Street, but I think she must have gone abroad. But to tell the truth, Austin, I haven't paid much attention to the matter for the last few weeks; I knew poor Herries intimately, and his terrible death has been a great shock to me, a great shock."

"I can well believe it," answered Austin gravely, "you know Argentine was a friend of mine. If I remember rightly, we were speaking of him that day you came to my rooms."

"Yes; it was in connection with that house in Ashley Street, Mrs. Beaumont's house. You said something about Argentine's dining there."

"Quite so. Of course you know it was there Argentine dined the night before—before his death."

"No, I had not heard that."

"Oh, yes; the name was kept out of the papers to spare Mrs. Beaumont. Argentine was a great favorite of hers, and it is said she was in a terrible state for some time after."

A curious look came over Villiers' face; he seemed undecided whether to speak or not. Austin began again.

"I never experienced such a feeling of horror as when I read the account of Argentine's death. I didn't understand it at the time, and I don't know. I knew him well, and it completely passes my understanding for what possible cause he—or any of the others for the matter of that—could have resolved in cold blood to die in such an awful manner. You know how men babble away each other's characters in London, you may be sure any buried scandal or hidden skeleton would have been brought to light in such a case as this; but nothing of the sort has taken place. As for the theory of mania, that is very well, of course, for the coroner's jury, but everybody knows that it's all nonsense. Suicidal mania is not smallpox."

Austin relapsed into gloomy silence. Villiers sat silent, also, watching his friend. The expression of indecision still fleeted across his face; he seemed as if weighing his thoughts in the balance, and the considerations he was resolving left him still silent. Austin tried to shake off the remembrance of tragedies as hopeless and perplexed as the labyrinth of Daedalus,[18] and began to talk in an indifferent voice of the more pleasant incidents and adventures of the season.

"That Mrs. Beaumont," he said, "of whom we were speaking, is a great success; she has taken London almost by storm. I met her the other night at Fulham's; she is really a remarkable woman."

"You have met Mrs. Beaumont?"

"Yes; she had quite a court around her. She would be called very handsome, I suppose, and yet there is something about her face which I didn't like. The features are exquisite, but the expression is strange. And all the time I was looking at her, and afterwards, when I was going home, I had a curious feeling that very expression was in some way or another familiar to me."

---

[18] In Greek mythology Daedalus designed a huge labyrinth to hold the Minotaur

"You must have seen her in the Row."[19]

"No, I am sure I never set eyes on the woman before; it is that which makes it puzzling. And to the best of my belief I have never seen anyone like her; what I felt was a kind of dim far-off memory, vague but persistent. The only sensation I can compare it to, is that odd feeling one sometimes has in a dream, when fantastic cities and wondrous lands and phantom personages appear familiar and accustomed."

Villiers nodded and glanced aimlessly round the room, possibly in search of something on which to turn the conversation. His eyes fell on an old chest somewhat like that in which the artist's strange legacy lay hid beneath a Gothic escutcheon.[20]

"Have you written to the doctor about poor Meyrick?" he asked.

"Yes; I wrote asking for full particulars as to his illness and death. I don't expect to have an answer for another three weeks or a month. I thought I might as well inquire whether Meyrick knew an Englishwoman named Herbert, and if so, whether the doctor could give me any information about her. But it's very possible that Meyrick fell in with her at New York, or Mexico, or San Francisco; I have no idea as to the extent or direction of his travels."

"Yes, and it's very possible that the woman may have more than one name."

"Exactly. I wish I had thought of asking you to lend me the portrait of her which you possess. I might have enclosed it in my letter to Dr. Matthews."

"So you might; that never occurred to me. We might send it now. Hark! what are those boys calling?"

While the two men had been talking together a confused noise of shouting had been gradually growing louder. The noise rose from the eastward and swelled down Piccadilly, drawing nearer and nearer, a very torrent of sound; surging up streets usually quiet, and making every window a frame for a face, curious or excited. The cries and voices came echoing up the silent street where Villiers lived, growing more distinct as they advanced, and, as Villiers spoke, an answer rang up from the pavement:

"The West End Horrors; Another Awful Suicide; Full Details!"[21]

Austin rushed down the stairs and bought a paper and read out the paragraph to Villiers as the uproar in the street rose and fell. The window was open and the air seemed full of noise and terror.

"Another gentleman has fallen a victim to the terrible epidemic of suicide which for the last month has prevailed in the West End. Mr. Sidney Crashaw, of Stoke House, Fulham, and King's Pomeroy, Devon, was found, after a prolonged search, hanging dead from the

---

[19] Reference to the Rotten Row thoroughfare that runs from Hyde Park Corner to Serpentine Road in Hyde Park, London and was frequented by the upper society during the nineteenth century

[20] Emblem having a coat of arms

[21] Reference to newspaper boys who used to shout headlines to sell papers on the streets

branch of a tree in his garden at one o'clock today. The deceased gentleman dined last night at the Carlton Club and seemed in his usual health and spirits. He left the club at about ten o'clock, and was seen walking leisurely up St. James's Street a little later. Subsequent to this his movements cannot be traced. On the discovery of the body medical aid was at once summoned, but life had evidently been long extinct. So far as is known, Mr. Crashaw had no trouble or anxiety of any kind. This painful suicide, it will be remembered, is the fifth of the kind in the last month. The authorities at Scotland Yard[22] are unable to suggest any explanation of these terrible occurrences."

Austin put down the paper in mute horror.

"I shall leave London tomorrow," he said, "it is a city of nightmares. How awful this is, Villiers!"

Mr. Villiers was sitting by the window quietly looking out into the street. He had listened to the newspaper report attentively, and the hint of indecision was no longer on his face.

"Wait a moment, Austin," he replied, "I have made up my mind to mention a little matter that occurred last night. It stated, I think, that Crashaw was last seen alive in St. James's Street shortly after ten?"

"Yes, I think so. I will look again. Yes, you are quite right."

"Quite so. Well, I am in a position to contradict that statement at all events. Crashaw was seen after that; considerably later indeed."

"How do you know?"

"Because I happened to see Crashaw myself at about two o'clock this morning."

"You saw Crashaw? You, Villiers?"

"Yes, I saw him quite distinctly; indeed, there were but a few feet between us."

"Where, in Heaven's name, did you see him?"

"Not far from here. I saw him in Ashley Street. He was just leaving a house."

"Did you notice what house it was?"

"Yes. It was Mrs. Beaumont's."

"Villiers! Think what you are saying; there must be some mistake. How could Crashaw be in Mrs. Beaumont's house at two o'clock in the morning? Surely, surely, you must have been dreaming, Villiers; you were always rather fanciful."

"No; I was wide awake enough. Even if I had been dreaming as you say, what I saw would have roused me effectually."

"What you saw? What did you see? Was there anything strange about Crashaw? But I can't believe it; it is impossible."

"Well, if you like I will tell you what I saw, or if you please, what I think I saw, and you can judge for yourself."

"Very good, Villiers."

---

22 Headquarters of the Metropolitan Police Service of London

The noise and clamor of the street had died away, though now and then the sound of shouting still came from the distance, and the dull, leaden silence seemed like the quiet after an earthquake or a storm. Villiers turned from the window and began speaking.

"I was at a house near Regent's Park last night, and when I came away the fancy took me to walk home instead of taking a hansom. It was a clear pleasant night enough, and after a few minutes I had the streets pretty much to myself. It's a curious thing, Austin, to be alone in London at night, the gas-lamps stretching away in perspective, and the dead silence, and then perhaps the rush and clatter of a hansom on the stones, and the fire starting up under the horse's hoofs.

I walked along pretty briskly, for I was feeling a little tired of being out in the night, and as the clocks were striking two I turned down Ashley Street, which, you know, is on my way. It was quieter than ever there, and the lamps were fewer; altogether, it looked as dark and gloomy as a forest in winter. I had done about half the length of the street when I heard a door closed very softly, and naturally I looked up to see who was abroad like myself at such an hour. As it happens, there is a street lamp close to the house in question, and I saw a man standing on the step. He had just shut the door and his face was towards me, and I recognized Crashaw directly. I never knew him to speak to, but I had often seen him, and I am positive that I was not mistaken in my man. I looked into his face for a moment, and then—I will confess the truth—I set off at a good run, and kept it up till I was within my own door."

"Why?"

"Why? Because it made my blood run cold to see that man's face. I could never have supposed that such an infernal medley of passions could have glared out of any human eyes; I almost fainted as I looked. I knew I had looked into the eyes of a lost soul, Austin, the man's outward form remained, but all hell was within it. Furious lust, and hate that was like fire, and the loss of all hope and horror that seemed to shriek aloud to the night, though his teeth were shut; and the utter blackness of despair. I am sure that he did not see me; he saw nothing that you or I can see, but what he saw I hope we never shall. I do not know when he died; I suppose in an hour, or perhaps two, but when I passed down Ashley Street and heard the closing door, that man no longer belonged to this world; it was a devil's face I looked upon."

There was an interval of silence in the room when Villiers ceased speaking. The light was failing, and all the tumult of an hour ago was quite hushed. Austin had bent his head at the close of the story, and his hand covered his eyes.

"What can it mean?" he said at length.

"Who knows, Austin, who knows? It's a black business, but I think we had better keep it to ourselves, for the present at any rate. I will see if I cannot learn anything about that house through private channels of information, and if I do light upon anything I will let you know."

VII
THE ENCOUNTER IN SOHO

THREE WEEKS LATER Austin received a note from Villiers, asking him to call either that afternoon or the next. He chose the nearer date, and found Villiers sitting as usual by the window, apparently lost in meditation on the drowsy traffic of the street. There was a bamboo table by his side, a fantastic thing, enriched with gilding and queer painted scenes, and on it lay a little pile of papers arranged and docketed as neatly as anything in Mr. Clarke's office.

"Well, Villiers, have you made any discoveries in the last three weeks?"

"I think so; I have here one or two memoranda which struck me as singular, and there is a statement to which I shall call your attention."

"And these documents relate to Mrs. Beaumont? It was really Crashaw whom you saw that night standing on the doorstep of the house in Ashley Street?"

"As to that matter my belief remains unchanged, but neither my inquiries nor their results have any special relation to Crashaw. But my investigations have had a strange issue. I have found out who Mrs. Beaumont is!"

"Who is she? In what way do you mean?"

"I mean that you and I know her better under another name."

"What name is that?"

"Herbert."

"Herbert!" Austin repeated the word, dazed with astonishment.

"Yes, Mrs. Herbert of Paul Street, Helen Vaughan of earlier adventures unknown to me. You had reason to recognize the expression of her face; when you go home look at the face in Meyrick's book of horrors, and you will know the sources of your recollection."

"And you have proof of this?"

"Yes, the best of proof; I have seen Mrs. Beaumont, or shall we say Mrs. Herbert?"

"Where did you see her?"

"Hardly in a place where you would expect to see a lady who lives in Ashley Street, Piccadilly. I saw her entering a house in one of the meanest and most disreputable streets in Soho. In fact, I had made an appointment, though not with her, and she was precise to both time and place."

"All this seems very wonderful, but I cannot call it incredible. You must remember, Villiers, that I have seen this woman, in the ordinary adventure of London society, talking and laughing, and sipping her coffee in a commonplace drawing-room with commonplace people. But you know what you are saying."

"I do; I have not allowed myself to be led by surmises or fancies. It was with no thought of finding Helen Vaughan that I searched for Mrs. Beaumont in the dark waters of the life of London, but such has been the issue."

"You must have been in strange places, Villiers."

"Yes, I have been in very strange places. It would have been useless, you know, to go to Ashley Street, and ask Mrs. Beaumont to give me a short sketch of her previous history. No; assuming, as I had to assume, that her record was not of the cleanest, it would be pretty certain that at some previous time she must have moved in circles not quite so refined as her present ones. If you see mud at the top of a stream, you may be sure that it was once at the bottom.

"I went to the bottom. I have always been fond of diving into Queer Street[23] for my amusement, and I found my knowledge of that locality and its inhabitants very useful. It is, perhaps, needless to say that my friends had never heard the name of Beaumont, and as I had never seen the lady, and was quite unable to describe her, I had to set to work in an indirect way. The people there know me; I have been able to do some of them a service now and again, so they made no difficulty about giving their information; they were aware I had no communication direct or indirect with Scotland Yard.

"I had to cast out a good many lines, though, before I got what I wanted, and when I landed the fish I did not for a moment suppose it was my fish. But I listened to what I was told out of a constitutional liking for useless information, and I found myself in possession of a very curious story, though, as I imagined, not the story I was looking for. It was to this effect. Some five or six years ago, a woman named Raymond suddenly made her appearance in the neighborhood to which I am referring. She was described to me as being quite young, probably not more than seventeen or eighteen, very handsome, and looking as if she came from the country.

"I should be wrong in saying that she found her level in going to this particular quarter, or associating with these people, for from what I was told, I should think the worst den in London far too good for her. The person from whom I got my information, as you may suppose, no great Puritan, shuddered and grew sick in telling me of the nameless infamies which were laid to her charge. After living there for a year, or perhaps a little more, she disappeared as suddenly as she came, and they saw nothing of her till about the time of the Paul Street case. At first she came to her old haunts only occasionally, then more frequently, and finally took up her abode there as before, and remained for six or eight months.

"It's of no use my going into details as to the life that woman led; if you want particulars you can look at Meyrick's legacy. Those designs were not drawn from his imagination. She again disappeared, and the people of the place saw nothing of her till a

---

23 Fictitious street associated with London's Carey Street and its bankruptcy courts. The term is used when a person is in trouble, typically financial, which Charles Dickens titled a chapter in *Our Mutual Friend* titled "Lodgers in Queer Street"

few months ago. My informant told me that she had taken some rooms in a house which he pointed out, and these rooms she was in the habit of visiting two or three times a week and always at ten in the morning.

"I was led to expect that one of these visits would be paid on a certain day about a week ago, and I accordingly managed to be on the look-out in company with my cicerone at a quarter to ten, and the hour and the lady came with equal punctuality. My friend and I were standing under an archway, a little way back from the street, but she saw us, and gave me a glance that I shall be long in forgetting. That look was quite enough for me; I knew Miss Raymond to be Mrs. Herbert; as for Mrs. Beaumont she had quite gone out of my head. She went into the house, and I watched it till four o'clock, when she came out, and then I followed her.

"It was a long chase, and I had to be very careful to keep a long way in the background, and yet not lose sight of the woman. She took me down to the Strand, and then to Westminster, and then up St. James's Street, and along Piccadilly. I felt queerish when I saw her turn up Ashley Street; the thought that Mrs. Herbert was Mrs. Beaumont came into my mind, but it seemed too impossible to be true. I waited at the corner, keeping my eye on her all the time, and I took particular care to note the house at which she stopped. It was the house with the gay curtains, the home of flowers, the house out of which Crashaw came the night he hanged himself in his garden.

"I was just going away with my discovery, when I saw an empty carriage come round and draw up in front of the house, and I came to the conclusion that Mrs. Herbert was going out for a drive, and I was right. There, as it happened, I met a man I know, and we stood talking together a little distance from the carriage-way, to which I had my back. We had not been there for ten minutes when my friend took off his hat, and I glanced round and saw the lady I had been following all day. 'Who is that?' I said, and his answer was 'Mrs. Beaumont; lives in Ashley Street.' Of course there could be no doubt after that. I don't know whether she saw me, but I don't think she did. I went home at once, and, on consideration, I thought that I had a sufficiently good case with which to go to Clarke."

"Why to Clarke?"

"Because I am sure that Clarke is in possession of facts about this woman, facts of which I know nothing."

"Well, what then?"

Mr. Villiers leaned back in his chair and looked reflectively at Austin for a moment before he answered:

"My idea was that Clarke and I should call on Mrs. Beaumont."

"You would never go into such a house as that? No, no, Villiers, you cannot do it. Besides, consider; what result..."

"I will tell you soon. But I was going to say that my information does not end here; it has been completed in an extraordinary manner.

"Look at this neat little packet of manuscript; it is paginated, you see, and I have indulged in the civil coquetry of a ribbon of red tape. It has almost a legal air, hasn't it? Run your eye over it, Austin. It is an account of the entertainment Mrs. Beaumont provided for her choicer guests. The man who wrote this escaped with his life, but I do not think he will live many years. The doctors tell him he must have sustained some severe shock to the nerves."

Austin took the manuscript, but never read it. Opening the neat pages at haphazard his eye was caught by a word and a phrase that followed it; and, sick at heart, with white lips and a cold sweat pouring like water from his temples, he flung the paper down.

"Take it away, Villiers, never speak of this again. Are you made of stone, man? Why, the dread and horror of death itself, the thoughts of the man who stands in the keen morning air on the black platform, bound, the bell tolling in his ears, and waits for the harsh rattle of the bolt, are as nothing compared to this. I will not read it; I should never sleep again."

"Very good. I can fancy what you saw. Yes; it is horrible enough; but after all, it is an old story, an old mystery played in our day, and in dim London streets instead of amidst the vineyards and the olive gardens. We know what happened to those who chanced to meet the Great God Pan, and those who are wise know that all symbols are symbols of something, not of nothing. It was, indeed, an exquisite symbol beneath which men long ago veiled their knowledge of the most awful, most secret forces which lie at the heart of all things; forces before which the souls of men must wither and die and blacken, as their bodies blacken under the electric current.

"Such forces cannot be named, cannot be spoken, cannot be imagined except under a veil and a symbol, a symbol to the most of us appearing a quaint, poetic fancy, to some a foolish tale. But you and I, at all events, have known something of the terror that may dwell in the secret place of life, manifested under human flesh; that which is without form taking to itself a form. Oh, Austin, how can it be? How is it that the very sunlight does not turn to blackness before this thing, the hard earth melt and boil beneath such a burden?"

Villiers was pacing up and down the room, and the beads of sweat stood out on his forehead. Austin sat silent for a while, but Villiers saw him make a sign upon his breast.

"I say again, Villiers, you will surely never enter such a house as that? You would never pass out alive."

"Yes, Austin, I shall go out alive—I, and Clarke with me."

"What do you mean? You cannot, you would not dare..."

"Wait a moment. The air was very pleasant and fresh this morning; there was a breeze blowing, even through this dull street, and I thought I would take a walk. Piccadilly stretched before me a clear, bright vista, and the sun flashed on the carriages and on the quivering leaves in the park. It was a joyous morning, and men and women looked at the sky and smiled as they went about their work or their pleasure, and the wind blew as blithely as upon the meadows and the scented gorse.

"But somehow or other I got out of the bustle and the gaiety, and found myself walking slowly along a quiet, dull street, where there seemed to be no sunshine and no air, and where the few foot-passengers loitered as they walked, and hung indecisively about corners and archways. I walked along, hardly knowing where I was going or what I did there, but feeling impelled, as one sometimes is, to explore still further, with a vague idea of reaching some unknown goal.

"Thus I forged up the street, noting the small traffic of the milk-shop, and wondering at the incongruous medley of penny pipes, black tobacco, sweets, newspapers, and comic songs which here and there jostled one another in the short compass of a single window. I think it was a cold shudder that suddenly passed through me that first told me that I had found what I wanted. I looked up from the pavement and stopped before a dusty shop, above which the lettering had faded, where the red bricks of two hundred years ago had grimed to black; where the windows had gathered to themselves the dust of winters innumerable.

"I saw what I required; but I think it was five minutes before I had steadied myself and could walk in and ask for it in a cool voice and with a calm face. I think there must even then have been a tremor in my words, for the old man who came out of the back parlor, and fumbled slowly amongst his goods, looked oddly at me as he tied the parcel. I paid what he asked, and stood leaning by the counter, with a strange reluctance to take up my goods and go. I asked about the business, and learnt that trade was bad and the profits cut down sadly; but then the street was not what it was before traffic had been diverted, but that was done forty years ago, 'just before my father died,' he said. I got away at last, and walked along sharply; it was a dismal street indeed, and I was glad to return to the bustle and the noise. Would you like to see my purchase?"

Austin said nothing, but nodded his head slightly; he still looked white and sick. Villiers pulled out a drawer in the bamboo table, and showed Austin a long coil of cord, hard and new; and at one end was a running noose.

"It is the best hempen cord,"[24] said Villiers, "just as it used to be made for the old trade, the man told me. Not an inch of jute[25] from end to end."

Austin set his teeth hard, and stared at Villiers, growing whiter as he looked.

"You would not do it," he murmured at last. "You would not have blood on your hands. My God!" he exclaimed, with sudden

---

[24] Strong cord made of woven hemp
[25] Tropical plant used for weaves but not very strong

vehemence, "you cannot mean this, Villiers, that you will make yourself a hangman?"

"No. I shall offer a choice, and leave Helen Vaughan alone with this cord in a locked room for fifteen minutes. If when we go in it is not done, I shall call the nearest policeman. That is all."

"I must go now. I cannot stay here any longer; I cannot bear this. Goodnight."

"Goodnight, Austin."

The door shut, but in a moment it was open again, and Austin stood, white and ghastly, in the entrance.

"I was forgetting," he said, "that I too have something to tell. I have received a letter from Dr. Harding of Buenos Ayres. He says that he attended Meyrick for three weeks before his death."

"And does he say what carried him off in the prime of life? It was not fever?"

"No, it was not fever. According to the doctor, it was an utter collapse of the whole system, probably caused by some severe shock. But he states that the patient would tell him nothing, and that he was consequently at some disadvantage in treating the case."

"Is there anything more?"

"Yes. Dr. Harding ends his letter by saying: 'I think this is all the information I can give you about your poor friend. He had not been long in Buenos Ayres, and knew scarcely any one, with the exception of a person who did not bear the best of characters, and has since left—a Mrs. Vaughan.'"

VIII
THE FRAGMENTS

[AMONGST THE PAPERS of the well-known physician, Dr. Robert Matheson, of Ashley Street, Piccadilly, who died suddenly, of apoplectic seizure, at the beginning of 1892, a leaf of manuscript paper was found, covered with pencil jottings. These notes were in Latin, much abbreviated, and had evidently been made in great haste. The MS. was only deciphered with difficulty, and some words have up to the present time evaded all the efforts of the expert employed. The date, "XXV Jul. 1888," is written on the right-hand corner of the MS. The following is a translation of Dr. Matheson's manuscript.]

"Whether science would benefit by these brief notes if they could be published, I do not know, but rather doubt. But certainly I shall never take the responsibility of publishing or divulging one word of what is here written, not only on account of my oath given freely to those two persons who were present, but also because the details are too abominable. It is probably that, upon mature consideration, and after weighting the good and evil, I shall one day destroy this paper, or at least leave it under seal to my friend D., trusting in his discretion, to use it or to burn it, as he may think fit.

"As was befitting, I did all that my knowledge suggested to make sure that I was suffering under no delusion. At first astounded, I could hardly think, but in a minute's time I was sure that my pulse was steady and regular, and that I was in my real and true senses. I then fixed my eyes quietly on what was before me.

"Though horror and revolting nausea rose up within me, and an odor of corruption choked my breath, I remained firm. I was then privileged or accursed, I dare not say which, to see that which was on the bed, lying there black like ink, transformed before my eyes. The skin, and the flesh, and the muscles, and the bones, and the firm structure of the human body that I had thought to be unchangeable, and permanent as adamant, began to melt and dissolve.

"I know that the body may be separated into its elements by external agencies, but I should have refused to believe what I saw. For here there was some internal force, of which I knew nothing, that caused dissolution and change.

"Here too was all the work by which man had been made repeated before my eyes. I saw the form waver from sex to sex, dividing itself from itself, and then again reunited. Then I saw the body descend to the beasts whence it ascended, and that which was on the heights go down to the depths, even to the abyss of all being. The principle of life, which makes organism, always remained, while the outward form changed.

"The light within the room had turned to blackness, not the darkness of night, in which objects are seen dimly, for I could see clearly and without difficulty. But it was the negation of light; objects were presented to my eyes, if I may say so, without any medium, in such a manner that if there had been a prism in the room I should have seen no colors represented in it.

"I watched, and at last I saw nothing but a substance as jelly. Then the ladder was ascended again... [here the MS. is illegible] ...for one instance I saw a Form, shaped in dimness before me, which I will not farther describe. But the symbol of this form may be seen in ancient sculptures, and in paintings which survived beneath the lava, too foul to be spoken of... as a horrible and unspeakable shape, neither man nor beast, was changed into human form, there came finally death.

"I who saw all this, not without great horror and loathing of soul, here write my name, declaring all that I have set on this paper to be true.

"ROBERT MATHESON, Med. Dr."

...Such, Raymond, is the story of what I know and what I have seen. The burden of it was too heavy for me to bear alone, and yet I could tell it to none but you. Villiers, who was with me at the last, knows nothing of that awful secret of the wood, of how what we both saw die, lay upon the smooth, sweet turf amidst the summer flowers, half in sun and half in shadow, and holding the girl Rachel's hand, called and summoned those companions, and shaped in solid form, upon the earth we tread upon, the horror which we can but hint at, which we can only name under a figure.

I would not tell Villiers of this, nor of that resemblance, which struck me as with a blow upon my heart, when I saw the portrait, which filled the cup of terror at the end. What this can mean I dare not guess. I know that what I saw perish was not Mary, and yet in the last agony Mary's eyes looked into mine. Whether there can be any one who can show the last link in this chain of awful mystery, I do not know, but if there be any one who can do this, you, Raymond, are the man. And if you know the secret, it rests with you to tell it or not, as you please.

I am writing this letter to you immediately on my getting back to town. I have been in the country for the last few days; perhaps you may be able to guess in which part. While the horror and wonder of London was at its height—for "Mrs. Beaumont," as I have told you, was well known in society—I wrote to my friend Dr. Phillips, giving some brief outline, or rather hint, of what happened, and asking him to tell me the name of the village where the events he had related to me occurred.

He gave me the name, as he said with the less hesitation, because Rachel's father and mother were dead, and the rest of the family had gone to a relative in the State of Washington six months before. The parents, he said, had undoubtedly died of grief and horror caused by the terrible death of their daughter, and by what had gone before that death. On the evening of the day which I received Phillips's letter I was at Caermaen, and standing beneath the moldering Roman walls, white with the winters of seventeen hundred years, I looked over the meadow where once had stood the older temple of the "God of the Deeps," and saw a house gleaming in the sunlight. It was the house where Helen had lived.

I stayed at Caermaen for several days. The people of the place, I found, knew little and had guessed less. Those whom I spoke to on the matter seemed surprised that an antiquarian (as I professed myself to be) should trouble about a village tragedy, of which they gave a very commonplace version, and, as you may imagine, I told nothing of what I knew. Most of my time was spent in the great wood that rises just above the village and climbs the hillside, and goes down to the river in the valley; such another long lovely valley, Raymond, as that on which we looked one summer night, walking to and fro before your house.

For many an hour I strayed through the maze of the forest, turning now to right and now to left, pacing slowly down long alleys of undergrowth, shadowy and chill, even under the midday sun, and halting beneath great oaks; lying on the short turf of a clearing where the faint sweet scent of wild roses came to me on the wind and mixed with the heavy perfume of the elder, whose mingled odor is like the odor of the room of the dead, a vapor of incense and corruption.

I stood at the edges of the wood, gazing at all the pomp and procession of the foxgloves towering amidst the bracken and shining red in the broad sunshine, and beyond them into deep thickets of close undergrowth where springs boil up from the rock and nourish the water-weeds, dank and evil. But in all my wanderings I avoided one part of the wood; it was not till yesterday that I climbed to the summit of the hill, and stood upon the ancient Roman road that threads the highest ridge of the wood. Here they had walked, Helen and Rachel, along this quiet causeway, upon the pavement of green turf, shut in on either side by high banks of red earth, and tall hedges of shining beech, and here I followed in their steps, looking out, now and again, through partings in the boughs, and seeing on one side the sweep of the wood stretching far to right and left, and sinking into the broad level, and beyond, the yellow sea, and the land over the sea.

On the other side was the valley and the river and hill following hill as wave on wave, and wood and meadow, and cornfield, and white houses gleaming, and a great wall of mountain, and far blue peaks in the north. And so at least I came to the place. The track went up a gentle slope, and widened out into an open space with a wall of thick undergrowth around it, and then, narrowing again, passed on into the distance and the faint blue mist of summer heat. And into this pleasant summer glade Rachel passed a girl, and left it, who shall say what? I did not stay long there.

In a small town near Caermaen there is a museum, containing for the most part Roman remains which have been found in the neighborhood at various times. On the day after my arrival in Caermaen I walked over to the town in question, and took the opportunity of inspecting the museum. After I had seen most of the sculptured stones, the coffins, rings, coins, and fragments of tessellated pavement which the place contains, I was shown a small square pillar of white stone, which had been recently discovered in the wood of which I have been speaking, and, as I found on inquiry, in that open space where the Roman road broadens out. On one side of the pillar was an inscription, of which I took a note. Some of the letters have been defaced, but I do not think there can be any doubt as to those which I supply. The inscription is as follows:

DEVOMNODENTi
FLAvIVSSENILISPOSSVit
PROPTERNVP_tia
quaSVIDITSVBVMBra

"To the great god Nodens (the god of the Great Deep or Abyss) Flavius Senilis has erected this pillar on account of the marriage which he saw beneath the shade."

The custodian of the museum informed me that local antiquaries were much puzzled, not by the inscription, or by any difficulty in translating it, but as to the circumstance or rite to which allusion is made.

...And now, my dear Clarke, as to what you tell me about Helen Vaughan, whom you say you saw die under circumstances of the utmost and almost incredible horror. I was interested in your account, but a good deal, nay all, of what you told me I knew already. I can understand the strange likeness you remarked in both the portrait and in the actual face; you have seen Helen's mother. You remember that still summer night so many years ago, when I talked to you of the world beyond the shadows, and of the god Pan. You remember Mary. She was the mother of Helen Vaughan, who was born nine months after that night.

Mary never recovered her reason. She lay, as you saw her, all the while upon her bed, and a few days after the child was born she died. I fancy that just at the last she knew me; I was standing by the bed, and the old look came into her eyes for a second, and then she shuddered and groaned and died. It was an ill work I did that night when you were present; I broke open the door of the house of life, without knowing or caring what might pass forth or enter in.

I recollect your telling me at the time, sharply enough, and rightly too, in one sense, that I had ruined the reason of a human being by a foolish experiment, based on an absurd theory. You did well to blame me, but my theory was not all absurdity. What I said Mary would see she saw, but I forgot that no human eyes can look on such a sight with impunity. And I forgot, as I have just said, that when the house of life is thus thrown open, there may enter in that for which we have no name, and human flesh may become the veil of a horror one dare not express. I played with energies which I did not understand, you have seen the ending of it. Helen Vaughan did well to bind the cord about her neck and die, though the death was horrible. The blackened face, the hideous form upon the bed, changing and melting before your eyes from woman to man, from man to beast, and from beast to worse than beast, all the strange horror that you witness, surprises me but little.

What you say the doctor whom you sent for saw and shuddered at I noticed long ago; I knew what I had done the moment the child was born, and when it was scarcely five years old I surprised it, not once or twice but several times with a playmate, you may guess of what kind. It was for me a constant, an incarnate horror, and after a few years I felt I could bear it no more, and I sent Helen Vaughan away. You know now what frightened the boy in the wood. The rest of the strange story, and all else that you tell me, as discovered by your friend, I have contrived to learn from time to time, almost to the last chapter.

And now Helen is with her companions...

W. C. Morrow
(1854-1923)

Along with Charlotte Perkins Gilman, W. C. Morrow is the only other American to pen a horror story rising to the level of this collection. Morrow was born in Alabama to an agrarian family that held slaves and backed the Confederacy.

After The Civil War, at the age of 25, Morrow left his family and travelled to Oakland, California. A few years later he moved to San Jose where he befriended fellow supernatural writer Ambrose Bierce, and other writers that helped open doors to the publishing world. He began submitting stories to various magazines for publication while making a living as a teacher of writing. Bierce, however, valued his stories more than his teaching as he told Morrow in an October 9, 1907 letter:

"Whether you 'prosper' or not I'm glad you write instead of teaching. I have done a bit of teaching myself, but as the tuition was gratuitous I could pick my pupils; so it was a labor of love. I'm pretty well satisfied with the results."[1]

William C. Morrow was soon having success at writing and by 1897 his first (and only) collection of stories was published—*The Ape, the Idiot and Other People.* It included such horror classics as "The Monster-Maker," and "The Permanent Stiletto." Morrow was 43 years old.

The Ape, the Idiot and Other People also included "His Unconquerable Enemy," which was originally called "The Rajah's Nemesis" when commercialized on March 11, 1889. It has been an

---

[1] *The Letters of Ambrose Bierce*, Bertha Clark Pope, 1922, pg. 139

unrelenting (or should I say "unconquerable") bringer of horror to readers ever since.

It's interesting to note that no dialogue exists in the story. It is told in complete expository fashion.

His Unconquerable Enemy
1889

I WAS SUMMONED from Calcutta to the heart of India to perform a difficult surgical operation on one of the women of a great rajah's household. I found the rajah a man of a noble character, but possessed, as I afterwards discovered, of a sense of cruelty purely Oriental and in contrast to the indolence of his disposition.

He was so grateful for the success that attended my mission that he urged me to remain a guest at the palace as long as it might please me to stay, and I thankfully accepted the invitation. One of the male servants early attracted my notice for his marvelous capacity of malice. His name was Neranya, and I am certain that there must have been a large proportion of Malay blood in his veins, for, unlike the Indians (from whom he differed also in complexion), he was extremely alert, active, nervous, and sensitive. A redeeming circumstance was his love for his master.

Once his violent temper led him to the commission of an atrocious crime,—the fatal stabbing of a dwarf. In punishment for this the rajah ordered that Neranya's right arm (the offending one) be severed from his body. The sentence was executed in a bungling fashion by a stupid fellow armed with an axe, and I, being a surgeon, was compelled, in order to save Neranya's life, to perform an amputation of the stump, leaving not a vestige of the limb remaining. After this he developed an augmented fiendishness.

His love for the rajah was changed to hate, and in his mad anger he flung discretion to the winds. Driven once to frenzy by the rajah's scornful treatment, he sprang upon the rajah with a knife, but, fortunately, was seized and disarmed. To his unspeakable dismay the rajah sentenced him for this offence to suffer amputation of the remaining arm. It was done as in the former instance. This had the effect of putting a temporary curb on Neranya's spirit, or, rather, of changing the outward manifestations of his diabolism. Being armless, he was at first largely at the mercy of those who ministered to his needs,—a duty which I undertook to see was properly discharged, for I felt an interest in this strangely distorted nature. His sense of help, combined with a damnable scheme for revenge which he had secretly formed, caused Neranya to change his fierce, impetuous, and unruly conduct into a smooth, quiet, insinuating bearing, which he carried so artfully as to deceive those with whom he was brought in contact, including the rajah himself. Neranya, being exceedingly quick, intelligent, and dexterous, and having an unconquerable will, turned his attention to the cultivating of an enlarged usefulness of his legs, feet, and toes, with so excellent effect that in time he was able to perform wonderful feats with those members.

Thus his capability, especially for destructive mischief, was considerably restored. One morning the rajah's only son, a young man of an uncommonly amiable and noble disposition, was found dead in bed. His murder was a most atrocious one, his body being mutilated in a shocking manner, but in my eyes the most significant of all the mutilations was the entire removal and disappearance of the young prince's arms.

The death of the young man nearly brought the rajah to the grave. It was not, therefore, until I had nursed him back to health that I began a systematic inquiry into the murder. I said nothing of my own discoveries and conclusions until after the rajah and his officers had failed and my work had been done; then I submitted to him a written report, making a close analysis of all the circumstances and closing by charging the crime to Neranya.

The rajah, convinced by my proof and argument, at once ordered Neranya to be put to death, this to be accomplished slowly and with frightful tortures. The sentence was so cruel and revolting that it filled me with horror, and I implored that the wretch be shot. Finally, through a sense of gratitude to me, the rajah relaxed. When Neranya was charged with the crime he denied it, of course, but, seeing that the rajah was convinced, he threw aside all restraint, and, dancing, laughing, and shrieking in the most horrible manner, confessed his guilt, gloated over it, and reviled the rajah to his teeth,—this, knowing that some fearful death awaited him. The rajah decided upon the details of the matter that night, and in the morning he informed me of his decision.

It was that Neranya's life should be spared, but that both of his legs should be broken with hammers, and that then I should amputate the limbs at the trunk! Appended to this horrible sentence was a provision that the maimed wretch should be kept and tortured at regular intervals by such means as afterwards might be devised. Sickened to the heart by the awful duty set out for me, I nevertheless performed it with success, and I care to say nothing more about that part of the tragedy. Neranya escaped death very narrowly and was a long time in recovering his wonted vitality. During all these weeks the rajah neither saw him nor made inquiries concerning him, but when, as in duty bound, I made official report that the man had recovered his strength, the rajah's eyes brightened, and he emerged with deadly activity from the stupor into which he so long had been plunged.

The rajah's palace was a noble structure, but it is necessary here to describe only the grand hall. It was an immense chamber, with a floor of polished, inlaid stone and a lofty, arched ceiling. A soft light stole into it through stained glass set in the roof and in high windows on one side. In the middle of the room was a rich fountain, which threw up a tall, slender column of water, with smaller and shorter jets grouped around it. Across one end of the hall, half-way to the ceiling, was a balcony, which communicated with the upper story of a wing, and from which a flight of stone stairs descended to the floor of the hall.

During the hot summers this room was delightfully cool; it was the rajah's favorite lounging-place, and when the nights were hot he had his cot taken thither, and there he slept. This hall was chosen for Neranya's permanent prison; here was he to stay so long as he might live, with never a glimpse of the shining world or the glorious heavens.

To one of his nervous, discontented nature such confinement was worse than death. At the rajah's order there was constructed for him a small pen of open ironwork, circular, and about four feet in diameter, elevated on four slender iron posts, ten feet above the floor, and placed between the balcony and the fountain. Such was Neranya's prison.

The pen was about four feet in depth, and the pen-top was left open for the convenience of the servants whose duty it should be to care for him. These precautions for his safe confinement were taken at my suggestion, for, although the man was now deprived of all four of his limbs, I still feared that he might develop some extraordinary, unheard-of power for mischief. It was provided that the attendants should reach his cage by means of a movable ladder.

All these arrangements having been made and Neranya hoisted into his cage, the rajah emerged upon the balcony to see him for the first time since the last amputation. Neranya had been lying panting and helpless on the floor of his cage, but when his quick ear caught the sound of the rajah's footfall he squirmed about until he had brought the back of his head against the railing, elevating his eyes above his chest, and enabling him to peer through the open-work of the cage.

Thus the two deadly enemies faced each other. The rajah's stern face paled at sight of the hideous, shapeless thing which met his gaze; but he soon recovered, and the old hard, cruel, sinister look returned. Neranya's black hair and beard had grown long, and they added to the natural ferocity of his aspect. His eyes blazed upon the rajah with a terrible light, his lips parted, and he gasped for breath; his face was ashen with rage and despair, and his thin, distended nostrils quivered. The rajah folded his arms and gazed down from the balcony upon the frightful wreck that he had made.

Oh, the dreadful pathos of that picture; the inhumanity of it; the deep and dismal tragedy of it! Who might look into the wild, despairing heart of the prisoner and see and understand the frightful turmoil there; the surging, choking passion; unbridled but impotent ferocity; frantic thirst for a vengeance that should be deeper than hell!

Neranya gazed, his shapeless body heaving, his eyes aflame; and then, in a strong, clear voice, which rang throughout the great hall, with rapid speech he hurled at the rajah the most insulting defiance, the most awful curses.

He cursed the womb that had conceived him, the food that should nourish him, the wealth that had brought him power; cursed him in the name of Buddha and all the wise men; cursed by the sun, the moon, and the stars; by the continents, mountains, oceans, and rivers; by all things living; cursed his head, his heart, his entrails; cursed in a whirlwind of unmentionable words; heaped unimaginable insults and contumely upon him; called him a knave, a beast, a fool, a liar, an infamous and unspeakable coward.

The rajah heard it all calmly, without the movement of a muscle, without the slightest change of countenance; and when the poor wretch had exhausted his strength and fallen helpless and silent to the floor, the rajah, with a grim, cold smile, turned and strode away. The days passed. The rajah, not deterred by Neranya's curses often heaped upon him, spent even more time than formerly in the great hall, and slept there oftener at night; and finally Neranya wearied of cursing and defying him, and fell into a sullen silence.

The man was a study for me, and I observed every change in his fleeting moods. Generally his condition was that of miserable despair, which he attempted bravely to conceal. Even the boon of suicide had been denied him, for when he would wriggle into an erect position the rail of his pen was a foot above his head, so that he could not clamber over and break his skull on the stone floor beneath; and when he had tried to starve himself the attendants forced food down his throat; so that he abandoned such attempts.

At times his eyes would blaze and his breath would come in gasps, for imaginary vengeance was working within him; but steadily he became quieter and more tractable, and was pleasant and responsive when I would converse with him. Whatever might have been the tortures which the rajah had decided on, none as yet had been ordered; and although Neranya knew that they were in contemplation, he never referred to them or complained of his lot.

The awful climax of this situation was reached one night, and even after this lapse of years I cannot approach its description without a shudder. It was a hot night, and the rajah had gone to sleep in the great hall, lying on a high cot placed on the main floor just underneath the edge of the balcony. I had been unable to sleep in my own apartment, and so I had stolen into the great hall through the heavily curtained entrance at the end farthest from the balcony.

As I entered I heard a peculiar, soft sound above the patter of the fountain. Neranya's cage was partly concealed from my view by the spraying water, but I suspected that the unusual sound came from him.

Stealing a little to one side, and crouching against the dark hangings of the wall, I could see him in the faint light which dimly illuminated the hall, and then I discovered that my surmise was correct—Neranya was quietly at work. Curious to learn more, and knowing that only mischief could have been inspiring him, I sank into a thick robe on the floor and watched him.

To my great astonishment Neranya was tearing off with his teeth the bag which served as his outer garment. He did it cautiously, casting sharp glances frequently at the rajah, who, sleeping soundly on his cot below, breathed heavily. After starting a strip with his teeth, Neranya, by the same means, would attach it to the railing of his cage and then wriggle away, much after the manner of a caterpillar's crawling, and this would cause the strip to be torn out the full length of his garment.

He repeated this operation with incredible patience and skill until his entire garment had been torn into strips. Two or three of these he tied end to end with his teeth, lips, and tongue, tightening the knots by placing one end of the strip under his body and drawing the other taut with his teeth. In this way he made a line several feet long, one end of which he made fast to the rail with his mouth. It then began to dawn upon me that he was going to make an insane attempt—impossible of achievement without hands, feet, arms, or legs—to escape from his cage!

For what purpose?

The rajah was asleep in the hall—ah! I caught my breath. Oh, the desperate, insane thirst for revenge which could have unhinged so clear and firm a mind! Even though he should accomplish the impossible feat of climbing over the railing of his cage that he might fall to the floor below (for how could he slide down the rope?), he would be in all probability killed or stunned; and even if he should escape these dangers it would be impossible for him to clamber upon the cot without rousing the rajah, and impossible even though the rajah were dead!

Amazed at the man's daring, and convinced that his sufferings and brooding had destroyed his reason, nevertheless I watched him with breathless interest. With other strips tied together he made a short swing across one side of his cage. He caught the long line in his teeth at a point not far from the rail; then, wriggling with great effort to an upright position, his back braced against the rail, he put his chin over the swing and worked toward one end. He tightened the grasp of his chin on the swing, and with tremendous exertion, working the lower end of his spine against the railing, he began gradually to ascend the side of his cage. The labor was so great that he was compelled to pause at intervals, and his breathing was hard and painful; and even while thus resting he was in a position of terrible strain, and his pushing against the swing caused it to press hard against his windpipe and nearly strangle him.

After amazing effort he had elevated the lower end of his body until it protruded above the railing, the top of which was now across the lower end of his abdomen. Gradually he worked his body over, going backward, until there was sufficient excess of weight on the outer side of the rail; and then, with a quick lurch, he raised his head and shoulders and swung into a horizontal position on top of the rail.

Of course, he would have fallen to the floor below had it not been for the line which he held in his teeth. With so great nicety had he estimated the distance between his mouth and the point where the rope was fastened to the rail, that the line tightened and checked him just as he reached the horizontal position on the rail. If one had told me beforehand that such a feat as I had just seen this man accomplish was possible, I should have thought him a fool.

Neranya was now balanced on his stomach across the top of the rail, and he eased his position by bending his spine and hanging down on either side as much as possible. Having rested thus for some minutes, he began cautiously to slide off backward, slowly paying out the line through his teeth, finding almost a fatal difficulty in passing the knots.

Now, it is quite possible that the line would have escaped altogether from his teeth laterally when he would slightly relax his hold to let it slip, had it not been for a very ingenious plan to which he had resorted. This consisted in his having made a turn of the line around his neck before he attacked the swing, thus securing a threefold control of the line,—one by his teeth, another by friction against his neck, and a third by his ability to compress it between his cheek and shoulder.

It was quite evident now that the minutest details of a most elaborate plan had been carefully worked out by him before beginning the task, and that possibly weeks of difficult theoretical study had been consumed in the mental preparation. As I observed him I was reminded of certain hitherto unaccountable things which he had been doing for some weeks past—going through certain hitherto inexplicable motions, undoubtedly for the purpose of training his muscles for the immeasurably arduous labor which he was now performing. A stupendous and seemingly impossible part of his task had been accomplished. Could he reach the floor in safety?

Gradually he worked himself backward over the rail, in imminent danger of falling; but his nerve never wavered, and I could see a wonderful light in his eyes. With something of a lurch, his body fell against the outer side of the railing, to which he was hanging by his chin, the line still held firmly in his teeth. Slowly he slipped his chin from the rail, and then hung suspended by the line in his teeth.

By almost imperceptible degrees, with infinite caution, he descended the line, and, finally, his unwieldy body rolled upon the floor, safe and unhurt! What miracle would this superhuman monster next accomplish?

I was quick and strong, and was ready and able to intercept any dangerous act; but not until danger appeared would I interfere with this extraordinary scene. I must confess to astonishment upon having observed that Neranya, instead of proceeding directly toward the sleeping rajah, took quite another direction.

Then it was only escape, after all, that the wretch contemplated, and not the murder of the rajah. But how could he escape? The only possible way to reach the outer air without great risk was by ascending the stairs to the balcony and leaving by the corridor which opened upon it, and thus fall into the hands of some British soldiers quartered thereabout, who might conceive the idea of hiding him; but surely it was impossible for Neranya to ascend that long flight of stairs!

Nevertheless, he made directly for them, his method of progression this: He lay upon his back, with the lower end of his body toward the stairs; then bowed his spine upward, thus drawing his head and shoulders a little forward; straightened, and then pushed the lower end of his body forward a space equal to that through which he had drawn his head; repeating this again and again, each time, while bending his spine, preventing his head from slipping by pressing it against the floor.

His progress was laborious and slow, but sensible; and, finally, he arrived at the foot of the stairs. It was manifest that his insane purpose was to ascend them. The desire for freedom must have been strong within him.

Wriggling to an upright position against the newel-post, he looked up at the great height which he had to climb and sighed; but there was no dimming of the light in his eyes. How could he accomplish the impossible task? His solution of the problem was very simple, though daring and perilous as all the rest. While leaning against the newel-post he let himself fall diagonally upon the bottom step, where he lay partly hanging over, but safe, on his side.

Turning upon his back, he wriggled forward along the step to the rail and raised himself to an upright position against it as he had against the newel-post, fell as before, and landed on the second step. In this manner, with inconceivable labor, he accomplished the ascent of the entire flight of stairs. It being apparent to me that the rajah was not the object of Neranya's movements, the anxiety which I had felt on that account was now entirely dissipated.

The things which already he had accomplished were entirely beyond the nimblest imagination. The sympathy which I had always felt for the wretched man was now greatly quickened; and as infinitesimally small as I knew his chances for escape to be, I nevertheless hoped that he would succeed. Any assistance from me, however, was out of the question; and it never should be known that I had witnessed the escape.

Neranya was now upon the balcony, and I could dimly see him wriggling along toward the door which led out upon the balcony. Finally he stopped and wriggled to an upright position against the rail, which had wide openings between the balusters. His back was toward me, but he slowly turned and faced me and the hall.

At that great distance I could not distinguish his features, but the slowness with which he had worked, even before he had fully accomplished the ascent of the stairs, was evidence all too eloquent of his extreme exhaustion. Nothing but a most desperate resolution could have sustained him thus far, but he had drawn upon the last remnant of his strength. He looked around the hall with a sweeping glance, and then down upon the rajah, who was sleeping immediately beneath him, over twenty feet below.

He looked long and earnestly, sinking lower, and lower, and lower upon the rail. Suddenly, to my inconceivable astonishment and dismay, he toppled through and shot downward from his lofty height!

I held my breath, expecting to see him crushed upon the stone floor beneath; but instead of that he fell full upon the rajah's breast, driving him through the cot to the floor. I sprang forward with a loud cry for help, and was instantly at the scene of the catastrophe. With indescribable horror I saw that Neranya's teeth were buried in the rajah's throat! I tore the wretch away, but the blood was pouring from the rajah's arteries, his chest was crushed in, and he was gasping in the agony of death. People came running in, terrified. I turned to Neranya.

He lay upon his back, his face hideously smeared with blood. Murder, and not escape, had been his intentions from the beginning; and he had employed the only method by which there was ever a possibility of accomplishing it. I knelt beside him, and saw that he too was dying; his back had been broken by the fall. He smiled sweetly into my face, and a triumphant look of accomplished revenge sat upon his face even in death.

Horror Short Stories Considered

Grant Allen
    1887 The Beckoning Hand

Gertrude Atherton
    1896 The Striding Place

Robert Barr
    1893 A Game of Chess

Ambrose Bierce
    1889 The Boarded Window
    1891 Chickamauga
    1891 The Man and the Snake
    1891 A Watcher by the Dead
    1893 The Secret of Macarger's Gulch
    1893 The Damned Thing

George Washington Cable
    1875 Jean-Ah Poquelin

Will Carleton
    1892 The Lianhan Shee

Anton Chekov
    1888 Sleepyhead

Kate Chopin
    1893 Desiree's Baby

Émile Erckmann and Alexandre Chatrian
    1870 The Invisible Eye
    1857 The Spider of Guyana

Charles Collins
    1866 No. 3 Branch Line: The Compensation House

Wilkie Collins
    1857 The Dead Hand
    1852 The Traveler's Story of a Terribly Strange Bed

Ralph Adams Cram
    1895 The Dead Valley

James DeMille
    1888 The Swamp Monster

Charles Dickens
    1860 Captain Murderer

Sir Arthur Conan Doyle
    1880 The American's Tale
    1890 The Ring of Thoth
    1892 Lot No. 249 (Mummy)
    1893 The Case of Lady Sannox
    1897 The Fiend of the Cooperage
    1899 The Story of the Brazilian Cat

Joseph Le Fanu
    1896 The Secret of the Two Plaster Casts
    1869 Green Tea

Elizabeth Gaskell
    1873 The Doom of the Griffiths
    1861 The Grey Woman

Theophile Gautier
    1882 The Foot of the Mummy

Charlotte Perkins Gilman
    1892 Yellow Wallpaper

Thomas Hardy
    1883 The Three Strangers
    1890 Barbara of the House of Grebe

John Harwood
    1861 Horror: A True Tale

Philippe-Auguste Villiers de l'Isle-Adam
    1883 Torture By Hope
    1883 The Very Image

Montague Rhodes (M.R.) James
    1895 Canon Alberic's Scrapbook

Jerome K. Jerome
    1893 The Dancing-Partner

Rudyard Kipling
    1890 The Strange Ride Of Morrowbie Jukes
    1890 At the End of the Passage
    1891 "The Finest Story in World"

Vernon Lee
    1890 A Wicked Voice
    1890 a lasting love

Jean Lorrain
    1895 The Holes in the Mask

Arthur Machen (Arthur Llewellyn Jones)
    1894 The Great God Pan

Guy de Maupassant
    1875 The Flayed Hand
    1883 The Hand
    1888 Who Knows?
    1884 The Spasm
    1885 The Mother of Monsters
    1886 *Le Horla*
    1887 Night: A Nightmare

Prosper Merimee
    1869 Lokis

William C. Morrow
    1897 The Faithful Amulet
    1897 The Gloomy Shadow
    1897 The Haunted Burglar
    1887 The Monster Maker
    1889 The Permanent Stiletto
    1889 His Unconquerable Enemy
    1897 The Woman of the Inner Room

Edith Nesbit
    1886 Man-Size in Marble

Fitz-James O'Brien
    1859 What Was It?
    1858 The Lost Room

Phil Robinson
    1889 Medusa

Marcel Schwob
    1892 Bloody Blanche

Henry Spicer
    1863 The Bird Woman

Robert Louis Stevenson
    1898 The Bottle Imp
    1886 Markheim
    1884 The Body-Snatcher
    1893 The Isle of Voices
    1896 The House of Eld

Bram Stoker
    1893 The Squaw
    1887 The Dualitists; or, The Death Doom of the Double Born
    1881 The Invisible Giant

E. W. Thomson
    1895 Red-Headed Windego

Leo Tolstoy
    1886 How Much Land Does a Man Need?

Basil Tozer
    1897 The Pioneers of Pike's Peak

Ivan Sergeyevich Turgenev
    1876 The Dream

H. G. Wells
    1894 Aepyornis Island
    1897 Pollock and the Porroh Man
    1896 In the Abyss
    1894 In the Avu Observatory
    1896 The Sea Raiders

Fred White
    1899 The Purple Terror

Other Titles by Andrew Barger

The Best Horror Short Stories 1800-1849 is a book for anyone who loves a classic horror story. Thanks to Edgar Allan Poe, Honoré de Balzac, Nathaniel Hawthorne and others, the first half of the nineteenth century is the cradle of all modern horror short stories. Andrew Barger read over 300 horror short stories and compiled the dozen best. A few have never been republished since they were first published in leading periodicals of the day such as *Blackwood's* and *Atkinson's Casket*. At the back of the book Andrew includes a list of all short stories he considered along with their dates of publication and the author, when available. He even includes background for each of the stories, author photos and annotations for difficult terminology.

'The Best Horror Short Stories 1800-1849' will likely become a best seller . . .What makes this collection (of truly terrifying tales!) so satisfying is the presence of a brief introduction before each story, sharing some comments about the writer and elements of the tale. Barger has once again whetted our appetites for fright, spent countless hours making these twelve stories accessible and available, and has provided in one book the best of the best of horror short stories. It is a winner. **—AMZ TOP TEN REVIEWER**

Through his introduction and footnotes, Barger aims for readers both scholarly and casual, ensuring that the authors get their due while making the work accessible overall to the mainstream. **— BOOKGASM**

A top to bottom pick for anyone who appreciates where the best of horror came from. **—MIDWEST BOOK REVIEW**

<u>BlooDeath</u>
<u>Best Vampire Short Stories 1800-1849</u>

Unearthed from long forgotten journals and magazines, Andrew Barger has found the very best vampire short stories from the first half of the 19th century, which are collected for the first time in this award-winning book on the origins of vampire lore. The cradle of all vampire short stories in the English language is the first half of the 19th century. Andrew combed forgotten journals and mysterious texts to collect the very best vintage vampire stories from this crucial period in vampire literature. In doing so, Andrew unearthed the second and third vampire stories originally published in the English language, neither printed since their first publication nearly 200 years ago.

Also included is the first vampire story originally written in English by John Polidori after a dare with Lord Byron and Mary Shelley. The groundbreaking book contains the first vampire short story by an American who happened to be a graduate of Columbia Law School. The book further contains the first vampire stories by an Englishman and German, including the only vampire stories by such renowned authors as Alexander Dumas, Théophile Gautier and Joseph Le Fanu. As readers have come to expect from Andrew, he has added his scholarly touch to this collection by including annotations, story backgrounds, author photos and a foreword titled "With Teeth."

<u>Shifters</u>
<u>Best Werewolf Short Stories 1800-1849</u>

Andrew has compiled the best tales from the period when werewolf short stories were first unleashed. The stories are "Hugues the Wer-Wolf: A Kentish Legend of the Middle Ages," "The Man-Wolf," "A Story of a Weir-Wolf," "The Wehr-Wolf: A Legend of the Limousin," and "The White Wolf of the Hartz Mountains." It is believed that two of these stories have never been republished in over 150 years since their original printing. Read *Shifters: The Best Werewolf Short Stories 1800-1849* by the light of a full moon.

A seminal work of impressive scholarship, "The Best Werewolf Short Stories 1800-1849: A Classic Werewolf Anthology" is highly recommended reading for fantasy fans, and a valued addition to academic library Literary Studies reference collections. **– MIDWEST BOOK REVIEW**

Best Ghost Short Stories 1850-1899
A Phantasmal Ghost Anthology

The fifty year period from 1850-1899 resulted in some of the best ghost stories ever written in the English language thanks in large part to the Victorians. It was during this period that ghosts started interacting with the living, a haunting trend kicked off by Charles Dickens's *A Christmas Carol* in 1843. The phantasms in this anthology follow the living and sometimes cause their demise. Classic authors are represented in the anthology including Joseph Le Fanu, Charles Dickens, Ralph Adams Cram, Bram Stoker, M. R. James, Francis Marion Crawford, Robert Chambers, and others.

Mesaerion
Best Science Fiction Short Stories 1800-1849

Looking for sci-fi stories that defined a genre? How about what is possibly the first science fiction story by a female or the first steampunk short story? There is the first voyage to the moon and a meeting with a lunar alien—Zuloc! What about a darkness machine and the first robotic insect? There is also the first story that deals with cryogenic freezing and reanimation. Andrew has searched two-hundred-year-old magazines and journals to find the very best science fiction stories from the period when the genre came to life, some of which are published for the first time in nearly 200 years.

More than just a simple anthology, 'Mesaerion: The Best Science Fiction Stories 1800-1849' significantly benefits modern readers with the editor's story back ground commentaries, annotations, author photos, and in informative foreword. – **MIDWEST BOOK REVIEW**

Phantasmal
Best Ghost Short Stories 1800-1849

Ghost short stories became very popular in the first half of the nineteenth century and this collection by Andrew Barger contains the very scariest of them all. Some stories thought too horrific were published anonymously like "A Night in a Haunted House" and "The Deaf and Dumb Girl," with the latter being anthologized for the first time since its original publication in 1839.

The other ghost short stories in this fine collection are by famous authors. "The Mask of the Red Death," is by Edgar Allan Poe; "A Chapter in the History of a Tyrone Family," by Joseph Sheridan Le Fanu; "The Spectral Ship," by Wilhelm Hauff; "The Old Maid in the Winding Sheet," by Nathaniel Hawthorne; "The Adventure of the German Student," and "The Legend of Sleepy Hollow," by Washington Irving; as well as "The Tapestried Chamber," by Sir Walter Scott. Andrew Barger has added his familiar scholarly touch to this collection by including annotations, story backgrounds, author photos and a foreword titled "All Ghosts Are Gray."

[A] unique perspective on this dawn of horror's early roots and their connections to our modern day. "The Best Ghost Stories 1800-1849" is a choice pick with stories from many legendary authors such as Edgar Allan Poe and Washington Irving, very much recommended reading. —**MIDWEST BOOK REVIEW**

<u>The Divine Dantes</u>
<u>Squirt Gun in Hades (Infernal Trilogy #1)</u>

An Indie Book Awards best second novel finalist, the first book in *The Divine Dantes* trilogy finds young rocker Edward T. Nad down on his luck after the other member of his two-person band (and girlfriend—Beatrice) leaves their small town for Europe. Once there, Beatrice has second thoughts about the breakup and asks their erstwhile manager cum travel agent, Virgil, to bring Edward to her without him knowing it. This sparks off the hilarious intercontinental journey of the staid, nerdy manager and the young rocker with an active and opinionated mind who struggles with the basics, like settling on a name for the band: "Grain of Sand and the Clams" versus "The Beelzebubbas." The novel contains the characters of "The Inferno" and tracks their movements through Hades in modern times. *Dante's Infernos: Squirt Guns in Hades* is the first in a trilogy of novels that parallel "The Inferno," "The Purgatorio," and "The Paradiso" of Dante's *The Divine Comedy* through modern times. Read the first chapter at the end of this book.

[A] lively and good-natured work . . .. —**PUBLISHER'S WEEKLY REVIEWER**

[R]eminds me a little of the fun I find in Carl Hiaasen or Christopher Moore, but he definitely has his own vibe . . .. —**AMZ BREAKTHROUGH NOVEL AWARD EXPERT REVIEWER**

<u>Coffee with Poe</u>
<u>A Novel of Edgar Allan Poe's Life</u>

Coffee with Poe brings Edgar Allan Poe to life within its pages as never before. The book is filled with actual letters from his many romances and literary contemporaries. Orphaned at the age of two, Poe is raised by John Allan—his abusive foster father—who refuses to adopt him until he becomes straight-laced and businesslike. Poe, however, fancies poetry and young women. The contentious relationship culminates in a violent altercation, which causes Poe to leave his wealthy foster father's home to make it as a writer. Poe tries desperately to get established as a writer but is ridiculed by the "Literati of New York."

The Raven gains Poe renown in America yet he slips deeper into poverty, only making $15 off the poem's entire publication history. Desperate for a motherly figure in his life, Poe marries his first cousin who is only thirteen. Poe lives his last years in abject poverty while suffering through the deaths of his foster mother, grandmother, and young wife. In a cemetery he becomes engaged to Helen Whitman, a dark poet who is addicted to ether, wears a small coffin about her neck, and conducts séances in her home. The engagement is soon broken off because of Poe's drinking. In his final months his health is in a downward spiral. Poe disappears on a trip and is later found delirious and wearing another person's clothes. He dies a few days later, whispering his final words: "God help my poor soul."

To give us a historical fiction look at Edgar Allan Poe is great. The start where we are at his mom's funeral gives a little insight into why he may write the way he does. It is very interesting the ideas the author has put into the story about Poe. I like the idea of detailing the life of Edgar Allan Poe into a historical fiction novel. . . . A great idea to give us some insight into why Poe may be the way he is. —AMZ **BREAKTHROUGH NOVEL AWARD EXPERT REVIEWER**

<u>Edgar Allan Poe</u>
<u>Annotated and Illustrated Entire Stories and Poems</u>
For the first time in one compilation are background information for Poe's stories and poems, annotations, foreign word translations, photographs of individuals Poe wrote about, and poetry to Poe from his many romantic interests. Here is a sampling of the tales and poems included: "Annabel Lee," "The Bells," "The Black Cat," "[The Bloodhounds]," "The Cask of Amontillado," "The Conqueror Worm," "A Descent into the Maelstrom," "The Fall of the House of Usher," "The Gold-Bug," "The Haunted Palace," "Lenore," "The Masque of the Red Death," "MS. Found in a Bottle," "Murders in the Rue Morgue," "The Oblong Box," "The Pit and the Pendulum," "The Premature Burial," "The Purloined Letter," "[The Rats of Park Theatre]," "The Raven," "Some Words with a Mummy," "The Swiss Bell-Ringers," "The System of Doctor Tarr and Professor Fether," "The Tell-Tale Heart," and "Thou Art the Man." The classic illustrations are by Gustave Dore and Harry Clarke, with a great introduction by Andrew Barger.

This is an ambitious work and one that immediately becomes the scholar's gold standard for research on this major writer of mystery and thrills. If for no other reason than to have a solid selection of the works of Poe on the shelf, this beautifully designed and handsomely printed book will serve that intent. But once the reader thumbs through this book, pausing to re-read favorites such as 'The Fall of the House of Usher', 'The Murders in the Rue Morgue', 'The Pit and the Pendulum', and 'The Raven', there are many little known gems of short stories, articles, essays, and poems in addition to the stories that are less familiar to the larger audience to discover.

Barger adds 'guidance' to his method of presenting these works by such devices as listing all of the poems under the subheadings of 'Women in Edgar Allan Poe's Life', 'Miscellaneous Poetry both Before and After Age 25', 'Autobiographical', and 'Men in Edgar Allen Poe's Life.' These may seem like minor adjustments to the collections, but in Barger's hands the divisions add meaning and context to the works.

This is simply a splendid book, handsomely written and produced, and a fine tribute to the literature of Poe - and to the scholarship of Andrew Barger! Highly Recommended. **—AMZ TOP TEN REVIEWER**

<u>Mailboxes – Mansions – Memphistophels</u>
<u>A Collection of Dark Tales</u>

A finalist in the International Book Awards anthology category, Andrew Barger's first short story collection unleashes a blend of character-driven dark tales, which are sure to be remembered. In "Azra'eil & Fudgie" a little girl visits a team of marines in Afghanistan and they quickly learn she is more than she seems. "The Mailbox War" is a deadly tale of a weekend hobby taken to extremes while "The Brownie of the Alabaster Mansion" sees a Scottish monster of antiquity brought back to life. "Memphistopheles" contains a tale of the devil, Memphis, barbeque and a wannabe poet. "The Serpent and the Sepulcher" is a prose poem that will be cherished by all who experience it. "The Gëbult Mansion" recounts a literary hoax played by Andrew on his unsuspecting social networking friends that involves a female vampire. Last, "Stain" is an unforgettable horror story about a stain that will not go away.

<u>Middle Unearthed</u>
<u>Best Fantasy Short Stories 1800-1849</u>

Long before *The Lord of the Rings* trilogy and the *Harry Potter* series, there were the ten best fantasy stories published in the early nineteenth century. In old magazines and forgotten journals,

Andrew read over 100 forgotten fantasy stories to find the very best. They include great tales by Charles Dickens, Mary Shelley, Washington Irving and many others. Read it today.

Connect with Andrew Online

Andrew's Email List:
media@AndrewBarger.com

Website:
AndrewBarger.com

Blog:
AndrewBarger.blogspot.com

Facebook:
facebook.com/AuthorAndrewBarger

Goodreads:
goodreads.com/author/show/1362598.Andrew_Barger